The RANI *of* JHANSI

Prince Michael of Greece is the author of a number of biographies and historical novels. Born in 1939, he studied political science in Paris before serving a term with the Hellenic army. His marriage to Greek artist Marina Karella led to his renunciation of any claims to the throne.

The RANI of JHANSI

PRINCE MICHAEL

OF GREECE

RUPA

Published in English by
Rupa Publications India Pvt. Ltd 2013
7/16, Ansari Road, Daryaganj
New Delhi 110002

Sales Centres:
Allahabad Bengaluru Chennai
Hyderabad Jaipur Kathmandu
Kolkata Mumbai

First published in French by Les Editions ORBANS 1984.

ISBN: 978-81-291-2962-8

10 9 8 7 6 5 4 3 2 1

Contents

PART I

A WOMAN IN LOVE

1

On 20 November 1853, at three o'clock in the afternoon—the day and the hour dictated by the court astrologer—the ceremony was commenced by the Raja of Jhansi for the adoption of his heir. To perform the ritual, the Raja had summoned from the holy city of Benares a priest of great renown, Pandit Vishnayak. Intoning the traditional incantations, the Pandit began by offering sacrifices to Vishnu and to the nine planets of the Hindu astral heavens: the sun, the moon, Mars, Mercury, Venus, Jupiter, Saturn, and Rahu and Ketu, which represent the rising and descending phases of the moon.

The people of Jhansi, a small state in central India, were delighted with the Raja's decision. The more devout among them rejoiced that their ruler, who was childless, was at last fulfilling his obligation to his ancestors by adopting a son, in accordance with the custom of Hindu princely families. Since the death of his only male child two years earlier, the Raja had had no more, and it had become clear to everyone that he never would. Rumours of his illness had been circulating for some time, and they had intensified in recent weeks. Aware that the Raja would not live much longer, his people had rushed to temples to pray. Not that they loved their ruler—far from it; but his death without a designated heir would have been even worse than his hated reign. It would have meant an end to the prosperity of Jhansi. The state would have been annexed by the British, devoured by its neighbours, and torn apart by quarrels of succession among the Raja's cousins. Now that he was adopting a son, the continuity and the future of Jhansi were assured.

The area around the palace had been overrun by a huge crowd of spectators, who had perched themselves on gables, cornices and corbelled balconies of the ornate houses. Below, the town square was packed so tight that people could scarcely breathe. Turbaned guards in red-and-gold uniforms, lances at the ready, kept the crowd at a respectful distance from the site of the ceremony.

The massed spectators stood on their toes, looking towards the arbour where the Raja and his retinue had taken up their positions. Following custom, the arbour had been erected in front of the residence of the adoptive parents, the royal palace. Twelve wooden pillars, painted red and white and adorned with garlands, supported a vast canopy of branches festooned with a vast array of colourful, strong-scented flowers.

From afar, the people were unable to distinguish between courtiers and guests from neighbouring princely states, between officers and escorts. All they could see was a patchwork of red turbans, black beards, gold swords, and jewel-studded brocade tunics of pink, red, mauve, yellow and pale blue. Only the British agent of Jhansi was recognizable. He stood out because of the simplicity of his uniform; he was the only man there who wore no gold or gems.

Enthroned in the midst of this glittering group, in full view of his subjects, sat the Raja of Jhansi, thin, greying, an impassive idol clad in pink and gold, who seemed alive only by the fleeting sparkle from a diamond in his necklace or from the bracelets on his forearms.

Was he really as ill as rumours claimed? At that distance, no one in the crowd could tell.

Thousands of curious eyes were turned to the Rani of Jhansi, who sat next to her husband on the gaddi.*

Because of purdah, the custom that shielded Hindu women from public view, she was an unfamiliar sight to her subjects. In the early days of her marriage to the Raja, they had caught mere glimpses of her at a few official ceremonies, through the muslin curtains of her howdah. But since that time she had seldom appeared in public, and it was said that her husband kept her virtually a prisoner behind the latticed windows of her apartments.

Today, the adoption liturgy compelled her, as the adoptive mother,

---

*A glossary of Indian words can be found at the end of the book.

to show herself unveiled. From a distance, the people could make out only her two large dark eyes that overshadowed a small conical face. A white sari—white was the Rani's favourite colour—clung tightly to her slender, elegant silhouette. Sitting very erect, Lakshmi, the Rani of Jhansi, followed the ceremony without moving. She was barely listening, however, to the incantations of the holy man from Benares. Her eyelids were lowered in order to glance undetected, every few moments, at her husband the Raja; it was crucial that no one suspect she had reason to watch him so carefully. She hoped the make-up she had applied to his features would deceive the guests of honour seated close to him. A mask of powder concealed the rings under his eyes and somewhat disguised his grimaces of pain; the rouge certainly hid his pallor. But no amount of kohl on his eyelids could dull the unnatural glitter of fever his eyes betrayed.

In anguish, Lakshmi prayed that he would bear up until the end of the ceremony, that he would be spared one of those terrible attacks that drained him, each time, of a little more life. Suddenly, her attention was drawn from him, for the most solemn part of the ceremony was about to begin. Pandit Vishnayak had already placed before the child's mother and father the traditional sum of one hundred and fifty silver coins.

In accordance with custom, the parents were distant cousins of the Raja, poor relations only too happy to give up a son if that would secure him an enviable position. The child's mother stood up; it was she, not the father, who would play the most important role in the ceremony. She took her five-year-old son, little Damodar, by the hand. As they walked towards the throne, Lakshmi was able to examine the child whom she had barely glimpsed until now, a little boy who, from this moment on, for reasons of state, was to be her son. His features, without expression, did not show much character, but the face itself was one of extraordinary beauty. Lakshmi thought she had never seen eyes so enormous. They seemed to contemplate the world with surprise and sweetness. When his mother, still holding him by the hand, stopped before the throne, the Raja of Jhansi asked her whether she was prepared to give him up.

It was a moment Lakshmi had dreaded, for she feared that the Raja's voice would betray his condition. But it rang loud and carried far.

Only its unusual pitch revealed the tremendous effort it had cost him.

Three times, so loud it was almost a shout, the woman cried, 'I give you this child; I no longer have any rights over him.'

The Raja drew Damodar to his side and lifted him onto his lap. From a bowl prepared by Pandit Vishnayak, he took some water mixed with saffron powder and drank. Lakshmi did the same. Then, together, they poured some of the water into Damodar's hand and made him drink. At length the Raja spoke the ritual formula:

'We admit this child into our household, of which he is now a part.'

Henceforth, Damodar would be the legitimate son of the Raja and Rani of Jhansi, heir to the throne. The religious ceremony was over.

And yet, to everyone's surprise, the Raja did not get up. He signalled to his Prime Minister, Diwan Naransin, who began to read from a document he had been holding.

'This is my testament,' he began.

Seated nearby on the dais, Sadasheo, the Raja's cousin and closest relative, was unable to conceal his surprise. If the Raja was having his testament read, then it was clear he did not expect to live. Was he really dying, despite all the denials? A base hope welled up in Sadasheo, only to subside almost immediately. It was not unusual, after all, for an adoptive father to make his testament public during such ceremonies, in order to emphasize the fact that the adopted child was now his heir. Feeling the pressure of Lakshmi's gaze, Sadasheo assumed a detached expression.

Lakshmi had only occasionally met this cousin of her husband's who lived on faraway estates, but their few encounters had been enough to make her realize that she had a staunch enemy in Sadasheo. He belonged to that dangerous breed of men who are both ambitious and complex. Lakshmi was well aware that he had always coveted the throne of Jhansi, and that for him, the adoption of a son by the Raja could only be an obstacle.

Without betraying his interest, Sadasheo was listening intently. The last sentence of the testament read by the Diwan was particularly interesting:

'Should I not survive, I trust that in consideration of the fidelity I have always displayed towards the British government, favour may be shown to this child, and that my widow, during her lifetime, may be considered the regent of the state and mother of this child, and that she may not be hindered in these duties in any way.'

At a sign from the Raja, the Diwan folded the document, crossed the dais under the leafy, flower-covered canopy, and offered it to Major Ellis. The Major was the political agent in Jhansi of the Most Honourable East India Company; in short, he represented England—that distant, mysterious, and yet undeniable power which for the past century-and-a-half, through successive wars and diktats, had been nibbling at India, state by state.

Seated next to Major Ellis was Kashmiri Mull, whose white beard concealed a wry smile. Kashmiri Mull was the Vakil, the Raja's legal counsellor. With his patriarchal appearance and benevolent expression, he was considered one of the most experienced minds among the wily, quibbling jurists who had sprouted all over India. Never would he have imagined his master the Raja capable of such shrewdness. Presenting his testament to the British...it was a master stroke!

Under the law of Hindu princes, the Raja had full rights to adopt a son and will him his throne. He did not need the approval of the British, who were only visitors in India, albeit increasingly demanding ones. By entrusting his will to Major Ellis, however, the Raja had placed the future of his lands, of his wife and son, under British protection. The power of England was now guarantor of the adoption that had just taken place.

Kashmiri Mull felt a twinge of sadness. Where were the days when even the most important princes could not make the slightest decision without begging, on bended knees, for consent from their suzerain, the Great Moghul, the emperor of India? What remained today of his once fearsome power? The present Great Moghul was but a feeble old man, universally despised, cloistered in Delhi inside a fort now far too large for him—a ghost, the last shred of a dynasty that had once amazed the world. Today, the real, the exclusive power was Britain; an army of administrators had replaced the magnificent tyrants. Manners change with the times. Other times, other customs.

Major Ellis ended his speech—which had been utterly incomprehensible to almost all in the audience—on an encouraging note: 'I shall do everything in my power to see that Your Highness's testament is accepted by the British government.'

This time the ceremony was truly over. The Raja of Jhansi tried to rise from his throne, but fell back, panting, motionless, his eyes closed. A shudder ran through the crowd, a silence, a moment of anguish that seemed interminable. Lakshmi placed her hand on her husband's, gently, as though it were a perfectly natural gesture, and the Raja got up. He walked to the edge of the dais and stopped. The people had moved closer. Slowly, in total silence, their irresistible pressure had forced the guards backward until they formed only a narrow ring around the arbour. The Raja swayed on his feet.

The crowd thought that he was waiting for something. The guests nearby worried that he might fall. He seemed at a loss, as though dazed by the sunlight. Lakshmi stepped forward and placed little Damodar's hand in her husband's. The Raja appeared to recover and, holding the hand of his new son, he began to walk ploddingly, like an automaton. Lakshmi held the child's other hand; the three of them stepped down from the dais and disappeared under the main portal of the palace. The people burst into cheers, saluting the arrival of an heir to the throne. Passive until the departure of their ruler, the crowd now broke through the guards, rushed to the walls of the palace, and scrambled onto the dais, jostling the officials in their joy. In an instant, all the dignity and pomp of the afternoon were swept away in a whirlwind of confusion.

The palace of Jhansi was not large by the standards of Indian princes. Yet, the walk to the Raja's apartments seemed to Lakshmi an odyssey without end. Holding her husband around the waist, she led him past the stables in the first courtyard, between two hedges of functionaries and servants, across the porch, then turned left and climbed the high steps of his private stairway. Once they reached the first floor, they had to navigate several more rooms crowded with courtiers. They made it to the Raja's room just before another seizure began. His Indian doctors rushed in, followed by Mandar, Lakshmi's faithful servant. On his low bed, supported by legs made of silver, the Raja writhed in pain. An iron hand seemed to be twisting his entrails, his heart seemed about to burst. At times the pain was so intense that his body arched from the bed, then fell back heavily, awaiting the next spasm. He had continuous attacks of diarrhoea and coughed up bile, spattering the silk covers of his bed with filth. There was no time to change them.

The physicians bustled about. Practitioners of Ayurveda with vast knowledge, they culled formulae for their potions, made of herbs and minerals, from the oldest Vedas, the most sacred texts of India. But they could not make the Raja swallow a sedative—he threw up everything they gave him—and the poultices they stuck to his body slid off with every spasm. Tirelessly, Lakshmi washed her husband's face with scented water and cleaned his soiled and stinking body without showing the slightest revulsion, without once losing her patience, her calm, her gentleness. She took care of him with the same grace she might have devoted to a religious rite, apparently unaffected by the terrible stench emanating from the bed, barely dispersed by the smell of incense and sandalwood rising from incense-burners. Only a small wrinkle between her eyebrows betrayed the tension inside her.

From time to time, her servant Mandar wiped away the beads of sweat on Lakshmi's face. Glowing embers in the braziers kept the small room as hot as a furnace.

Mandar had asked many times to relieve her mistress at the Raja's bedside, but Lakshmi always refused, aware of the fact that, far more than the scented water, it was her hands that brought relief to her husband. Thrice, the physicians, thinking the Raja's heart would collapse, feared that it was all over.

At last the attacks seemed to subside. The Raja fell into a heavy torpor. For the moment there was nothing more to be done. The Raja's room was jammed with people—his closest servants who slept on the floor beside his bed, physicians, secretaries, a few chamberlains, the bearer of the fly-swatter, the waver of the fan and the bearer of the hookah. Even the sword-bearer managed to slip in, unnoticed, behind the others. All these bystanders looked on in silence, immobile, with that apathy which was a sign of deep and painful emotion.

'I'll watch over him, leave us,' Lakshmi ordered. 'You too, Mandar.'

Alone with her husband, Lakshmi glanced about the room looking for her pillbox, a little case made of enamel and gold, its diamond-studded lid decorated with a peacock, the emblem of the dynasty of

Jhansi. Mandar had left it on a cushion. Flicking the lid open, Lakshmi took a pinch of opium, brought it to her mouth, and then, suddenly, threw it away.

'Aren't you taking your drug, Lakshmi?'

The Rani started guiltily. Her husband had not moved, nor opened his eyes. But he was conscious, and he had guessed at Lakshmi's temptation.

'I no longer need it, my lord,' she answered.

For years she had found in opium the comfort and happiness she could find nowhere else. But she had sworn to herself that when her husband died, she would give it up forever. And now the moment had arrived. Hope seized Lakshmi and carried her off, a terrible hope of which she was ashamed, but one she was unable to stifle.

The Raja had not fully understood his wife's answer.

'Of course, you don't need it anymore because you don't have to worry about the future. I've provided for you by adopting a son and I've saved you from a terrible fate. You know what a crime it is, in the eyes of our society, to be a childless widow. You would not have been allowed to remarry. You would have had to shave your head, wear an undyed sari, sleep on a bare floor.'

The Raja had become animated as he spoke, almost relishing the prospect.

'How often you must have thought of it! You would have been reduced to less than nothing, almost a servant, a constant target for the insults and contempt of my family. You would have lost your rank, been thrown out of your apartments into some vile corner, to vegetate in darkness, forgotten by everyone, mistreated and laughed at by your inferiors.'

The Raja was right. Lakshmi had indeed shuddered at the thought of such a life; and yet, paradoxically, she had never believed she would have to endure it. In her deepest self, she had always felt that she was destined for other things.

And yet, it was not for her sake, nor to respect the wishes of his subjects, that the Raja had adopted a son. It was simply a question of pride. He could not bear to see his dynasty die out with him, young and undistinguished though it was. And if he had, in his will, appointed Lakshmi regent, it was only because he could not go against the traditions of Indian princes, which demanded that the mother of a sovereign still in his minority should rule in his place until he reached manhood. Moreover, the Raja had refused to make the necessary dispositions until the very last moment. 'There's still time, I'm not really that sick, we'll see about it later,' he would tell his advisers who, becoming increasingly frantic, had time after time begged him to assure the continuity of his kingdom.

As though to avenge himself for having succumbed to their pressure, the Raja now took pleasure in twisting the knife in the wound.

'I could feel your fear and that of the others. My ministers, my courtiers, your father Moropant, and even my faithful Naransin were afraid of losing their sinecures if I died without an heir. That's why I stretched out the pleasure of postponing my decision. Their fears—and yours in particular, Lakshmi—were so amusing to me...'

And yet, disgusted by the multiple intrigues that she had seen being woven about her husband's deathbed, Lakshmi had refused to exert the slightest influence on his decision, despite the repeated pleas of the Raja's advisers. The unfairness of the Raja's insinuations so annoyed Lakshmi that she was unable to restrain herself.

'You are wrong, my lord. I never worried about my future. The horoscope drawn at my birth predicted that I would rule.'

The Raja's reply spewed forth, 'I know that's all you've ever wanted, I know how you've been awaiting this moment, how you've been longing for me to die. But I don't envy you, Lakshmi. The moment you climb on to the throne you'll be surrounded by suitors who'll try to force themselves on you, by relatives who'll make constant claims on your power, by courtiers who'll do their best to take advantage of your lack of experience. Neighbouring states will see weakness in the regency—your weakness, Lakshmi—and they'll attack you and try to carve up Jhansi between them. Your only companions will be ambition, greed and treason.'

Lakshmi allowed him his prophecies, indifferent to his words. She took stock of how disease had ravaged his body. Always thin, he had become skeletal; his body, once well-shaped, had shrivelled away. He had always looked somewhat like a bird of prey; now he reminded her of a moulting old vulture. The pinched nostrils enhanced the hook of his nose. His eyes, small, round and usually sparkling with malice, were covered with a colourless film. Unlike other Indian princes, he had never grown a moustache or a beard, and his smooth skin, always bilious, had turned entirely yellow. His lips, once fleshy and well-drawn, were now merely two grey threads. Lakshmi was happy that he could not see what had happened to him, for he had always been vain about his appearance. She felt deep contempt for this man who, even at the edge of death, still sought to humiliate, to discourage, to destroy her; but now that she felt beyond his reach, she pitied him and allowed him to continue without interruption.

'In order to govern well, one must be vigilant, harsh, even merciless. But you think you will do better with smiles and charm. You think that the people love you. No, Lakshmi, the people hate us.'

'The people hate you, my lord.'

Fortunately, the Raja had not heard his wife's answer. A weak, complicated man, the Raja had tried, early in his reign, to make his power felt through a kind of irascible harshness. That had earned him only the hatred of the people of Jhansi. Sensing their feelings, he took revenge in extreme cruelty. His petty and bloody arbitrariness had so increased the animosity of his subjects that they had given his name to the dungeon in the fort where the hangman worked tirelessly.

Exasperated by his inability to disturb his wife's calm, the Raja sharpened his spiteful attacks.

'And then there are the British. Are you sure they'll allow you on the throne?'

He had struck home.

'Everything is settled,' Lakshmi answered, but it sounded almost like a question.

The Raja sighed.

'Will the British government accept the adoption? Will they recognize you and Damodar as my successors?'

Lakshmi heard, behind the satisfaction of tormenting her, a sincere anxiety in his voice.

'Your family has always been an ally of the British,' she protested. 'It's the British who kept them in power. Every time there was a war or a rebellion, your family sent its army to fight for them. It's the British who recognized Jhansi as an independent state and your family as its hereditary rulers. They granted your predecessor the title of Raja. They defended you against your cousins when they contested your right to the throne. Why do you think they would change their policy now and not recognize the adoption of our son?'

The Rani had taken some pleasure in describing the continual and, in her eyes, shameful servility of the Rajas of Jhansi towards the British invaders. But her husband was too absorbed in his own thoughts to take offence.

'Don't forget,' he said, 'that the British are the real masters, the masters of Jhansi and the masters of all of India, even if they aren't officially yet. Today they are friends, tomorrow they could be enemies.'

The Raja was afraid of the British. He always had been. Lakshmi saw more clearly than ever how deeply that fear was ingrained in him. He had not forgotten the treatment the British had inflicted on him fifteen years earlier, before his marriage to Lakshmi. Fed up with his peculations and his acts of cruelty, they had simply dethroned him for three years, returning him to power only after he had promised to mend his ways.

Lakshmi wanted to allay her husband's pessimism, but she was interrupted by the arrival of Mandar bringing oil lamps; night had begun to fall. Mandar approached the bed and offered a small bottle to the Raja.

'Major Ellis himself brought it to the palace. His friend, Doctor Allen, made this medicine and begs you to take it to make you feel better.'

The Raja tried to raise himself on his elbows.

'I will never swallow medicines made by unclean foreign hands.'

'But,' Mandar insisted, 'Doctor Allen prepared this medicine with water from the Ganges in order to purify it.'

'It was prepared by a foreigner and I don't want to die impure.'

The Raja's voice had risen to an almost feminine pitch. He was terrified by the idea of suffering in the hereafter, the consequences of dying in a state of impurity; but Lakshmi wondered whether he didn't also retain, even near death, his fear of poison. Falling back on his pillows, the Raja renewed his monologue.

'And even if that medicine might have cured me, I wouldn't have taken it. I'm tired of life. I lost my taste for it two years ago...since the death of my son...'

The Raja had said 'my' son, as if the boy had been his alone. Lakshmi felt her heart contract. In a flash, she relived the joy she had felt at the birth of her child. Her happiness had been no greater than that of the people of Jhansi. The entire city had been illuminated, the Raja's army had paraded through the streets in their smart red-and-gold uniforms, the royal elephants had distributed the symbolic sugar to every household. The celebrations had lasted for days, during which the poor, by the thousands, had eaten their fill. Her child had died three months later. The people's grief had been profound, and for a long time afterwards nothing had been able to raise Lakshmi from her own despair.

She wished the Raja had not aroused that painful, ever-present memory.

'Since the death of my son,' he continued, 'nothing has gone well for me. That's why I let myself die.'

The Rani protested, 'You didn't let yourself die. You have a well-known disease, dysentery.'

Furious at being contradicted, the Raja spat out more lies.

'No, Lakshmi. I let myself die. Because I knew you wouldn't give me any more children. Because I knew you'd remain barren...'

The Raja's accusation wounded Lakshmi deeply, all the more because she knew it was false. The fault lay with him. A life of debauchery had worn away his health. She was unable to contain her bitterness.

'You never tried to have any more children. You never found out if I really was sterile.'

But the Raja was no longer listening to her. His face had contorted and his eyes rolled back into his head. A new attack was on the way. Lakshmi shouted. The physicians, who were waiting in the next room came running and with them courtiers and servants, all of whom thought themselves indispensable. Lakshmi knew that this was the end. The attack came, as horrible as the last. The sight of his suffering made Lakshmi suffer. She knew that red-hot irons were tearing at her husband's insides. She could do nothing for him. Even the touch of her hands, which in the past had given him solace, was no longer effective. Now, along with the tiny wrinkle on her brow, heavy bluish circles appeared under her eyes. And yet, she continued to care for him, with a gentleness and patience that seemed inexhaustible.

This attack was more violent than the previous one, and shorter. Suddenly, the Raja fell into a coma-like trance. His heart was giving out. The servants cleaned the bed, and Lakshmi helped them place her husband on cool, clean silk sheets.

Lakshmi dismissed all the attendants and again was alone with the dying man.

The few oil lamps Mandar had placed on the floor bathed the room in soft golden light, thickened by the sweet-smelling smoke of the incense-burners. Her gaze lingered on the large religious paintings, haphazardly hung, whose orientalism contrasted with the profusion of mirrors imported from Europe, testimonials to the Raja's vanity. In a niche in one wall, the gold statue of the goddess Lakshmi, the tutelary divinity of the dynasty of Jhansi, glowed softly.

The Rani stared at her husband as though fascinated by his unconscious form. The resentment that had welled up over the years against him, for everything he had put her through, was subsiding as his death approached.

At the very beginning of their marriage, eleven years earlier, a clash of personalities had set the fourteen-year-old adolescent and the forty-year-old man against each other. He had wanted to rule her the same way he ruled his subjects, by fear. But he had soon been forced to recognize his failure. The popularity of the Rani among the people had grown in proportion to their hatred of her husband. She was not well-known, for she rarely emerged from purdah, but she was said to be generous and devout, though an unhappy wife. Her success, through no fault of her own, had enraged the Raja. He had literally locked her up, stiffening the rules of purdah specifically for her. Perhaps the Raja was also jealous of this woman—beautiful, attractive, elegant—whom he neglected, whom he no longer even touched. He preferred to indulge in various eccentricities which, in the early years of their marriage, Lakshmi had found highly disconcerting. His passion for theatre was such that he would even assign himself a role in the plays he staged, and it was always a woman's role, since there were no actresses in his country. From dressing up as a woman for the stage, his taste for female clothing, little by little, had spread into the rest of his life. In his apartments he often dressed as a woman, and Lakshmi suspected that, sometimes, he ventured into the streets of Jhansi in female disguise. She also wondered whether this penchant—and what lay behind it—were responsible for the lack of ardour he showed her. He liked to cover himself with jewels—excessively, in Lakshmi's opinion. One day, she remembered, an Englishman touring Jhansi had been unable to refrain from asking why the Raja wore bangles, symbols of feminine docility. Unfazed, the Raja had answered that since the British were masters of India, all Rajas ought to wear bangles.

For years, the Rani had remained confined within purdah. Burning with energy, thirsty for the outdoors, she had instead been condemned to utter inactivity in small rooms with latticed windows on the first floor of one of the palace wings. A lover of solitude, she had been forced to endure the constant chattering company of women servants, who, she knew, spied on her for the Raja and reported to him every word she spoke.

To sustain her, to understand her, the Rani had been able to rely only on one servant, Mandar, her companion since childhood. Over the years, Mandar had naturally become a confidante and almost an adviser, whose frankness and verbal explosions stimulated the Rani. And yet a subtle but boundless distance always separated the lady-in-waiting from the queen.

The Rani's long years of imprisonment had been all the more painful because her childhood and adolescence had accustomed her to the freedom Maratha women traditionally enjoyed. Frustration and the apparent hopelessness of her situation had somewhat affected her mind. She had begun to smoke the hookah in a sort of frenzy, and from there she had slipped into the use of opium. She had numbed herself into resignation, but she had not been broken.

Suddenly, the Rani became aware of the deathly silence around her. No sound came from outside the palace, although normally the people of Jhansi would have been spending the night in noisy celebration of the adoption. Perhaps they had been warned of their sovereign's imminent death; perhaps they were merely waiting silently, with the anxiety one feels when faced with any sudden change.

Life seemed to have ebbed completely from the Raja's twisted body and contorted features. He was dying as he had lived, in torment. For his wife, his death meant the freedom he had always denied her. Soon the gates of purdah, her prison, would open before her. In her imagination, Lakshmi compared herself to a caged bird that had long been trained to fly freely. She felt herself capable of handling freedom, for she knew it would give her life a purpose, a meaning.

She raised her eyes and looked out the window. On the horizon, the black sky had turned dark blue. Dawn was not far off.

At four-thirty in the morning, on 21 November 1853, Gangadhar Rao, seventh Raja of Jhansi, died without having regained consciousness.

2

As she left the Raja's room, Lakshmi found three people at the door; three questioning faces—her father Moropant, her servant Mandar and Prime Minister Naransin. Addressing Naransin by his title, she said, 'Diwan, please assemble the High Council at eight o'clock this morning.'

It was not her words that surprised her listeners, but the tone of her voice; it was that of a master, permitting no argument.

The Rani had already walked on, taking the interior corridor that led to the purdah, which connected with the Raja's apartments. There she found her female relatives waiting for her. Although an only child, the Rani had a vast collection of aunts, cousins and nieces, who after her marriage to the Raja had followed her to Jhansi in the hope of getting sinecures. All of them were sobbing loudly in the traditional display of mourning.

Aunt Anahita, her father's older sister, stepped up.

'From now on, Lakshmi, you must shave your head. And you must go on a pilgrimage to Benares, like all childless widows.'

'I will not shave my head, because I have a son, and I will not go to Benares because I must govern.'

Her voice was dry and cutting. Aunt Anahita insisted, 'Your son is adopted. Your husband died without leaving you a living child. You must submit to tradition.'

In a sharp, almost hysterical voice Lakshmi answered.

'All my life, I've been forced into a mould. You put me there at birth—you, my aunt, you, my father, and later, my husband. Now the mould is broken. I'm out of it now, and I will never go back.'

The old lady seemed deeply shocked.

'Do you mean to say, Lakshmi, that you look upon your husband's death as a liberation?'

Without answering her, Lakshmi continued, 'During all those years that my husband kept me locked up without mercy, not one of you made the slightest effort to convince him to lighten my imprisonment. You found it more convenient to amass privilege and riches by taking advantage of my position. From now on, none of you, nor anyone else, will dictate my behaviour. You may think or say whatever you wish. I'm a widow, but I am also a mother, and I am a queen. *I am free.*'

She had almost shouted the last sentence. She stopped and looked at the walls of what had once been her prison. Purdah among Hindu families, zenana among Muslims, the harems of the Middle East—the women's quarters, no matter what their name—were always a prison. Lakshmi stared at the faded tapestries on the whitewashed walls, their gold and their colours dulled with the years. Then she noticed her relatives, who surrounded her in silence, stunned by the scene they had just witnessed. Lakshmi felt an urge to laugh, along with a desire to rush at them and shake them by the shoulders.

Moropant, who had joined them, was watching his daughter thoughtfully. It was he who broke the silence.

'Is that how you regard the education I gave you with so much love? As a mould, a prison?'

'Yes...no,' Lakshmi answered. 'I'm tired, I don't know any longer what I'm saying, what I'm thinking.'

In fact, she was utterly exhausted. She felt a sudden and violent desire for opium. Despite the fatigue that sapped her will, she resisted the temptation, as she had promised herself. From now on she would have no need to dull her mind. She turned to her servant.

'Come, Mandar, come help me. I must get ready for the council.'

The throne room was not large. Like the rest of the Jhansi palace, it had been designed in the days when architectural tastes of the princes had not yet turned to the gigantic scale that would eventually become the fashion. High windows giving onto the palace's two main courtyards illuminated the hall. On the walls were frescoes in which delicately painted bouquets stood out against a burgundy background. Garlands of flowers were painted on the beams of the ceiling. An immense Lahore carpet with Persian designs covered the entire floor. At the rear of the room two columns supported an arch, forming an alcove for the gaddi, the same silver throne that had been used outside for Damodar's adoption ceremony. A semi-transparent muslin curtain had been hastily hung in front of the alcove, to shelter from masculine eyes the place where the Raja's widow would now sit.

Although the meeting had been called at the last minute, they all came, not wanting to miss this historic council. Next to the Prime Minister, Diwan Naransin, was the minister of finance, the secretary of state, the guardian of the seal and the minister of justice. The officers of the army of Jhansi mingled with advisers, secretaries, scribes and other court officials. Nearby were the great landowners, those talukdars and zamindars who were the social backbone of Jhansi. The banias, the powerful merchants responsible for the prosperity of the town, an important commercial centre, had sent their representatives.

The heads of the noble families had also rushed over. Warriors of ancient stock imbued with military tradition and a deep sense of their prerogatives, they belonged to the race of the Maratha. They were the heirs of the conquerors who, in centuries past, had caused so much trouble for the Moghuls and later for the British, and who had carved out for themselves kingdoms, large and small, in the region. The Raja of Jhansi, like the ruling caste of his state, was a Maratha.

They all settled cross-legged on small brocade pillows, facing each other in long rows. During the years of purdah, Lakshmi had met very few of these men. Nevertheless, she began her speech with assurance, in a voice that was soft but carried.

'By virtue of the testament of my late husband, Raja Gangadhar of blessed memory, and in order to obey his expressed wishes, with which you are all acquainted, I hereby assume power. I shall reign until our son, your Raja Damodar, comes of age.'

There was nothing in this to surprise the Rani's listeners. The history of India, their history, was filled with women of all kinds who, at various times, had ruled either directly, as regents, or indirectly, by dominating, through the senses or through character, a husband or a lover.

Lakshmi's next words, however, came as a shock to the council:

'In order to fulfil my duties better, I have decided to emerge from purdah forever. I will not wear the traditional veil when I receive my dignitaries. Furthermore, as I do not want to remain confined within this palace, I shall visit my subjects both in town and in the countryside. My face will not be veiled.'

Lakshmi made a sign to Damodar who was sitting very erect next to her on the gaddi. The child stood up, grabbed the muslin curtain in his little hands and tugged on it with all his strength. The thin material tore from the columns and fell in a heap to the ground.

The Rani's audience showed no emotion except a brief shudder. Then in an extraordinary breach of protocol, they all turned their heads towards the throne, towards the woman they had never seen before. No one said a word. Then Kashmiri Mull, the legal counsellor, a faithful among the faithful, without stirring from his pillow, his head lowered, eyes glued to the carpet, spoke in a trembling voice.

'Leaving purdah, Rani, has never been done before. You will violate one of our most sacred traditions.'

Lakshmi waited a few moments before answering.

'This tradition you speak of, Kashmiri Mull, is not ours. It is not derived from our religion. Purdah was brought to India by Muslims, foreigners, when they invaded our country centuries ago. The Indian woman is free. Our religion grants her the same rights as men. In leaving purdah, I am doing no more than respecting our true tradition.'

Lakshmi suspected that the argument would not be enough to convince all those men. She began again, quietly, almost humbly, 'I will never be close to my subjects if I cannot show myself to them. I will not be able to know their problems, their wishes and their hopes if I do not seek them out and speak with them. This is why I have decided to leave purdah.'

The minister of finance, the furnavese, voiced an objection.

'And what about the foreigners, Rani—what about the British? How will you receive them? You know that you will have to see the representative of Britain stationed here, and the British administrators who have controlled our treasury since the bankruptcy of the previous reign. Will you show yourself to them?'

'Never. The rules of purdah will be kept inviolate for foreigners. I shall never appear unveiled before an Englishman.'

Her case was won. And when Naransin stepped forward to shout, 'Long life to Lakshmi, Rani of Jhansi', his cry was taken up with enthusiasm by the entire audience, their voices echoing loudly throughout the throne room.

The funeral procession of the Raja of Jhansi, Gangadhar Rao, had already reached the cremation site, a field on the shore of Lake Lakshmi, named for the goddess of plenty who had a temple built to her by the water. Holding Damodar by the hand, the Rani, followed by her relatives and her court, had walked through the narrow streets of Jhansi, lined with silent crowds, behind the stretcher that bore the remains of her husband. He had been dressed in his richest clothes and his most precious jewels. Garlands of flowers were piled high around his body; the traditional betel leaves had been placed in his mouth.

Pandit Vishnayak, who had come from Benares for Damodar's adoption, was the officiating priest. Placing logs of sandalwood on the funeral pyre, he recited a prayer:

Without essence, without death, immutable is our soul.
He who thinks it dies is ignorant of the truth.
How could it die, when never did it condescend to be born?
Above change, above death, the soul is contemporary with God.

The crowd that had watched the procession march through the streets had followed it from the town and now stood by, impassive, silent, curious. The Raja's corpse was placed upon the pyre after being stripped of its jewels, which were to be returned to the state treasury. Pandit Vishnayak passed a burning torch to Damodar, the dead man's heir and closest relative, whose duty it was to light the pyre. Holding the torch, Damodar walked around the pyre seven times, not in the usual clockwise, astrologically benefic way but counterclockwise, malefic. He carried out his part of the ritual with a mixture of childlike docility and adult gravity. Not a tremor shook the crowd when he touched the torch to the four corners of the pyre while reciting the prayer the Pandit whispered in his ear:

Here you are in the celestial fields.
Neither wind nor earth nor any of the living worlds
could hold you back.
Go, go to the kingdom of eternal life whence you came.
The ancestors of your race, the ancient Diwani, welcome you.
Don the cloak of divine splendour.
To the star-studded valleys, among flowers of light, go.
Stay forever there where all your desires are fulfilled.

Lakshmi stood very still before the pyre. Like Damodar, she was dressed in white, not just because she was in mourning but also because it was her favourite colour, almost her symbol. She herself had chosen the site for the cremation where, according to custom, she was to have her husband's cenotaph erected. It was located next to the temple of Lakshmi, her own protector as well as that of the dynasty of Jhansi, where she had liked to perform her devotions whenever her husband let her out of the palace. She had always loved the calm lake and the bucolic aspect of its shores, dotted with temples and chapels.

Lakshmi thought of her husband. By now his soul had already become a 'pret'; it had entered a body, small as a human thumb, and was in the custody of Yama, the judge of the dead. In exactly thirteen days a ceremony would mark his reincarnation, his return to earth in a new body. The good and the evil deeds of the life he had just left would determine the caste into which he would be reborn. Lakshmi wondered which caste he would draw. A high caste was out of the question, after the injustices and cruelties he had committed for so long. Although she had her doubts, she hoped he would, at least, be reincarnated as a human being, that he would not be condemned to live his next life as an animal. Still, even if he did return as an animal, the evil he had done would destine him to take the shape not of a noble animal like the elephant, but of a lowly one such as the pig, the ultimate disgrace.

The Raja's ashes would be collected in an urn and taken to Benares to be cast into the sacred Ganges, a custom reserved for the ashes of the high-born in order to facilitate their travel into the afterlife, but would this passport be enough to improve his future existence?

Had she married a Rajput instead of a Maratha, Lakshmi would have had to obey the custom of Rajasthan and lie down on the pyre to be burned alive next to the corpse of her husband, a notion that would have delighted him. She did not even grimace when a whiff of burnt flesh, borne by the breeze, overwhelmed odours from the garlands of flowers and the sandalwood. With her husband the detested past was going up in smoke; it had taken the Raja's death to return her to life. Those were her thoughts as she watched the cinders swirl, climbing in a shower of sparks into the reddening sky of evening.

An observant woman, the Rani had been surprised by the absence at the Raja's funeral of his cousin Sadasheo, his closest relative after Damodar. She mentioned it to Diwan Naransin during their daily meeting.

The reappointment of Naransin as prime minister had been her first political decision; her husband had recommended it before his death. For many years, Naransin had been the Raja's right hand and Lakshmi sometimes wondered if they had been lovers. But that was no longer important. Naransin knew the workings of the state better than anyone else, and from the very start, he had served her with the same effectiveness and devotion he had shown the Raja.

Because of her choice, she had been subjected to veiled complaints from her father, who had wanted the post of diwan for himself, in order that he might better give his daughter the benefit of his experience. But Moropant's solicitude could sometimes be as burdensome as his greed. Had he not forced the inclusion into his daughter's marriage contract of the pensions and honours he expected from his son-in-law? Nevertheless, the Rani did not completely shunt him aside; she kept him close by, as much for the value of his advice as out of filial duty. That, too, had been the Raja's idea. 'Your father is a good politician,' he had told her, the day before his death. 'He'll be useful to you, and he'll derive even greater advantage from you than he could during my reign.'

Naransin merely shrugged when she mentioned Sadasheo. 'It would be fairly strange,' he said, 'if Sadasheo had come to pay his last respects. So far, he's done nothing but insult the king's memory and contest his will.'

That was how Lakshmi learned that Sadasheo had been in touch with a number of Jhansi's nobles and dignitaries to protest Damodar's adoption, which he claimed was illegal, and to ask them to place him on the throne that was his by right. Wasting no time, he had already assumed the title of Raja Sadasheo Rao of Jhansi.

Before Naransin could arrest the troublemaker and throw him in prison, he had fled far from Jhansi to take refuge in his lands at Parola. There was nothing much to fear from his base intrigues, which would soon die a natural death. Still, the Rani wondered where that weak, insecure man had found the courage to launch such an enterprise, and it occurred to her that he might have had hidden support from other quarters. In fact, Sadasheo's sole impetus was the horoscope drawn at his birth, which predicted he would one day be king.

'Sadasheo has an astrologer behind him,' the Rani said. 'I have the people of Jhansi.'

Naransin, after a long silence, answered, 'There is one point that needs our attention. Sadasheo has written to the British Governor General of India to protest the late Raja's testament and to claim the throne for himself.'

'The British know very well the adoption is legal.'

'That's true, Rani. Still, it would perhaps be wise if you wrote to the Governor General yourself and reminded him of it.'

'Why? An adoption like this is strictly a matter of our own customs and religion.'

'Your husband, Rani, the late Raja, wrote to the British when he decided to adopt Damodar. Perhaps you ought to follow through. Keep in mind that when your husband came to power, he was opposed by his cousins and managed to keep the throne only because the British backed his claim.'

'Diwan, the less we involve the British in our affairs, the better.'

'I know, Rani. But if we don't involve them, they'll involve themselves. You know how the new Governor General, Lord Dalhousie, likes to meddle in the affairs of the independent states. He is said to be a brutal man, and he has already shown that he has little respect for our desires and traditions. You lose nothing by writing to him.'

Under her coolness and pride, the Rani concealed a certain anxiety.

Every time she heard the British mentioned, she felt her heart stabbed by a vague worry and uncertainty. Hesitating between her instincts and political necessity, she was unsure of how she must behave towards them; and she hated indecision.

After weighing the matter carefully, she gave in to the Diwan's arguments, but she refused his offer to compose the letter she would send Lord Dalhousie. She wrote it herself, in Persian, the language all Indian courts had used since the invasion and occupation by the Great Moghuls. When she gave her first draft to Naransin and old Kashmiri Mull, both were dazzled by the precision and accuracy of the text, from a woman so young and inexperienced. After studying, article by article, the treaty of alliance between Jhansi and Britain, she had extracted every point that legitimized the adoption of Damodar and her succession to the throne.

Since custom dictated that no ruler should ever actually write an official document, a scribe employed his most beautiful calligraphy to copy the letter in golden ink. The parchment was placed in a red silk pouch embroidered with gold flowers, then inserted into another pouch made of muslin and fastened by gold ribbons from which hung the great seal of the Rani of Jhansi.

The Diwan solemnly presented the document to Major Ellis, the British representative at Jhansi, with a request that he send it on to the Governor General in Calcutta. He reported to the Rani that Major Ellis had spoken highly reassuring words upon being informed of the contents of the letter. 'We have a treaty of friendship and alliance with Jhansi,' he had said, 'and nothing could allow us to contest the ruling dynasty's privilege of adopting an heir. To do so would be to deny the liberal spirit that informed the treaty.'

For centuries India had been an aggregation of hundreds and hundreds of kingdoms and principalities of varying size and importance, some of them as large as European countries, others just a few square miles in area. Attempts had been made to unite them—but only by foreign invaders like the Delhi Sultanate and the Great Moghuls. Their authority had never extended to the whole of India, and in fact, depended entirely on the energy of each successive ruler. Anarchy and secession reappeared every time a weak or inept emperor held the throne. Then, in the eighteenth century, the British arrived. As invaders, they showed themselves better organized and more efficient than their predecessors, subtler and also more patient. They had first moved in under the cover of the Most Honourable East India Company, whose only avowed purpose was trade. Little by little, the Company had insinuated itself into the affairs of the Great Moghuls and the Indian kingdoms, taking a hand in numerous local wars, and finally, it had begun to annex various states. Thereupon, the Company collapsed; its affairs were gradually taken over by the British government, a development accompanied by a change of attitude on the part of the British, who became more direct in their interventions and more open in their colonialism.

Located in central India, the state of Jhansi could not be called ancient. A hundred years earlier, in the middle of the eighteenth century, a Maratha warrior, who had distinguished himself in various wars, had been granted this territory with the title of Raja. It was not very large. Compared to more important Maratha states such as Gwalior, Indore or Baroda, it was, in fact, tiny. Nevertheless, the rule of successive Rajas had transformed it over the years into a state that was both prosperous and envied. A large army guarded it from attack and from any eventual upsurge in banditry, one of the region's more lucrative industries. Its capital, the town of Jhansi, housed no fewer than sixty thousand inhabitants. Its merchants and artisans, famous throughout India, attracted wealth to the land like a magnet.

Dotted here and there with rocky hills, the flat and arid land of Jhansi remained ungenerous, but thanks to dams built by the Rajas and thoroughgoing irrigation, oases had emerged. The capital and the villages were surrounded by vast belts of opulent fields, kitchen gardens and orchards. Vegetables and fruit flourished in abundance, but Jhansi was especially famous for its flowers.

Rani Lakshmi had been ruling Jhansi for several weeks. First, she had brought her son and her court to the palace in the fort, the traditional seat of power, which her husband had abandoned in favour of the town palace, a secondary residence. Dominating Jhansi from the crest of a hill, the fort, with its impressive assembly of towers and ramparts, was the physical symbol of authority.

Although she had gone without transition from the mind-numbing idleness of purdah to the constant activity and demands of power, the Rani had immediately found a rhythm that suited her. She had always known that, unlike the immense majority of Indian women who are crushed by submission, she had been born for action. It was so much a part of her nature that she had immediately organized her life for it. She rose at five o'clock and performed her puja. The mornings were spent, with the help of Diwan Naransin and her officers, supervising the work of the political and military departments. After that, she granted audiences to anyone asking to see her or went into town to determine for herself the needs of her people.

Every afternoon at three o'clock, she took her place in the throne room, on the silver gaddi that had been her husband's, to listen to reports, receive petitions, give instructions, working with the ministers and the employees of the various departments. She did this with an efficiency and wisdom well beyond her years, having been prepared for these tasks, paradoxically, by the man who had done most to humiliate and debase her—her late husband. He had cruelly imprisoned her, but he had also never failed to consult her before making political decisions. Often the walls of purdah had resounded with the noise of their arguments. This had not discouraged the Raja, who continued to seek her advice, while at the same time growing resentful of his dependence on her. Thus, gradually and without wanting to, he had given her a political education.

Lakshmi never stopped working until sunset. After a light, healthy supper, she went to bed early. As she had vowed, she had stopped taking opium at night. This prodigious act of will was, at first, accompanied by painful attacks of nervousness, which she fortunately managed to control. And although she had not given up tobacco, she used it sparingly, smoking her hookah only during private audiences.

Often she rode on horseback into town or out into the country, accompanied by her faithful Mandar and a small guard. She sought a dialogue with the common people, the peasants, dealing with them with simplicity and concern. Struck by the contrast between her reign and her husband's, her subjects idolized her. They praised her charity, her piety, her irreproachable lifestyle, her conscientiousness. They were not far from regarding her as a saint.

The frequent audiences she granted Major Ellis and his subordinates took place according to the strictest rules of purdah. But despite those restrictions, she always managed to display a consideration towards the British that did not go unnoticed. They praised her courtesy and her remarkable abilities all the way to Calcutta, the British capital of India.

'She's a highly respected and well-liked woman, and I believe her perfectly suited to her lofty responsibilities,' Major Ellis reported to Lord Dalhousie.

Every day she set aside time to work privately with Diwan Naransin. She did not like to admit to herself that she would await the hour of his arrival with a certain degree of impatience. Naransin was handsome, lively, intelligent, and there was something equivocal about him that was far from unattractive. Sometimes, although he never for an instant forgot the deference due his sovereign, she would notice in his eyes a gleam directed not to the queen but to the woman.

This perfectly innocent aspect of their meetings disconcerted her. Yet she was careful to admire him only for his professional qualities.

She was particularly grateful to him when he successfully negotiated a treaty of friendship with Orchha. The principality of Orchha was Jhansi's southern neighbour and hereditary enemy. In former times it had owned Jhansi and still claimed rights over it. Orchha was currently ruled by the fearsome and merciless Rani Lakri Bai, who had secured for herself a solid reputation for ambition and ruthlessness. A change of regime in Jhansi was fertile ground for the intrigues that had made her famous throughout the region.

Although Lakshmi remained sceptical of Diwan Naransin's chances of success, she allowed him to leave for Orchha. He did not have far to travel; the capitals of the two states were only fifteen miles apart. He came back a week later with a treaty of alliance in his pocket. Orchha had abandoned all its territorial claims on Jhansi and promised eternal friendship.

On the night of his return, Lakshmi received Naransin with less formality than ever before. Instead of letting him sit cross-legged on the carpet, she invited him to sit next to her on the low couch that ran along the wall. She called for a hookah so that he might smoke with her.

Their conversation took place in her favourite spot in the palace, the private audience chamber behind the throne room. It was a corner room, rather small, located on one of the upper floors of the fort with an extraordinary view of the countryside and the jungle. Less sumptuous than the throne room but more refined, it was decorated with small niches in the Persian style, and entirely painted over with flowers and bouquets in the strong lines and vivid colours characteristic of the local school of painting.

'Well, Diwan, how did you work this miracle?'

'I did it thanks to you, Rani. Rani Lakri Bai is well-informed. She has heard of your extraordinary popularity. She knows how much energy and concentration you devote to your work. She has also understood that you usually get your way.'

'You're too modest, Diwan. You overlook your own cleverness and powers of persuasion. Even so, I find the Rani of Orchha's amenability surprising. She has hated me for years, even though we've never met. It has even been said that she was jealous of me. Perhaps she has changed? What kind of woman is she? Tell me about her.'

'It is a strange coincidence, Rani—the Rani of Orchha never stopped asking about you. She wanted to know everything—just as now you want to know everything about her. The Rani of Orchha is neither young nor beautiful, but she is an intelligent, active, decisive woman and she listens to reason.'

'All this is very different, Diwan, from the image I had of her. Didn't she refuse to give up the throne to her son, even though he came of age a long time ago? She keeps him away from power, spies on him, and keeps him besotted with sensual pleasures. She is a monster, mad for power and won't let anything or anyone stand in her way. And they say that the means she uses to fulfil her unfathomable designs are both subtle and terrible.'

'You ought not to believe your courtiers, Rani—any more than the Rani of Orchha has believed her own, who tried to please her by telling her terrible things about you. The Rani of Orchha sincerely wants your friendship.'

Suddenly, the Rani turned towards Naransin.

'Could it be you're in love with her, Diwan? I hear that she has traces of her former beauty.'

Naransin burst out laughing.

'Even if the Rani of Orchha were young and beautiful, which she's not, I couldn't love her—I love another queen.'

Imperceptibly, Naransin had been edging closer to Lakshmi on the couch, and now he placed his hand gently on her thigh. Lakshmi gave a start. Glancing up into Naransin's eyes, she saw violent, uncontrollable desire.

'You can't be serious, Diwan.'

'I've been this serious for years, Rani, ever since the first time I saw you when you arrived in Jhansi, when you were yet a child.'

Lakshmi was so bewildered that all she could say was, 'But, Diwan, you are married.'

'The chains of my passion are far stronger than the ties of marriage, Rani.'

He had taken Lakshmi's hand. She wrenched it away quickly and stood to face him.

'It's out of the question, Naransin.'

'How often have I seen complicity in your eyes, Rani! You knew of my love, and you didn't forbid it.'

'That's not true. I admire you as a competent minister, and I'm fond of you because you're a devoted collaborator—that's all.'

'You're alone, Rani—you need a man.'

'I enjoy my solitude, Diwan, and I don't need anyone.'

'Your life is too austere. All you do is work and pray. Don't tell me you never wish for diversion. If you don't want to respond to my love, at least take it for your amusement. Let me offer you the pleasures this love could give you.'

'Educating my son and ruling are enough. I have no need for diversions.'

'So many women who lack your beauty or your position have lovers. There's not a Rani in all of India, not even the oldest and the ugliest, who doesn't have several. And you, who are young, beautiful, and passionate, you won't take one? And besides, your life, until now, must not have been particularly fulfilling in that area.'

The allusion to her husband made the Rani blush in spite of herself.

'I shall see you tomorrow, as usual.' The Rani tilted her head to the side, her habitual gesture that meant the meeting was over.

As he left the room, Naransin said, 'I await the day, Rani, when you will take a lover. I know that day will come, and I hope that when it does, you will choose me. I'm as worthy of it as anyone else—probably more so.'

Left to herself, the Rani, at first, felt disgust for the Diwan's vulgarity. She found it surprising that a man so refined and intelligent could commit such a blunder. Even the most gifted men have moments of stupidity, Lakshmi realized. How could Naransin believe for one moment that she would fall into his arms? And to think that she had suspected him of being her husband's lover!

Embarrassment and modesty kept the Rani from telling anyone, even her faithful Mandar, of the incident. She decided to ignore it. Yet it was with some apprehension that she went to her meeting with Naransin on the following day. She was reassured, however, for it was soon clear that he, too, had chosen to ignore and, if possible, forget what had happened. He was completely unselfconscious, having recovered the subtle deference he always showed despite the informality of their interviews.

She could not detect in him any trace of shame at having exposed himself so ridiculously, nor any resentment at having been rejected. Lakshmi, too, tried to remain natural. She only momentarily exaggerated, perhaps, that courtesy which is peculiar to royalty, and she made a point of asking the Diwan's opinion on various matters as often as possible, in order to show him that he had not lost her trust. Either Naransin had already forgotten her refusal, in the manner of ladies' men who have been rejected as often as accepted, or else, the Rani thought, he was a genius at dissemblance.

Without settling on either explanation, the Rani fell back into her close collaboration with the Diwan. Both had a taste for politics and hard work. Both loved Jhansi and were working for the kingdom's welfare.

3

On the morning of 15 March 1854, shortly before eleven o'clock, Major Ellis, the British agent, appeared at the gates of the fort of Jhansi. He had requested an audience with the Rani, not an unusual occurrence, but on this occasion he had also suggested that she have her ministers attend the meeting, which was unusual.

Each time Ellis entered the throne room he was shocked by what he considered its barbarous garishness. The walls and the ceiling were entirely covered by frescoes. Painstakingly primitive portraits of former Rajas of Jhansi and heroes of Indian history, as well as miniatures of mythological scenes stood out from an intricate background of arabesques and rosettes painted in ultramarine, burgundy and poison-green. In the profusion of colour, there was nowhere for the eye to rest. The vogue of European fashion that had flourished in India half a century before had also left its mark on the room. Above the frescoes were hung huge Venetian mirrors and more portraits of the Rajas of Jhansi, these last painted in oil on canvas in a vaguely English style. Against the walls stood a row of massive Victorian furniture, dressers and tables of heavy mahogany groaning under knick-knacks of silver and Bohemian crystal, more of which hung from the ceiling in the form of chandeliers.

Treading on vast Lahore carpets, Major Ellis passed slowly between rows of the Rani's ministers and courtiers sitting on low cushions. He declined the tall mahogany armchair that had been set out for him facing the muslin curtain that marked the boundary of purdah, shielding the Rani from his gaze. Instead, he remained on his feet, staring at the cloth, through which he made out the outline of the silver throne and seated on it a thin silhouette. He could see the Rani's head tilted slightly to one side, a position often assumed when she was listening.

Lakshmi was not overly surprised to find that Major Ellis was accompanied by his aides-de-camp and his secretaries. The British enjoyed solemnity, and when surrounded by his assistants, the major seemed better able to summon the assurance necessary in his dealings with Indians. Protected by the shadows behind the muslin curtain, Lakshmi had a very clear view of Ellis, who stood in the light cast by a window. The military uniform, the famous red coat, did little to lend stature to this rather dumpy-looking official. A disciplined and efficient administrator, he was also a peaceful, kindly man. His relations with the Rani had always been simple and straightforward. She liked the broad smile that so often lit up his square face.

Today, strangely silent, he was unsmiling. Although surprised, the Rani waited patiently for him to speak. At length, having straightened himself to his full height, Major Ellis cleared his throat and began:

'I have received a communiqué from Calcutta.'

He stopped short. Immediately, Lakshmi sensed this was a serious matter. A few seconds slipped by before Major Ellis spoke again, in a low and rapid voice:

'The Most Noble Governor General of India has decided in council, for various reasons, to refuse to confirm or sanction Damodar's adoption. Consequently, the state of Jhansi is to be taken over by the British government. Henceforth, the subjects of the said state of Jhansi will consider themselves to be under the authority of the said British government, to which they will pay all revenues formerly due to the said state.'

The interpreter's monotonous voice and the familiar sounds of the Maratha language into which he rendered Major Ellis' speech only increased Lakshmi's astonishment and her fury. Damodar's adoption was refused, Jhansi annexed; she was no longer queen. At the first words spoken by Major Ellis, she had turned white with rage. Her entire body was shaking. She began to rise. Mandar, who stood at her side, fearing an explosion, gently placed a hand on her arm to restrain her. The Rani sat down again. After a silence that seemed endless, she spoke a single sentence, slowly, in a soft but strong voice:

'Meri Jhansi nahin dungi!—I will never give up my Jhansi.'

Major Ellis had been shifting his weight from leg to leg. Now he straightened up, raised his head and said, 'I will do everything in my power to see that Your Highness is properly provided for and treated with all due respect by the British government.'

No answer came from behind the curtain. Major Ellis glanced furtively at his assistants, and then, summoning all his courage, added, 'May I take the liberty to tell Your Highness how much I deplore this decision and how much I regret having been ordered to inform you of it.'

Still, Lakshmi remained silent behind the curtain. Neither Major Ellis's sympathetic understanding nor his obvious embarrassment could do anything to soften the blow. At last, the Rani barked an order. Diwan Naransin stepped forward and bowed before Major Ellis, signalling the conclusion of the audience. Ellis clicked his heels, bowed sharply at the muslin curtain, and left the room much faster than he had entered, at once relieved and ashamed. The Rani dismissed everyone—ministers, councillors, relatives and retainers—and locked herself alone in her room. The surprise, the humiliation, the anger and suffering were too great. For hours she could not stop weeping.

Waiting in the anteroom, Mandar heard the Rani's sobs through the closed door. Then silence. Her servant could just make out the sound of her slippers on the carpet as she paced up and down.

Evening came. Several times Mandar scratched at the door and asked permission to bring food. The Rani continued to pace, refusing even to answer. Moropant arrived in a state of high agitation and knocked on the door. Again, there was no response.

'Lakshmi, open up,' he said. 'The people of Jhansi have gathered at the palace gates.'

The door swung open, and Moropant and Mandar saw Lakshmi standing before them, her cheeks streaked with tears, her eyes red and blazing.

News of the annexation had spread through the city like wildfire. The people had closed their shops and, as a sign of mourning, had not lit their lamps at nightfall. The entire city lay shrouded in darkness. Thousands of people had left their houses and climbed the hill to the fort. They had gathered in the areas separating the different enclosures and in the vast square before the palace. All were bareheaded and barefoot, witness to their sorrow. They waited in silence and despair, their eyes on the shaded facade of their queen's palace.

The Rani seemed to awake from a nightmare and said to her father, 'Go speak to them in my name. You will say exactly what I tell you, "Go home peacefully, good people. All is not lost. We are living in difficult times, but your Rani will find a solution."'

The people's spontaneous demonstration of support had rekindled the Rani's energy. She summoned the closest of her advisers, Diwan Naransin, Kashmiri Mull and her father, Moropant, to the audience chamber.

'I have decided to resist,' she announced. 'We have an army, and the people of Jhansi are behind me. I will place myself at their head and fight the British. Perhaps we shall be beaten, but at least we won't be dishonoured.'

Diwan Naransin warmly approved.

Out of filial duty and respect, Lakshmi asked her father what he thought.

'I'll do whatever you decide,' answered Moropant. 'If you choose to defend yourself, I'll fight at your side.'

In the context of Indian law, this display of submission by a father to a daughter was so astonishing that Lakshmi remained speechless with gratitude. It made up for all the greed and indifference Moropant had so often demonstrated. Moreover, his answer showed that he disapproved of Lakshmi's decision. Had he expressed his disapproval more clearly, especially in the presence of witnesses, she would have been forbidden by filial respect to contradict him openly or even argue her point.

It was old Kashmiri Mull who took it on himself to speak the bitter truth, 'Resisting would serve no purpose. Just a few minutes ago, I learned that a British army is on the march towards Jhansi. Several regiments, with artillery. They're only two days' march from here.'

'So the British do know me after all,' the Rani could not refrain from saying.

Kashmiri Mull continued, 'Besides, resistance would only worsen the situation and ruin any hope for the future...if there still is any hope...' he grumbled to himself.

Who would come to their rescue? Her neighbours, her allies? All of them, north and south, were thinking only of grovelling before the British in the hopes of being spared themselves. They were symbols of an India that had been rendered apathetic by a methodical, inexorable conqueror. Little Jhansi would not hold out very long against the formidable power of the British Empire. The city shelled, the inhabitants looted, the Rani and her ministers exiled, the country reduced to slavery... India had learned the fate England reserved for the vanquished, and among those vanquished in the past few decades had been states far greater than Jhansi and rulers infinitely more powerful than Lakshmi. Kashmiri Mull was right. The British would make short work of Jhansi. They all knew it, even Naransin who had welcomed Lakshmi's proposal of resistance with such enthusiasm, even Lakshmi herself, who did not want to subject her people to a ruinous, hopeless war.

'What have I done to deserve this?' she asked. 'What did my poor Jhansi do to be punished this way?'

Kashmiri Mull shook his head and explained that the iniquitous action by the British had not been directed personally at her. She was merely another victim of Lord Dalhousie's long-term political strategy.

'He started by annexing the principality of Satara, where the ruler had died childless. Remember what he did to your childhood friend Nana Sahib. He, too, was an adopted son, and when his father, the Raja of Bithur, died two years ago, Dalhousie refused to recognize the adoption and seized the country. Believe me, Rani, the annexation of Jhansi is just one more step in his plan to add as many princely states to British territory as he can.'

Kashmiri Mull's explanation was obviously correct, but resignation was an attitude unsuited both to the Rani's age and her character. She ordered him to discuss the matter with Major Ellis in order to gain time.

Though sceptical, Kashmiri Mull was anxious to oblige the Rani, and during the following days, he met several times with Major Ellis. The meetings were interminable—Kashmiri Mull, as a jurist, enjoyed nothing so much as splitting hairs, and Major Ellis, out of respect for the Rani's painful situation, listened with commendable patience. Kashmiri Mull cited the treaties between Jhansi and Britain, quoted the correspondence between the British government and the Rajas and analysed similar cases. Ellis took refuge behind Lord Dalhousie's arguments. Based as they were on the most outrageous bad faith, Kashmiri Mull had no trouble tearing them apart.

One evening, the exhausted Major Ellis finally shoved at him the notes Lord Dalhousie had written in justification of his actions.

'The people of Jhansi never expected nor asked their Raja to adopt an heir. The incorporation of Jhansi into British territory will bring its inhabitants numerous and immediate benefits sufficient to convince them.'

In the face of such shameless lies, of such contempt for the wishes of the people of Jhansi, there was nothing to do but give up.

But Kashmiri Mull had to speak his mind to Major Ellis.

'It is just as I thought; the annexation has nothing to do with the law. It is no more than a brutal, arbitrary act without the slightest basis in legality.'

Still, Kashmiri Mull did battle again the following morning. On his own initiative, Major Ellis had recommended to Lord Dalhousie a number of measures which he thought might soften the blow to the Rani. The Governor General's refusal to adopt them saddened and angered him. No pension would be granted to the Rani's courtiers and servants, who would have to be dismissed. The Rani would leave the palace at the fort of Jhansi and turn it over to the British. Moreover, she would be instructed to present the new British administrator with the crown jewels and her private funds as well as the contents of the public treasury.

The Governor General's cynicism stunned Major Ellis, even though he had by then grown accustomed to Lord Dalhousie's methods. Pointing out that the late Raja had designated his adoptive son Damodar as sole heir, Dalhousie declared himself unable to transfer the legacy of jewels and money to the widow. Thus, in order to finish plundering the Rani, he based his claims on the very testament he had refused to sanction. He did grant her, however, a yearly pension of five thousand rupees.

Major Ellis's sense of shame was such that he did not dare transmit the Governor General's answer to Lakshmi. Instead, he entrusted the mission to Kashmiri Mull. Lakshmi burst into contemptuous laughter,

'Five thousand rupees! Let the British keep their five thousand rupees! I'd rather be completely destitute than have to live off their charity!'

The Rani had already dismissed her army, her court, her aides and administrators. She delivered the crown jewels to Major Ellis along with the balance of the exchequer, which amounted to 245,738 rupees in gold and silver. Although she was well aware of the efforts he had made for her cause, she was unable to restrain her sarcasm.

'Perhaps, Major, you will allow me to keep the books my late husband collected? Unless, of course, you think you might get a good price for them!'

Major Ellis blushed before agreeing. The Rani did not inform him that she had ordered the removal of an enormous ancient bronze gun, nicknamed Kadak Bijli (Fierce Lightning), which had become, over the years, a sort of mascot to the fort. Not wanting it to fall into British hands, she had had the gun buried in one of the courtyards of the town palace, her new residence.

The moment came for the Rani to leave the fort where she had so briefly reigned. The commander of the British army that had occupied Jhansi after the annexation had ordered that she leave by night in order to avoid popular demonstrations. To make up for that final show of pettiness, Major Ellis had decreed that the former ruler and her retainers be transported by the royal elephants, which were now the property of the British government. Zealous grooms had decorated the animals in their finest ornaments, used only for official ceremonies.

The Rani was surprised to find, in the fort's main courtyard, her albino elephant, a fluke of nature which was the envy of all the neighbouring Rajas. She wore her usual white sari, without a single jewel. Between her eyebrows she had a black tika of mourning. Widow of a Raja, the Rani was now the widow of a kingdom. Despite Major Ellis's entreaties she had declined to remove anything from the palace in the fort; her baggage was as meagre as her retinue. She stopped for a moment at the threshold of the palace, looked around, and saw only British soldiers where, just the day before, her servants had been milling about. Then she stepped forward and lightly ascended the steep marble steps of the stairway that permitted easy access to the elephant's back. With Damodar, she settled into the large ceremonial howdah, made of solid silver, roofed with a purple-and-gold canopy.

When the albino elephant lumbered off, Major Ellis, deliberately or by habit, came to attention and gave a military salute.

The fort's main gate, reserved exclusively for royalty, swung open. The procession passed under the arch and then travelled through the three enclosures that traditionally protect a king. The elephants trudged down the steep hillside and, once they reached level ground, turned left towards the city. Damodar leaned out of the howdah for a last look at the dark mass of the fort with its potbellied towers. Roughly, the Rani pulled her son back into his seat. 'Look forward,' she said. 'The past is gone.'

She had spoken sharply and regretted it immediately.

The royal elephants carrying the deposed queen and her suite tramped through the town. Their tusks and their feet circled with gold, their backs covered with saddle blankets of gold-embroidered velvet hanging to the ground, the beasts trudged forward slowly. Their resplendent finery and their majestic pace reminded the Rani of ceremonial parades during which they had carried her through cheering, enthusiastic crowds, now an insignificant, cruel memory.

She was now a completely powerless ruler, incapable of doing anything for her subjects, who called her 'mother'. What was to become of them? All her dreams for their happiness, for increasing their prosperity, for preparing Damodar for the throne had crumbled. Nothing would ever erase from her name or the reputation of her family the humiliation she had undergone at the hands of the British. She felt the cruelty of her situation all the more for having briefly known the satisfaction of acting and expending herself towards a goal. Had she emerged from prison only to fall back into a drab and idle existence?

The town was shrouded in silence and darkness. The few torches carried by the servants who led the Rani's elephants barely added to the cold light from the moon. Sitting very erect in her silver howdah, the Rani maintained the majestic and gracious bearing she had always shown during official ceremonies. But she could see nothing around her except closed doors and shutters. There was no one outside and only the stars saw her pass by.

The Rani lived the following weeks in a state of constant exasperation, burning with feelings of humiliation and injustice. The British army that had marched on Jhansi at the time of the annexation and occupied the town without resistance had now retired, leaving behind a small garrison composed of troops from the Twelfth Bengal Native Infantry, the Fourteenth Queen's Cavalry, and a detachment of artillery. The soldiers and non-commissioned officers were sepoys, Indians serving under the British flag. In all, there were 881 native soldiers under eight British officers commanded by one Captain Dunlop.

The British garrison, of course, occupied the fort of Jhansi, the seat of authority, but it set up its living quarters in a newly-built cantonment outside the walls of the city.

British power, after the recall of Major Ellis, was now represented by Captain Alexander Skene, the political agent, who was seconded in legal matters by Deputy Superintendent Captain Gordon. Both lived in bungalows in the town, not far from the Rani's palace. The other Englishmen who had come with the occupation force stayed outside the city in a civilian compound built especially for them. There, in pleasant little bungalows, lived Doctor Phipps, the British surgeon and his wife, the comptroller, the tax inspector, and several other administrators with their assistants and their families. Altogether, the compound housed about fifty British civilians.

Never, during her daily horseback ride, did the Rani go south of the city, for it was there that the British had built their military camp and civilian compound. She did not want to see any of the signs of occupation. Damodar, whom she took with her on her rides in order to train him in horsemanship, asked her a thousand questions about this forbidden region. She answered vaguely, out of ignorance and distaste. In the child's imagination, the area had become the terrifying and enticing lair of legendary monsters.

The people of Jhansi were suffering the consequences of the annexation. The Rani saw this only too clearly whenever she went to perform her devotions at the sanctuary of Lakshmi, her tutelary goddess, or at some other temple. These outings were accompanied by a certain pomp; she was surrounded by guards and a retinue came with her, giving the illusion that she had not entirely lost her rank. No sooner had she left the palace than she would find herself surrounded by townsmen who came to tell her of their misfortunes.

Noblemen of important local families that had traditionally provided courtiers and functionaries to the Rajas of Jhansi had lost their positions and their pensions. The soldiers of the Raja's disbanded army had been reduced to idle penury. The merchants and artisans complained that since the removal of Jhansi's court, their main source of trade had dried up. 'There is no more movement, no more activity, no more prosperity,' one of them complained. 'Our town has fallen very low,' another sighed.

Many showed no reticence in comparing the British to the thugs, those religious fanatics who banded together in secret societies and included looting and murder among their holy rites.

'The annexation of Jhansi,' the Rani heard, 'is worse than the murders committed by the thugs. Dalhousie has put a noose around the neck of an entire people.'

Everyone wanted help from the Rani—a pension, a favour, an intercession on their behalf; the British had not succeeded in uprooting the age-old instinct that made people turn to their ruler—in power or not—for assistance in case of need. Their complaints and petitions reminded the Rani cruelly of her own misfortune and powerlessness. How could she help her former subjects except by lending a compassionate ear and trying to comfort them?

She herself was constantly humiliated by the occupiers. The British seized the lands whose rents used to provide the maintenance of her husband's cenotaph; they ruled against her in a lawsuit involving some orchards and gardens; they refused her permission to make a pilgrimage to Benares, India's sacred city. They absorbed into their treasury revenues of the two villages that had always been allotted to Jhansi's most sacred temple, that of the goddess Lakshmi. Violating the country's religious beliefs, they even authorized the slaughter of sacred cows. These measures resulted not from deliberate brutality, but from the pettiness and stupidity of the British bureaucracy. The Rani simmered with indignation and, whenever she was about to boil over, she would summon Captain Skene.

The latter had expected to confront a furious ex-queen. Instead, he found a serene and courteous woman, and Lakshmi soon won him over, as she had Major Ellis before him. Captain Skene praised her docility and her virtue, even to Calcutta. Invariably, he agreed with the Rani's views, expressed his regrets, apologized, promised to correct the situation, wrote to Calcutta, and was rebuffed. Sometimes he received no answer; sometimes, he was given reconfirmation of the measures taken, no matter how outrageous or unjust. What could he do but sigh and yield?

Within her own apartments, Lakshmi could not escape her relatives' concert of complaints. Her father mourned his lost sinecures and bewailed his daughter's sad fate. He had not allowed himself to be corrupted by the British, rejecting their offer of a post in the new administration. Lakshmi's aunts and cousins complained of penury, painting themselves as victims even while continuing to live off her.

In order to escape from these constant lamentations assailing her from all sides, the Rani had taken to burying herself in her favourite retreat, a partly-fortified pavilion at the gates of the city, built on the old dam that separated the Narayan gardens from Lake Lakshmi. The harmony of the landscape, the calm that belied the passage of time, and her own solitude gave her some peace.

The Rani sat on the carpet, leaning back against purple and gold cylindrical pillows in the little room that had been converted into a library to house the books she had saved, thanks to Major Ellis. The volumes, protected by slipcases of rich brocade, were carefully piled on the floor or lined up in niches in the walls. Sucking the amber mouthpiece of the hookah Mandar would prepare for her, the Rani would immerse herself in the poets made fashionable by the court of the Great Moghuls. Or else, she would read to Damodar. Her son was all she had left. She needed to love, and since she could no longer love a whole people, she loved a child. Although she could no longer train him to rule, she wanted to make of him a warrior worthy of his military caste. She read to him from the national epics in order to inspire him with the courage of their heroes and help him acquire a taste for great deeds. Although he had a tendency to gain weight, the child still had an extraordinary face, its central feature being his enormous eyes. He still did not exhibit any strong personality traits, but he was an open, affectionate, engaging child. Seated next to his mother, he was afraid to move, and yet, both of them sometimes allowed their attention to wander. Lakshmi stopped reading and gazed out the window to the quiet bronzed waters of the lake, the exuberant vegetation of its green banks...

One incident, however, broke the monotony of her days. Sometimes, especially in the early months of her banishment, the Rani would lose her temper. One morning at the palace, while she was dressing with the help of her retainers, one of them, Mira, pricked her lightly with a pin. Lakshmi exploded. 'Damn you, you clumsy girl!' she screamed, and slapped her on the arm.

When she saw the terror in Mira's face, she immediately composed herself. She held out the gold rings she had been about to put in her ears and said, 'Take these, Mira, and forgive me.'

Mira refused the jewels and burst into tears. 'You are so good to me, Rani,' she stammered, 'and I have been so bad!'

Thinking that Mira had simply been terrified by her anger, Lakshmi tried to calm her. But Mira, growing more and more upset, kept repeating, 'I've been so bad, I've done you so much harm, I've done you such harm'—and finally, she fled from the room.

Astonished, Lakshmi told Mandar to run after her and see what was wrong. Mandar was unable to draw a single coherent word from Mira, who was now in a state of total hysteria. Returning to the Rani's room, Mandar said, 'She's completely mad. She says that she poisoned your husband, the late Raja, and that she has been tortured by remorse ever since.'

Lakshmi was immediately interested.

'Bring her back to me,' she ordered, 'even if it's by force.'

Dragged in by Mandar, Mira threw herself at Lakshmi's feet.

'Mercy, Rani, mercy, don't have me killed!'

Lakshmi made her get up. In a firm voice, she said, 'I won't have you killed, Mira. But you say that you poisoned my husband. Why?'

Wracked by sobs, Mira said nothing.

'You didn't poison him of your own free will, right? Someone told you to do it. Who gave you the order?'

'Ask me anything you want, but not his name. He would kill me.'

Lakshmi tried another tack. Her eyes locked into Mira's, she said, 'Tell me how you poisoned my husband.'

'Every day I put in his food small amounts of a poison that produces the same symptoms as dysentery. Everyone had to believe the Raja was dying of a disease.'

'Who ordered you to do it?'

'I cannot speak. He would kill me. I cannot...'

Lakshmi recognized the uncontrollable terror that dominated her servant.

'Go away, Mira, and think about it. You'll have plenty of time. Think about what you did. Eventually you'll realize that the only way to redeem yourself is by telling me what I ask you. Go now, I'll send for you tomorrow.'

Lakshmi ordered that Mira be locked up alone in a room in the now-empty purdah, and that she be guarded discreetly in order to discourage any attempt at escape. Lakshmi remembered now that a suspicion had come over her while she was watching over her dying husband. He had said that he had let himself die, and moreover, he had displayed all the symptoms of dysentery. And yet, Lakshmi had experienced a flash of doubt as though something had told her there might be another cause, and the thought of poison had presented itself to her mind.

But why murder? True, he had always been hated, but Lakshmi did not think it could have been an act of vengeance by the family of one of his numerous victims. Besides, if Mira really had poisoned him, she had done so at a time when it was common knowledge that his health was failing. Why would anyone have precipitated the death of a man already condemned?

That evening, Lakshmi told her former Prime Minister, Diwan Naransin, what had happened. She started by reproving him, in a roundabout manner, for his lack of vigilance.

'You were the best-informed man in Jhansi. If what Mira says is true, if there really was a plot to assassinate the Raja, you would have heard about it.'

Not only did Naransin admit his negligence—the Raja's illness had swamped him with work—but he also removed the Rani's last doubts.

'I believe Mira. The late king was poisoned.'

'But why? By whom?'

'It's not difficult to name the guilty party, Rani. Only one man could have profited by the Raja's death—his cousin Sadasheo. His protests against Damodar's accession and his attempt to steal the throne are proof enough of his guilt.'

'Why would he have poisoned my husband when everyone knew he was already dying?'

'Sadasheo couldn't inherit the throne unless the Raja died before adopting an heir.'

Naransin offered to open an inquiry that would unmask the culprit, but the Rani refused. There was no point in stirring the mud. The past no longer mattered. Besides, she would interrogate Mira herself, in a tête-à-tête, and force the girl to talk.

The following morning, having finished her puja, the Rani, followed only by Mandar, went to the room where Mira had been locked up. She pulled the bolt, opened the door, and then gagged. Mira was hanging, lifeless, from the ceiling on a chain that had once held a lamp. Unable to move, the Rani stared with a mixture of pity and revulsion at the girl's purple face, the dead eyes staring out of their sockets, the swollen tongue, the graceful neck bent at an impossible angle. Alongside, Mandar, rooted to the spot, was shaking uncontrollably.

'Remorse probably drove her mad,' Mandar said with an effort, 'and she committed suicide.'

'Or else someone "suicided" her so that she couldn't talk,' the Rani said slowly. 'Have you noticed that her feet are touching the ground? That's a strange way to hang oneself!'

Mira had definitely been silenced. And what if Sadasheo were not the one? Everything pointed to him, yes; but was it perhaps just a little too obvious? But then, who else might have wanted the Raja's death? For several days Lakshmi drifted between various suspicions, most of them appearing highly improbable. Then they faded, and the incident as well as its implications were swallowed up by Lakshmi's indifference, sinking into a curious fatalism from which she had thought herself exempt.

Every morning, two Indian women, small and graceful, dressed in men's clothes (white trousers, shirt and turban) could be seen crossing swords with consummate skill in the palace gardens. They moved with such speed and precision that they seemed to be gliding on the raised paths between the flower beds. It was the Rani training with Mandar. From childhood, Maratha women were submitted to the same warlike discipline as men, and Lakshmi and her servant had long experience in the virile sports of wrestling, fencing and marksmanship.

But at the high point of the duel, the Rani sometimes would feel a sudden weariness and throw down her sword, clattering on the flagstones of pink granite.

It was not her body that was weary, but her soul. Physical exercise made her forget for a moment the dullness of her existence, but only for a moment. Almost immediately she would once again be overwhelmed by the pointlessness of her life.

In the afternoon, in a corner of the audience chamber in the town palace, the Rani pored over a tattered copy of Walter Scott's latest novel. Eyebrows furrowed, her finger running along the print, she conscientiously droned out the words she read. She had decided to learn English, as much to fill the hours as to better understand the unwelcome guests who played such an important role in her life and that of her people. For her teacher, she chose the wife of the British surgeon residing at Jhansi, Doctor Phipps. Annabelle Phipps had been born in India, knew its customs and spoke its language. Several times a week, one of the Rani's carriages drove to the civilian compound to bring her to the palace.

Annabelle Phipps was a woman of breathless, voluptuous beauty. Her skin was so dark, she might have passed for an Indian. She was intelligent, and it did not take her long to teach the rudiments of English to the Rani. She applied herself to her task, proud to have a former queen for her pupil.

The novels of Walter Scott, those medieval stories of fearless knights, besieged castles and noble blood feuds reminded the Rani strongly of the India of princes and warriors. But she was impatient with her progress and often became nervous and distracted. Mrs Phipps would reprimand her with delight, not bothering to conceal her contempt.

When Mandar was surprised by the Rani's tolerance of Mrs Phipps's behaviour, the Rani explained, 'She's delighted to be able to look down on us Indians. Don't mind her; she has her complexes. She was born into a low English caste and is terrified that people might mistake her for one of us because of her dark skin.'

The Rani's only recreation was to watch Damodar and his friends playing kit-kit, gilli-danda or chota lathi in the courtyard of the outbuildings. Often she could not resist joining in the games, running and shouting with the little boys and laughing so hard when attacked that she let them win.

Her monotonous routine had begun to affect the Rani. The attitude of her former subjects did not encourage her to bestir herself. She stopped up her ears in order not to hear the bad news against which she could do nothing. She had virtually no reaction upon learning of the annexation by the British of the kingdom of Oudh.

Oudh was no little Jhansi. Located in the north east, it was one of India's wealthiest and most important kingdoms. Its capital, Lucknow, the busiest, most cosmopolitan city in the country, was legendary for its opulence. The court of its kings surpassed that of any other in luxury and extravagance.

Until then, Oudh had been protected by the British, who, a century before, had encouraged, if not orchestrated, its creation. It had worked out to their advantage, for the kings of Oudh had lent the East India Company considerable sums which, needless to say, had never been reimbursed. One day in February 1856, claiming that the current king, Wajid Ali Shah, was incompetent, Lord Dalhousie dispossessed him, exiled him to Calcutta and seized his kingdom.

'It's just as I told you,' said Kashmiri Mull to the Rani. 'The Governor General is following a deliberate policy. The annexation of Satara, of Bithur, of our Jhansi were only practice. He was preparing himself for his masterpiece, Oudh. And I have to admit,' the Vakil added grimly, 'that I never would have imagined he would dare do it.'

Diwan Naransin interrupted, 'It has shaken all of India. Emotions are running high everywhere. Even among the sepoys of the British garrison here, almost all of whom come from Oudh,' he added, his voice vibrant with hope.

'India won't lift a finger,' the Rani answered, playing distractedly with her jade-handled fly-swatter.

Events soon proved her right—the agitation died down, the rumours disappeared. Oudh remained in British hands, and the Rani felt justified in her indifference.

Soon afterwards, Lord Dalhousie left India and was replaced by a new Governor General, Lord Canning. He was an open, generous and kindly man, but the damage had already been done. The effects of his predecessor's brutal and provoking policies could no longer be erased.

The Rani's own helplessness seemed to her a reflection of the helplessness of India, and she did not regard Lord Canning's arrival as any reason to emerge from her hibernation.

Two years had passed in such inactivity, and the Rani gradually lost all hope.

4

One afternoon in September 1856, two riders moved slowly along the dusty road leading from Kalpi to Jhansi. Both were dressed alike; white jodhpurs, a loose shirt tied at the waist by a belt that held two pistols, and a white silk turban, part of which hid the lower half of the face.

The Rani of Jhansi and her faithful Mandar were returning from their daily ride. The sandy soil muffled the sound of their horses' hooves. A low jungle of skinny shrubs stretched to the horizon, some of them thorny, others with waxy dark leaves; here and there, an old majestic bushy tree towered above them. The many shades of green shone brilliantly, as though polished by the rainy season that was now coming to an end. On the horizon, piles of rock formations looked like squat natural fortresses. The dull red earth saturated by rain harmonized with an incandescent red sky in which the sun had begun its descent.

The two riders stopped on a bridge spanning one of the many waterways that crossed the Kalpi road. Scanning the muddy waters, they saw a masculine head bobbing up and down, a few dozen yards upstream. The man was swimming vigorously; he had to be a foreigner, presumably an Englishman. At first, the Rani was surprised by this unexpected sight. Then, she gave in to a sudden urge for mischief. In a falsetto voice, speaking English with the accent of Indian servants of the British, which she could imitate to perfection, she shouted, 'Be careful, sahib, there are crocodiles in the river!'

Startled, the swimmer snorted, clumsily raised his arms, and almost vanished underwater. The two accomplices burst into laughter. The man swam fast for the closer bank and clambered out of the water, completely naked. For a moment he stood still, trying to catch his balance in the ankle-deep mud, blinded by the rays of the setting sun.

The Rani took time to examine him, absorbing the young, expressive face, dark hair plastered to his skull by the water; a well-proportioned body with a muscular torso, strong legs and a flat stomach.

Thinking that his witnesses were only two boys, the man did not attempt to cover himself. The Rani turned toward Mandar, saw that the latter was quite as fascinated as she, and collected herself.

'Aren't you ashamed, Mandar?' she remonstrated her sharply, and shaking her reins, the Rani clattered off the bridge at a gallop.

Throughout the evening Lakshmi managed not to think of the encounter. But when she retired for the night, when she lay alone on her big silver-footed bed, the image of the naked man in the river took hold of her mind and would not let go. She tossed on the silk covers while her treacherous memory fed her, one by one, the details of that masculine body. Contrary to her habit, the Rani did not fall asleep until very late.

The day had been long and hot, and Roger Giffard had been in the saddle since dawn. When he saw the river, he could not resist a swim. The water was muddy, but it refreshed him nonetheless. He was lucky the two young Indians had happened upon him and warned him of the dangers lurking underneath. Had they not seen him, he might have been devoured by a crocodile. But on second thought, it occurred to Roger that they might have been making fun of him. In this region crocodiles lived only in the larger rivers. Pranksters or not, the two Indians were excellent horsemen, and Roger had been able to admire their seat as they galloped away.

He reached the fort of Jhansi at nightfall and reported to Captain Alexander Skene who would henceforth be his superior. Roger Giffard was twenty-five years old. He came from a very old family of Norman origin, long settled in Wales and very poor. His father, a schoolmaster, with considerable financial sacrifice, had sent Roger to the best schools—Harnwell College near London and then Oxford, where Roger had studied law. He had then undergone training with a barrister of great repute in one of London's most famous law firms, Gray's Inn. One day he had decided to present his credentials to the board of directors of the Most Honourable East India Company, and his application had been accepted.

Upon his arrival in India he had entered Fort William College in Calcutta. All new recruits were automatically enrolled there to learn the history, laws and languages of India. Roger stayed only two years instead of the usual three, since his degree and the training he had undergone in London allowed him to finish his studies faster than his companions. He had left the college with the degree of Writership.

Captain Skene was aware of all this; he had read it in Roger's file which had been sent up from Calcutta.

'Only your brilliant results at the exams got you this job, Giffard. As you've no doubt heard, we prefer army men in the civilian posts.'

'Why, Captain?'

'The government feels that men with military training are more suitable, especially in India. Your immediate superior, by the way, the man you'll be assisting, is an officer—Captain Gordon. But let's get back to you, Giffard. Why on earth did you interrupt your training at Gray's Inn to ship out to India?'

Roger admitted the truth—he had no means of his own, and salaries were higher here than in England. Also, he wanted to travel before settling down, and lacking the funds to do so as a tourist, he had decided to see India at Her Majesty's expense. His superior's warm greeting had encouraged Roger to be frank.

Alexander Skene was slightly over forty years old. He was tall, thin, with a hatchet face, pointed nose and a pointed chin. His small blue eyes shone often with a sort of fond amusement. Although inflexible about duty and principles, he was a tolerant, understanding and warmhearted man. He had greeted Roger more like a friend than a superior. He offered him a glass of whiskey and put him at ease, not just to make the new arrival comfortable but also to get a glimpse of Roger's character behind the barrier of formality. Not entirely satisfied with Roger's answer, he asked, 'But why Jhansi? I'm told you asked to be stationed here. No one ever asks for Jhansi. They all want to be sent to Lucknow, Cawnpore or even Delhi—if, of course, they have to leave Calcutta at all. When they're chosen for a spot like Jhansi, they think they're being exiled.'

Upon finishing his studies at Fort William, Roger, like all his companions, had drawn up a list of places where he wanted to be stationed. He had chosen all the smallest towns, placing Jhansi, on a whim, at the head of the list.

'I chose a small town because I want to get to know India. I couldn't do that in one of the big cities, surrounded by other Englishmen.'

An Englishman who wanted to learn about India—this was quite a rarity. The captain was now thoroughly intrigued, but he preferred not to ask any more questions, sensing he could not pry anything else out of Roger. 'Interesting fellow, but needs to be watched,' he thought. And then he set about telling Roger of his new duties as assistant to the district commissioner.

Skene had also made arrangements for Roger's lodgings. There were no unoccupied bungalows in the civilian compound. Captain Skene had therefore taken the liberty of renting a room for Roger in the house of the British surgeon and his wife, Doctor and Mrs Phipps, whose house was too large for their needs, and who would be delighted to have him.

Soon after his arrival, Roger requested an audience with the Rani in order to pay his respects. As he told Captain Skene, it seemed only normal that a newcomer to Jhansi should introduce himself to the former ruler. The captain approved. He only wished that all Englishmen arriving in Jhansi would do the same, and although he usually made that suggestion, it was not in his nature to force them.

'Strictly between us, Giffard—and for God's sake, don't quote me—the annexation of Jhansi was not our government's soundest act. The people of Jhansi never wanted British rule and the manner in which we behaved toward the Rani was utterly unjust.'

The Rani of Jhansi granted Assistant Magistrate Roger Giffard's request for an audience. The sight of a new face was for her a welcome diversion.

On the appointed day, Roger dressed with care, donning his only suit of evening clothes: a tight-waisted black frockcoat, black trousers, black boots, a white waistcoat on a white shirt, a black silk tie. The clothes were worn but well-cut and highly flattering.

It took Roger ten minutes to ride his horse from the civilian compound to the walls of the city. As soon as he passed through the Orchha Gate, he was swept up into that Indian swarm that so disgusted Mrs Phipps. Roger's landlady had boasted that she never set foot in town. Through a labyrinth of narrow streets, he made his way toward the Rani's palace.

Without dismounting, Roger knocked on the heavy wooden door. A peephole opened, a face appeared, Roger gave his name, the peephole shut. After five minutes had gone by, he began to think he had been misunderstood, and he was about to knock again when the doors slowly swung open. Roger rode into a vast courtyard bordered by empty elephant-stalls. Carefully tended flower beds, brightened by the sun, attempted to lend the area the appearance of a garden. Across the courtyard rose the palace's yellow facade, two storey high, its windows framed by over-elaborate stucco columns and arcades; above each window stood a stucco peacock, its tail fanned out. A servant appeared and casually took hold of the horse's reins. Roger dismounted.

Several dozen ragged-looking men, probably servants, were sitting on the steps or loitering in the shadow of the stalls, savouring their complete idleness. Roger was surprised by their number, having heard that the British annexation had bankrupted the Rani. He had not yet learned that with Indian royalty, poverty was relative, and that among their retainers, there were not only servants who had a definite function but also parents, brothers, children, cousins, nephews, uncles—people who affixed themselves to the household like barnacles, without any specific responsibilities. At the Rani's palace, there were several hundreds of these parasites satisfied with bed and board and an occasional modest handout.

Roger was not sure what to do. No one seemed to be paying any attention to him. Finally, a man dressed in worn brocade came up and instructed Roger to follow him. In an approximation of English, the man explained that he was one of the Rani's chamberlains. Roger also half-understood that the man was vaguely related to the Rani.

They passed under the porch of the palace. After climbing a steep staircase, they walked through the throne room and the audience chamber, turned right, crossed another five or six small rooms, and then stopped before a closed door of carved wood inlaid with copper. The chamberlain knocked.

A feminine voice answered through the door in Marathi, 'Who is it?'

'The Sahib Feringhi,' answered the chamberlain.

After a few moments' wait, the door was opened by invisible hands and Roger followed the chamberlain into a room slightly larger than the previous ones. A carpet with a leafy design covered the floor. The walls were scalloped with little Persian niches in which mirrors, all of them too large, had been placed carelessly. From the ceiling hung a crystal chandelier, obviously imported from Europe and also too large for the room, and a punkhah, wielded by a servant to fan the air. The room was bare of furniture except for an English mahogany armchair sitting in the centre of the carpet and surrounded by garlands of sweet-smelling flowers.

The chamberlain motioned Roger to the armchair. Facing it was a curtain of semi-transparent muslin strung across a sort of alcove. Roger could see only silhouettes behind the cloth, a woman seated on a low sofa, another standing next to her, and a child who came and went restlessly.

Even if he had seen the Rani unveiled and close up, Roger would probably not have recognized the former queen as the youth who, a few days earlier, had frightened him with imaginary crocodiles. She spoke a few words in Marathi to the chamberlain, who suddenly began to examine Roger with a deeply grieved expression. Roger was both puzzled and embarrassed. No one had told him that the black of his clothes was a colour Indians considered a very ill omen. After a brief silence, the Rani snapped an order, again in her own language.

The chamberlain jumped and approached Roger with the deference due a guest of the queen. In his vague English he whispered that there was a rather delicate matter he had omitted to mention. Would the sahib consent to remove his boots, since protocol required that no one enter the queen's apartments wearing shoes?

Roger frowned. He had no desire to take off his boots, and moreover, he worried that the socks he had put on that morning might have holes at the toes. Noting Roger's obvious displeasure, the chamberlain hastened to add that if Roger so wished, he could put on the hat he was holding in his lap. The Rani, he explained, would see in it a gesture of respect. Suddenly, Roger almost laughed out loud. He resigned himself to pulling off his boots, but found they were too tight. He pulled at the left one, but it would not come off. He pulled harder, grew red in the face and winded with the effort, and finally managed to tear it off. He then went through the same agony with the other. His socks were indeed worn through, but he had already made such a ridicule of himself that it could not possibly matter. He placed the boots next to his chair, tugged on his waistcoat, put his hat on in accordance with the chamberlain's instructions, and assumed as dignified a pose as he could manage.

It occurred to him that women had a knack, independent of protocol, for making men appear ridiculous.

The Rani had been watching her visitor closely. She had recognized him immediately. He had the pointed chin, the high cheekbones and the slightly bent nose. His hair was very black, straight and carefully combed. In his gestures she saw a certain intensity, perhaps even fervour.

'To what do we owe the pleasure of your visit, Sahib?'

The Rani's voice was soft, and the quality of her English surprised him. He explained that having just arrived in Jhansi, where he had been appointed assistant magistrate, he had wanted to pay his regards to Her Highness. After thanking him, the Rani launched on the trivial questions that all royal personages are in the habit of asking any newly-introduced stranger—how long had he been in India, what places had he seen, what part of England did he come from, did he have brothers and sisters, where did his parents live, where had he been to school, how long had he lived in London? Roger answered all these questions carefully.

At one point during the exchange, the child, who had been fidgeting behind the curtain, suddenly pulled it toward him, and Roger was able to catch a glimpse of the Rani. It lasted no more than a second, but it was time enough for him to etch every detail of her silhouette, her clothes and her face on his memory. It seemed to him that the Rani took her time before telling the child to let go the curtain, as if she had not been displeased to be seen.

The Rani's stream of trivial questions appeared to be slowing. The chamberlain thought the audience was over. But after a silence, the Rani asked, 'Tell me, Sahib, what strikes you most about India?'

'The birds, Your Highness.'

Mandar, who was standing next to the Rani, noticed that she lost her poise for a moment and showed surprise.

'The birds?' asked the Rani.

'Yes, Your Highness. They are far more numerous and far noisier than those in England.'

The Rani smiled.

'Why are you interested in birds, Sahib? Do you hunt them?'

'I don't hunt birds, Your Highness. I draw them. In my free time I'm a painter—an amateur painter, of course. And if I am to do justice to my sitters, I have to learn to know and understand them.'

And, without being asked, he began to speak about them with enthusiasm, not as an ornithologist might, but as though the birds were friends of his. He described his encounters with them, explained their characters and their habits. He became so absorbed in his subject that he completely forgot where he was and whom he was talking to.

The Rani was slightly annoyed at hearing this Englishman describe Indian birds as though he knew them better than she, but she found the love with which he spoke of them almost moving.

'I must say,' she interrupted, 'that for a foreigner, you have admirable knowledge of our fauna. But you haven't mentioned vultures. This country is swarming with them. We even have red ones.'

It was a transparent allusion to the British uniform. Pretending he had not caught it, Roger answered, 'I did not mention vultures because in India, they are birds of ill-omen, Your Highness.'

The Rani bit her lip and fell silent. Seeing that he had scored a point, Roger thought he might flout protocol and ask the Rani a question.

'Your Highness seems to like birds. Does she have many caged ones?'

'In India, Sahib,' she answered in her soft voice, 'we do not put birds in cages. They are tame and do not need to be behind bars. The birds, at least, are free.'

The allusion to the British had slipped from her unintentionally.

'We hope you will find time to paint our fauna, Sahib, and may your stay among us be a happy one.'

The chamberlain, who had been standing motionless in a corner, stepped over to Roger's seat. Roger understood that the audience was over. He rose, picked up his boots, bowed at the curtain, and retired.

That evening Roger wrote a letter to his closest friend, Roderick Briggs. Born in the same year, they had met at Harnwell College. At first, they had hated each other and fought as often as possible; then, their childish hatred had turned into a friendship that had endured and even deepened as they grew out of adolescence. The son of a member of parliament from Devonshire, Roderick belonged to the local gentry. Family tradition and a taste for the army had brought him to the Woolwich Military Academy, from which he had emerged as a second lieutenant in the Eighth Hussars. He had been sent to Crimea, where England, in alliance with France and Turkey, was at war with Russia. When the war ended, Roderick returned to garrison life in England. He found it a boring existence, from which Roger's letters were always a welcome distraction.

Mrs Phipps, the wife of the doctor with whom I board, has given the Rani English lessons; she had described her as a sort of a tiny Indian doll, commonplace and black-skinned. Mrs Phipps also told me that her former student, in spite of her twenty-eight years, had remained an undisciplined, capricious, spoiled child. I saw the Rani only for a short moment—her child had accidentally, while playing, pulled aside the curtain of the purdah—but what I saw was a queen. She sat very straight on her throne, which is wide and low, with great natural dignity. Her face showed kindness and vivacity.

Painting has taught me to see things quickly. Therefore, I can tell you, I saw a finely-drawn face, a small nose which I think might be slightly hooked. Her skin is rather fair. What struck me most are her eyes. They're enormous, slightly drawn toward the temples, very dark, of course, but sparkling and always in motion. She was wearing a white sari of very thin material—perhaps muslin—and only gold earrings for jewellery. Her sari was so tight that I could guess at a shapely body. She has neat ankles and wrists, and tiny feet. And her greeting was quite as seductive as the rest—reserved, as befits a queen, but sincerely warm where I had expected coolness and distance. Either Mrs Phipps, contrary to what she says, doesn't know the Rani well, or else she deliberately denigrated her for reasons unknown to me.

Soon afterwards, the Rani received a large envelope containing a watercolour of a bird of paradise. The artist had admirably rendered the green sheen of its black feathers, its famous tuft, and the two long white feathers in its black tail. The bird was shown drinking out of a cup of tea, just as the artist had seen it.

In response, a messenger from the Rani came to Doctor Phipps's bungalow to invite Roger to paint the Rani's domestic birds in her gardens whenever he wanted.

The Rani felt a need to explain her gesture to Mandar.

'I feel bad about that young man. I didn't treat him well when he came to present himself, and then he sends me one of his paintings which, besides, shows genuine talent. At least I can give him the opportunity to practise his art.'

'There are plenty of birds to be painted elsewhere than in your gardens,' grumbled Mandar, looking away.

Needless to say, Roger took full advantage of the Rani's invitation. His work left him with quite a bit of free time. Jhansi was a quiet, sleepy post, and neither Roger nor his superior, District Commissioner Captain Gordon, were particularly busy. Roger soon got into the habit of painting in the Rani's gardens. He was known at the palace gate; a servant would let him in and lead him to the second court. Because it was so small, the palace of Jhansi had no real gardens; their role was filled by flower-planted courts. Both Roger and his feathered models preferred the second court to the first, a passageway filled with loiterers. The second court had a garden in the Moghul style introduced by the Muslim conquerors of India; raised rectilinear paths paved with pink granite separated vast square flower beds of roses, jasmine, tuberose, marigolds and verbena.

At the far end of the garden, nature had been allowed to take over. Several large mango trees shaded a lawn. Kachnars, bushes covered with white and purple flowers, grew haphazardly. The walls of the seldom-used outbuildings hugging the court were covered with exuberant bougainvillea of all colours—scarlet, purple, yellow, orange, pink. This was the Rani's domain, visited only by her intimates. The gardeners bothered neither Roger nor the birds. They did not seem surprised by his presence, and at times they appeared not to see him at all—an Indian habit that sometimes makes newcomers uncomfortable but suited Roger perfectly. Their quiet indifference allowed him to work in peace.

He had not seen Lakshmi since the audience, and this annoyed him. As Mandar had said, there were birds everywhere, and if he came to paint those at the palace, it was in the hope of seeing their owner. One day, his paintbox under his arm and a convincing expression of artistic absent-mindedness on his face, he wandered towards the porch that led straight to the queen's private apartments. An old woman sprang at him from the shadows, jabbering in dialect and waving her arms, and Roger had been forced to retreat.

The scene had not been missed by the Rani; she watched Roger every day.

In the late morning when her audiences were finished for the day, she would retire to the library to hear bhajans, during which a singer from the palace's temple recited the Gita, a holy book of Hindus, accompanied by musical instruments. As though by chance, the Rani would sit by the window, and sometimes her mind would wander. Then she would look outside and see, at the other end of the garden, a young man seated cross-legged on the grass, in shirtsleeves, bending over his sketchbook. Often he would turn and stare at the library window as if he knew the Rani stood behind it. Instinctively, she would step back, so as not to be caught.

That day, Roger was painting one of the white peacocks strutting among the flower beds. He had always found these birds stupid and their cries sinister, but the Indians were fond of their national bird, a symbol of nobility and fertility, and the Rani set great store by this emblem of the dynasty of Jhansi. Suddenly, the peacock turned its head anxiously, folded its fan, and hopped away as fast as it could. Roger looked over his shoulder—the Rani was standing behind him.

'You have scared away my model, Your Highness,' he said in a tone of amused reproach.

The Rani apologized and then asked to see his work. Her eyes did not leave Roger's, whose sparkle she was noticing for the first time. Wide-open under thick arched eyebrows, they were an indefinable mixture of gold, green and brown, a changing colour that made his gaze sometimes intense, sometimes sweetly gentle.

He opened his portfolio. She sat down next to him on the lawn with a simplicity he found charming. He had already painted a tailorbird building its nest, a dark-backed weaver, a white pigeon which is supposed to bring good luck, and a white dove—all the Rani's doves were white. He had even done a portrait of the Rani's favourite bird, a white owl that lived in one of the mango trees.

Every time he handed her one of the watercolours, the Rani gave little cries of joy like an amazed child and made comments in Marathi. It was a language Roger could not speak, but he understood from the tone of her voice that the Rani admired his work.

'How did you become a painter?' she asked, in English.

Roger explained that he had been taught to draw by his mother who had painted, not without talent, portraits of the local gentry at home in Wales.

'But you're much too good a painter to have chosen to become a barrister!'

Roger answered that he liked the law and its practice. He did not tell the Rani that his parents had practically forced him into it. For them, it represented the social advancement they had wanted for him, the goal for which they had worked so hard all their lives.

'An artist like you, Sahib Giffard, was not made for the dry dialectics of the law. You were made to paint, not to live among files,' the Rani said in a peremptory tone. Then, as though wanting to be forgiven such a personal remark, she asked, almost humbly, 'May I keep the portrait of my white owl?'

'All these drawings belong to you, Your Highness,' answered Roger.

She thanked him, picked up the portfolio, and hurried away like a child who has just been given a long-coveted present and runs off to gloat over it in her secret hideaway.

5

The Rani decided to take Roger along on one of her excursions on horseback. Only a few servants were to go with them.

After crossing the belt of gardens and orchards surrounding Jhansi, they were suddenly in the jungle. Winter had not yet stripped the leaves from the trees, whose appearance seemed to Roger quite familiar and European. But the density of the shrubs forming the dark underbrush had something disquieting and repellent about it.

The sandy path ran through an inextricable tangle of branches and wild rhododendron bushes, some of which were still in bloom. They spurred their horses and galloped at the breakneck speed the Rani liked, all the way to the village of Burah where they were to stop for lunch.

Burah was built on a height, dominating fields carved out of the jungle. From afar, the long, low houses with mud walls of pale ochre seemed a single rampart. A leafless coral tree and a few palms rose from among the thatched roofs. When they entered the village, Roger was surprised by the cleanliness of the haphazard, winding streets.

After being led to the village elder, they sat down in front of his house on a small uneven square, across from a squat, recently-whitewashed temple. Water was brought, and Roger noticed that while the Rani drank, she was careful not to let her lips touch the rim of the earthenware cup in order to avoid any impure contact.

Then they were served a typical Indian peasant's meal: a plate of dal, potatoes and chapattis. Naturally, they ate with their fingers, and the Rani watched Roger from the corner of her eye, amused by his clumsiness. When he reached out for the dish with his left hand, she stopped him suddenly.

'You are going to horrify the peasants. Never eat with your left hand—it is considered impure.'

She explained that proper table manners consisted of scooping up the food with three fingers of the right hand without dirtying them beyond the first knuckle.

Since Indians do not drink during meals, the buffalo milk was not brought until they had finished eating. Roger had some difficulty swallowing the thick, creamy liquid.

Having drained her cup, the Rani noticed in the village square an elephant that was harnessed not for work in the fields, which would have been normal, but for travel. She asked the elder who was the traveller who had just arrived by elephant.

'It's a fakir, Rani,' answered the old man.

'A fakir!' the Rani exclaimed. 'But all fakirs take a vow of poverty and travel on foot!'

The old man was reluctant to show ignorance.

'Perhaps,' he said, 'it was given to him by one of the faithful.'

'And why has he come here?'

'Like all fakirs, he goes from house to house spreading the good word.'

A fakir on an elephant, who had come all the way to preach in this lost little village... It all seemed very strange to Lakshmi. The elder watched her anxiously.

'Don't worry about it, Rani. A fakir is a welcome distraction for our women.'

In India, only holy men are allowed into the part of the house reserved for women, to see them unveiled and speak to them.

'You will bring me this fakir,' the Rani ordered.

Then her attention was distracted by a troupe of travelling entertainers setting up their stage on the little square, where the villagers had already begun to gather.

'Have you ever seen our tamashagars?' she asked Roger. 'They travel from village to village with their puppets, staging the most famous episodes of India's great epics.'

The peasants knew these episodes by heart, having heard them read so often in the temples, but the puppeteers nevertheless remained their favourite entertainment.

Followed by Roger, the Rani had walked up to the stage. Roger noticed that although the villagers made way for her respectfully, they showed neither excessive eagerness nor servility. She explained the scenes as they unfolded on the stage. It was one of the most popular episodes from the epic known as the Ramayana.

The hero, Prince Rama, in fact an incarnation of the god Vishnu, had landed in the fabulous island of Lanka, where his betrothed, Sita, was being held by the king of demons, Ravana. There followed a terrible battle, during the course of which Rama himself killed the evil Ravana.

Lakshmi knew every word of the epic. Suddenly, she perked up her ears. Victorious Rama was addressing the audience.

'Thus we shall confound the demons who have concocted diabolical machinations against us; thus we shall destroy the demons and rid ourselves of the calamity that has taken hold of our country. If one day you tell yourself, "My religion is dying, my people have been reduced to a state worse than dogs," then take up arms, as I, Rama, have done.'

The Rani knew very well that what she had just heard was not part of the epic. The allusions to the British occupation were transparent. She sensed suddenly that the audience had grown tense. Roger had not understood the words spoken by the marionette but, a sensitive man, he could not help but feel a strange current of hostility coursing through the crowd. He remained still and continued to smile, as if fascinated by the spectacle. Finally, the Rani tugged at his sleeve.

'Let's go,' she said. 'They're really not very good.'

She walked off at an easy pace, followed by Roger and surrounded by her servants. When they reached the edge of the village and their waiting horses, the Rani turned to the elder and asked, 'Where do those tamashagars come from?'

'From the east, from the kingdom of Oudh.'

'And where is that fakir I asked you to bring me?'

'He left, Rani.'

Absorbed in the puppet-show, the Rani had not noticed that the elephant and its mysterious rider had disappeared.

'And what did he preach?' the Rani asked casually.

No less lightly, the old man answered, 'He said that if Swadharma and Swaraj, religion and freedom, were insulted, we would have to defend them by force.'

The Rani carefully concealed her surprise. She took leave of the elder and with her escort, left the village at a trot.

That evening she summoned Naransin, her former Diwan, to the palace. He did not seem surprised by what she told him.

'I've heard of this sort of thing happening recently in several villages in the region. It is always sparked by the preaching of fakirs or by travelling puppet-shows. All the speeches are pretty much like the one you heard.'

'What does it mean?' asked the Rani.

'Nothing important,' answered Naransin. 'The incidents are probably provoked by the exaltation of a few very small groups of fanatics such as we have always had in this country.'

The Rani did not seem convinced. Naransin reassured her.

'India, as you know, has always been like a pond of dark water, Rani. From time to time bubbles form at the surface, expand, and then burst.'

The Rani knew very well that in India, it was best not to try to explain everything.

One day, while rummaging through Roger's portfolio, the Rani came upon a sketch that made her frown. It was a portrait of a very young woman, almost a child. She wore a blue cotton blouse that ended just below her breasts and a skirt of the same cloth knotted on her hips. In her hair was a flower made of gilt paper and little fake pearls. She wore a great deal of paint on her face, but the artist had rendered perfectly the innocent, almost frightened look in her eyes.

'And who is this winged creature, Sahib Giffard? I don't recall having seen it in my gardens,' asked the Rani, amused.

'Her name is Kiraun.'

'Your mistress, Sahib Giffard?'

Roger hesitated a few seconds before answering, 'Yes, Your Highness.'

'No doubt one of the camp followers who live in those shacks at the edge of the cantonment.'

'No Indian woman of a condition higher than Kiraun's would have me, Your Highness—as you know, she would be too afraid of losing her caste by having any relations with a foreigner, a man of impurity. Only girls like Kiraun accept us Englishmen. They are so poor they have nothing to lose, not even their caste.'

Roger had scored a point, as he saw from the Rani's reply, 'I know that those girls, in spite of their trade, are often kind and devoted.'

And she felt pity for Kiraun. No doubt the girl was hopelessly in love with Roger. She felt for him too; to take comfort from the likes of Kiraun he must have been lonely indeed, far from his family and his country, in a mysterious, elusive empire he was trying to understand and wanted to love.

That afternoon, they rode all the way to the river Puhaj, north of Jhansi. They galloped a good part of the way back and stopped to rest only once they had passed the village of Bhogla. They sat down in the shade of a giant tamarisk. Around them, at a respectful distance, crouched the servants who usually accompanied her on such excursions. The setting sun had tinted the peaceful fields red. The slope they were on offered an immense view of the countryside; they could clearly make out the towers of the fort of Jhansi in the distance. Somewhere a turtledove cooed, and high in the blue sky, bands of herons flew northward.

Still out of breath after their gallop, Roger and the Rani admired the beauty of the evening without speaking. Roger gazed absent-mindedly at a small hole in the ground about a yard away from him. Although the hole was half-covered by a stone, it seemed to Roger that something was moving inside it. Intoxicated with fatigue and pleasure, he paid no attention. A few seconds later, he saw the head of a cobra emerge slowly from the hole. Roger was petrified. Almost half the snake's body had slithered from the hole by the time the others noticed it. Like Roger, the Rani froze, her eyes fixed on the reptile. Her servants leaped up and fled in all directions, shouting. The noise and the movement alarmed the cobra; now fully out of its hiding-place, it raised its head and began to sway from side to side, flicking the air with its tongue. Still, Roger was too terrified to move.

Her voice thick, the Rani said, 'Whatever you do, stand still.' Very slowly, she rose to her feet. The snake had not calmed down; it continued to sway back and forth, an arm's length from Roger, its tongue darting from its mouth like a whip. As slowly and smoothly as she could, the Rani reached for one of the pistols in her belt. She was about to pull it out when the cobra, in a single movement, sprang at Roger and bit him in the calf.

Then it shrank back and slithered away almost immediately, but the Rani, having drawn her pistol, aimed and shot it in the head. Roger, who had shouted in pain when he was bitten, was slowly sinking to the ground.

The Rani did not lose a moment. She ran to his side and tore open the leg of his trousers. Two tiny drops of blood formed a bead on the calf muscle where the cobra had struck, just above the boot top. The Rani drew the small jewelled dagger she always carried, and without hesitation cut into the wound, widened it, squeezed it in order to make it bleed, and sucked at it avidly, spitting out the poisoned blood. She went about it methodically, without haste, with impressive composure.

In spite of the pain, Roger swore to himself that he would not cry out or even sigh in front of the Rani. He found it ironic to consider that he had been cut open with the dagger that Mrs Phipps said was poisoned.

When the Rani had sucked the wound as clean as she could, she improvised a bandage. Her servants, their panic subsiding, had returned. With their help she hoisted Roger, who could barely move his leg, onto her own horse.

She jumped up behind him, and they rode back to Jhansi at a slow walk.

Night had already fallen when they reached the palace. Roger was pale and sweating heavily, but he did not complain. The Rani had him placed in a litter drawn by oxen and taken back to the civilian compound.

As she watched it trundle off under the porchway, Mandar, standing next to her, muttered, 'The cobra, our sacred animal, attacks a foreigner...it's symbolic.'

'Don't be silly. I feel responsible for what happened. I shouldn't have taken him along.'

'Is he going to die?' asked Damodar, who had come out to join his mother, attracted by all the excitement. His voice shook and his eyes were filled with tears. Damodar was very fond of the Sahib Feringhi, the foreign gentleman. He had accepted Roger's presence far better than Mandar had. At first he had been curious. For the Hindu child, the Englishman was an unknown creature, impure, perhaps dangerous, and therefore fascinating. Roger's kindness and openness had done the rest. When Damodar, watching Roger paint, asked to be taught to draw, Roger set to it patiently. The child and his friends often invited him to join in a game and Roger accepted willingly, not with the condescension of an adult that children would immediately detect, but with the genuine enthusiasm of an adolescent. He made them explain the rules of the game in detail. He did not let the children win when he could beat them, and when he made a mistake, he was the one who laughed the loudest. He had become very popular with them.

'Is he going to die?' Damodar asked again.

'No, he isn't,' the Rani answered.

Two hours later, she sent a messenger to Doctor Phipps's bungalow to inquire after Roger. The news he brought back was not good. Roger's fever was rising, and he was not only very weak but also in great pain. To her attendants' surprise, the Rani did not go to bed, as she always did, at nine-thirty. She retired to the library, ordering them not to wait up for her.

In a quiet voice the Rani read, or rather recited, the holy texts she knew so well; again and again, the thought of Roger came to break her concentration. She turned over and over in her mind the events of the afternoon; she saw him, wan and bloodless, being taken away on the litter.

At midnight, gnawed by anxiety, she sent another messenger to the compound. It seemed to the Rani that he took years to return. He found her pacing the floor, unable to settle down anywhere. This time, the news was worse—Roger's fever had risen to one hundred and four degrees. He had fallen into a coma, from which he emerged only in delirium. His life was hanging by a thread.

It must have been about one-thirty in the morning, and Doctor Phipps was sitting at Roger's side when one of his Indian servants came in to announce that two riders had come from the palace asking to see him. Muttering to himself with annoyance, Doctor Phipps stepped out into the hallway to meet the two riders, one of whom, to his great surprise, he recognized as the Rani of Jhansi herself. He was still trying to collect himself when she said, 'I am here to see Sahib Giffard.'

The doctor asked her to wait a moment and then vanished. The Rani paced from room to room. Despite her anxiety, she examined the Phipps house with curiosity—the dark heavy furniture, the rocking-chair, the large family photographs on the wall, the Staffordshire crockery, the potted plants, the periodicals spread haphazardly around the whiskey-tray on the dining-room table created an atmosphere she found stifling. It was the first time she had come to the civilian compound. In the moonlight she had seen the perfect rows of bungalows, all alike, each surrounded by a little garden. The whole layout seemed to her boring and depressing.

When she entered Roger's room, she found Annabelle Phipps standing next to the brass bed. With her long dark curls tumbling down her back, a vast dressing-gown of silk and lace floating over her full form, anguish in her features, she was the very image of tragedy. A single glance was enough to show the Rani that Roger's life was in danger. His skin was yellow; sweaty strands of black hair were plastered to his forehead. His face had hollowed, his eyes were sunken, his nose pinched. He seemed unconscious, breathing arhythmically with an ugly wheeze. At times, his chest would rise so violently that it seemed ready to burst; at others, it seemed completely still, as if the heart had stopped.

After staring at him for a few moments, Lakshmi turned to her servant and said, 'Go fetch Natva. Quick!' In whispers, she explained to Doctor Phipps that Natva was a hatha-yogi, a member of a highly-praised holy brotherhood of healers. Doctor Phipps did not have the foggiest idea what a hatha-yogi might be. He imagined the Rani was speaking of a fakir, an illusionist, one of those Indian charlatans whose cures were a mockery to medical science. Nevertheless, Doctor Phipps was in awe of the Rani and did not dare oppose her. Uncomfortable in the presence of the two women, he left the room.

Annabelle Phipps sat down on Roger's bed. She wiped the sweat from his forehead with her lace handkerchief, she caressed his face and his hair; tears streamed down her cheeks.

'Don't die, Roger, don't die,' she moaned.

She was doing everything she could to show the Rani she was madly in love with the young man.

The Rani found the exhibition distasteful and Annabelle beneath contempt. She too wanted Roger to live. But instead of crying, she fortified her will against his death. 'I don't want him to die, I don't want him to die,' she kept repeating to herself. Shaken, she stared at his body, its contours traced faithfully by the light covering sheet, that body she had once seen naked in all its vitality and beauty.

Suddenly, Roger smiled. The Rani imagined it was meant for Mrs Phipps. She was too exasperated with the Englishwoman to realize that Roger, despite his open eyes, could see nothing. He seemed to be emerging from his coma. He muttered a few incomprehensible words, and then clearly spoke Mrs Phipps's name—'Annabelle'. His face stiffened, and he fell back into unconsciousness. He had called Mrs Phipps, she was in love with him, they must be lovers, the Rani thought. Rage and jealousy welled up in her like a wave of heat and she was preparing to leave when the door opened to admit Natva, the hatha-yogi.

Natva was completely bald except for a small tuft of hair in the middle of his skull. He wore a white robe that left his chest and one of his arms uncovered. His skin was light, his eyes large and round, his nose narrow and very hooked. His thin lips muttered a prayer. Only a few small wrinkles on his forehead and the grey tuft of hair indicated that he was over fifty. He gave an impression of calm, authority, saintliness, extraordinary youth. Annabelle Phipps stood up and shouted, 'I don't want any sorcerers! Take him away! He'll kill him!' and then burst into loud sobs.

Doctor Phipps led her out of the room. The hatha-yogi stepped to the bed, placed a hand on Roger's forehead, and muttered, 'This is not, this is not, this is not.'

From the depths of his unconsciousness, Roger felt a sudden freshness. Like a drop of icy water, it poured from his forehead over his skull, down his spine, down, still down, all the way to the soles of his feet.

The hatha-yogi remained perfectly still, his hand on the patient's head. Slowly, the vice of pain loosened. The freshness continued to radiate through him and began to clear his brain.

A curious feeling came over the Rani, who was still standing at the foot of the bed; it seemed to her that the moment, her anguish, even time itself were receding.

How long did the feeling last? She was never to know.

Gently, the hatha-yogi withdrew his hand from Roger's head, stood up, and said, 'He's cured.' Indeed, a little tinge of colour had returned to Roger's cheeks, His breathing was light and regular. On the other hand, the hatha-yogi seemed exhausted, even feverish. His skin had taken on that yellow tint that the Rani had seen in Roger's; icy sweat was forming on his skull and forehead, and his entire body was trembling. He had absorbed all of Roger's illness. The Rani followed him from the room.

In the corridor, Annabelle Phipps, her features altered by grief, threw herself in their path and shouted, 'You're leaving, he is dead, you have killed him!'

The Rani stared at her so coldly that she stopped abruptly. Then, as if his wife did not exist, the Rani turned to the doctor and said, curtly, 'He'll be all right by morning.'

It was not the next day but the day following that Roger rose from his bed. He had been so exhausted that he had slept straight through a day and a half. He woke up cured. He stayed at home another week, recovering his strength.

6

One evening soon afterwards, a travelling jeweller, a personage familiar to Indian palaces, presented himself at the gates of the Rani's palace. Like many of his colleagues, he peddled his wares from court to court, travelling with an escort of guards armed to the teeth. The Rani received him in the audience chamber. Her fortune had been considerably depleted by the British, but she had always liked jewels and still enjoyed admiring them. The jeweller was rather fat, unctuous and servile.

'You're wasting your time, jeweller, I have no money to buy your merchandise,' the Rani said.

'I ask only for the privilege of showing it, Rani. Your gaze alone will lend it incomparable sparkle.' With almost feminine gestures, the jeweller began opening the drawers of his travelling chest made of precious wood inlaid with ivory. On a sheet of dark velvet he had spread on a low table, he placed the jewels one by one, spouting flowery, poetic explanations. He had night-blue enamel torques with diamond stars; breastplates of large triangular, round and rectangular diamonds; necklaces with a dozen rows of enormous emeralds; brocade bracelets embroidered with articulated diamond baguettes; pompoms made of a string of pearls holding a ruby to hang from a cap; aigrette-holders inlaid with cabochons; chokers, forearm bracelets, hairnets, and so on. Assuming an air of disgust, as was customary in these matters, the Rani, who had an eye for jewels, itemized for Mandar the qualities and faults of each one, the purity of a stone, the finesse of a setting. She turned them over delicately, for the value of Indian jewels is determined by their enamelled backs. She examined the delicacy of the designs, which represented flowers, birds, arabesques. She spurned the red and the green enamels, seeking instead the pinks, yellows or periwinkle blues, which are far more difficult to obtain.

When the jeweller had finished emptying his chest, he said, 'And now, Rani, I must beg a favour. I have here a jewel of such value, of such rarity, that I wish to show it to you alone.' Although surprised by this request, the Rani asked Mandar to leave the room. Once they were alone, the jeweller, his head lowered, his fingers playing with the emeralds and diamonds spread out before him, murmured, 'In fact, Rani, I have come to give you the opportunity to recover the most beautiful jewel in the world—Jhansi.'

The Rani's surprise was such that she was unable to hide it. The jeweller continued, 'I have come, Rani, to give you the means to recover for yourself and for your son the throne that is yours by right and from which you were unjustly deposed.'

'And through what magic do you plan to do this, jeweller?'

'Through a revolt against the British oppressors.'

The Rani's heart was beating wildly. Was she dealing with a fanatic, a madman, a joker or an agent provocateur? She needed to know more.

'And with whose help shall I rebel, jeweller? You don't want me to rise up against the British Empire with the few servants I have left?'

'Oh no, Rani! You will not be alone. With you there will be kings who were robbed as you were, artisans, peasants, all those who suffer under the British occupation and fear for their traditions and their religion.'

'But in order to fight you need soldiers!'

'We have them, Rani—they are the British's own soldiers, our Indian brothers who they recruited into their armies. Of all those who have decided to throw off the yoke, the sepoys are the most determined.'

'I assume that you settled the matter among yourselves before coming to make this proposal.'

'Everything is ready, Rani. For months and months, we have been recruiting people all over India. Our network is spread throughout the country. There are millions of us who are dissatisfied, millions who await only the signal for rebellion.'

'Have you thought of the British reaction?'

'The British! Do you know how many there are across India, Rani?

39,352 troops and 6,170 officers, altogether 45,522 Englishmen—against one hundred and fifty million Indians.'

'And who will be your leader?'

'Our legitimate master, Rani. The Great Moghul, the Emperor of India.'

The Rani began to laugh. All of India knew that the current Great Moghul, Bahadur Shah, was an old man without character, without power, without prestige or money; a miserable recluse in his ruined palace at Delhi. He passed his time writing poetry and teasing the women of his harem, harassed by his favourite wife, a harpy called Zinat Mahal, and torn apart by the quarrels of his sons, who rivalled each other in greed and incompetence.

'Do you mean to tell me, jeweller, that Bahadur Shah would lead a general revolt against the British? You must be joking!'

'He will be a symbol, Rani. His name will be enough to unite the rebellion around him and lead us to victory and independence.'

That kind of language was making the Rani more and more sceptical. 'I am well placed, alas, to know how India has been humiliated, despoiled and threatened in her religion and her traditions—but a general revolt!'

'India, Rani, has not only been humiliated. She has been reduced to slavery. The annexation of princely states that has already taken place on doubtful pretexts is only the beginning. The British intend to seize all the princely states, with or without pretext. They want to crush our freedom, our traditions, our religion under their boots. They have only one goal—to reduce all of India to slavery. Only rebellion can spare us that slow death.'

'Tell me, jeweller—who sent you here?'

The jeweller smiled and answered softly, 'Destiny, Rani, your destiny.'

'But what you say is so unexpected. I would need some proof.'

'You will have it, Rani. Soon you will see, in Jhansi as well as in the rest of the country, signs that you cannot fail to recognize. They will show you clearly that we are all united, and the time is coming.'

'Why did you choose me, jeweller?'

'Because of your prestige. In the hearts of the people of Jhansi, you are still the queen. A single word from you and they will all flock to our cause, they will all rebel. And then we know that you have contacts with the British. You can gather information we need. Your help will be priceless.'

'You speak as if I had already accepted, jeweller.'

'Think about it, Rani. Take your time, but make sure it is not already too late when you make your decision.'

'Aren't you afraid that I might betray you to the British?'

'Perhaps you might refuse, against duty and your own interests, to join us—but betray us, your country and your countrymen? I know you will never do that.'

The Rani was deeply shaken, prey to conflicting emotions. She did not want to give the jeweller the slightest indication of her reaction. Moreover, the man so intrigued her that she became insolent.

'I thought the banias, the merchants of your caste, were interested only in getting rich.'

'There are times when we must forget the miserable preoccupations of daily life. I have answered India's call, as we all must.'

'How much for this necklace, jeweller?' the Rani asked suddenly, pointing to an object that had struck her the moment she saw it. It was a very long necklace, for a man, made of twists of large pearls; thick rings of gold set with rubies were set at intervals of a few inches.

'A thousand rupees. It's worth three times more, but I will let you have it at that ridiculously low price as proof of my admiration for you.'

'You're dreaming, jeweller. It's worth four hundred and fifty at most.'

'Your legendary knowledge of gems misleads you this time, Rani. There are not two necklaces in India as beautiful as this one.'

In an instant, conspirator had changed back to tough merchant. The Rani and he bargained at length, she for her pleasure, he with age-old science. Finally, he let the necklace go for four hundred and seventy-five rupees. He repacked the jewels into the drawers of his chest, humbly took his leave of the Rani, and departed without once again alluding to the matters he had first spoken of. The Rani knew she had obtained the necklace at a price far below its actual value. No doubt the merchant knew this as well. Had he wanted to secure her good graces? At any rate, the transaction had been to her advantage.

The meeting with the jeweller did not make the Rani change her daily routine. During her hour of leisure, she walked to the pillared pavilion that opened onto pools and flower beds to listen to the evening concert of sacred music. The musicians did not play from scores. With drums and sitars they improvised on a given theme in order to create the essence of a raga, the atmosphere of the moment.

Golden-brown shadows were invading the far end of the garden. Night was falling. It was the hour when each tree became an insane aviary in which thousands of birds chirped, screeched, cooed and cackled together. The birds of India are noisier than any others. Their din covered the familiar sounds of the street and distracted the Rani.

She could think of nothing but the jeweller's words... The British driven away, Jhansi freed, she and her son back on the throne—those were her fondest wishes. She had never been resigned to her present state, even though the passing years had made her apathetic. And now a stranger had come suddenly to rekindle her hope. It was true that discontent and a kind of disquiet were widespread throughout India. But from that to hatching a careful plot, reaching every caste and every province, from that to making India shake off her age-old lethargy and burst into flames! The Indian kings taking up arms...well, not a single one had protested her dethroning or the annexation of Jhansi. As for the people, her people, rebelling, they whined about the occupation but they also made the best of it. She did make the connection between the jeweller's visit and the subversive speeches she had heard in the village of Burah. Fakirs and puppeteers had nothing in common with banias and merchants. The latter were said to act, live and breathe only for personal gain, and the patriotic words of the jeweller reawakened in the Rani her habitual suspicion. She was well-acquainted with the intrigues that twisted day and night through every Indian court. She knew that even off the throne she remained a target, surrounded by spies and shadowy designs.

She smelled provocation in the jeweller's visit. Someone was trying to compromise her. It could be a neighbouring state, Orchha for instance, wanting to harm the former ruler, or the British trying to test the sincerity of her submission. She saw trouble both for herself and for Jhansi in the jeweller's invitation. Better not to respond to it and especially not to speak of it to anyone.

As servants bustled about the Rani in her room, they whispered with more excitement than usual. All they could talk about was the scandal caused the day before at the ball given by the British officers to celebrate Roger's recovery. News travelled fast between Indian servants, those of the British and those of the palace. For a long time the Rani had paid no attention to such gossip, but recently she had been lending an ear to the rumours concerning the British colony and sometimes she went as far as to ask a question or two.

That day her servants did not refrain from mentioning Roger by name, since he had been the reason for the ball.

Sahib Giffard had danced all night with Mrs Phipps. Doctor Phipps had left early, while Sahib Giffard and Mrs Phipps had been the last to leave, and when they had walked out to the steps, he had kissed her on the mouth. They had ridden home together in the same carriage.

The Rani grew pale, but she had enough power over herself to remain impassive. Of Kiraun she was not jealous. A queen cannot be jealous of a camp-follower. But Mrs Phipps...Annabelle was a beautiful woman, voluptuous and frustrated. She belonged to the same race as Roger, they spoke the same language, and he lived under her roof, which could only facilitate their liaison. But after all, the Rani asked herself, why should I be jealous? I am not in love with Sahib Giffard.

After breakfast she went down to the courtyard to wait for him. He arrived out of breath, in an expansive mood. 'How I've missed our rides, Your Highness!' he cried.

It was the first time she had seen him since the night he almost died. She noted immediately in his face the fatigue wrought by last night's ball. His features were drawn, his eyes small and circled by dark rings—and his pallor owed nothing to his recent illness. The Rani greeted him with icy courtesy.

She glanced with barely-concealed contempt at the Indian clothes he had donned; although far better suited to the climate than British flannels, none of his compatriots would have brought themselves to wear them. She appeared not to notice that he addressed her servants in Hindi, a language he had decided to learn and already spoke tolerably well, having left far behind the few words other Englishmen condescended to gibber. She climbed onto the saddle without saying a word, and they rode off silently onto the countryside. They maintained an even, easy pace, for Roger was still weak and could not indulge his urge to gallop. Lakshmi remained silent, in contrast to her usual animated volubility.

At last, Roger asked, 'What's wrong today, Your Highness?' There was a trace of a caress in his voice.

'What's wrong? What's wrong is that I'm tired of watching the British shock and offend my compatriots by their behaviour.'

Surprised, Roger said nothing. Lakshmi continued, 'Last night's party created quite a stir in town.'

'The officers simply wanted to celebrate my recovery,' answered Roger, who did not understand what she was getting at.

'I cannot allow that in the presence of Indians, whom you use as slaves. You devour impure food, you get drunk in noise and disorder, and you behave indecently with women by embracing them.'

'Perhaps some of the men had too much to drink, Your Highness. Chances are that I did too. But I can assure you there wasn't anything untoward about that friendly—I might even say familial—gathering.' Having understood what the Rani meant, Roger explained that eating ham, which Indians consider impure food, and holding women by the waist to dance were British customs. 'They're not indecent customs,' he added, 'they're just different from yours.'

'In that case, Sahib Giffard, it would have been best if you hadn't brought them from Britain.'

Lakshmi had not, of course, even mentioned Annabelle Phipps, who was not unrelated to her annoyance. The patience with which Roger had answered, far from appeasing her exasperation, had only increased it. She was also nervous because of the jeweller's visit, and all the memories, vague hopes and uncertainty it had stirred in her. Suddenly, she felt her countrymen's complaints and her own bitterness float to the surface.

'The British really mistreat India. Not a day goes by without my people coming to tell me of a new insult to our traditions or our religion, a new offense, a new depredation.'

Lakshmi continued with the first example that came to mind.

'You brought the railroad, which is a good thing, but the cars are not arranged in accordance with our caste system. A Brahmin risks finding himself sitting next to an untouchable, which would make him forever impure.'

'The British, Your Highness, cannot accept the caste system. They see that sort of segregation by birth as a profound injustice.'

'That is because they don't understand the first thing about it, Sahib Giffard. The British pity the untouchable, whom they accuse us of mistreating—but he accepts his condition, because he knows that his good deeds will allow him to be reborn in a higher caste. I myself, who am a Brahmin, could be reborn as an untouchable if I act wrongly. That is the justice of our religion.'

And without giving him time to answer, she threw at him the injustices the British were compounding by their policies. The peasants could no longer meet their rents. The great landowners, crushed by taxes, stripped of part of their holdings, were being forced to sell what was left to bankers and merchants, those vultures who often came from elsewhere. The sepoys were getting little more than starvation wages. In the states that had been annexed, entire professions were being reduced to virtual famine. Nobody could meet the taxes the British were drowning the country in.

'You know what my compatriots keep saying: "*Company sarkar choron ki jamaat hai*...The administrators of the Company are no more than a band of thieves."'

Roger defended himself, step by step, against this avalanche of accusations; but he did not forget for a moment that this woman who was attacking him, this woman he was in love with, had been victimized by his countrymen. He did not deny the imperialism of the British government. He knew how brutal and rapacious its functionaries could be. Yet he remained convinced of the superiority of his country and its civilizing mission.

'The British want to pull India from her ancient stagnation—shake up her worn-out institutions, curtail her inequalities and evil customs—they want to bring modernism, progress and prosperity to drag India from the Middle Ages into this century. They have devoted themselves to that task. But such a transformation, because of its magnitude, necessarily entails friction, clashes and occasional injustice.'

'Those are excellent intentions,' the Rani replied with a bitter laugh. 'But perhaps the British ought to begin by getting to know us, to understand us, instead of treating us as though we were an inferior race.'

Roger lost patience. 'And Indians, don't they look down on us, even as they submit? Don't they consider us only slightly better than untouchables? Don't they, to boot, claim we have no hope of being reincarnated?'

'You are mistaken, Sahib Giffard. Indians do not despise the British, they fear them. They fear for their beliefs, for their faith. They are convinced the British want to convert them all by force to Christianity.'

'That's absurd!' Roger said. 'All the British have done has been to put an end to certain religious practices they thought particularly cruel. They've forbidden infanticide, suicide by widows, and they've allowed those widows to remarry.'

The Rani changed tack with lightning speed. 'And what about your missionaries, Sahib Giffard? What do you think of them? They are multiplying like crickets before the monsoon. They preach, they insist and they bribe. Your government encourages them, showers them with gold. And whose gold, Sahib Giffard, but ours.'

'British priests consider it their duty to make the religion of love and charity known to everyone.'

'We too have such a religion. So let the British keep theirs!'

'In any case, Your Highness, the British will never use force to convert the Indians.'

'Then why does one read in the newspapers of British officers who claim to have enlisted in the Indian army with no other goal than to convert Indian soldiers to Christianity? Do they use gentleness and persuasion for that purpose? Why is it that, in the barracks, sepoys who have fallen low enough to deny their religion are rewarded and promoted more quickly than the others? The British are only encouraging renegades. How could we ever trust them?'

The Rani dug her heels into her horse's flanks and raced away. She was so exasperated with the British, with Roger, that she had only one desire—to gallop straight ahead on the dusty road until sheer exhaustion took over.

Roger watched her disappear, followed by her servants in a cloud of dust. He continued at a walk, leaving the reins slack, sunk in thought. The stingy light of a December afternoon darkened the ochre earth and the solid green of the leaves. The sky was covered with thick motionless clouds, a grey shell. Roger felt tired, discouraged, somewhat troubled. He had wanted to make the Rani understand his country's intentions, he had tried to explain Britain to India, and he was fully aware of the uselessness of his efforts.

During the following days, he did not join the Rani on her afternoon rides. He was disturbed by her unexpected bitterness and by his own thoughts. However, he did send her a present he had prepared for her during his convalescence.

She received an album of watercolours depicting, in caricatural fashion, the adventures he had just lived through: Roger face to face with the swaying serpent, petrified with fear; the Rani's servants in flight; the snake dying from the Rani's bullet; Roger grimacing and gritting his teeth while the Rani operated; Annabelle Phipps at his bedside, exhibiting operatic grief; Roger convalescing in his chaise-longue, enduring the visits of all the wives in the civilian compound. Every face and attitude was rendered with such accuracy and humour that even the most dramatic scenes seemed comical. The Rani was present in these caricatures, but she was always shown from the back.

The pictures made her laugh out loud.

With the album came a note that moved her deeply, 'I owe Your Highness my only possession—my life. Henceforth, it is yours—you may do with it as you please.'

7

Deepavali, or festival of lights, the most important celebration on the Hindu calendar, was held around this time of the year. The joyous animation which seized the town, and from which the British were excluded, made Roger's heart even heavier. It had been a week since he had seen the Rani and he missed her grievously. As he left the office of the district commissioner, which, like all the buildings of the British administration, stood within the town walls, he began to wander through the streets instead of returning home to the civil station. He allowed the movement of the crowd to carry him, and thus, almost without realizing it, he found himself passing through one of the city gates and heading for the lake. As he approached the temple of Lakshmi, the crowd became thicker. Suddenly, Roger saw the Rani leaving the temple.

Like all Jhansi's inhabitants, she had gone to perform her devotions to the goddess Lakshmi, the patron deity of Deepavali. Relatives, councillors, former courtiers and servants, all in their finest apparel, formed around her a halo of brocade, turbans, and aigrettes. By her side was her son Damodar. He and his friends had fashioned the traditional torches by wrapping oil-soaked rags around sticks of bamboo.

Although Roger stood apart, the Rani noticed him immediately. She whispered a few words into Damodar's ears. The little boy then began to make his way towards his friend, the Feringhi. The crowd stepped aside respectfully at the little boy's approach. Damodar smiled at Roger and handed him an unlit torch. Then he set it alight with his own and spoke the traditional words, 'My spark touches your torch, your spark touches mine. The torch is the cosmos; the spark, you or me. One day, we shall light up again elsewhere. Why die?'

The Rani had drawn close to them and Roger was able to admire her elegance. On her head she wore a toque of red silk around which were woven strands of pearls and rubies. Her brocade waistcoat, generously open, slightly bared her cleavage. She wore a necklace of large diamonds, and in her gold belt were two pistols with damascened grips. The wide legs of her trousers enhanced the petiteness of her feet.

The splendour of her attire made her seem even more desirable. She thanked Roger for his gift with her usual graciousness, but in the presence of the crowd surrounding them, her thanks were those of a queen to a loyal supporter. Already, she was walking away.

She climbed into her silver palanquin and set off for the town, surrounded by her courtiers and followed by the crowd. Roger remained behind along with the last of the faithful. His encounter with the Rani had been frustratingly short and saddening in its lack of intimacy. He sighed. It was time to return to the Phipps's house for dinner, something he would have given anything to be spared from.

Contrasting with the animation of the town, where every house sparkled with thousands of oil-lamps, the civil station was wrapped in its usual gloom. Roger was about to enter the Phipps's bungalow when something rustled in a nearby syringa bush. He made out Kiraun's little face, half-hidden behind the flowers. He walked up to her. With a humble gesture she held out her gift; Indian custom dictated that on the night of Deepavali presents should be given to one's parents, friends and loved ones. It was a roughly-carved wooden statuette of the goddess Lakshmi. The unfortunate deity, painted in garish colours, looked hideous.

And yet its purchase must have meant hardship for Kiraun. Embarrassed, Roger took all the rupees he had in his pocket and put them in her hand. He would have wanted to give her a present, to buy her a jewel, but all he had for her was a few coins. Kiraun counted them carefully, and then, ecstatic, threw her arms around Roger's neck, kissed him lightly, and ran off into the bushes.

Dinner with the Phippses seemed duller than ever to Roger. The joyful sounds of the town in fete, the beating of drums, the triumphant blasts of conches blown by Indian women, drifted into the civil station, borne by the night, and enhanced the heavy atmosphere that blanketed the Phipps's dining-room.

Roger had thought it advisable to show up for dinner. Recently, he had come to feel that his hosts viewed him with suspicion because of his growing love for India. His wearing of Indian clothes, his taste for Indian food, his use of the Indian language seemed to them acts of impropriety. Doctor Phipps only raised his eyebrows and stared at Roger with bitter irony, but Annabelle did not refrain from speaking her mind. That evening he was late, and that was enough to set her off.

'I don't understand, my dear Roger, why you have such affection for the native quarter, where you spend so much of your time. Those natives frighten me, with their stares. You never know what to expect. They look as though they might cut your throat at the first opportunity.'

Roger protested. He had never sensed the slightest hostility from Indians.

'Don't tell me you don't mind the sight of their misery. Those skeletal beggars, those legless men, those lepers who hang on to your clothes, who spit their blood at your feet...'

'You know very well, Annabelle, that what they spit is not blood but the juice of the betel nuts they chew. And you also know that behind this facade that horrifies you, there is a very ancient civilization, admirable, incomparable.'

'Which doesn't prevent them from being filthy,' Mrs Phipps shot back.

'Indians are the cleanest people in the world. Even the British could learn from them on that score.'

When he saw his hosts' scandalized expression, Roger sensed he had gone too far. He added, 'Dirty or not, it seems to me that it's their country and we ought to spend some time with them and get to know them.'

'We're here above all to educate them,' grumbled Doctor Phipps.

'Perhaps,' Roger answered. 'But we ought to be able to do that without destroying their structures and their beliefs, which seem to suit them perfectly well. We claim to have come here to better their condition, but did it occur to us to wonder whether they're satisfied with it, and whether they appreciate the alternative we are proposing—or imposing?'

'You're quite an original, I must say,' sighed Annabelle. 'It's true you are an artist.' She pursed her lips to pronounce that last word with as much contempt as she could muster.

'I once knew a painter who came here, a Swede,' Doctor Phipps recalled. 'Made a tidy little packet painting Maharajas. Perhaps you ought to change careers, Giffard, leave the Company...'

The remark, uttered kindly, did nothing to alter his wife's acerbity.

'At any rate, we regret, we're sad to see that you prefer the company of Indians—Indians of both sexes—to ours. That's your choice. But I like you and I don't like to hear people gossip about you. Everybody here knows that you go to the palace everyday, and the ex-Rani has such a bad reputation...'

Roger was about to answer sharply but decided against it, not wanting to start a quarrel that would only feed Annabelle's jealousy. The atmosphere became charged with embarrassment. The meal dragged on.

Doctor Phipps gave a detailed description of the cases he had seen during the day, expatiating on the barbarity of Indian medicine and the obscurantism of the people. Annabelle complained incessantly of the noise from the town.

'Those savages won't stop until dawn, they're going to keep me up all night.'

Roger said nothing.

Dessert had just been served when a servant informed Roger that messengers from the palace were waiting outside to see him. Running out to the verandah, Roger came upon Lakshmi herself. She had exchanged her festival finery for one of those composite ensembles only she could create. Around her body she had wound a long piece of white muslin that hid half her face, covered her torso, and ended in the shape of breeches. Around her waist was a red embroidered shawl through which she had slipped her pistols and her dagger with the gem-studded handle. She had slipped a heavy silver bracelet on one ankle.

'I did this so that no one will recognize me. I want to go see the celebration in town,' she explained.

It did not take Roger long to rush back to the dining-room, take a hasty leave of the dumbfounded Phippses, bound into his room to slip on his Indian clothes and his turban, and leave with the Rani on horseback.

The entire city was awake and joyfully celebrating Lakshmi, the goddess of wealth and prosperity who, on this day, blessed every household. The streets had been carefully swept and cleaned, a considerable change from their usual aspect. In front of every house, as well as on the facades lit by the little earthen lamps, powders of all colours formed many different designs and patterns, the most common being the swastika, the emblem of the goddess. Through the windows open onto the street Roger saw many families playing games of cards or dice.

'We believe,' the Rani explained, 'that if we win on the night of Deepavali, our luck will last all year. So gamblers always try their luck—as do thieves, who are all at work right now, convinced that if they manage to fill their pockets on this night, the whole year will be favourable to their activities.'

The bazaar, normally deserted at night, was crowded and animated. Every shop had been transformed into a reception room with silk draperies on the walls, floors covered with rich carpets, and chandeliers of Bohemian glass hanging from the ceiling. The owners and their families were receiving guests, eating, drinking, laughing. The whole bazaar shone with light and resounded with music played by orchestras at alley intersections.

Pressed close together, Roger and the Rani let themselves be carried along by the crowd. Roger noticed she was wearing a scent he had never smelled before. Lakshmi explained that it was her custom every year on this day to scrub herself with a mixture of sand, sandalwood, and scented herbs, so that she would be clean of all impurities. The Rani sounded like a happy child, and Roger surrendered himself to the intoxicating atmosphere of the bazaar, whose colours, smells and animation were like a drug. At one intersection, the Rani found herself in front of a poster pasted on a wall in plain view. The text, crudely printed, was repeated in three columns, in Hindi and Urdu, the two main languages of India, and in Marathi, the regional tongue.

> *Hindus and Muslims of India! Arise! Brethren, arise! Of all the gifts of God, the most gracious is that of liberty. Will the oppressive Demon who has robbed us of it by deceit be able to deprive us of it forever? Can such an act against the will of God stand forever? No! No! The English have committed so many atrocities that the cup of their sins is already full. To add to it, they now have an evil desire to destroy our holy religion. Are you going to remain passive? God does not want that. For He has inspired the heart of Hindus and Muslims, He has filled them with courage, and soon, the British will be so completely defeated that in our India there will remain not even a trace of them!*

The Rani could not take her eyes off the poster, as though she wanted to pierce its secret. Then, sensing someone was looking at her, she turned to see a cloth-seller staring at her intently. He was alone in his shop, apparently preferring to do business than celebrate.

The Rani stepped up to his stall and pretended to examine his cotton fabrics. The merchant was not fooled.

'Foreigners might soon be having a rough time of it. Not that that should please me. They're good customers. The English ladies who send for me and my merchandise from the civil station are always polite. And they don't ask for credit. I have nothing against the British. Nor do my colleagues in the bazaar.'

'But then, merchant, who is it that hates them so? Who wrote this? Who posted it here?'

The merchant shrugged.

'Who am I to know? In any case, they're not from around here. In Jhansi, people might not like the British foreigners, true, but they certainly don't want any trouble.'

While listening to the merchant, the Rani noticed that no one in the crowd stopped to read the incendiary poster, but that many gave it a furtive glance as they walked by, as if they already knew what was written there.

'In any case,' the merchant continued, his eyes lowered, 'no matter what happens, we'll all follow our queen and do what she tells us.'

Lakshmi blushed. The merchant had recognized her beneath her veil. Quickly, she walked away with Roger and left the bazaar for less crowded streets. Only then did she slow her pace. Breaking the silence, Roger asked, 'What did that poster say?'

Offhandedly, she answered, 'It said that India will soon rebel against the British.'

The enormity of the answer, coupled with its casualness, made the young man burst out laughing.

Slowly, they walked on. It was clear to Roger that she did not feel like speaking, and so he left her to her thoughts. What had struck the Rani most about the poster was its call for the union of the two religions, Hinduism and Islam, which divided India. Their centuries-old rivalry and their conflicts had brought about the weakness of the empire. United, India would be invincible. Was it possible? Could the unthinkable be accomplished, could India recover her strength and her freedom and throw out the British?

The Rani's thoughts returned to the jeweller. He had not been lying after all. Something was indeed afoot—but in India there were always plots in the making, most of them aborted or still-born.

Tomorrow she would try to gather more information. Tonight was a night for celebration, tonight she was with Roger.

They had now left the town and taken the road that led to Lake Lakshmi, between the temple and the mausoleum the Rani had built to the memory of her husband. They arrived at the jetty where the Rani's servants waited to carry her across the lake to her pavilion, where she planned to spend the night.

It was then that she remembered the present she had brought for Roger, an antique Moghul dagger, its handle the shape of a horse's head completely inlaid with rubies. Again, Roger felt ashamed of not having known the custom of giving presents on the night of Deepavali. He took from his finger a family ring, a simple Hellenistic intaglio set very simply in gold, representing Venus. He offered it to the Rani.

'My mother gave me this ring the day I left home to go to school. It depicts our goddess of beauty. It is yours by right.'

The Rani slipped the ring onto her finger. For a moment, both felt a sense of embarrassment. Roger began to take his leave but Lakshmi stopped him.

'I presume, Sahib Giffard, that you have never seen the temple of Lakshmi,' she said, drawing him towards the buildings that arose from the shadows nearby.

The tour did not take long. Lakshmi and Roger sat down on a stone bench in a courtyard lined by monks' cells, illuminated only by the milky light of the evening. In front of them a wide, high staircase led to the sanctuary, its open portal a patch of light cut out of the dark facade. From inside came the voice of an invisible Brahmin humming religious verses. From time to time, one of the faithful crossed the courtyard noiselessly and disappeared into the sanctuary. Then they would hear the tinkling of the bell he rang to chase away evil spirits. The night was especially mild, almost hot.

'At home in England now,' Roger said, 'it's terribly cold. Roderick's last letter said it was the hardest winter they've had in several decades.'

'Who is Roderick?' the Rani asked.

Roger replied that Roderick was his best friend. Lakshmi wanted to know everything about him—what he did, how long he and Roger had been friends, where they had met.

'Does your friend look like you, Sahib Giffard?'

'Not at all.'

Roderick was very tall, much taller than Roger. Despite his height, he looked like a cherub gone to seed, with a small upturned nose, round blue eyes, light curly hair and freckles.

'Is he a painter like you?'

Roderick Griggs was drawn more to literature but his only real passion was the army—excluding, of course, Sarah Brandon, his eternal fiancee. Who was Sarah Brandon? Roger tried to explain that Roderick's betrothed had been born into an inferior caste. With her long blonde hair and her open expression, she seemed the picture of innocence, but in fact, she was a young woman who knew what she wanted. She had decided she would marry Roderick, and in order to reach her goal, she played him on her line with consummate skill. Roderick was completely taken.

Lakshmi asked a hundred more questions about the love affair of Roderick Briggs and Sarah Brandon. Then, suddenly, she said, 'And you—are you in love with Mrs Phipps?'

Roger's only answer was to laugh out loud.

'And yet you sleep with her.'

Roger had grown accustomed to the crudeness and directness with which the Indians expressed themselves, a startling contrast with their extreme prudery.

Roger looked at Lakshmi and smiled before answering, 'We've never been lovers. All I did was kiss her one night at a ball—and besides, I was drunk.'

'But you sleep with Kiraun.'

'I made Kiraun my mistress in order to forget you. I couldn't stand loving you without hope. From the first moment I saw you, when you received me at the palace and made a fool of me, I've loved you.'

He had put his arms around Lakshmi. She shuddered, but did not resist. Slowly, he brought his face to hers and gently kissed her. Submitting to his embrace, she returned his kiss with passion, but then she turned away suddenly and lightly ran off towards her boat, her bare feet silent on the stone slabs.

For a time Roger remained on the bench, staring at the Rani's pavilion on the opposite bank. Hundreds of small oil lamps lined the cornices, windowsills, balconies, terraces and turrets. They caressed every opening, every relief, colouring the stucco, warming the stone and glittering on the water like a shower of falling stars. Against the dark mass of trees, the brilliantly-lit pavilion, resting on the black satin of the lake, was a magical apparition. To Roger it seemed an unreachable promise.

Straining his ears, he could just hear the sound of the Rani's boat, invisible in the darkness, gliding through the water.

'Why didn't I make her stay, if she was willing?' he wondered. 'When will we have another moment of such intimacy?'

'Why didn't I give in to him?' Lakshmi asked herself, rocked by the rhythm of the rowers. She did love him; he had won her over with his openness, his high spirits, his zest for life, his kindness. He was the only one who regarded her neither as a strange animal, as other Englishmen did, nor as an idol, as her former subjects did. The British—all the British—treated the whole of India as a loose woman. She was an Indian, she was a Brahmin, she was a queen. She could not fall into the arms of an Englishman. Roger might be different, but he was still one of those who were responsible for India's misfortune, the misfortune of Jhansi as well as her own.

When she reached the pavilion, she examined the ring Roger had given her. Venus was engraved on a sapphire, a stone Indians consider unlucky. Her first impulse was to tear it from her finger. But then she told herself that love was stronger than auguries, and that a stone, whether evil or not, would not change her destiny.

8

As he entered the Rani's private audience chamber, Roger said, 'I've brought Kiraun. She wanted to talk to you. She's waiting outside.'

'This will be the first time a whore crosses my threshold,' the Rani grumbled.

Roger's casualness had gone too far this time. She had no difficulty imagining the horrified disapproval of her servants at this girl who had dared enter the palace. In her most regal manner, she ordered, 'Bring her in.'

Her prejudice melted away as soon as she saw Kiraun, a child's face on a woman's body.

'She can't be eating more than one good meal a day,' thought Lakshmi, for the tricks of Kiraun's profession could not quite disguise her thinness.

She bowed down before Lakshmi, her hand grazing the ground in front of her in a gesture of respect. Her caste was too low to allow her to touch the Rani's foot.

'What have you come to tell me?'

Kiraun's large frightened eyes stared at the Rani; her mouth opened, her lips trembled, but she was unable to utter a single word. Lakshmi's voice took a gentler tone.

'Don't be afraid, my child. Speak.'

'They want to kill them all. They told me. I don't want him to die. You alone can do something. They're going to massacre all the British.'

Kiraun's words, almost inarticulate cries, came out all at once, elbowing one another out of the way.

'Calm down, my child. Explain yourself slowly.'

Lakshmi's voice had a soothing effect. Kiraun regained her composure.

'Who is going to kill whom?' the Rani asked.

'The sepoys. They're going to kill all the British in Jhansi.'

'When? How?'

'I don't know. They're holding secret meetings at night to organize the massacre.'

'All the sepoys?'

'No. Only some.'

'How do you know?'

Kiraun bowed her head. Almost inaudibly, she whispered, 'It's one of my customers. A sepoy. He came yesterday. He was drunk. He told me horrible things about what they're going to do.'

'Why did you come to tell me this?'

'Because I don't want Sahib Roger to die. I love him, Rani. I know he's not for me. It's you he loves, Rani. I'm well aware of that. And only you can do something to stop him from being killed with all the others.'

Kiraun sounded sincere, but Lakshmi was not convinced. A child, a prostitute—could she be trusted?

'I believe you, Kiraun, but...'

'I've brought you proof, Rani. While my customer slept, I went through his clothes. I found this letter. When he left, he was still too drunk to remember it.'

Lakshmi took the crumpled piece of paper Kiraun held out. She had difficulty deciphering the almost illegible handwriting:

This letter is sent from the Kalpi garrison to the men of the Twelfth Bengal Infantry and the Fourteenth Cavalry stationed at Jhansi. May it reach Rissaldar Kale Khan. This letter is written in order to convey from the men of the Kalpi garrison the blessings of the Brahmins and the greetings of the Muslims. The state of affairs is the following: on the third day of the coming month, cartridges will be distributed to the Jhansi garrison. Let me repeat this again: the cartridges will have to be bitten on the third day of the coming month. Of this you are informed by reading this letter—whatever your opinion, answer

> *us. We have informed you of this in advance because we consider you our people. This letter is sent to you by the entire cantonment. The religions of the Hindus and the Muslims are one. And therefore all of you soldiers must be made aware of this—here, all the sepoys, regardless of their rank, are displeased over this matter. What more is there to say? Do what you think best. Here everyone, officers and men alike, send you their greetings and their blessing.*

Kalpi was a little town on the banks of the Jumna, about hundred miles east of Jhansi. The British, after annexing the surrounding territory, had turned it into an important military garrison. The Rani was puzzled by the letter's confused style. What was to happen on the third day of the following month, on 3 January 1857? What was this story about cartridges? There was one sentence that struck her more than any other: 'The religion of the Hindus and the Muslims are one.' She had read that call for the unification of the two faiths once before, in the subversive poster that had mysteriously appeared in the bazaar on the night of Deepavali.

Putting aside these thoughts, Lakshmi turned to Kiraun.

'You said that your customer and his friends held secret meetings. Where do they gather?'

'At night, outside the cantonment. That's what he told me.'

'Do you know when the next meeting is?'

'Tonight.'

The Rani thanked Kiraun for coming to speak to her, gave her a purse, and dismissed her. Kiraun stared at Lakshmi with an air of reproach, refused the gold, and quickly left the room. Roger had not intervened at all, and the Rani was too preoccupied to wonder how much of the conversation he had even understood.

Ten o'clock struck in the little neo-Gothic church built by the British in the centre of the civil station. In her wooden shack on the edge of the neighbouring military cantonment, Kiraun was dispatching the night's first customer, a very young British sub lieutenant just arrived in India. There was a knock at her door. Opening it, she was astonished to recognize the Rani disgused as a peasant. She began to abuse the young Englishman, who was still straightening his uniform, insulting him profusely, and after roughly sending him on his way, invited her new visitor in. The coming of the queen made Kiraun delirious with terror and pride. The Rani immediately noted the meticulous cleanliness of Kiraun's hovel.

'You are going to take me to the sepoys' secret reunion,' she announced. Kiraun drew back in fright.

'Don't ask me that, Rani. They would kill me if they found out.'

'With me you have nothing to be afraid of. I'll protect you.'

Mustering her courage, Kiraun asked a question, 'Why do you want to go, Rani?'

'I want to know. I want to see this with my own eyes. I don't trust anyone else's information.'

The Rani led Kiraun outside and motioned to her to jump up behind her on the horse.

'I can't touch you, Rani.'

The Rani simply held out her hand to help her up. They rode by the gates of the garrison and saw sepoy sentinels marching up and down in impeccable order, rifles on their shoulders. They saw the officers' mess blazing with lights, they heard English voices and laughter wafting from the open windows. Perhaps Roger was among them. They rode along the embankment that served as a rampart around the camp and reached an area where the sandy dunes became steeper and the thorny bushes thicker.

On the other side of the embankment, everything seemed to be asleep. The two women dismounted. The silence was thick around them. Lakshmi followed Kiraun, who walked without hesitation, making a detour around a cluster of bushes, bending over to dodge a branch. She seemed to know exactly where she was going. Lakshmi wondered whether she was merely following her customer's directions or whether she had actually come here before to spy on the plotters.

Suddenly, Kiraun turned around and signalled to the Rani to stop. Close by, men were talking leisurely, the sort of sound one overhears in the evening coming from a terrace. Very slowly, the two women went down on their hands and knees to clamber up a dune that rose before them.

When they reached the top, they raised their heads cautiously. There was nothing to be seen on the other side. The voices had seemed much closer than they actually were. They continued forward on the path as silently as they could, brushing aside dead leaves with their hands. Whenever a spiny branch on the ground caught their clothing or scratched them, they would unhook it carefully, in silence. At the crest of the next dune, they saw what they had come for. Twenty or thirty men were crouched in a large hollow between the dunes. They wore peasant's clothing, and all had pulled down a piece of their turbans to hide the lower part of their faces. Only their eyes were uncovered. There was one man, thin and frail, who had not hidden his features. He wore a British uniform, a red tunic buttoned as per regulations, black boots, a red turban. The pallor of his face sharply contrasted with his black moustache. He gestured nervously as he spoke and his eyes darted from side to side.

Pointing him out to the Rani, Kiraun whispered, 'That's the leader, Rissaldar Kale Khan. And the fat one next to him is my customer, Gulab Singh.'

Kale Khan was finishing his speech.

'Brothers, if we rise up, success is ours. From Calcutta to Afghanistan, there will be victory, freedom, celebration. Remember the prophecy—all of you, from the snows of the north to the seas of the south, have heard it. A thousand and a thousand and another thousand years ago, one of our sages predicted that the empire of foreigners would end exactly one hundred years after its creation. In a few months it will be one hundred years to the day since the accursed Feringhi won the decisive battle that gave them our country. In a few months we shall throw them out, fulfilling that age-old prophecy.'

'Plassey,' the Rani thought. It was there, on 23 June 1757, that Lord Clive had crushed the army of the Nawab of Bengal, handing England the key to India.

A slight noise made her turn; Kiraun had disappeared, crawling backward to take shelter behind a bush. The Rani continued listening to the plotters. She held her breath to better hear the questions Kale Khan was being asked. A light rustle of leaves behind her once again drew her attention. A few steps away in the shadows, a man, an Indian, was crawling towards her. Her heart stopped beating. Terror staked her to the ground. The man was drawing closer, taking every precaution to make no sound. When he reached Lakshmi, he signalled to her to be silent—it was Roger. Having understood most of what Kiraun had told the Rani, he had known she would not let the matter drop. He had not wanted to allow her to go off alone, but he knew that she would not let him come with her on an expedition to spy on her own countrymen. All evening he had loitered near the palace and he had caught a glimpse of her leaving through a little door hidden in the wall. Taking great precautions not to be detected, he had followed her.

Side by side, they watched the conspirators.

Kale Khan showed his men a bottle and a book. 'Now you will take an oath, on the water of the Ganges or the Koran, depending on your religion. You will swear to do what we tell you to do when we tell you to do it and, if necessary, to die for our country.'

One by one, the men rose to their feet, walked up to Kale Khan, took the oath, and returned to sit in their places. It was the turn of a sepoy who was seated slightly apart from the others. Kale Khan motioned to him. The sepoy remained seated.

'I will not take the oath,' he said. 'I want to uphold my freedom and my religion, but I will not kill the British. They've always been good to me. Lieutenant Taylor has never mistreated me. He's even been generous. I will not kill Lieutenant Taylor. I will not betray you, but I won't take the oath.'

The man bowed his head and remained motionless.

Kale Khan said nothing and made a simple sign. A man, already sworn in, who was sitting closest to the one who had just finished speaking, rose, stepped silently to his side. Suddenly, he tore off the man's turban, pulled his head back by its hair, and slit his throat. It happened so quickly that the victim made no sound. The Rani saw only the blade snapping through the air and the victim's body slowly sagging to the ground, blood spurting from his neck, then seeping into the sand.

Paralyzed with horror, the Rani stared wide-eyed at the corpse slumped on the sand. At last, Roger touched her shoulder and indicated it was time to leave. Spurred by curiosity, Kiraun had returned to

Lakshmi's side; she did not seem particularly affected by the brutality of the scene they had just witnessed. Lakshmi pulled herself together, and with her two companions, slithered away through the bushes.

They had gone not a hundred steps when they came face to face with a sentinel who had not noticed them on their way out. The man seemed as astonished as they were.

'Who are you? What are you doing here?' he asked.

'We're lost,' the Rani muttered. Kiraun stepped in to save the situation. With extraordinary calm, she approached the man with her most suggestive walk, and said, 'Help me, handsome. I have here two customers, greenhorns. They don't know how to go about it, and besides, they don't have anything in their pants. Make love to me to show them how it's done and for you it'll be free.'

The sepoy began to laugh. 'Not tonight, I'm on guard duty. Now go away…no, wait!'

Something in Roger's appearance, in his stance, had caught the man's attention. He stepped up to Roger and, with a sudden movement, knocked off his turban. A Feringhi! The sepoy grabbed for his sword and tried to shout the alarm, but no sound came from his throat. His mouth twisted into a terrible rictus, he fell face down to the ground. The Rani, slipping silently behind him, had plunged her dagger into his back. She bent over the man to make sure he was dead, coldly pulled out her weapon and wiped it on the corpse's shirt.

Hurriedly, they made their way back to the clearing where they had left their horses. Kiraun jumped onto the saddle. Lakshmi remained standing next to her horse, shaking from head to toe, incapable of moving. Gently, Roger took her in his arms.

'Once again you've saved my life, Lakshmi,' he whispered, his lips grazing her hair.

She seemed neither to see nor hear him, she kept hiccupping, 'I killed a brother. I killed a brother!'

From under her skirts Kiraun pulled out a brass flask from under her skirts.

'Take this, Rani. It's guj, it'll do you good.'

The Rani had never tasted that popular alcohol, but after swallowing several gulps of it, she felt definitely better.

She mounted the horse with Kiraun and soon they reached the road that passed by the military camp. The mess was still as brilliantly lit and as noisy.

The following day, the Rani tried to minimize the significance, in Roger's mind, of what they had witnessed.

'Those we saw last night are only a small band of fanatics. I can assure you sepoys do not want to kill their British masters. I see them right here in Jhansi with their officers, with the wives and children of their officers. They are filled only with respect, devotion, even affection.'

Was she trying to convince herself, or was it simply that she did not want to alert the British?

'I presume, Sahib Giffard, that you have informed Captain Skene?'

Roger had seen it as his duty. Of course, he had not mentioned the Rani's name.

'What was the captain's reaction?' she asked.

'He wanted to arrest Kale Khan, the head of the conspirators—but he slipped through our fingers and disappeared. Skene is convinced the others weren't his soldiers. He trusts his sepoys, and like you, he's convinced that not one will revolt. Only one order has been issued: from now on Englishmen must not stray from the cantonment and the civil station without an escort of sepoys.

'But it's not in the countryside that the danger lies,' answered the Rani, in spite of herself. 'The peasants are peaceful.'

She refrained from adding that she thought Captain Skene's order completely irrational.

It was a wintry day, one of those rare occasions on which central India experiences truly cold weather, carried down from the distant Himalayas. Over her shoulders the Rani had thrown a beige shawl woven from the finest, rarest cashmere.

After a long and exhausting ride with Roger, she had stopped to see the headman of a village. She was watching two sepoys, seated some distance away; on Captain Skene's orders, they now accompanied Roger during their excursions. They were crouched on the ground with her guards, chatting and joking, sharing a few betel leaves and chewing peacefully. 'How on earth,' the Rani wondered, 'could these gentle, simple souls turn into rebels with daggers in their teeth, ready to murder the British?'

Night was about to fall and peasants were already coming in from the fields. A sweeper walked up to the sepoys and pointing at one of their flasks, asked for a drink of water. The sepoy, a Brahmin, assumed an expression in which astonishment mingled with disgust. How could an untouchable like the sweeper not know that, by merely holding the flask, he would pollute not only the vessel but also its owner?

Instead of bowing to the sepoy's brutal refusal, the sweeper struck back, 'That's enough now, with the arrogance of your caste. Do you know you've lost that caste of yours? The new cartridges you've been issued are covered in cow-fat and when you bit them, it is you who became impure—not me.'

And the sweeper began to laugh.

The sepoy leapt to his feet, brandishing his rifle. He seemed to have gone mad, running off down the street, uttering inarticulate cries. The sweeper resumed his work, sweeping the street with feigned thoroughness, an air of sly satisfaction on his face. The Rani summoned Roger's other sepoy, who had not moved or spoken during the scene.

'What's this about cartridges?' she asked him.

'Recently we were issued new rifles and new cartridges. Before loading them into the chamber, we have to bite them to remove the grease. It's a mixture of cow-fat and pork-fat,' the sepoy answered, crestfallen.

'Who told you what the grease was made of?'

'A friend in the regiment. He wanted to warn us.'

'Are you quite sure it's a mixture of cow-fat and pork-fat?'

'Yes, Rani, that's what we were told.'

Touching cow-fat would make a Hindu lose his caste; touching pork-fat was sacrilege for a Muslim. All sepoys, no matter what their religion, were committing a crime against it by biting the new cartridges.

'When were these cartridges issued?'

'Some time ago. I can't remember when.'

'Try to remember. When was it?'

'I think it was in January.'

'3 January...new cartridges...they will have to be bitten...do what you think best...' Those were the words in the letter to the conspirators that Kiraun had spirited away from her customer. What had seemed a mystery to Lakshmi now became clear. She called to the sweeper. He stopped his work, dropped his broom, walked over and knelt, touching his forehead to the ground.

'Tell me, sweeper, who spoke to you of those new cartridges?'

'A fakir who came through the village one day. He told us that all the sepoys who had touched those cartridges had become impure. We are no longer the only untouchables,' he added, raising his head triumphantly. 'All the sepoys have become untouchables.'

Back at the palace, alone with Mandar, the Rani exploded. She was scandalized by the business of the cartridges, by the sacrilege the British were forcing on their sepoys. The injustice they had committed towards Jhansi and herself, the rage and stifled hatred smouldering in her for so long, rose to the surface again and poured out in a vehement speech bristling with threats and imprecations.

'And if the sepoys rebel, so much the better.'

'I thought those who wanted to revolt were thugs,' Mandar said with irony, a flash of triumph in her eyes.

Thugs who, in the name of God, strangled sacrificial victims, had for centuries terrorized India and their deeds continued to feed innumerable legends.

'Thugs' was the word the Rani had used to describe the conspirators when she returned, shuddering with horror and disgust, from her nocturnal expedition. Since then, the information about the cartridges had made her change her opinion.

'If I were a sepoy, I'd join the conspiracy myself,' she said.

'Why don't you? You were asked to—you were called.'

So Mandar knew about the jeweller's visit. She always knew everything about the Rani.

'I have nothing in common with the sepoys. I don't pretend to be the submissive slave of the British in order to then creep up behind them in the night and stab them in the back. That is not how our ancestral tradition tells us to fight. If we're to attack in the open, in daylight, then I'll accept. I will be ready.'

Mandar shrugged at the Rani's evocation of the Maratha ideals of chivalry. Gravely, she said, 'We must help our brothers.'

'I'll think about it,' the Rani answered; in an instant, she had recovered her usual prudence.

The next morning, she summoned Captain Skene. In order to preserve her distance, she received him ceremonially in the throne room instead of the audience chamber, with Diwan Naransin at her side. She had no army, but she still had guards. She had no court or ministers, but she still had courtiers and advisers. As for protocol, it remained as strict as ever. Skene might have thought she was still the ruler. He knew immediately that something was wrong; instead of addressing him directly in English through the purdah curtain, she spoke in Marathi, using an interpreter.

She protested against the cartridges and demanded that they be withdrawn from the territory under Captain Skene's control, her former kingdom.

Although she spoke harshly, she remained polite, for she was not entirely without esteem for the captain. He tried to appease her.

'The Governor General in Calcutta has already been informed of this regrettable incident. Orders have been given throughout India to withdraw those cartridges from circulation and replace them immediately with others greased with mutton-fat, the use of which will offend neither Your Highness's religion nor that of the Muslims.'

It was obvious that Captain Skene considered the matter closed.

Outraged by his offhandedness, the Rani said, 'There has, however, been some violence in the Calcutta area.'

She had heard that in the small town of Raniganj several fires had been set and telegraph wires cut. Again, very near Calcutta, at Barrackpore, the British army's largest station, some sepoys had refused to bite their cartridges. General Hearsey, the garrison's commanding officer, had had to assure the sepoys solemnly that the sacrilegious cartridges had been replaced.

'As Your Highness knows, everything has been straightened out. The incidents have had no consequences and must be attributed wholly to the admittedly honourable sensitivity of your compatriots.'

Skene's unaccustomed self-importance infuriated the Rani.

'If you and your people continue to mistreat your sepoys you will have their just anger to fear.'

'Our sepoys are faithful to us. Moreover, Britain is prepared to put down any subversion, no matter where or from whom.'

'Let us understand one another, Captain. India is at peace and I hope it stays that way. But your compatriots are endangering that peace. Speak to your masters, write to them. Stop them from insulting our religion and our traditions. Encourage them to look after the prosperity and well-being of Indians.'

Given his position and the Rani's, Skene resented being lectured. Without answering, he saluted and withdrew.

Diwan Naransin, who had been silent throughout the interview, spoke up. 'Do you know the poem, Rani, recently written by the Great Moghul, Bahadur Shah, that has mysteriously spread throughout the country? One line is of particular significance: "The powerful British who boast of having vanquished Russia and Persia were driven from India by a simple cartridge."'

The Rani laughed. 'He's not as senile as they say, old Bahadur Shah... May he speak the truth!'

During the next few days, the Rani sent word to Roger that she was too busy to see him. He was not taken in by such excuses. From Doctor Phipps he had heard all about her audience with Captain Skene, who had been struck by the Rani's unprecedented animosity, a serious matter. Roger felt that she was including him in her resentment of the British, he felt dejected.

9

Doctor and Mrs Phipps were having guests that night, and Roger could not pass up a dinner to which his superiors had been invited. Among them were Captain Skene, Captain Gordon, the commanding officer of the garrison Captain Dunlop, his adjutant Lieutenant Taylor, and Taylor's gentle, timid wife.

Annabelle Phipps was particularly elegant, and for once, she had eschewed the ruffles for which she had such a weakness. A simple dress of ruby-coloured velvet trimmed in black brought out her clear, lustreless complexion and the darkness of her hair. All the guests were secretly jealous of Roger, for all but Captain Skene keenly suspected that she was his mistress.

Roger had grown to hate the interior of the Phipps's bungalow a little more each day. It reproduced in detail the horror of a petty bourgeois London apartment. The porcelain, the silver and the linen had been imported from England. The Indian servants attempted with painful difficulty to serve meals with the precision of English butlers, under a barrage of reprimands from Mrs Phipps for their many mistakes. They brought in the vegetable soup, which was too hot, boiled fish, roast beef with potatoes, and several quivering aspics whose appearance and taste were nauseating. Utterly delighted, the guests praised to the skies Annabelle's talents as a hostess. Their enthusiasm knew no bounds when a surprise arrived for dessert—a plum pudding that had travelled all the way from London in an iron box, and which Roger was alone in finding terribly indigestible.

Upon that triumph Annabelle retired discreetly with Mrs Taylor, leaving the men to their port and cigars. Conversation immediately came around to a strange phenomenon that had recently appeared in the region. It involved chapattis, those flatcakes of unleavened bread that are a staple of the Indian diet. It seemed that the village watchmen, the chowkidars, familiar figures in any Indian agglomeration, had become chapatti-mad. One of them would suddenly appear in the neighbouring village with two chapattis, which he would give to his local colleague with instructions to make six more. The latter would then take two to his colleague in the next three villages and relay the same order.

Within a few days, the watchmen of all the villages in the province had received their two chapattis. These they would cut into little pieces which they distributed to anyone who asked for them. Captain Skene had already alerted the Governor General of India, and Calcutta answered that the same phenomenon had been observed in every province.

Captain Dunlop, wanting to demonstrate his zeal, had had several of the travelling chapattis confiscated and had personally dissected them, looking for revealing components. They contained none; they were no different from those eaten all over India every day.

Lieutenant Taylor spoke up, 'I asked the headman of one of our villages about the meaning of the chapattis. He told me it was an old Indian custom that when the leader wants something from his people, he uses this method to warn them that orders will soon be arriving.'

Captain Gordon suggested another explanation. 'You remember, a few months ago, some of our districts were hit by cholera. Perhaps this distribution of chapattis is some magic spell to fight the disease.'

Doctor Phipps, an old India hand as well as a scholar, told his guests of two similar cases in the history of central India: a distribution of sugar in 1806 and one of coconuts in 1818.

'Nothing happened afterwards, and no one ever found out the meaning behind these distributions.'

Why should there be anything to worry about? The gentlemen rejoined the ladies in the drawing-room, where Annabelle Phipps did everything she could to make the guests understand that she was a happy, well-loved mistress. She sat on the arm of Roger's chair, whispered in his ear, pouted, smiled dreamily, and laughed throatily. Roger was tense; these evenings bored him, as did Annabelle's antics. The guests all admired the coolness with which he feigned indifference towards Mrs Phipps. They knew the rules of the game and would have thought any sign of infatuation on his part in the worst possible taste.

Someone again mentioned the mysterious chapattis. Annabelle piped up, 'All that is just a new mania caused by the superstition of backward, ignorant people.'

Roger, already annoyed by her flirtatiousness, responded, 'It might mean that something enormous is being readied—an uprising against us, a rebellion.'

The guests stared at Roger, some with amusement, others in consternation.

'And where on earth did you come up with that idea, Giffard?' asked Doctor Phipps. 'I've known this country much longer than you. Jhansi—indeed, all India—has never been more quiet.'

'You're forgetting, Doctor, the conspiracy among the garrison's sepoys.'

Dunlop and Gordon protested in unison. Roger didn't know their men as they did. There was no possibility of rebellion.

'You're worried over nothing, Giffard,' Skene added. 'India is always criss-crossed by mysterious signals which, if they have some meaning for the Indians, have no consequence for us. A conspiracy in the whole country, a rebellion? To me it seems out of the question. We would have been already warned. Imagine a rebellion organized by the public distribution of chapattis! Come, come, Giffard, a little common sense....'

But Roger insisted, 'The Indians are restless. They're awaiting something, something important. They see signs of something coming.'

'The men you're getting your information from—or the women—are losing their heads over nothing,' said Captain Skene, alluding, almost against his will, to Roger's relations with the Rani.

'Why would the Indians rebel against us, anyway?' asked little Mrs Taylor with a frightened expression.

Captain Dunlop, red with anger, shouted, 'If those niggers rebel against us, after everything we've given them, they'll have proven they're the most ungrateful wretches on earth.'

Roger lost his temper.

'How dare you call the Indians niggers, sir! It's with precisely that mentality—that ignorance and superciliousness—that you and your kind are ruining this country and shaming our own!'

Before Dunlop could answer, Skene stepped in and spoke calmly to Roger, 'Don't forget, Giffard, that you're an Englishman and that you're talking to an officer.'

Roger rose from his chair and left. While saddling his horse he could hear through the window the comments that followed his exit.

'The climate's driven him mad!'

'Don't forget he comes from a very humble background.'

'Perhaps he's hiding a shameful love affair!' After that last 'kind' remark by Annabelle, Captain Dunlop issued a warning, 'You ought to beware of him, Skene, you'd better think of having him transferred.'

Roger's anger and despair over his compatriots' blindness and narrow-mindedness were such that, for a long time, he galloped aimlessly in the night. When he calmed down, he saw that he had ridden around the town walls and was now on the bank of Lake Lakshmi.

Windows were lit up in the Rani's pavilion on the other shore. So she, too, was still awake. The desire to see her again, sharpened by each day of separation, proved too much. He undressed, knotted his clothes into his jacket, tied the bundle on his head like a turban, and plunged into the lake. The water, which Indians thought freezing, was fairly comfortable to the Welshman. It had a pleasant smell of earth and reeds. With each of his movements the reflections of the moon and stars on the water broke up into hundreds of silver sequins. He swam vigorously, propelled by rage and impatience. As he drew near the pavilions, he was able to make out a small tunnel dug into the foundations, for boats to dock. He swam into the tunnel and hoisted himself out of the water onto a sort of landing-stage; he was exhausted by the effort and by the alcohol he had drunk in order to get through the Phipps's dinner. Suddenly, the cavern filled with light. The Rani's guards, hearing his splashing, had come out with torches, jabbering and gesticulating furiously. One of them removed the brown wool shawl in which he had wrapped himself for the night and threw it over Roger's shoulders. Then, not knowing quite what to do with him, the guards brought him to the Rani.

Lakshmi had enough self-control to show no surprise at the sight of an almost naked man appearing out of the night, dripping water, with long weeds stuck to his skin. Panting, but no less composed, Roger asked a single question, 'Tell me Lakshmi—couldn't two people who love one another place their love above the conflict between their races?'

The Rani did not answer. With a flick of her hand she dismissed the guards. Then she had Mandar bring a liqueur of rose-water and opium, a tonic that was also an Indian love-potion. While he drank in long gulps, Roger kept his eyes on the Rani. 'Tell me, Lakshmi,' he said, 'I want to know, I want...'

He never finished the sentence. The silver cup slid from his fingers and his head fell back on the pillows. He had suddenly fallen asleep, exhausted by the night's emotions. For a long time Lakshmi gazed at the sleeping body on the brocade, and at last, she murmured, 'You're right, Roger. Love is stronger than racial differences. It has to be.' Next to her, Mandar nodded gravely.

The next afternoon they went, as usual, for a ride. Lakshmi took Damodar with them and he was delighted by the unexpected treat. She feared being alone with Roger, for his presence troubled her. As they trotted along, she asked, innocently, what had caused his impulsive nocturnal visit, suspecting that behind it lay something other than the simple desire to see her again. Roger did not want to confess his quarrel with his compatriots.

'I was bored,' he said simply, 'I just couldn't stand their chapatti stories any longer.'

'What chapatti stories?' the Rani asked.

Roger told her about the conversation at the Phipps's dinner. Lakshmi was immediately intrigued. She had heard nothing about this strange distribution of chapattis.

They had reached the village of Unnao, its entrance guarded by a gigantic solitary tree. Under its low branches lived a fakir, a holy man. The Rani and Roger had often seen him there, always at the same spot, perfectly motionless during his meditation. That day, too, they found him at his post. The fakir was frighteningly thin and entirely naked. His long matted beard and hair were greying. On his forehead esoteric signs were painted in white. Sitting on the ground in the lotus position, he was smoking hashish in his chillum. He did not move as they came up. Roger, Lakshmi and Damodar crouched down a few yards away, waiting for him to speak. Without changing his position or looking at them, the fakir suddenly said, 'You have come, Rani, to ask me about the chapattis.'

Although she was accustomed to holy mens' gifts of divination, the Rani gave a start. The fakir continued in an even, slow voice, 'Those spirits with their invisible wings fly throughout the country to its most remote corners, setting fire to the minds of the people by the very vagueness of their message. Whence they come and where they go, no one can tell. Yet for those who await them, the strange symbols bring a precise message and speak a limited truth. For the ignorant, the information they bear is unlimited. Hurry on, O spirits with invisible wings, hurry on, preach the holy word to all the children of India and tell them the land is ready.'

The fakir stopped and Lakshmi knew he would say no more. 'Will those spirits run the British out of India?' asked Damodar, who had attentively followed the holy man's speech.

The fakir had spoken in Sanskrit, a scholarly language Roger did not understand. He did not question the Rani, however; India had taught him to wait silently until his partner chose to speak.

Later, while Damodar was galloping ahead, Lakshmi said brusquely, 'Go away, Roger, leave India. There is going to be trouble. I don't want the storm to catch you. You understand my people and respect them. I don't want you to have to pay for those who don't.'

'I don't want to be separated from you, Lakshmi. Especially if there's danger.'

'For me there's no danger, I am Indian. But for you...for all the British... Get away, Roger! You can come back afterwards, when everything has calmed down.'

'It's too late. I can't leave your country.'

He tried to explain to the Rani that India had allowed him to discover himself, that India had brought him a freedom infinitely richer than that which he had sought to gain from his studies, from his profession, from money and success. He had become a different man.

He was not even certain he could readapt to England.

'But this isn't your country,' the Rani protested.

'India has become my country. She is beautiful and unhappy, strong and gentle, mysterious and sensual. Like you, Lakshmi.'

She smiled before answering wistfully, 'India is generous, but she can also be cruel and pitiless.'

'I know there's a threat hanging over the British. But for me, happiness lies here.'

She hesitated for a moment before asking, 'Would you stay if a rebellion broke out and you knew I was going to be involved?'

'Whatever you may do, Lakshmi, I shall always love you.'

The following morning seemed endless to Roger. The atmosphere at the deputy superintendent's office weighed on him more and more. Ever since his explosion of frankness during the Phipps's dinner, Captain Gordon regarded him with a certain distrust and had put a palpable, if barely perceptible, distance between them. As soon as he could get away, Roger ran to the Rani's palace, only to learn that she had left Jhansi at dawn. No one knew where she had gone or how long she would be away.

10

The Rani travelled in a palanquin as large as a small room, fanned by a punkha manipulated from above by a servant seated on the roof. With the Rani were faithful Mandar and several servants, who had brought baskets filled with fruit, various foods and refreshing drinks. The enormous machine was pulled by two powerful horses that had been imported from France by the Rani's late husband at the extravagant cost of fifteen hundred pounds sterling each.

The Rani was on her way to Gwalior. That kingdom, one of the largest, richest and most powerful in the Indian empire, was the prestigious beacon of central India. It was ruled by an inexperienced young maharaja, but the real power belonged to his Prime Minister, Diwan Dinkar. Faithful to Gwalior's traditional policies, the Diwan had shown only kindness to his small neighbour, Jhansi. The old fox was considered one of the ablest and best-informed politicians in India. It was he whom the Rani wanted to consult. No one could better guide her and help her make her decision.

The sun was beginning to sink when, emerging from behind a rocky hill, the Rani was able to make out the formidable rock of Gwalior in the distance. A very long plateau rimmed on all sides by sheer cliffs studded with temples and palaces, it dominated the plain and was visible from miles around.

The Rajas of Jhansi kept a villa about a mile north of Gwalior, on the main road from Agra. No sooner had the Rani arrived than a messenger came from the court of Gwalior. Maharaja Sindhia hoped for the honour of her company at dinner in his palace, and had sent an escort to bring her there—a detachment of guards and six elephants, dressed as if for a ball, with silver howdahs, saddlecloths of embroidered velvet, gold necklaces and bracelets. Surrounded by guards on horseback, the procession of glittering pachyderms left the villa and set off, bearing the Rani and her suite to dinner.

Disdaining the superb old palaces of the fort, the rulers of Gwalior lived in the centre of the new town, in the Gurki Palace. This was a relatively modern building erected on a uniform pattern, consisting of numerous square or rectangular courtyards bordered by low rectilinear buildings. Some, planted with flowers and trees, served as gardens.

The Rani entered the new wing built a few decades earlier in the neo-classical style that was the fashion in Europe. She was led to the throne room, an immensely long room with a very high ceiling. Indian lavishness showed itself in the frescoes—swarms of arabesques, divinities, royal portraits, and scenes in miniature—drawn in a heavy style with slightly garish colours.

At least three hundred tribal chieftains, the Maharaja's vassals, had taken their places in the throne room. The colour of their clothes ranged from pink to scarlet. The nobles of the court all wore red Maratha turbans, gold-embroidered frock-coats and steel arm-plates—vestiges of medieval armour dripping fringes of gold that covered their hands.

The Rani took her seat next to Maharaja Sindhia—a friendly young man, with quite handsome features but without much character—under a very low canopy of ornate stucco. A brocade pillow was the only throne used by the rulers of Gwalior; their courtiers had to be content with the carpet. The feast was sumptuous, worthy of one of India's richest and most powerful rulers. An army of servants, in green-trimmed scarlet livery, orange trousers, pink belts and turbans, brought in the various dishes while singers and dancers displayed their talents.

The Rani was rediscovering the luxury, the sense of ease of a royal court. More subtly, she was steeping herself, once again, in the atmosphere of a ruling monarchy, impressed in spite of herself by the pomp and prodigality surrounding one of India's most prestigious kings. Sitting next to her, Diwan Dinkar limited himself to uttering the customary compliments and exchanging a few platitudes with the Rani. He seemed to prefer conversing with his other neighbour, Sir Robert Hamilton, the British government's agent for all of central India and Captain Skene's superior, who was stationed at Gwalior. Sir

Robert had greeted the Rani with the distant, slightly absent-minded politeness that British officials used towards those they considered to be negligible quantities.

Treated with the utmost deference by the Maharaja, he was obviously on the closest and most cordial of terms with Diwan Dinkar. The evening was drawing to a close when, on a sign from the Maharaja, servants in dark blue velvet and gold came forward, two by two, bearing on gold platters gifts from their ruler to the Rani—necklaces, belts and aigrettes, all of them much too big for the Rani, impressive but with stones that were not of the best quality. There were also piles of multicoloured silk, gold and silver brocade and sequinned muslin.

All the Rani was able to accomplish that evening was a whisper in Diwan Dinkar's ear that she hoped to see him alone in order to profit from the wisdom of his advice.

'Here we go,' thought Diwan Dinkar, very curious to learn the reasons for the Rani's visit.

The following morning, while the Rani was being dressed, Diwan Dinkar arrived at her villa unannounced. Had she been unable to receive him, he would have waited or left as he had come. But the Rani had no intention of letting him get away. She found him in the garden. 'Garden' was too grand a word for that small area planted with flowering bushes which flowed, without walls or transition, into the sandy plain.

They sat down on an ornamental marble bench facing a fountain long since run dry. The mild temperature made it pleasant to be out of doors and they would be safe there from eavesdroppers. Lakshmi took a good look at Diwan Dinkar as he settled down. A frail, sickly old man, his movements were slow, his skin white, his eyes blue. His gaze, haughty and discerning, lit up at times with a benevolent but sly glow. He found a comfortable position, and began to chew betel leaves a servant had offered. The Rani went straight to the point.

'Have you heard of the great revolt, Diwan?' she began.

'Perhaps it would be best, Rani, if you told me why you ask.'

Without hesitation, the Rani told him about the puppets and the mysterious fakir, the incendiary poster on a wall during the night of

Deepavali, the sepoys' secret meetings, the cartridges and the chapattis. The Diwan listened silently, deep in thought. The Rani saved the conspirator-jeweller's visit for last. Once she had finished, the Diwan simply said, 'We too have received similar visits.'

The Rani pressed him further, 'In spite of these portents, do you really think, Diwan, that the great rebellion will break out? India seems so calm—so resigned?'

'India is like sleeping water. Nothing is more reassuring than its calm surface, and yet, sudden, unexpected, terrible storms can rise at any moment.'

The Rani then attacked head-on. 'What is the extent of the conspiracy?'

'Hundreds of thousands of people are involved. They've been preparing for months; they're perfectly organized. They have their codes, their messengers, their agents. Fakirs and Pandits, the holy men of our religion, as well as maulvis and mullahs, the Muslim leaders, have been preaching rebellion from town to town, village to village, barracks to barracks. It is the sepoys who are the main hatchery for recruits to the conspiracy. They're organized into a network of secret societies. You cannot imagine, Rani, the number of letters circulating throughout the country, all of them describing the crimes of the British and calling for rebellion. We have trouble reading them because they're in code and I'm surprised that the one that found its way to you was in Hindi. The conspiracy has sent its feelers inside the royal courts. It is even said that the conspirators have been encouraged by Russia and Persia, two powers who would be delighted to see the British kicked out of India.'

'Do the British know all this is happening?'

'They don't have the slightest inkling, incredible as it may seem. Their ignorance of our country, their aloofness from our people and their trust is so great that they're completely unconscious of the danger.'

'Tell me, Diwan, who is at the head of all this?'

For the first time, Diwan Dinkar dropped his air of detachment and looked surprised.

'What! Do you mean, Rani, that you don't know? You, of all people?'

He stopped, as thought he had already said too much, and with unexpected agility, he rose to take his leave.

'Will I have a chance to see you again before I leave, Diwan?'

'Of course, of course,' he answered absent-mindedly. The Rani did not ask when their next meeting would take place. The Diwan was not a man to be pressed, and now he seemed in a hurry to leave.

He did not appear again the rest of the day, nor the next morning. Waiting for word from him, the Rani spent idle hours wandering about her house and the surrounding countryside. Then, in the late afternoon, bored and annoyed with waiting, she decided to go into the city in her coach. She went to pay devotion at the temple of the reigning dynasty of Gwalior, in the Gurki Palace. This holy place was unique in India in that it was also consecrated to the Muslim cult of a local prophet, Mansoor Sahib, who was buried there. It was said that under the temple lay labyrinthian cellars that housed fabulous treasures of the Maharajas of Gwalior.

From the temple the Rani went on to the tombs of Chatry Bazaar, where the imposing cenotaphs of the late rulers of Gwalior rose, side by side. Each had its own temple, within which a black marble statue of the dead ruler sat surrounded by white marble statues of his wives.

Every day the statues were dressed, hung with jewels and presented with food and drink. The Rani visited the cenotaphs conscientiously, lighting a joss stick in each.

On her way back, she took the long street that wound from one end of the new town to the other. She was almost at the ramparts when her coach had to slow down in the midst of a crowd. At least a thousand men and women had gathered to listen to a preacher standing on the steps of a seventeenth century mosque built of white stone.

The throng was so thick that the Rani's coach was unable to move. When she saw the preacher, she was struck by his appearance. Although slightly stooped, he was obviously very tall, over six feet. His loose clothes did nothing to hide his extreme thinness. Although his face was deeply lined, it was difficult to tell how old he was. An aquiline nose curved down over thin lips and his pointed chin was lengthened by a thin black beard. Set deeply in their orbits under thick dark eyebrows, his eyes seemed lost in contemplation, oblivious of the crowd.

He spoke in a compelling voice, which carried far even though it was not loud.

'Brothers of my land, faithful believers, rise up and throw out once and for all the foreign strangers. They have crushed all the foundations of justice under their boot. They have stolen our freedom. They are determined to turn our land to dust. There is only one way now to rid India of their unbearable tyranny. And that is to start a bloody war. A war for independence, a religious war for justice. Those who fall in its battles will be the heroes of their country, and the gates of Heaven will open wide for them. But the flames of Hell are burning already to annihilate the miserable cowards and traitors who turn away from their duty.

'Brothers of my land, choose now.'

The Rani had never seen such serene power in a man. Despite the bitter smile that distorted his features, despite the violence of his speech, he emitted warmth and humanity. Every man and woman stood hypnotized by his words. The Rani knew that he belonged to the race of prophets.

He was, quite simply, calling for jihad—a holy war.

The Rani's coachman was worried.

'Let us go, Rani. Let us turn back. There is going to be trouble.'

Nothing could have made the Rani leave. But the coachman was right. Soon a regiment of sepoys, led by their British officers, appeared at the end of the street. The crowd did not even look at them. The preacher, unperturbed, continued his speech. When the first ranks of the soldiers reached the crowd, people appeared to shudder slightly. Nothing more.

On an order from their officers, the sepoys tried to open a path to the preacher. The crowd did not move, allowing itself to be jostled without breaking ranks. A new order and the sepoys drew their swords. In seconds, there was indescribable confusion. Men and women fled in all directions, screaming. They threw themselves at the sepoy, to try to break out and knocked them down. The soldiers struck back with the flat of their sabres, intensifying the people's panic and rage. Daggers were drawn to try to hamstring the sepoys' horses. The sepoys defended themselves, now slashing their swords at heads, shoulders and arms.

The Rani's coach was drowned in this screaming tide. The horses neighed and reared up. A British officer, followed by a few men, fought through the crowd, trying to reach the preacher, but part of the crowd had fallen back towards the mosque, hiding the preacher from sight. By the time soldiers had finished clearing the steps of the mosque with their sabres, he had disappeared. Taking advantage of the confusion, he had vanished under their very eyes.

The crowd had finally dispersed. Only the sepoys were left, tending to a score of wounded. At last, the Rani's carriage was able to move on, driven by a very discomposed coachman.

The following day the Rani had still not received a message or a visit from Diwan Dinkar. She suspected he was trying to avoid her. In the afternoon she sent a messenger to the Maharaja's court to inform him she would be leaving tomorrow. One hour later, Diwan Dinkar presented himself at her villa, again unannounced. He did not offer any explanation or excuses. The Rani began by telling him of the incident she had witnessed in town; the Diwan, of course, had already heard all about it. She told him of the extraordinary impression the preacher had made on her. It turned out he was an old acquaintance of the Diwan.

'That Muslim holy man is Ahmedullah Shah. They call him the Maulvi of Faizabad, after the city where he normally resides. His origins are cloudy. He has travelled a lot in Arabia, and some say he has been as far as Europe. In any case, he does speak English.

'My police are aware of him because, on an earlier visit to Gwalior, he disturbed the peace. He's a dangerous fanatic, devoured by ambition, who preaches violence in order to reach his own ends. He's all the more dangerous for his undeniable gift for arousing crowds. I've had my eye on him for a long time, and although yesterday we let him get away, measures have been taken, and I hope we'll soon get our hands on him.'

The Rani now saw the preacher the way rulers regard troublemakers; her enthusiasm for him was considerably diminished.

Changing the subject abruptly, the Diwan asked, 'You have decided then to join the conspiracy?'

'I want your advice, Diwan.'

'Your wisdom will tell you, Rani, what you must do. But you are young and ardent. I know that you are burning to fight and to avenge the injustice the British perpetrated against Jhansi, against you. But wouldn't it be safer to wait before enlisting your people in such a venture? You are aware of the terrible repression they would suffer if they failed.'

'Fail, Diwan? The English number exactly 45,522 in India, against one hundred and fifty million of our compatriots.'

'That is true, Rani. And when the great revolt breaks out, let us expect that the British will at first be routed everywhere and driven off. Their very presence in India will be threatened.' He paused for a long time, which made the Rani grit her teeth with impatience. Then, in his weary, monotonous voice, he continued, 'England is the most powerful nation on earth. She has inexhaustible resources and, what's more, unconquerable determination. She will never give up this choice morsel—India. She will send reinforcements, more reinforcements, and still more reinforcements. And in the end, she will win, even if it takes decades.'

'Thus I am to believe that when the great revolt breaks out, Gwalior will side with the British.'

The Diwan hesitated before answering, but the Rani's frankness had disarmed him. He divulged his plans.

'We will maintain good relations with the British, no matter what happens. Nonetheless, we have not shut the door against the conspirators of today, and we will not slam it on the rebels of tomorrow. And if it becomes necessary, if circumstances require it, we will reach an understanding with them, we will even lend them aid—discreetly of course; but we will never enter the great rebellion at their side, and we will never cut our ties with the British.'

'And you will warn the British of what is about to happen?'

'No. That's their responsibility—to keep their eyes open.'

The Rani fell silent and the Diwan knew that she was somewhat disconcerted by the twists and turns of his policy.

'Allow me to give you one piece of advice, Rani; see nothing, hear nothing, say nothing—and nothing will happen to you. Don't forget that the British can also be generous. They could very well put back on the throne a deposed queen who hadn't abandoned them in their hour of need. If you stay out of this, you'll be spared, you and your people...and you might even gain by it.'

The Rani said nothing, but the Diwan sensed that his reasoning had had an effect. He asked the Rani to remain in Gwalior for a few more days. Both he and his master, the Maharaja, would be delighted to entertain her, offer her a few banquets. The Rani thanked him but declined. She was in a hurry to return to Jhansi where, on the following day, she went directly to the pavilion on Lake Lakshmi, without stopping in town.

'I need to rest after the trip,' she told her attendants. Almost immediately upon arriving, she sent a messenger to the civil station to invite Roger to dinner that evening. Then she turned herself over to the expert ministrations of her servants to get ready.

Under Mandar's directions, two of them brushed coconut oil into her hair, the recipe Indian women use from childhood to condition their hair, and later, prevent it from turning white. Then they stuck jasmine flowers in it, their scent blending into that of the attar with which they had oiled her body after her bath. Two other servants painted the palms of her hands and the soles of her feet with mehandi, in complicated motifs derived from stylized flowers, an art transmitted from generation to generation. All this took a great deal of time, during which the Rani quietly smoked her hookah, its water scented with orange-blossom; she always claimed that tobacco sharpened her mind.

And now, the Rani needed to think. She had been happy, on her trip to Gwalior, to renew her ties with that world of princely courts that was hers. And yet, she had returned in a state of bitter disappointment. Under the pretext of asking Diwan Dinkar for advice, she had really gone to seek his approval. But he had counselled caution, and unfortunately, he had convinced her. She would not involve herself in the conspiracy. Her responsibility to her former subjects took precedence over her urge to wash away with blood the humiliations and injustices the British had made her suffer. Reining in her impatience to fight to free her people, she must do her utmost to shelter them from the coming storm, which meant she would have to continue to tolerate the hated occupier and remain a fallen queen.

If reason forbade her to act, she still had the right to entertain herself and the power to love. She had missed Roger even more than she could have imagined.

The boat she had sent for the young man glided on the jade-coloured lake. The old oarsman, his toothless gums parted in silent laughter, pulled slowly at his oars, too slowly for Roger's impatience.

The day was waning, and a red sun sank behind the towers of the fort. The uneven banks of the lake were covered in luxurious vegetation. Here and there, a temple emerged from bristling palm trees. At distant intervals, clusters of dark round rocks formed hills on each of which stood a narrow pagoda-shaped chapel.

Roger's eyes were glued to the Rani's pavilion which, because of its four conical turrets, looked like a fortress despite its modest proportions.

Roger's boat slid into the tunnel under the pavilion where Roger had swum in a week before. A servant was waiting. Roger climbed a narrow staircase, crossed a miniscule courtyard darkened by branches of a single large tree, and entered the familiar drawing room.

Disdaining the white sari, or the masculine clothes she usually favoured, the Rani was wearing a sari bronzed in red and gold, red being the symbol of long life and of love. Her astrologer had told her that today she should wear rubies and pearls, and so she had donned the necklace she had bought from the jeweller-conspirator; she wore no other jewels. The splendour of her attire enhanced the sparkle of her beauty and lent it a touch of mystery.

They sat on a sofa before low tables of rosewood inlaid with ivory.

'I've ordered an Indian dinner for you, Sahib Giffard,' she said. 'I refuse to be like all those Rajas who serve the British atrocious imitations of their own dishes.'

She clapped her hands; servants appeared bringing the thali, a silver tray holding a number of very small dishes of strongly-flavoured vegetables.

Indians set great store by the appearance of food, which must be made pleasing to the eye by subtly associating its colours. But what is most important is that the food be healthy and well-balanced. Ancient recipes dictate the size and the order of the dishes, their texture, the introduction of an acid and the digestive base in the form of tomatoes, vinegar or lemon. Spices, all of which have medicinal properties, play an important role. The Rani liked best of all the hot peppers from Kashmir, India's favourites; she quenched their fire by drinking yoghurt.

Although she herself was a vegetarian, the Rani had ordered meats for Roger—skewers of mutton, tandoori chicken macerated in spiced yoghurt and daubed with a paste made of crushed red peppers.

The splendour of an Indian meal is judged by its desserts. Servants carried in pyramids of pineapples, cinnamon-apples, guavas, bananas, mandarin oranges, coconuts and, of course, pomegranates, which are regarded as harbingers of good fortune. With them came the sweets—rasgullas, balls of casein cooked in fruit-syrup; payasam, a cream of milk and flour boiled down with cashews and sprinkled with raisins; and halva, a paste of sesame seeds and nuts. They were wrapped in edible gold leaves, a royal luxury that is also a potent vitamin.

The Rani and Roger said very little; Indian protocol does not mix food and conversation.

Both were in a hurry to finish the meal. At last, in boxes of wrought gold, came the paan, which concludes Indian meals; they mixed ground areca nuts with lime, added a clove, wrapped the mixture in betel leaves, and chewed them. The servant withdrew, carrying away the trays.

The Rani had ordered for Roger a decanter of sherat, an Afghan wine imported by the Moghuls. For herself she had poured a little guj into the gold kalian of her hookah, which made the tobacco slightly heady. Night had fallen, and the darkness enveloping the house cut them off from the world. The Rani described her trip to Gwalior, the Maharaja's palace, his court and his feasts.

Roger complained of the stifling boredom of life in the British community, which had seemed even more painful to bear during her absence—the five days she had been away had felt like five months. He painted comical descriptions of breakfast at the Phipps's—with the doctor reading his newspaper and Annabelle demonstrating her superiority by harassing her servants; the mornings spent poring over the boring files of the rare lawsuits assigned to the district magistrate; the afternoon siesta on the verandah, under a punkha waved by a servant; the hours of whist and billiards in the officers' mess; the evenings spent sipping claret and exchanging the same platitudes over and over again; the interminable dinners at the Phipps's or other households in the civilian compound, where there were never less than ten dishes served. His compatriots clung tightly to British ways, and their tiny community retired into itself. The climate, together with their own sloth or idleness, had made them sink into an intellectual and physical torpor.

Roger and the Rani were talking faster and faster, laughing louder and louder; and then, a sudden silence settled between them. The moon had risen and through the windows night crept in, silent and luminous. The lake seemed a milky surface bordered by strange black cut-outs traced by temple roofs and by treetops under the dancing glow of the stars. In the room, perfumed odours rising from the burners charged the atmosphere with sensuality. The Rani leaned back dreamily on the brocade pillows with the provocative grace of a model for a Moghul miniature. Never had Roger sensed in her such abandon. His body vibrated and blood beat in his temples. He stretched out his arm and took the Rani's hand, which trembled in his like a trapped bird.

Lakshmi bowed her head. Her heart beat wildly. She had waited so long for this moment, and now, she was afraid. Her emotion was such that for several minutes she could neither speak nor move.

At that moment, Mandar knocked at the door.

'An urgent message from Diwan Naransin.'

Lakshmi took the note and read it. Her eyes opened wide in surprise and horror. In a strangled voice, she said, 'They have executed Mangal Pande.'

Roger had heard of him; the name had been all over the *India Gazette*. A fortnight before, at Barrackpore near Calcutta, a sepoy of the 34th Native Infantry, Mangal Pande had appeared in the middle of the military cantonment in a state of excitement bordering on madness, shouting to his comrades to rise up against the British in the name of their religion. He had shot down a sergeant-major who had rushed up to arrest him, and wounded two officers as they tried to disarm him. The sepoys, despite orders, had refused to raise a hand against Pande, a Brahmin of the highest caste. General Hearsey, the garrison's commanding officer, had then ridden with a handful of British troops into the group of sepoys surrounding Mangal Pande, still shouting, his raised hands stained with English blood. When he saw that he would be arrested, he tried to kill himself with his own gun, but managed only to wound himself. The sepoys had then dispersed, and Mangal Pande was hauled before a court-martial.

'They executed him,' the Rani repeated. 'They couldn't find anyone in all Barrackpore to do their dirty work. They had to send for a hangman all the way from Calcutta.'

'They had to execute him,' Roger answered. 'General Hearsey had to make an example of him.' He was deeply annoyed at the interruption to such a promising evening and was not particularly concerned by the fate of Mangal Pande.

'He acted for his faith and he died for his faith!' The Rani shot back.

'He was drugged, Lakshmi. He said so himself at the trial.'

'If he took drugs, it was from despair.'

'Come, Lakshmi. Do you think the British should allow anyone to stand up and call for rebellion? What would the Indian kings do in their place?'

The tone of his voice was light, placatory. Once again, he took her hand, trying to recover the intimacy they had lost. Lakshmi tore it away. 'I shall never belong to an Englishman!'

She was all the more vehement for having been, a few minutes earlier, on the point of giving in to him.

'The British are nothing but murderers!' she shouted.

The insult wounded Roger. He cursed Mangal Pande, the sepoys, even General Hearsey. Laying aside for once his natural gentleness, he said, 'Be careful, Lakshmi. The British will crush anyone who rises against them.'

'I thought you liked India and Indians.'

'And I thought you placed love above racial differences,' he replied.

She wanted to throw him out, but she lacked courage. It was he who rose to leave. Standing before her, his lips tight and eyes burning, he spoke with rage in his voice, 'I love India and I love you, Lakshmi.'

And he left without another word.

Sadness and frustration kept the Rani from sleeping. Pacing up and down in the pavilion's drawing room, she noticed Roger's waistcoat lying among the cushions; he had taken it off after dinner and left it behind in his hurried departure. She held it for a moment, fingered the cloth, brought it to her face and inhaled its strong manly smell. A letter slid from its pocket to the floor. Picking it up, Lakshmi saw from the signature that it came from Roger's closest friend, Roderick Briggs. Unable to resist the temptation, she opened and read it.

Roderick had been forced to postpone his wedding to Sarah Brandon, for he had asked to be attached to the army in India. His superiors had assured him that serving there for a time would lead to faster promotion, and besides, Roger had convinced him of the country's attractiveness. He would be landing in Bombay in a few weeks and was looking forward to seeing Roger again. The letter finished thus:

> *Your last few letters greatly surprised me. You claim to be so deeply in love that you couldn't care less about your future, your career, your life. You, Roger, swept away by passion! You, who boasted of being incorruptible by love, you who made fun of the love I bear Sarah. You have changed a great deal, my friend, and I am curious to see what ravages passion has wrought—and also to meet its object. You don't tell me anything about her, except that she is Indian. Are you quite sure the tropical climate hasn't made you lose your head and that what you say is the love of your life is not just a simple little exotic adventure? Falling in love with an Indian...really, Roger!*

11

At the district magistrate's office, Roger tried to stay interested in his files. It had been a fortnight since he had seen the Rani. A fortnight since he had given her sign of life, though the temptation had gnawed at him every day. He had plunged into work but nothing seemed to register. He had not touched his brushes, having lost all desire to paint. He had taken to lounging about the mess at the cantonment, listening to the officers' talk without hearing it and drinking considerable amounts of whiskey. Struck by the regularity of his attendance at the mess, his colleagues imagined he had experienced a change of heart, but his brusqueness soon discouraged their attempts at friendliness.

Suddenly, a bustling and the sound of shouts roused him from his torpor. A crowd was gathering in the street. Passers-by hauled themselves by the bars onto window-ledges to get a better view. Between turbans Roger saw the red-and-gold canopy of the Rani's palanquin, and then he heard, coming from Captain Gordon's office, the noise of scraping chairs, the rattle of a sword being hurriedly readjusted, the squeak of a door thrown open. Suddenly, he heard Lakshmi's voice.

'Captain, as we were returning from the temple, it occurred to us to come see you. We know with what conscientiousness you and your aides administer justice for the good of the citizens.'

Roger had not moved. He heard Captain Gordon mutter an answer, not knowing what to make of this visit, the first the Rani had ever paid him.

'Would you give me a tour of your offices?'

With Captain Gordon on her heels, Lakshmi entered Roger's office and greeted him silently, her hands clasped in front of her bosom.

Roger stood at attention. Gordon signalled him to join them. Together, they walked from room to room. The Indian assessors and scribes went into shock, waving off that day's petitioners to rush to the Rani, kneel before her and kiss the ground or the hem of her sari. Some of them had once worked at the palace. Lakshmi recognized them, asked after their families, had a word for each one. They gazed at her with veneration, and Roger understood that for them, she would always be the real queen. As she walked away, they all wanted to follow her. Gordon, jostled, found himself separated for a moment from the Rani. She used the opportunity to turn to Roger.

'We hope, Sahib Giffard, that you will soon come to see us at the palace.'

And she climbed back into her palanquin in the middle of a milling crowd.

Shielded from sight by the gold-embroidered muslin curtains, Lakshmi broke into a smile. How many times during the last two weeks had she thought of summoning Roger! Each time she had held back, hoping that he would make the first move, and giving in to vague anxiety, caused not only by her feelings for him but also by the events that she sensed were brewing.

And that morning she had received pleasant and unexpected news. Her childhood friend, Nana Sahib, the former Raja of Bithur, had sent word that he was coming to Jhansi. He had undertaken a long pilgrimage which led him from city to city. Before going home, he would make a detour to Jhansi in order to see his spiritual sister.

His timing was perfect. Never had Lakshmi felt a greater need to see Nana Sahib, her friend, her older brother who, though he too had been deposed by the British, had reportedly remained their friend. Her joy at the news of his visit, which she wanted to share with Roger, had convinced her to give in and personally fetch him at his office.

Roger did not show up that afternoon to ride with her as she had hoped. He came to the palace only in the evening, for a brief visit. His look, his smile belied his reserve, but she too was slightly self-conscious at being alone with him. To dispel this slight uneasiness, Lakshmi described to him memories of her childhood, which had been awakened by Nana Sahib's imminent visit.

'There were three inseparable friends in Bithur: a fat one, young Raja Nana Sahib; a dark one, his cousin Rao Sahib; and a thin one, their playmate, Tatya Tope. Although they were ten years older than I, they adopted me. They treated me as a boy and included me in their male warlike games.'

Lakshmi recalled their races on horseback along the sandbanks of the lazy, almost motionless river, the target-shooting with pistols, the mock sabre-duels in an abandoned courtyard of the palace of Bithur.

'At first we hated each other, Nana Sahib and I. I'll never forget the time I asked him to take me on his elephant and he refused and made fun of me. My father tried to calm me by saying, "You weren't born to ride elephants. Now be quiet." But being quiet was the last thing I could be. I remember shouting at Nana Sahib, "You'll see—one day I'll own ten elephants to each one of yours. Remember what I'm telling you." And I was right, because after my marriage, I did own ten elephants and more.

'It was only during my last years in Bithur that we really became friends. He would confide in me, tell me his troubles. He had fallen in love with one of his father's slaves, Husseinee Hanum. He must have been eighteen or nineteen, and she was a great beauty—very tall, very light skinned with a regal bearing. I was fascinated by her. I wonder if she's still with him....'

Nana Sahib arrived at Jhansi in the early afternoon one day at the end of April. The arrival of a ruler, even a deposed one, was a choice distraction for the people of Jhansi, who had scrambled atop the town walls to watch for his procession. The first thing they saw in the distance, between the trees lining the Kalpi road, was a cloud of brilliant colours with banners flying above, and behind, an indistinct mass of elephants and camels. Gradually, the picture became clearer. The shimmer of bright colours divided into the turbans, shawls, and robes of nobles astride richly-caparisoned horses. They carried huge flame-shaped banners embroidered with gold. Then came the musicians playing silver drums and trumpets, and the dancers, the astrologers, and the Raja's servants in yellow and red livery. These were followed by the heralds of the court wearing the Raja's arms embroidered in gold on their chests and shouting in unison the Raja's innumerable titles and no less innumerable virtues. In the front walked the chamberlains, gold staffs in hand. At the tail end, surrounded by their keepers, was a string of twelve elephants, each with a silver howdah set on long blankets of gold-embroidered velvet.

Nana Sahib rode the first elephant. A servant holding a vast silk parasol with gold tassels protected him from the sun. Another servant, swishing a black and gold fly-swatter, kept insects away from his master. A group of eighty to a hundred camels, loaded with the baggage of the Raja and his suite, brought up the rear.

The Rani awaited her guest in the forecourt of the palace. Nana's elephant stopped by the narrow marble staircase designed for dismounting. In honour of the queen of Jhansi, the Raja of Bithur was completely covered in gems. Bracelets of emeralds and diamonds circled his arms. Around his neck were rows of emeralds, each the size of a pigeon's egg, dangling over a breastplate of enormous diamonds. The hilt of his sabre was a patchwork of diamonds and rubies. His turban was fastened by a plaque of diamonds and emeralds. Each of his fingers wore a silver ring set with rubies, diamonds and emeralds. Even his belt was inlaid with precious stones. Following Maratha custom, he had hung from his ear a large gold ring, ornate with heavy pearls. In his hand he held a pair of European gray suede gloves that contrasted strangely with that grand Oriental display of opulence.

Tall and imposing, the Raja was incontestably a man of noble bearing. The Rani recognized the same pale aristocratic tint of his skin, the large round eyes, the impeccable teeth his smile revealed; but he had become a lot fatter since his adolescence. Disregarding protocol between Indian princes, Nana Sahib and Lakshmi threw themselves into one another's arms. It had been fifteen years since they had last seen each other.

Nana Sahib's munificence was legendary. He had brought gifts for everyone, from Diwan Naransin to the lowest servant, in the palace. For Lakshmi, he had chosen not jewels but a man's gifts, weapons she would appreciate more than ornaments. He offered her a sharp-bladed military sabre with a steel hilt damascened in gold, and a brace of pistols made in England, the finest product of British gunsmiths, their handles filigreed in silver. To Damodar he gave a dagger, not a child's toy but an adult weapon, with an emerald-studded hilt. To this he added a miniature rifle with which the child could practise shooting. These presents delighted Damodar as much as Nana Sahib's two favourite animals, a lion-tailed monkey and a rabbit-sized squirrel, that he took with him everywhere he went.

Nana Sahib and Lakshmi spent the entire afternoon exchanging news and memories.

'How is Husseinee Hanum?' Lakshmi asked.

Nana Sahib hesitated and then answered briefly, 'I took her into my service after my father died.'

The Rani concluded that Husseinee Hanum was still in favour, although public rumour attributed numerous feminine conquests to Nana Sahib.

Changing the subject rapidly, Nana Sahib asked Lakshmi's permission to give a dinner that evening for the British civilian and military authorities in Jhansi. Lakshmi made a face. She had no desire to receive the British into her palace, but it was the request of a friend, and moreover, the rule of purdah would give her legitimate reason not to attend. She was unable, nevertheless, to hide her surprise.

'I've heard of the sumptuous receptions you've given them in Bithur. They all praise your hospitality and congratulate themselves on having such a friend. But how can you still be friendly after they refused to recognize your adoption and deposed you the way they deposed me?'

'Not all the British are bad. Many are even rather charming.'

Then he teased the Rani, 'You're not going to give those Englishmen an Indian meal? They wouldn't know how to eat it, and what's more, they'd think they were being poisoned. Don't worry—I brought everything with me.'

'Where do you think you are? Among savages?' the Rani replied. 'I have everything you need right here.'

A former Raja of Jhansi, a great-uncle of Lakshmi's late husband, had imported a large amount of furniture and crockery from London. Lakshmi and Nana Sahib merrily explored the palace's storage rooms, and supervised the transformation of a ground floor waiting-room into a banquet hall.

The Rani's curiosity proved too strong for her to stay in her apartments; she concealed herself behind a slightly opened door and watched as the banquet progressed.

The table was a splendid display. The china, the glassware and the silver sparkled among the brilliant, variegated flowers that were Jhansi's pride. Nana Sahib presided at one end of the table, his back to the door behind which Lakshmi was hiding. At his request, the men had come without their wives.

The Rani had eyes only for Roger, who sat at the other end of the table. Nana Sahib was speaking with his neighbours, Captain Skene and Captain Dunlop. He spoke correct English and even read the London newspapers, but the Rani noted, with a touch of satisfaction, that he handled the language less well than she, since he needed to have at his side a translator, a Eurasian named Todd, to help fill in the gaps in his vocabulary.

The other guests, who were not participating in the august conversation of the Raja and their superiors, compensated as usual by criticizing the details of the meal. The tablecloth might be cut from the finest European damask, but instead of napkins, they had been given hand-towels. The soup had been served in dessert-plates, the beer in cheap cups one might buy at any fair, and champagne glasses had been used for the claret. To top it all, the pudding had been brought in a soup-plate. In short, these Indians simply had no idea.

After brandy, the servants, on a sign from Nana Sahib, entered bearing gifts for each of the guests: sabres, daggers, revolvers and rifles were distributed to all. The Rani wondered what Roger would do with the hunting-rifle he had been given, for he did not hunt.

The distribution of presents meant that dinner was over. Captain Skene gave the signal to rise. Roger was the last to thank the Raja of Bithur and take his leave.

Once the British had left and the servants retired, Lakshmi emerged from her hiding-place and entered the banquet hall. Only Nana Sahib was still there, his back to her, seated at the long, deserted table. He brought a glass to his lips, and Lakshmi was surprised that he should have taken to brandy. Nana Sahib had heard Lakshmi come in, but he did not move or turn around. Staring at the amber liqueur at the bottom of his glass, he said calmly, 'We will run them all out of India.'

The Rani stopped in her tracks. Nana Sahib, still not looking at her, repeated, 'Yes, Lakshmi, we'll soon be rid of these Englishmen.'

'You want to kill all the British!' Lakshmi exclaimed.

'I'm not cruel, Lakshmi, you know that. We won't kill them if we don't have to.'

Gradually, Lakshmi understood what Nana Sahib had just said.

She walked to the table and stared hard at him. 'So, you're part of the conspiracy,' she said, her throat tight.

'A part! You underestimate me, Lakshmi.'

The Rani laughed nervously. 'You, the leader of the conspiracy! But you're only interested in pleasure, Nana Sahib!'

Nana Sahib disregarded her disdainful remark.

'You didn't like the chapattis? And the cartridges? How easy it was just to make use of the clumsiness of the British! Although I must admit, we'd already begun to form secret societies among the sepoys.'

Suddenly, Lakshmi remembered Diwan Dinkar's surprise in Gwalior when she had asked him who was the leader of the conspiracy. He had been amazed that Lakshmi did not know it was her best friend.

'You will be at my side,' Nana Sahib said simply. 'Do you remember when we used to play at war as children and I'd make you my lieutenant? You'll be one again tomorrow to free our country. You refused to answer the invitation of the jeweller I sent you, but I know you, Lakshmi. You'll come around to our side.'

The Rani remained silent, and Nana Sahib, mistaking this for assent, continued, 'You'll be with me at the head of the movement. The others are just accomplices. The former Nawab of Oudh, the old Great Moghul, the Maulvi of Faizabad, the Diwan of Gwalior—all accomplices, nothing but accomplices.'

'What are you saying?' Lakshmi interrupted. 'Diwan Dinkar is part of the plot?'

'Dinkar is in full sympathy with us, even if his position prevents him from showing it openly. He came to Bithur expressly to speak to me about it, during a tour he was making with his master the Maharaja.'

'Tell me, Nana Sahib, why are you playing this game with the

British? You pass yourself off as their best friend, you even force me to receive them. Why this hypocrisy?'

'But I don't detest them, Lakshmi. I very much enjoy the company of the British. I admire their qualities. I even like their innocence when they make fun of me without realizing that I'm aware of it. And then, one learns a lot about the British by spending time with them. In that respect this recent pilgrimage was highly instructive. I needed to evaluate their strength. That's why I asked you to receive them this evening.'

Lakshmi remained silent for a few moments. Then, in a low, hoarse voice, she asked, 'Why you, Nana Sahib?'

Nana Sahib took his time before answering, 'My father was humiliated when the British deposed him. I was humiliated when the British refused to recognize my adoption and dethroned me. As for you, you were humiliated when they dispossessed you. All of India has been humiliated. That's enough.'

'So you're rebelling out of bitterness. That's not how wars are won.'

'No, but that's how revolutions are made.'

Lakshmi turned and quickly left the room.

Early next morning Nana Sahib and his suite left Jhansi to return to Bithur. The Rani did not come out to bid him goodbye, breaking one of the sacrosanct laws of Indian hospitality.

Once the procession had disappeared, a servant approached the Rani, who was with Mandar in the palace garden, and held out a chapatti.

'The Raja of Bithur left this for you. He ordered me to give it to you and say, "From North to South, from East to West, the wind is blowing."'

When the servant had left, Mandar said, 'Of course you're going to answer the Raja's call.'

Mandar knew. Perhaps she had listened from behind the door the night before, like any well-trained servant. Without looking at her, the Rani spoke somberly, 'I've seen my best friend, my brother, drink with the British, laugh with them, and pat them on the back, only to learn that he's the leader of the conspiracy that wants to throw those same people out of India. I abhor this kind of falseness.'

Mandar assumed a deeply shocked expression. The prestige of kings was deep among people of her station, and it wounded her to hear one spoken of so harshly.

'Do you think,' she asked, 'he'd be able to rid us of the British by charging them at the head of his puny army? If he operates in the shadows, it's only because the power of the enemy forces him to do so. You accuse him of betraying the ideals of our ancestors, but what about you? Are you worthy of them, when all you do is bewail your fate while acquiescing in British oppression? For us Indians, Nana Sahib has shown himself to be the leader we need.'

'If only he were! I'm convinced he's exaggerating his role. The conspiracy has not one head but a thousand.'

'Because the whole country's involved! You're the only one who has refused to join the fighters for religion and freedom.'

To hide her confusion from Mandar, the Rani unsealed the letter she was holding. Although she had recognized Diwan Dinkar's seal, she had not yet opened it.

In flowery prose the Diwan related the recent pleasure tour he had just made with his master the Maharaja of Gwalior. Their itinerary had taken them as far as Calcutta. There, Governor General Lord Canning had received them with the greatest ceremony, and Dinkar described at length the feasts that had highlighted their stay in the capital of British India. At the Calcutta Botanical Gardens, Maharaja Sindhia had given a banquet for the British colony that had been a huge success.

The Diwan of Gwalior's letter surprised the Rani. Dinkar had never written her before, and he was not a man to do anything without precise reasons. What was he hiding behind all these touristic descriptions? The Diwan went on to describe the many monuments the Maharaja and he had admired in Calcutta. On the Governor General's orders, they had visited almost all the British military installations in the city and its surrounding area.

'His Majesty, my master, was deeply impressed by the formidable power and inexhaustible resources of the British army. One understands why England in the past has vanquished all those who attacked her.' The Rani reread the sentence and remained pensive until Diwan Dinkar's message became clear. He had dragged his master all over the country not to see the sights but to gauge British strength. His conclusion was clear-cut and, once examined, the same as he had told the queen when she had gone to consult him at Gwalior. Whatever happened, the British would come out on top.

This reminder of the Diwan's warning came at a time when the Rani was already irritable enough.

She began to walk at a rapid pace, feeling a need for movement and solitude. But her servant remained at her side, curious about the contents of the letter that had so altered the mood of her mistress.

They entered the courtyard which Damodar used for a playground. He was running about shouting with other boys his age. Roger had joined in the game while he was waiting to go on his daily horseback ride with the Rani. Damodar ran over to greet his mother. He was very excited.

'The British are going to be thrown out and I'll be put back on the throne.'

How had he heard? Loose talk among the servants, no doubt. The child had already run off to resume his game with Roger. 'And that's how it is,' the Rani said. 'Damodar's delighted to hear the British are going to leave, and all he wants is to be Sahib Giffard's friend. His child's instincts are correct. If you hate the English, must you hate them all? If you love an Englishman, does that mean you're on their side?'

Roger had at last extricated himself from the children, who did not want to let him leave the game. Grinning with joy, he told the Rani he had just learned that his friend Roderick had landed at Bombay; before taking up his post, he had asked for leave to visit Roger. Then Roger thanked the Rani for last night's dinner, at which all the British guests had been completely won over by Nana Sahib.

'Captain Skene was particularly charmed. He's been telling everyone that, just as his colleagues say, the British don't have a better friend than the Raja of Bithur.' The Rani turned pale and walked on. Once she and Mandar were out of earshot, she turned to her servant and said in a tired voice, as though continuing a long conversation, 'No, Mandar! I shall not join the conspiracy!'

It was more than Mandar could bear.

'The British have done their work well. They've destroyed the flame that burned in you, they've destroyed your conscience. You have forgotten your people, you have forgotten India. You're betraying them. And all that because you love an Englishman.'

The Rani looked at Mandar and found her ugly, with her angular face, her long teeth and her purple gums bared in anger.

'If I love Roger, that concerns no one but me. Have I betrayed our secrets to him? Have I defied our beliefs, our traditions?' And she finished with a bitter cry, 'I'm not even his mistress!'

12

Late spring brought weather that grew hotter each day. It became impossible to ride in the afternoon, and the Rani napped instead. When evening brought the illusion of slightly cooler air, she would walk in the park with Roger.

The pavilion at the lake stood on a dam built a century earlier by a Raja of Jhansi. Behind it stretched the Narayan Bagh, the vast gardens. Clusters of palm trees were planted close together in large squares separated by avenues of orange and lemon trees. From their branches rose the intense chatter of birds, unleashed by the waning day. Brown shadows crept along the ground as the rays of the setting sun bathed the majestic palms in orange.

Lakshmi, worried about the present, sought refuge in telling Roger about the past.

'I don't have many memories of Benares where I was born. We left there when I was three. I vaguely remember the palace in which we lived and which seemed to me immense. I used to run through suites of empty, dusty rooms. I would lean over the parapet of the terrace to watch the muddy Ganges flowing below. The palace belonged to Nana Sahib's uncle, Prince Chimaji. He had been thrown out of Poona when the British deposed the Peshwa. My father, who had always served him, had followed him into exile in Benares.

'I see by your expression that you don't know much about the Peshwa, although his fame and glory echoed throughout India for centuries. The Peshwa, Roger, was the hereditary chief of the confederation of Maratha kings and princes who, in western India, had made up a formidable and flourishing empire. Then the British came. They slithered into the Maratha Empire like a worm into fruit.

Then came division, weakness, and finally, disintegration. The British eventually deposed the last Peshwa, Baji Rao II, Nana Sahib's adoptive father, and expelled him and his family from Poona, his capital.

'My father, who came to Benares with Prince Chimaji, had lost almost all his fortune in the disaster. He managed to feed us on a salary of fifty rupees a month, all that Prince Chimaji could afford to give him. Several maharajas and even the British offered him posts that were both honourable and lucrative. "It is better to live in honest poverty than immoral prosperity," he told them, refusing their offers.'

Had her father really been that disinterested? Little by little in the course of her story, the Rani invented a Moropant very different from reality, not in order to hide the shameful truth from Roger, but rather to create for herself the kind of paternal figure she wished she might have had.

'My father didn't disgrace his long lineage. We come from a very old Brahmin family from Way, a small city south of Bombay. It's a holy place where the people are traditionally faithful, pious and proud. When Chimaji died, my father, who was left without a roof and without employment, was taken in by the prince's older brother, Baji Rao, the former Peshwa, the last of his glorious line. When the British deposed him, they gave him, out of charity, a tiny principality called Bithur, not far from Cawnpore.

'And so we went to live at Baji Rao's palace in Bithur. The Raja of Bithur's palace was infinitely more luxurious than his brother Chimaji's; the former Peshwa had managed to hang on to some of his fortune. I was bowled over by our new residence. It was the first time I'd seen anything like it—the large mirrors with gold frames and the crystal chandeliers imported from Europe, the furniture inlaid with ivory and mother-of-pearl, the porcelain from China, and a whole series of gigantic portraits of ancestors that Baji Rao had commissioned. All this was new and extraordinary to me.

'I had great fun in Bithur with the three friends I've told you about, and yet I felt very lonely. My mother died when I was three. She was extremely beautiful. She could neither read nor write, but she recited for me our religious texts and national epics. And then she'd often take me with her to the temples of Benares. When we went to

Bithur, she had already died. I had no brothers or sisters. I felt quite alone, but I've always liked solitude or, at least, I've gotten used to it.

'The old Raja of Bithur, the former Peshwa, had taken a liking to me. He was a bitter man; he had never come to terms with having been deposed and exiled by the British. He insisted on maintaining at tiny Bithur a court as large and as rich as the one he'd had in his former capital, Poona. But behind that facade, he hid a deep resentment. I'm the only one, I'm told, who ever found favour with him. He treated me like an adopted daughter, had me educated with care, and decided to find a brilliant match for me. He turned down on my behalf several offers from parties he didn't think important enough—he wanted to marry me to a ruler. The horoscope drawn at my birth had said I would be a queen, and queen was what the old Raja of Bithur wanted me to be.

'Finally, he settled on the Raja of Jhansi, who was a widower and wanted to remarry in order to have an heir. At the start, the Raja was hesitant—I didn't have a dowry.'

'Why did he finally marry you?'

'Because, although I was poor, I belonged to the highest caste, the Brahmins. He was a wealthy king but only a Kshatriya of the warrior caste, which is inferior to that of the Brahmins. It was my protector, Baji Rao, who settled all the expenses of the wedding.'

'But your fiance had never seen you and you had never seen him!'

'In India, Roger, all marriages are arranged.'

'So there are never love-matches?'

'That's not important, because for us, marriage isn't what it is for you. We don't grow up expecting romantic love. Marriage is not an end in itself but a natural means to a specific goal. For the ambitious, it's a way of raising one's status. In their eyes, my wedding to a ruling prince was an unhoped-for success. And then, our idea of happiness is so different from yours. As one of our sages put it, "Happiness does not derive from happiness. A woman attains it only through pain. A woman who hasn't been touched by sorrow is not complete, for only suffering can make her whole."'

Try as he might, Roger still could not understand.

'How could you, with your character and your independence, agree to marry a man you hadn't chosen, a man you'd never seen?'

'It was an idea I'd been accustomed to since my childhood. And then, I was only fourteen years old. Besides, it seems that I gave everyone quite a shock on the day of the wedding. As you know, bride and groom must walk seven times around the ritual fire before the priest ties them together by their clothes. At that moment, apparently, I said aloud, "Make sure that knot is tight." The priests and the royal guests were very shocked by my effrontery. A bride is supposed to be timid and reserved. Everyone decided I had been badly brought up.'

One evening as Lakshmi and Roger were returning to the pavilion, at the hour when the setting sun darkened the walls of Jhansi and cast a pearly gloss over the lake, they saw Mandar running out to meet them. Out of breath, she shouted, 'The revolution has begun, the revolutionaries have taken Delhi. The Great Moghul is back on his throne.'

Was it true? The news had just reached the British by telegraph. Their Indian subordinates had passed it on to Diwan Naransin, who had sent Mandar out to find the Rani. She immediately rode back to town with Roger, rushing to the palace while Roger raced to his office.

Separately, they learned the details of what had happened.

Meerut, a small city located forty miles northeast of Delhi, was considered by the British as India's safest station. It was the only city where they were a majority. The garrison consisted of two regiments, exclusively British, well-equipped with artillery.

And yet, on 8 May, the Third Regiment of native cavalry refused the new cartridges issued to them by their superiors, on the pretext that they were greased with sacrilegious fat. Trouble with cartridges had by then become commonplace and no one worried about this particular incident. The authorities merely had eighty-five of the mutineers arrested and thrown in prison. A military tribunal condemned them to several years of forced labour. In the middle of squares formed by troops on parade, the mutineers were stripped of their uniforms and put in irons. The matter was considered closed.

The next day, 11 May 1857, was a Sunday. In the late afternoon, while the British colony was praying in church, the sepoys suddenly mutinied in their cantonments. They set fire to their barracks and killed

British and even native officers who tried to oppose them. Then they spilled out into the town, opened the gates of the jails, and released the eighty-five sepoys who had been imprisoned a few days earlier.

In no time at all, the upheaval reached the bazaar. The population set fire to all the buildings associated with British domination—public buildings, offices, hotels—and within a few hours, they had cleared Meerut of the British and were masters of the city. The rebel sepoys formed a column, left Meerut and set off towards Delhi.

They marched in typically British order and discipline and took only one night to cover the forty miles separating the two cities. On 12 May, at seven in the morning, they stood at the walls of India's former capital. Mysteriously, the gates swung open before them. The mutineers raced through the streets, shouting, 'Deen, deen'—the Indian war-cry. The sepoys of the Delhi garrison overpowered their officers and rallied to the Meerut contingent. Thousands of Delhi's inhabitants took to the streets, welcomed the rebels with open arms and helped them hunt down the British, who were attempting to flee the city in all directions. The rebels then made for the Red Fort, invaded the former imperial palace, threw themselves at the feet of old Bahadur Shah, the Great Moghul, and proclaimed him their ruler. That night, Delhi was rid of the British occupiers, and the Great Moghul, 'Light of the World, the Badshah, the suzerain lord of twenty kingdoms', ruled once again.

Upon hearing the news, the Rani's first impulse was to rush to the palace temple, located near the main portal and open to the faithful. There, she found only a few women sitting in a corner and an old peasant deep in meditation. Before the silver statue of goddess Lakshmi, the Rani placed her offerings—garlands of flowers, grains of rice and wheat—and prayed, with enthusiasm and hope, that the rebels succeed, and that the movement spread quickly to Jhansi and free 'Bharat Mata', Mother India. The rebellion was no longer just a matter of fanatics and deposed kings. The whole army had risen in the garrisons of Meerut and Delhi, and the people of those cities had followed them. India had finally taken her destiny in her hands.

The following morning, the Rani summoned Captain Skene. In the meantime, more news had arrived, chilling her exaltation. At Delhi, the revolutionaries had been unable to capture an important arsenal.

A group of British officers had managed to blow it up, setting off a huge explosion that rocked the entire city. The Great Moghul, the octogenarian Bahadur Shah, had shown the greatest reluctance to return to the throne. His champions had had to run him to ground in his harem and practically drag him out. In both Delhi and Meerut, the rebellious sepoys and the prisoners they had freed, many of them common-law criminals and highway robbers, had indulged in widespread looting, and not just of British possessions. It was not only British military personnel who had been massacred; civilians, women and children had also been the objects of a hideous manhunt, chased from house to house, dragged from their hiding places to have their throats cut, to be slashed and hacked to pieces on the spot. The two cities were awash in violence and confusion. At Delhi, the rebels had brought fifty British prisoners to the Great Moghul, who barely glanced at the men and women standing before him, haggard with fatigue and fear. He himself was trembling like a leaf, absolutely terrified by the rebels. He had simply murmured, 'Do whatever you want with them,' and turned away. The rebels had led their prisoners to a courtyard on the edge of the palace, butchered them with sabres and bayonets, and thrown their bodies down a well.

The Rani received Captain Skene in the audience chamber, privately, without witnesses. She asked his opinion of the events.

'Our army will have the situation in hand at any moment now and will crush the mutineers without difficulty. As Your Highness knows, apart from Meerut and Delhi, the country is calm. No one has moved.'

'You were certain there would be no rebellion, Captain. Yet, it did break out.'

'Only locally, Your Highness—and, may I add, to my shame—only because of the incompetence of some of our officers.'

The Rani knew that Skene was alluding to General Hewitt, the commander of the Meerut Division, who, all throughout that fatal day of 11 May, had taken no action. He had not even ordered his British regiments and their artillery out of the cantonment; the sepoys had been allowed to torch, loot and massacre without interference.

'And you don't fear anything will happen here in Jhansi, Captain?'

'I answer for my troops, I'll answer for Jhansi, and my colleagues in other stations are prepared to do the same. My sepoys, I am happy to say, continue to be completely faithful to us. I have always had complete trust in them, and I still do.'

'How can you be so certain of their feelings?'

'Because they came on their own initiative to me and my aides to tell us the shame and horror they felt for what their companions have done at Meerut and Delhi.'

'Nevertheless, Captain, I feel responsible for the security of my former subjects, and I must ask your permission to raise, at my own expense, a small army to maintain order in case of need and protect the population against any eventual trouble.'

Skene thought for a few moments and finally consented. The Rani, who had sensed his hesitation, was unable to keep from asking, 'You're not afraid, Captain, of allowing me a weapon I could turn against you?'

'I know you, Your Highness. You are loyal and frank and incapable of any treasonable act.'

The Rani was touched. She always had a certain respect for Skene. He too was loyal and sincere, even quite naïve. In a gentle voice, she asked, 'Where do you find such trust?'

'I have faith in God and my country. I believe in my mission. We are bringing India progress, justice and hope. Like so many of my compatriots serving in this land, I like Indians.'

'And the Indians like you, Captain. You are popular in Jhansi.'

And it was true; despite the resentment harboured by the inhabitants of Jhansi towards the British, Captain Skene had gained their affection through his simplicity, his attention to their needs and his genuine kindness. His confidence, however, provoked the Rani and she continued attacking.

'So, according to you, there are in Jhansi no supporters, no accomplices of the Meerut and Delhi rebels?'

Skene took offence at her insistence, which seemed to cast doubts on his information and his authority. Dryly, he replied, 'Certainly, there are people here who would like to see us driven out and dream of seeing anarchy take over. Your Highness needs only to ask Diwan Naransin. My services have informed me that he is in touch with a number of agitators we have had our eye on.'

From the Rani's dumbfounded silence, he saw that he had scored a point. Recovering from his anger, he bowed before her and left her to her thoughts.

'Diwan, are you part of the conspiracy?'

The Rani had not even given Naransin time to sit down. For a moment, disconcerted, he stiffened; then he smiled, almost amused.

'Yes, Rani. I've joined it in order to look after your interests. If the revolution spreads to Jhansi and triumphs, I will be there to make sure that its architects put you back on the throne.'

'The revolution will not triumph. In a few days, the British will retake Meerut and Delhi and unleash a pitiless repression. It will not be confused sepoys or dispossessed kings, like this Raja of Bithur, who will kick them out of this country.'

'You are forgetting the people. They have already begun to rattle their chains, and soon they will break them. And then they will turn on the kings who failed to understand their wishes and stayed faithful to the British, and sweep them aside...'

Haughtily, the Rani replied, 'My popularity, Diwan, matters less to me than my duty to maintain peace in Jhansi.'

'You were cautious and wise not to join the conspiracy when you were asked to. If the British keep the upper hand, you will be uncompromised in their eyes. And if it becomes necessary, you can sacrifice me to their anger. In the meantime, allow your humble minister to remain in touch with the revolutionaries in order to prepare your future should they win.'

Anxious questions tumbled from the Rani.

'Will there be a rebellion in Jhansi? When? Who will lead it?'

'The less you know about it, the better. For your own protection, I would rather you remained aloof from what is going to happen.'

What Naransin said was reasonable; what he was doing seemed to be in the Rani's best interests. Still, she was angry that he should have allowed her to learn of his involvement through Skene. The Rani hated anything that people did behind her back, even when they did it for her own well-being.

Captain Skene's authorization to the Rani to raise an army drew heated criticism from the British colony. Jhansi was and would remain calm; the docility and fidelity of the garrison's sepoys were not in doubt. Why then would the Rani need an army except to serve a secret ambition to retake her throne from the British by force? By entering into her game, Skene had shown amazing gullibility. Annabelle Phipps was particularly blunt in voicing her opinion. She was Britannia herself, draped in the Union Jack, shaking with indignation before Roger.

'That native woman! We give her a generous pension, we allow her to keep her palaces, her servants, her honours, and now she turns against us, betrays us! We should shake her up immediately, if only as a precautionary measure. When I think of all the cajolery she's lavished on us all these years! When I think of how she made those eyes at Skene—who, besides, fell for it... But I've never been taken in by her hypocrisy. I never trusted her. And you all fell in love with that unspeakable woman, that enemy of our country, that harlot—because you ought to know, Roger, that before you, there were others, many others, Englishmen, Indians...'

Roger understood that Annabelle was waving the flag of patriotism only in order to vent her jealousy. He interrupted the flow of insults.

'Enough, Annabelle—you're talking nonsense. Besides, anger makes you look ugly.'

Mrs Phipps dissolved in loud sobs.

Thereupon, Roger was summoned by Captain Skene to his office at the fort.

'I know, my dear Giffard, that you're often at the palace and at the pavilion on Lake Lakshmi. I want you to keep your eyes and ears open and report to me on the Rani's activities.'

Roger protested that he would never spy on the Rani. If the Company was no longer satisfied with his service, he was prepared to tender his resignation.

'Listen to me, Giffard. I don't think the Rani is making any plans against us. On the other hand, we are living in uncertain times. We have to be particularly vigilant and we have to keep every possibility in mind. After all, it would hardly be surprising that a ruler we deposed should think of making use of the circumstances to recover her throne...

Who mentioned spying? Just continue to see the Rani as you have in the past, and if you notice anything suspicious, simply let me know.'

Roger was less than enthusiastic about the idea, but he had to pretend to accept. Wasn't it the only way he could continue to see Lakshmi often without appearing to betray his countrymen?

Instead of gliding into the tunnel, the boat docked at a small pier below the pavilion. Roger jumped out and hurriedly climbed the granite steps. As soon as he had arrived at the vast lawns surrounding the pavilion, he recoiled.

The area was swarming with men, sinister as hangmen. Their clothes were dirty, motley and they were literally weighed down with weapons: daggers, knives, sabres, rifles, powder horns, bandoliers. Their faces were enough to give one the shivers—thin, dark, with aggressive moustaches, bristling beards, and eyes fierce as wolves peering out from under turbans jammed low on their foreheads. When Roger appeared, several of them reached for their daggers. All stared at him with suspicion and hostility. Had the pavilion been attacked by these brigands? Were they holding the Rani prisoner? Roger was slightly reassured when he saw a small group of these new soldiers of the Rani playing with Damodar. The child was shaking with laughter, and the warriors were treating him with surprising consideration and tenderness.

Roger found the Rani in her sitting room.

'Have you seen my dacoits?' she asked. Roger had heard of those inhabitants of the jungle, the elusive bandits, the scourge of India who sometimes controlled entire regions and eagerly hunted all policemen, Indian or British.

'They're good people,' the Rani said. And she explained to Roger that these outlaws, the survivors of a troubled period of Indian history, had a long and old tradition.

They lived hidden in the jungle, from which they burst forth to ransack farms of big landowners or caravans of merchants. Robbing the rich to give to the poor, they had as allies the peasants they protected. Whenever they overstepped their bounds, the Rajas would send an army to teach them a lesson. The dacoits would disappear for a time, and then resume their activities more quietly. In spite of everything, they remained devoted and respectful to the rulers, whose call they always answered. Bold and elusive, faithful to their word and their honour, the dacoits were the heroes of a thousand popular legends.

'I could never find soldiers more seasoned or obedient,' the Rani insisted.

'And how did you manage to find them?'

'All I had to do was send a message to Sanghar Singh, the most famous dacoit chieftain in the region, a talukdar who, one day, insulted an Englishman and then thought it wise to take to the jungle. But don't be afraid, he and his troops would never attack the British...unless I ordered them to,' she added, smiling slyly.

Activity, even of a modest kind, made the Rani happy. Having an army gave her the fleeting illusion that she was a ruler again. She was surprised by Roger's dark mood.

Roger still believed in the possibility of a mutiny at Jhansi, but he was convinced that the British would put it down with extreme brutality, a policy decision he already disapproved of. Why then did the Rani need an army? To maintain order, as she claimed? To Roger, these dacoits seemed more likely to create disorder.

To cheer him up the Rani took his hand between hers, an unheard of gesture on her part, which was not an invitation but an expression of love. Roger's hand remained inert and cold between Lakshmi's small palms. With a sigh, he said, 'Could it be that, one day, we'll find each other in opposite camps as enemies?'

Her answer rang out as sharply as a cry of victory, 'Never! Our love is too strong.'

'But still, it isn't stronger than all that keeps us apart and prevents it from fulfilling itself.'

Suddenly, Lakshmi allowed Roger's sadness to affect her.

'You're unhappy and so am I. It's neither your fault nor mine. It's just the circumstances. Be patient still, and let time do its work.'

She held out a kind of rosary of delicately-carved wooden beads.

'You call this a rosary, we call it a mala. Each bead has written on it the name of our warrior-god Rama, and we repeat his name as we tell each bead. My mother gave it to me when I was born and it hasn't left me since.'

Roger slipped the rosary around his neck and said, 'From now on, it will never leave me.'

A few days later, the army assembled by the dacoit Sanghar Singh settled in the palace courtyards and in abandoned outbuildings. It numbered three or four hundred men issued with rumpled and incomplete uniforms from the old army of the Raja. Some wore the regulation tunic over dhotis. Others had brought their old hunting blunderbusses of local manufacture instead of muskets. Many had kept their own rather gamey turbans instead of wearing the sumptuous red-and-gold ones of the Raja's army. And almost all claimed to have been unable to find boots in order to remain blissfully barefoot.

Although suspicious of dacoits, the inhabitants of Jhansi made them feel welcome. The presence of this force seemed a guarantee against any possible unrest. They also saw in it a resurrection of the Rani's power, a symbol of Jhansi's independence; she derived from the dacoits prestige and popularity.

During the burning hours of the afternoon siesta, bamboo screens on the windows bathed Lakshmi's room in golden darkness. Her body dripping in sweat, she spent long hours lazing on the red-and-gold bed which was far too big for the narrow room. In her torpor, she heard the faraway shouts of children playing in the lake, and closer, the voices of guards under a shade tree, and horses, plagued by flies, pawing the ground with their hooves.

It was there that Roger came to see her in the evening. He sat down beside her, his back resting on the silk pillows, and for Lakshmi, these peaceful hours seemed the prolongation of her dreams. They sipped their sherbets, their light conversation interrupted by long silences. What united them, they had no need to speak of; what kept them apart, they did not want to mention. She did not tell him that she feared for him. They watched as the rays of the setting sun flooded the walls, as the shadows slipped from the corners, slid under the furniture, climbed to the ceiling, almost enveloping them. Sometimes their hands would touch, their legs brush lightly; Roger's arm slid around Lakshmi's waist, Lakshmi's arm draped itself over his shoulder. The desire that lived within them made no other demand. They had probably never been closer, never happier. Sometimes Roger wished this happiness would never end; sometimes he wished the storm would burst right then, hoping that in the calm that would inevitably follow, he would at last be united with Lakshmi.

On 4 June, the Rani received unsettling news. The British had still not reacted to the taking of Delhi by the rebels, and now Lucknow, the former capital of the state of Oudh and one of India's largest and busiest cities, was coming to a boil. There had been persistent rumours that a mutiny was to break out at nine o'clock on the evening of 30 May. The Chief Commissioner, Sir Henry Lawrence, had ordered all Europeans in Lucknow to move into the Residence, which he had had fortified and stocked to withstand a siege.

30 May went by without incident. That evening Sir Henry, somewhat reassured, had a quiet dinner with his aides. Over dessert he turned to his principal informant and said, 'Your friends aren't punctual.'

At that very moment, the guests heard the sound of musket-fire. It was nine o'clock and the sepoys had begun their mutiny.

There was also tension at Cawnpore, a city close to Lucknow and almost as important. Even Gwalior was in ferment. Diwan Dinkar no longer dared set foot in the native troops' cantonment for fear of what they might do to him because of his unconditional support of the British. As a precautionary measure, British women and children living in the city had been transported to the fort in the Maharaja's palace, under the protection of his personal troops.

And even in Jhansi the night before, two barracks had mysteriously burned down in the military cantonment.

The Rani summoned Captain Skene to the palace, cancelling all appointments, and asked him what measures he planned to use to forestall any further incidents that were stirring up the people.

'None, Madam. The fires in which Your Highness sees arson are attributable, without any possible doubt, to accidents.'

'So you see no possibility of a mutiny in Jhansi?'

'I must admit there is a feeling of unrest among Jhansi's wealthier class. But I am absolutely certain that all this will quieten down as soon as news of British successes reaches Jhansi. Your Highness can be quite sure that we are all safe here...for the moment,' he added, in a voice so low the Rani did not hear it.

'As for those successes—how do the British intend to achieve them?' she asked.

'A British army is being readied to march on Delhi. As for the trouble spots, Lucknow and Cawnpore, every precaution has been taken. My friend Wheeler, the commanding officer at Cawnpore, writes that he has asked the Raja of Bithur, Nana Sahib, to come live there in order to protect our compatriots in case of need. I'm happy to say, Madam, that your friend Nana Sahib came to Cawnpore immediately with troops and several guns, and he has been entrusted with guarding the city's treasury.'

The Rani was speechless. Nana Sahib, the leader of the rebellion, summoned by the British to protect them! Had their blindness not been so tragic, it would have been laughable. The Rani knew, then and there, that they were running headlong towards disaster. She rose to her feet and said, 'Go, Captain, there is nothing left for you but to fulfill your destiny and do your duty as I know you will. May God keep you—your God, our gods and all gods. There will never be enough of them to watch over you. Farewell, Captain.'

Puzzled by the Rani's solemnity, Captain Skene left without answering. The Rani then sent a messenger to fetch Roger immediately, even though she knew he was busy at his office. He arrived, rather surprised and perhaps somewhat annoyed by the Rani's inconvenient summons.

'Listen to me, Roger. You are in danger here. You must ask for leave and go to Bombay. It is securely held by your army. There shouldn't be any trouble there. I hope it's not already too late. But you really must go before tonight. '

Roger did not know quite what to make of the Rani's advice but the anxiety he sensed in her shook his confidence.

'I can't leave Jhansi, Lakshmi. I don't want to leave you. And there are my countrymen. No matter what I think of them, I'd feel I was deserting them.'

'Then come live at the pavilion on the lake and avoid going into town for a while. In my house, at least, you'll be safe.'

'If you were to extend that invitation to all my countrymen, I'd be able to accept it.'

The Rani shrugged impatiently. She knew the absurdity of her offer and how impossible it was for Roger to accept. She let him leave after they had decided to see each other again several hours later.

But that evening Roger did not come. For once, his superior Captain Gordon had given him work that could not wait. Roger sent a message to the Rani to tell her about it and to say he would come the next evening.

PART II

A QUEEN

1

The following afternoon Roger finished his lunch at the Phipps's bungalow around three o'clock. The meal had seemed longer than usual. Annoyed that he had been unable to see the Rani last night, he still had an hour or two to kill before leaving to join her at the pavilion. Coffee was served and Doctor Phipps immersed himself in his newspaper. Annabelle gazed absent-mindedly at the bamboo screen covering the window.

Suddenly, gunshots were heard in the distance, coming from the direction of the military cantonment. Roger and the Phippses put their cups down and remained silent, frozen in surprise. They heard someone running in the street and a voice, probably that of an Indian servant, shout: 'The dacoits! The dacoits are attacking the cantonment!'

'The dacoits? Impossible!' Doctor Phipps grumbled. 'They were pushed back from the towns years ago. They wouldn't dare attack us.'

'Could those dacoits be the ones the Rani hired for her army?' Roger wondered. 'Would she really have turned them loose against the British?' He stifled the thought, angry that it should even occur to him. To his surprise, Annabelle remained calm.

'Savages!' she said simply. 'One day, an example will have to be made. Skene is much too lenient with them.'

Roger abruptly pushed his chair back. 'I'm going to see what's happening.' Doctor Phipps also got up.

'Go ahead, Giffard, and let us know. Those dacoits aren't going to keep me from my nap.'

Roger put on his top and stepped outside, which seemed like a furnace due to the blistering heat. He saddled his horse and set off at a trot towards the cantonment.

Unable to sleep, the Rani tossed and turned on her bed in the pavilion on the lake. She sat up with a start, astonished, as her father Moropant burst into the room, unannounced.

'The sepoys have rebelled in the cantonment. They're hunting down the British!' he cried.

Lakshmi's heart stopped. A name rose to her lips but remained unspoken—Roger. Rushing out to the skiff that had brought her father, Lakshmi climbed in and hurried the old oarsman, whose slowness made her tremble with impatience. Her horses were on the other bank, near her husband's mausoleum. Jumping onto the saddle, she galloped off towards town.

Kiraun was trying to sleep on the pallet in her hovel, seeking respite from the intolerable heat, when the first shots made her jump up and run outside. They had come from the Star Fort at the rear of the cantonment, behind the soldiers' barracks. It was a square, squat building used as an arsenal and treasury, and it owed its name to the star-shaped earthworks that protected it.

Running along the cantonment's outer embankment, Kiraun stopped opposite the Star Fort, which was under attack from a group of sepoys. Kiraun recognized their leader, Sergeant Gurlash Singh, the man whose letter from a rebel she had read a few months earlier, and who had since become one of her most frequent customers. She saw him as a hero leading the attack, and she began to applaud from the height of her observation post. But the rebels lacked spirit. They did not aim their muskets; some were even shooting up into the air. The artillerymen guarding the Star Fort quickly opened the gates and welcomed them inside.

The rebels had been in possession of the arsenal for only a few moments when Kiraun saw soldiers of the Fourteenth Cavalry, to which the rebels belonged, ride up between the barracks. They advanced in impeccable order, led by the garrison's eight British officers. On an order from Captain Dunlop, they halted a few hundred yards from the fort. Dunlop rode to the front of the ranks, followed only by Lieutenant Taylor. In a few short sentences he tried to convince the insurgents inside the fort to surrender. In reply, he came under rifle fire. The rebels either aimed too high, or else they had deliberately spared him, for at that range, Captain Dunlop was an easy target. He and Taylor returned to their lines and were replaced by Captain Skene, who had just arrived from the town, winded from his gallop. Skene also tried to negotiate, making appeals to the rebels' common sense, promising to examine their demands and not punish them harshly. He too was shot at—inaccurately. He returned to his troops and gave the order to attack the fort. For a moment the soldiers hesitated. They had just seen a piece of light artillery, which the rebels had taken from the arsenal, appear on the earthworks.

Kiraun trembled with excitement. She did not like the British. Her rare British customers always shocked her by their crudeness, and she had decided, once and for all, to forget that Roger was their compatriot. Besides, she had never seen a spectacle as fascinating. The soldiers of the Fourteenth Cavalry had begun to ride in perfect formation towards the arsenal.

One shot, a single shot, rang out. The riders stopped. Captain Dunlop shouted the order to advance. No one moved. Stiff in their saddles, they seemed to be waiting. None of them looked at the officers. From her observation post, Kiraun was jumping for joy. The climax was coming. It was with deep disappointment, then, that she saw Captain Dunlop gesture out of weariness, or perhaps of resignation, and order his men to make an about-face, an order they carried out flawlessly.

Roger had not been able to get further than the officers' mess, just inside the gates of the cantonment. The native guards had been issued instructions to admit no civilians. He had to watch the roll-call from the verandah of the mess. There were thirty-five men missing, thirty-five cavalrymen, the ones who had seized the Star Fort, thirty-five insurgents out of eight hundred and eighty-one native soldiers.

When the roll-call was finished, Captain Skene stepped into the middle of the square formed by his men and spoke a few words. He excoriated the rebels, promised they would soon be made to toe the line, exhorted his audience not to imitate them, and made them swear to remain faithful to the British flag. As one man, the soldiers shouted—'We promise.'

Captain Dunlop then ordered them to return to their barracks; they did so in calm and orderly fashion. The British officers repaired to the mess, rushed to the bar and ordered stiff whiskies. They had not experienced a single moment of fear; rather, they seemed puzzled and angry. Still, they avoided commenting on the seizure of the arsenal, and instead congratulated themselves on how smoothly the inspection had gone and on the loyalty of their soldiers.

When he came home, Roger told the Phippses what had happened. It was about six o'clock in the evening and he yearned to join the Rani. Was she waiting for him at the pavilion, or had she come to town? Was it decent for him to abandon his colleagues at that moment?

He was still hesitating when an officer appeared at the door, bringing orders from Captain Skene. All British families were to move into the Jhansi fort at once. This precautionary measure caused great agitation in the bungalows.

Annabelle Phipps railed against Captain Skene's weakness. 'What he should do is fire guns, not show our fear by taking refuge in the fort.'

She tormented her servants more than ever, making them pack a thousand useless objects, including evening gowns, as though she expected balls to be held at the fort.

Doctor Phipps gathered up his files and books, which he thought indispensable, even for a short absence from his home. Roger quickly packed a few clothes and his sketchbooks. In the street between the bungalows, a line of palanquins, large-wheeled oxcarts, were waiting to transport the British families and their baggage. An escort of native cavalrymen, the same ones who had refused earlier to attack the arsenal, surrounded them. Leaving the civil station, the procession crossed a large empty stretch of land called the Jokhan Bagh, and avoiding the city, reached the fort by climbing a ramp that ended outside the walls of Jhansi.

The fort had ample room to accommodate the civil station's sixty men, women and children, who settled quietly into the apartments they were assigned, some in the former palace of the Rajas of Jhansi, others in barracks built along the ramparts.

No accessory, no ritual would be lacking for the refugees' meals. Their cooks had brought from the abandoned civil station all the victuals and implements necessary to their art. Their servants had carried over the many articles indispensable to British comfort. Following protocol and custom in the British community, the officers' wives, civilian families and the children with their ayahas all took their meals in different rooms.

The officers dined separately in what had been the throne room of the palace. As a bachelor, Roger was invited to join them.

The prevailing opinion among the men was that their superiors had panicked. The sepoy escort, led by their junior officers, had now returned to the cantonment and retired to their barracks. The cantonment and the town were quiet.

The rebels still held the Star Fort, but they were not giving any signs of life. They would be dislodged the following morning with ease because Captain Skene had made his plans. He had sent for reinforcements from the nearby stations of Datya, Orchha and even Gwalior. These were expected to arrive tomorrow afternoon. In twenty-four hours order would be completely restored.

This opinion was reinforced at the end of dinner, when Sanghar Singh, the former dacoit who had become the leader of the Rani's army, entered the room with several aides. He had brought two hundred men to ensure the safety of the British.

Captain Skene was triumphant.

'I had sent a message to the Rani asking for some of her troops. She lost no time in complying. I knew I could count on her. She's our ally and a considerable asset because she's still popular and influential among her former subjects.'

Sanghar Singh walked to Roger's seat and handed him a note. Roger blushed as he took it, and waited for the others' attention to be diverted from him before reading it.

The Rani had written in English, sprinkled with a number of spelling errors—'Come join me at the palace. An escort of my soldiers will accompany you.'

The officers rose from the table and took their leave of Captain Skene. They planned to return to the cantonment for a night they hoped would be peaceful.

Roger took advantage of the noise to whisper to Sanghar Singh that he would go to the palace tomorrow, as soon as everything had returned to order.

Later, long after curfew had sounded, he strolled along the ramparts. At distant intervals he would pass one of the Rani's soldiers on guard-duty. The stars shone with that intensity peculiar to warm nights. Below, the military cantonment was shrouded in darkness and silence. Nothing stirred in the town spread at the foot of the ramparts. Only the barking of a dog broke the silence.

Roger could make out the dark mass of the Rani's palace within the tangled network of the town's terraces. He saw the campfires of Sanghar Singh's soldiers burning in the courtyards.

He could not see the lighted windows of the private apartments of the former Raja of Jhansi where Lakshmi was keeping watch in the library.

No sooner had the Rani arrived at the palace, in the mid-afternoon, than her informants contradicted the alarming news relayed by her father. In the cantonment there had been only a limited incident, and the vast majority of the sepoys had remained steadfast.

Despite her distaste for collaboration and the pleas of Diwan Naransin she had gone to the help of the British, as Captain Skene had demanded. Refusing to do so would have constituted an act of rebellion. Despite her wishes, she had been unable to shelter the only Englishman she wanted to protect, the man she loved. Roger had not accepted her invitation as she had hoped, and it was him she was thinking of as she wondered what tomorrow would bring.

No one slept late at the fort on the morning of 6 June. There was reassuring news for the British refugees when they awakened. Captain Dunlop had sent a message from the military cantonment. The night had been perfectly quiet. At six o'clock in the morning, there had been the usual inspection of the troops, which had gone off without a hitch. As they had done the day before, the sepoys had responded to his brief speech by professing their loyalty; they had even shown, in no uncertain terms, their disapproval of their rebel comrades.

The rebels were still masters of the Star Fort. Dashing the hopes of their officers, they had not stolen away in the night. Captain Dunlop meant to seek out Skene at the first opportunity to discuss various means of subduing them. From the ramparts the refugees were able to observe that calm prevailed also in the town, whose familiar sounds wafted up to the fort. Captain Gordon decided to go to his office as usual. Roger offered to go with him.

After walking into town, they went first to Gordon's house, where they were served their morning tea, and then to their offices in a building behind the Rani's palace. No unusual excitement could be detected in the crowded streets; the inhabitants of Jhansi were going about their usual business. At most, Roger, while walking, might have felt he was being stared at, but the stares were more curious than hostile. The two men found their native employees waiting for them at the office, and spent their morning bent over their files. The only difference this day was that petitioners who usually filled their waiting room were absent.

Several times Roger had the urge to leave the office and step over to the nearby palace to call on the Rani, but he did not. Such a visit would have seemed improper to his superior. He would wait until afternoon to see Lakshmi again.

The two men returned to the fort for lunch. The only discordant note came from the tax-collector, Robert Andrews. He had gone to the town prison to collect munitions kept there and had got a very cold reception. The darogha, a man named Bakshish Ali, had treated him with barely disguised hostility, and claimed to have lost the key to the munitions store. Andrews had not challenged the obvious lie; he had negotiated with infinite patience, and in the end, the darogha had allowed him to take only a very small part of the munitions.

The incident did not cause much anxiety among the refugees; they were expecting the arrival of the reinforcements Captain Skene had requested from the neighbouring states at any moment.

It was the hour of siesta, but in her hovel Kiraun was not asleep. Her peasant's instinct told her that something was about to happen.

Shortly after two o'clock, confused noises drew her outside. Two to three hundred of Jhansi's inhabitants, most of them men, were heading for the entrance to the cantonment. Were their intentions hostile, or did they simply want to find out what was going on at the Star Fort?

Among them Kiraun recognized several evil-looking faces. They were petty thieves, fast-talkers who frequented the taverns, always on the lookout for some shady opportunity, especially if it involved the possibility for loot. They belonged to that slum population that hides from daylight in normal times and suddenly appears at the slightest sign of trouble, like rats climbing out of sewers.

Kiraun was surprised to notice among them the head-jailer of Jhansi's prison, Bakshish Ali. The crowd walked unhurriedly to the entrance of the cantonment and passed casually through its portal. The native sentries did nothing to stop them.

Kiraun joined the group as it walked around the officers' mess, followed the long alley between the sepoys' barracks, and reached the area in front of the Star Fort. A good number of sepoys were already there, standing at ease, listening to Sergeant Gurlash Singh, Kiraun's customer. 'Listen! Listen to what our brothers in Delhi have written!'

He was brandishing a piece of paper from which he began to read:

'We have conquered the capital of the Empire and restored the Emperor of India to his throne. The entire Bengal Army has risen up against her British masters. She has run the British out of Calcutta, Lucknow and Cawnpore. Why haven't you done the same, our brothers of Jhansi? If you don't expel the British now, you will lose your castes or your faith."

The orator stopped. Then Bakshish Ali, a Muslim, shouted, 'Pray, my brothers!' And all the Muslims in the crowd began to pray. Standing, their hands open in a gesture of adoration and offering, they intoned the first verses of the Koran.

At that moment, the cantonment's eight British officers rode up on horseback. The crowd of spectators broke ranks to let them through. When the officers reached the last sepoy ranks, Captain Dunlop ordered them to return immediately to their barracks.

The sepoys, without undue haste, turned, raised their rifles and fired on their British officers. Kiraun saw Captain Dunlop, his face covered in blood, emit a drawn-out sigh and slide slowly from his saddle to the ground. He was dead. Another officer seemed to twitch under the impact of the bullets and then fell back, his arms in the air. Lieutenant Taylor, wounded only in the shoulder, managed to push his horse to a gallop and escape. Kiraun watched him clatter off, a large dark stain spreading on the back of his red tunic. The crowd approached the bodies of the seven British officers curiously and surrounded them in silence.

Roger, who had lain down on a camp-bed without undressing, was roused from his daydreaming by shouts and calls for help. Leaning out the window, he saw Lieutenant Taylor being carried in, gravely wounded. His red tunic was a deep maroon; blood dripped onto the pink granite flagstones.

Running from his room, Roger found the refugees surrounding Captains Skene and Gordon on the ground floor. Lieutenant Taylor had managed to make his way to the fort, where he described what had happened.

Skene summed up the situation in a few words. He had received no answer to his request for help from the neighbouring states, and the reinforcements he expected had not come. Since the sepoys had passed over to the rebellion, it would be necessary to defend the fort. The heavy, steel-riveted wooden gates were shut, and male civilians were posted on the ramparts with the Rani's soldiers. Roger was assigned a place in the first enclosure, above the large portal that faced south. From there he could see part of the town as well as the Jokhan Bagh, the vast empty area that stretched all the way to the town walls.

Natural barriers of large rocks hid the cantonment from his sight, but he could hear noise coming from that direction, a sort of rumble interspersed with shouts.

Soon, he saw plumes of black smoke rising on his right from behind the trees that hid the civilian compound; the rebels were burning the British bungalows. For the first time, Roger was afraid. The great revolt, which had been hinted at many times, was now reality. It had broken out right here in Jhansi. The massacre of the officers who had so often been his dinner companions, the sight of Lieutenant Taylor in his bloodied uniform brought home to him the fact that all Englishmen, including himself, ran the risk of meeting the same fate.

And yet, he could not quite believe that the Indians he knew, gentle and warm, could transform themselves into murderers. And he trusted the Rani; she had authority and she detested violence. She had promised to protect him and she would find the means to do so.

The sounds of a violent argument wrenched him from his thoughts. Women and children were emerging from the portal of the second enclosure surrounded by the Rani's soldiers. In the middle of the group, Doctor Phipps was dragging his wife along by force.

'Help me convince Annabelle,' he said to Roger. 'The Rani has offered to take our women and children into her palace for their safety. Skene accepted immediately, of course, but Annabelle doesn't want to hear any of it.'

His wife was screaming hysterically.

'She'll betray us! It's a trap! I want to stay here.'

The doctor tried without success to calm her, to convince her to leave. When Roger stepped up to her she shouted, 'Your whore's going to have us all massacred...'

Then Roger did something he would never have expected himself capable of. Calmly, he slapped Annabelle Phipps in the face. She quieted down immediately, stared at him with a look of utmost venom and said, 'You'll regret what you've done. Your Rani won't get away with it, either.' And head held high, she resumed her position in the group of women and children who, escorted by the Rani's soldiers, set off towards the palace.

Returning to his post, Roger soon caught sight, between the rocky heights, of a shouting, gesticulating mob that had gathered on the road leading to the cantonment. They were the rebel sepoys, surrounded by onlookers who had now begun to cheer them. They passed quite close to the fort. Roger could see them waving from their bayonets the bloodstained British uniforms of the officers they had massacred. They were shouting, 'Deen ki jai!—Victory to religion!' as they made their way to the town.

When they drew near the town walls, the Orchha gate opened mysteriously before them. They streamed in and disappeared from Roger's sight. For a long time he continued to hear their cries of 'Deen ki jai! Deen ki jai!'

He would not have been able to make out, in the tumultuous crowd, the dainty little silhouette of Kiraun. She had never left the rebels; she had followed them all the way to the deserted civil station. She had watched them run through the deserted alleys, rushing in and out of bungalows and setting them afire, shouting encouragement to one another. There had been little looting; the impulse to destroy had been much stronger. They had cheered as they watched the bungalows blaze up, the flames rising very high, the walls crumbling and collapsing to the ground.

Then, Bakshish Ali had given an order and the rebels had set off towards the town, followed by their sympathizers. There, they had made straight for the jail, freed prisoners, bandits, thieves and murderers, who joined them enthusiastically. The procession, growing larger by the minute, then headed for the administrative buildings, the physical manifestations of the British occupation—the post office, the police station, the tax building, the deputy superintendent's offices—and merrily set fire to them all. The merchants who had not shut their shops stood at their doorsteps, laughing and clapping their hands. The people of Jhansi would not have rebelled against the British on their own; but since the sepoys had undertaken the task, they exulted in being rid of the occupiers. In the streets it was holiday time.

Torches in hand, wholly absorbed in their work of destruction, the rebels ran shouting past the Rani's palace. Kiraun, tired of running behind them, stopped. She sat down on the ground against a wall, and stared at the closed gates of the palace.

2

The uneventful night and morning had done nothing to dissipate the Rani's anxiety. Her powerlessness to do anything had been a constant torment. She had been forced to wait and to be idle, two conditions she abhorred.

No sooner had the women and children of the British families arrived at the palace than the Rani had the gates shut. She posted her soldiers at the latticed windows on the first floor and on the terraces. She personally supervised the installation of the refugees, assigning them rooms in the deserted wings of the second court, where her private gardens lay. She had bedding, food and drink brought in. Her domestic animals took this intrusion into their territory very badly, fleeing into the trees and onto the terraces.

As she walked past the Rani, Annabelle Phipps stopped, stared her down, and spat on the ground before her feet. Lakshmi was too preoccupied to allow her rage to get the upper hand. She simply shrugged. The resignation, anxiety and fear of the refugees increased her feeling of helplessness. Shortly after, she heard the shouts of the rebels as they entered the town, the cheering of the crowd, the roar of the fires. She saw, above the walls of her palace, plumes of black smoke stretching into the sky.

Anarchy was spreading to the town, but she wanted to believe that her palace would remain the sanctuary it had always been. Then, the terrible noise abated. The rebels had marched to the west of the town, heading for the fort.

Roger had not left his post above the fort's main portal. He strained his ears, but from where he stood, he could hear only a confused hubbub coming from the town.

Once or twice, a brief crescendo in the shouting made him shudder. Suddenly, shots rang out way off to his left. Someone ran by behind him and shouted, 'We're under attack! Regroup!'

Regroup. It was easier said than done. Roger followed a few of the Rani's soldiers as they ran precipitately down the stairs flanking the rampart. Heading towards the sound of gunfire, he crossed the courtyard, climbed another stairway, and emerged into the swarm of defenders on the ramparts of the first enclosure. He elbowed his way to a battlement, leaned over, and looked out.

The rebels were attacking the fort. They were scrambling up the slope, shouting and firing towards the ramparts. Roger judged them to be at least a thousand strong. In fact, they were no more than a few hundred. Behind them came part of Jhansi's population, yelling encouragement from a cautious distance. Roger raised his rifle, aimed carefully at one of the assailants, and pulled the trigger. The rebel fell backwards, struck dead.

A volley of bullets answered Roger's shot, flying by just inches from his head. He ducked immediately, then straightened up, shot rapidly at random into the crowd of rebels, and again took refuge. He thought of his friend Roderick, the soldier, and wondered how he could possibly enjoy battle. The smoke from their guns was interfering more and more with visibility, which suited Roger who preferred not having to see the attackers.

The noise of the firing and the smell of gunpowder began to intoxicate him, and little by little his fear subsided. The attack lasted half-an-hour; then, surprised by the defenders' stubborn resistance, the rebels fell back and disappeared into the town. Behind them they left several dozen of their dead and wounded companions, dark stains on the ochre earth. Roger pulled his silver watch from his pocket. It was five-thirty in the afternoon.

The day was beginning to wane in the audience chamber, where the Rani sat with her advisers. A soldier whom she had sent to the fort had just returned with a hastily-written note from Captain Gordon.

> *Your Highness, it seems certain that tomorrow the worst will happen to us. We suggest that you take charge of your kingdom and govern it, along with adjoining territories, until British authority is re-established. We shall be eternally grateful if you will also protect our lives.*

She could hear the shouts of the crowd and the howling of bands of rebels running by from the street. The racket did nothing for the equanimity of her advisers, who were breathing with difficulty because smoke thick with ashes was gradually seeping into the room.

Naransin begged her to take power, but to side with the revolutionaries instead of helping the British.

Kashmiri Mull pleaded with her not to abandon the British, and warned of the consequences that would befall both Jhansi and herself if she did.

'What British?' Naransin protested. 'There are no British in Jhansi and soon there won't be any left in all India.'

Her father Moropant wanted her to take power without siding with the revolutionaries.

The Rani raised her hand to quiet them and spoke bitterly, 'The British give me the house to maintain just as it's burning down. They give me power because they can no longer exercise it. How can I assume power with what's going on outside?'

She had no time to hear her advisers' answers. Three men burst into the room, followed by the Rani's servants who, having failed to stop them, had stuck to their heels. One look at the intruders was enough to tell the Rani whom she was dealing with. Ferocious-looking men with sabres in their hands, covered with dust, one of them still showing streaks of blood on his filthy clothes, they were the three leaders of the rebellion. The Rani recognized their chief from the secret meeting of the conspirators, Rissaldar Kale Khan, who had vanished then and now had reappeared with perfect timing. She did not know Bakshish Ali and did not recognize Kiraun's customer, Gurlash Singh.

Kale Khan said, 'Order your soldiers to keep the British from leaving the fort and give us your cannons.'

The last order astonished the Rani.

'But...what cannons?' she asked. 'I don't have any.'

'Don't try to trick us. You've hidden some cannons and we need them.'

Only then did the Rani remember that when Jhansi was annexed, she had, on a whim, buried an enormous old bronze cannon in one of the palace yards; the fort's mascot nicknamed Kadak Bijli. Collecting herself, she answered Kale Khan curtly, 'I'll do what I think best, and neither you nor your accomplices will impose your will on me.'

More threatening than ever, Kale Khan took a step towards the Rani, his hand on his sabre.

'We know that you're helping the British, the enemies of our religion and our freedom. If you persist, we will burn down your palace and slaughter you along with all the British wives and children you're sheltering.'

The Rani stood firm. She stared the three rebel leaders straight in the eye and calmly told them to get out.

Surprisingly enough, they obeyed. During the brief exchange, the Rani's councillors had remained petrified. The Rani fumed against the bandits, those thugs who had dared violate the home of a queen and presumed to give her orders.

'The rebels' threats don't impress me. If anything, they make me lean towards helping the British.'

She was answered by a concert of protests.

'Your soldiers would rather side with the rebels.'

'Helping India's enemies would be an infamous act.'

'Have you forgotten how the British have humiliated you?' asked Mandar, who had been drawn into the room by the noise made by the rebel leaders.

Moropant spoke gently to his daughter, 'Lakshmi, your people are with the patriots.'

The Rani shrugged. 'I'll make my decision alone,' she said, dismissing everyone.

The emotion dominating her at that moment was bitterness. She felt resentment towards the British. It was they who had sown discord among her people by annexing the kingdom. It was they who, through their blindness, had allowed the rebellion to ripen and burst. It was they who stood between Roger and her. And now, it was they who were presenting her with a cruel dilemma by demanding that she intervene. Impulsively, she grabbed her writing-case, scribbled a few lines to Captain Gordon, and placed her seal on the paper.

At the fort the British dined with the usual ceremony, even though protocol had been disrupted. The women had gone to the shelter of the Rani's palace, and the officers had been massacred. There were about twenty-five men sitting in one room, being served dinner by perfectly-dressed servants. That afternoon's attack had been repulsed, but what about tomorrow?

There was no longer any hope of receiving help from the neighbouring states of Datya, Gwalior or Orchha. Captain Skene had been clear on that score. On the other hand, there were the Rani's soldiers. The British could even count on further aid from her, if necessary. The rebels lacked plans, organization and artillery. They could be defeated easily.

The optimistic banter at the dinner-table masked, in fact, their profound anxiety.

Halfway through the meal, one of the Rani's chamberlains, who had easily slipped through the rebel lines, entered with a letter from his queen for Captain Gordon. Gordon read it aloud, translating from Marathi to English.

When in peacetime I asked for my kingdom, you refused. Now that you can no longer keep it, you give it back to me. You did not deem it necessary to consult me when, in council in Calcutta, you settled the fate of Jhansi. The best thing you can do now is take care of your own fate. The rebel troops will burn down my palace and slaughter me and everyone in it if I offer you protection. It would be best if you tried to save your own lives.

With the note was a verbal message which the chamberlain now relayed to Captain Skene. His ruler, the Rani had only one piece of advice for the British—let them disguise themselves in native clothes, steal out of the fort during the night, and take refuge in the neighbouring city of Orchha, which was still calm. Her guides were ready to lead them there. In the meantime, she promised to keep their women and children in her palace and protect them, no matter what happened.

The Rani's advice was judicious. Yet the British came up with every reason for ignoring it. They feared the shame of fleeing before the rebels, of having to blacken their faces, of pulling on rags that natives wear.

These men were used to comfort, and even those who were trained to fight were reluctant to embark on an uncomfortable adventure. Routine, fatigue and the heat held them back.

Roger was on tenterhooks during the discussion, because the Rani herself was not spared. Without going as far as to accuse her of betrayal, some did not hesitate to claim she was playing a double game. Thus, he welcomed gratefully the diversion offered by one of the Rani's soldiers who came up to Roger and asked him to follow him. Although surprised, he did not hesitate and discreetly slipped out of the room.

They left the palace, walked down the slope, and crossed the second enclosure. The soldier pointed towards the small temple of Ganesha, a small, rough structure standing out against the rock.

As he stepped in, Roger saw two women apparently in prayer. He recognized Mandar first. It was only when she turned around that he saw Lakshmi. Her presence here was so unthinkable that the possibility had not occurred to him. By the weak flicker of the lamp burning before the elephant-god, he saw that she was trembling with emotion, staring at him, unable to speak.

Trying to reassure her, he asked by what miracle had she managed to enter the fort. In a barely audible voice she answered that for centuries there had been an underground passage linking the town palace to the fort. She regained a semblance of composure to tell him how, weak with terror, she had followed Mandar through the dark tunnel, accompanied by swarms of bats. Suddenly, her voice became firm, 'I've come to fetch you. Come back with me.'

'I can't Lakshmi. I have to stay.'

She lost her patience.

'It's useless for you to stay here. There is nothing you can do for your compatriots.'

'I know, Lakshmi.'

'You're not responsible for their errors. Why should you pay for them?'

'Would you respect me, would you love me if I abandoned them to go with you?'

'Then force them to take my advice. Tell them to escape.'

'They won't do it.'

'But I cannot help them.'

'I didn't ask you to help them.'

The Rani stamped her foot, indignant. Then, in tears, she threw herself into Roger's arms. Gently, he stroked her hair.

'Whatever may happen, Lakshmi, nothing can destroy our love.'

'Come, Rani,' said Mandar tenderly. 'We can't stay here any longer. It's time to go.'

Lakshmi gained control of herself enough to say to Roger, 'I'll come back tomorrow.'

His eyes followed her as she left the temple and disappeared in the darkness.

Roger's guard duty lasted from two to four in the morning. Walking up and down the rampart, stopping sometimes to lean on the parapet, he thought of Lakshmi. Would he see her tomorrow, would he ever see her again? The worst was now possible. And yet he did not want to give up hope, for hope was named Lakshmi. She would assume power, she would bring the rebels to heel, she would free him and all the British in Jhansi.

At that moment the Rani, in torture, was pacing the floor of her room. The British were pressuring her, the rebels were threatening her, her people had gone mad, and Roger was in mortal danger. What was she to do? What could she do? From time to time, she heard coming from the street, now close, now faraway, shouts and sounds of celebration—the rebels too were wide awake.

At nine o'clock in the morning, tired from his watch, Roger was still in bed. In a half-sleeping state he heard the voices of women. Then he realized he was not dreaming. He rushed outside to hear the news; Captain Skene had called the women and children back from their refuge in the Rani's palace. He had pulled them from a shelter Roger considered impregnable to expose them to the dangers of an attack. Skene no longer trusted the Rani, Roger gathered, and he was horrified.

Annabelle Phipps was delighted. She described her impressions to the men surrounding the small group. The Rani had treated her and the other women with a contempt that spoke volumes about her intentions. The Rani had received the leaders of the rebellion. With her own eyes Annabelle Phipps had seen them on their way to the throne room. The Rani had made herself an accomplice to the rebels, and Annabelle had no doubt of the fate she and her companions would have met had they remained at the palace.

In order not to listen to Annabelle's nonsense Roger questioned Mrs Taylor, a drab, self-effacing woman with large sad eyes. Skene's order to return had reached them at dawn. They had been escorted back to the fort by the Rani's soldiers. Avoiding the main streets of Jhansi, they had been fortunate enough to meet no rebels; they must have been sleeping off the debauchery of the night before, for they had looted the Englishmen's wine-cellars and got prodigiously drunk. The population seemed calm. And yet, Mrs Taylor noticed a certain excitement in the air. The passage of the British wives and children had caused no incident, but she had sensed in the inhabitants of Jhansi a definite, though unaggressive, hostility. One of her children had suddenly begun to cry, and an Indian had slipped to her side and whispered, 'Don't be afraid, we hold no grudges against women and children.'

'And now, Mr Giffard,' asked Mrs Taylor, 'what is to become of us?'

Roger lacked the presence of mind to make up a reassuring lie. He too wondered what would happen.

When Roger returned to his post on the rampart, he saw servants of the Rani, clearly recognizable by their livery, making their way up to the fort by a roundabout path. On the orders of their mistress they were bringing provisions for the besieged. Captain Gordon refused to admit them into the fort. Ropes were thrown down and the food hauled up in baskets.

On the way back, despite their precautions, the Rani's servants bumped into a rebel patrol. They were stopped, questioned, insulted for having brought provisions to the British, threatened with death, and somewhat roughed up. They extricated themselves by explaining that they had acted only on express orders from their queen.

The rebels then returned to the Rani's palace—but this time, in numbers. Led by their chiefs, a hundred of them surrounded the buildings and parlayed with the Rani's men guarding the walls and terraces. The rebels assured them that, far from having evil intentions towards the Rani, they had come to defend her from the British.

The soldiers, only too happy to believe them, opened the gates allowing the rebels to invade the courtyards, the outbuildings, the ground floor and even the throne room. But they did not dare enter the Rani's private apartments, where she had taken refuge behind locked doors. She had also had Damodar brought there and forbade him to leave. Restless from confinement and the agitation he sensed in the air, the child had become unruly, running around, throwing tantrums and adding to the tension.

With heavy irony, the rebel leader Kale Khan reassured Moropant; he had no intentions of harming the Rani if she stopped helping the British. Sniggering, he added that they had been extremely foolish to have their women and children brought back to the fort, since neither he nor his companions would have violated the hospitality offered them by the Rani. These declarations, passed on to her by Moropant, increased the Rani's rage against Captain Skene's stupidity.

Moropant also brought her news that made her tremble—aided by information from her servants, the rebels had unearthed the fort's mascot-cannon and thrown in prison Sanghar Singh, the dacoit leader of the Rani's army, whom they considered more loyal to her than to their ideals.

The insurgents occupied the streets and the houses surrounding the hill atop which stood the fort; they held the city walls and gates, and constantly patrolled behind the fort to make sure the British could not flee, but they were still not numerous enough to lay siege to the fort itself.

Kiraun had been wandering among them since dawn. All of a sudden, walking by not far from her, an Indian drew her attention. In spite of his dark skin, in spite of his clothes, everything in his posture and his walk branded him a foreigner, an Englishman. Kiraun recognized him under the disguise as an occasional customer of hers, young Andrews, who was training for the Bar and worked with Roger under the orders of Captain Gordon. He hurried past her, and Kiraun was surprised that no one else identified him as a feringhi.

The rebels patrolling the streets were far too busy stealing and destroying to take notice of passers-by. The bungalows of Captain Skene and Captain Gordon, the only Englishmen to live inside the town, had been reduced to ashes. The rebels had also begun to ransack the houses of Bengalis, turncoats who, at the time of the annexation of Jhansi, had come from Bengal with the British in order to serve as their intermediaries, and who were particularly hated by the local population.

They also attacked the houses of a few banias. Guided by townspeople, they chose those who had grown rich on the backs of local landowners by buying up the lands the British had forced them to sell. From the selective destruction of British property, the crowd was slipping towards simple, indiscriminate looting.

The young Englishman had reached the square in front of the Rani's palace when a cry made him turn around involuntarily. An Indian was running towards him, shouting, 'That's Andrews! I know him! He is my enemy!'

The crowd closed in around the young Englishman. Kiraun saw sabres rise in the air. She heard a loud scream. Andrews had been slaughtered in front of the gates of the Rani's palace. Kiraun understood that a messenger sent from the besieged fort to the Rani had just been intercepted. Listening to the rebels' conversation, she learned that three other Englishmen, Michael Scott and the Purcell brothers, sent out in disguise by Captain Skene, had also been recognized and put to death.

She made her way to the fort and walked along its walls until she found a lightly-guarded gate.

Hailing the soldiers of the Rani posted on the ramparts, she enticed them with all the resources of her art and the freshness of her youth. The soldiers made sure there were no officers about, then slipped down, and let her in. They were about to take advantage of this unexpected bounty when she literally slipped through their fingers and bounded away, followed by their shouts of rage. Instinct led her straight to the post guarded by Roger, who scarcely had the time to be surprised at her appearance.

In a flood of words she told him what she had seen and heard. It was more her obvious distress than her almost incomprehensible pidgin explanations that made him understand that something serious had happened. Without hesitation he led her to Captain Skene to repeat her story. Skene was crushed. He had sent those four men to ask the Rani for safe-conduct passes out of Jhansi for himself and his besieged companions. They had been his last hope. He looked at Kiraun thoughtfully, and abruptly asked whether she would accept to carry a message to the Rani.

Kiraun wavered—helping the British! Then she looked at Roger. He simply smiled, and Kiraun accepted.

Leaving the fort, slipping through the rebel lines, making her way through the growing chaos in town was no difficulty for her. She found the gates of the Rani's palace wide open. Its courtyards, its stairways, its rooms were overrun with dusty, dirty, armed rebels openly fraternizing with the Rani's soldiers. The curious and the sympathizers wandered in and out, not just to see the rebels but also to stroll around the palace they had never entered before,

Kiraun made her way easily through the disorderly throng. She met no obstacle until she reached the doors of the Rani's apartments. There she had to knock repeatedly, argue and plead. The door opened, but the servants, staring with disgust at the young prostitute, still refused to take her to the Rani. Kiraun was forced to shout and stamp her feet before they led her into the Rani's library.

When the Rani saw her come in, she smiled for the first time since the day before. Kiraun's youth, her expression of anxiety and determination, touched her. Kiraun delivered her message. The Rani told her briefly how to answer Captain Skene, and then added, 'Make sure they know what's going on in town and in my own palace. Tell them you found me a prisoner in my apartments. Go, Kiraun.'

Kiraun's return to the fort was as easy as leaving it.

Roger had been watching for her from the ramparts. He had the main gate opened for her and led her to Captain Skene.

'The Rani will do her best to help you, even though she'll be running a terrible risk if she does it openly.'

At that moment Captain Gordon came to warn Skene that the rebels had completed their encirclement of the fort and were preparing to attack. In the confusion that followed, Kiraun grabbed Roger by the sleeve and whispered into his ear that, once again, the Rani begged him to come take refuge in her palace before it was too late. Kiraun herself would bring him there. Roger shook his head and ordered her to leave the fort before the attack began. Kiraun refused to move.

The rebels opened fire around two in the afternoon. The main attack took place at the fort's eastern walls. Roger was posted on the west, looking out over open country from atop the steepest side of the hill. Only a few small bands of rebels had ventured there, clinging to the rocks and shooting haphazardly.

With the handful of soldiers allotted to him, Roger repulsed them easily. Several times he tried to send Kiraun away, but she refused to leave his side. No one could take her Englishman from her now, not even the Rani. She sat next to him humming, indifferent to the danger. Sometimes she would stand up suddenly and peer over the parapet, following the rebels' intermittent attacks with interest.

From the other end of the fort Roger could hear the noise of musket-fire, which continued uninterrupted until nightfall. Then he went to join Captain Skene, who was holding council. There were only twenty Englishmen left around him. The attack had been repulsed, but at what cost!

The rebels had brought within sight of the fort an enormous cannon. Why had they not used it? No one knew. No doubt they would put it to work tomorrow. Where had they found it? At the Rani's palace? Had she given it to them? Had she joined the rebels? Many thought so. For the first time Roger dropped all reserve and defended her vehemently. Skene and Gordon backed him; they refused to doubt the Rani's loyalty.

'And yet her army is abandoning us,' Doctor Phipps pointed out.

During the attack, the soldiers sent by the Rani to defend the fort had obeyed orders, but they had fought without vigour and even with some reserve. They had carefully refrained from shooting at those of their companions who had gone over to the rebellion and constantly exhorted them to change sides, trying to shame them for serving the enemies of freedom and religion. Whether or not it was the Rani's fault, her soldiers were no longer to be counted on.

'I've decided to dismiss them,' Skene announced.

The soldiers left immediately, without arguing and in good order. Now the fort had for its defence only a handful of Englishmen and their Indian servants, altogether about a hundred men. They were completely surrounded by the insurgents—the sepoys from the garrison, soldiers of the Rani's army and fanatic inhabitants of Jhansi—a total of more than two thousand men.

Night had fallen. At his own request Roger had been transferred to the most dangerous guard station, the one closest to the rebels, below the small temple of Ganesh in the first enclosure. From there he could keep an eye on the hole, hidden by a rock, through which the Rani had slipped into the underground passage leading to the palace the night before. He waited for her, but she did not come.

He grew impatient, then waves of unhappiness began to surge inside him, bringing with them absurd doubts. He was too exhausted to imagine simply that since the palace was occupied and she was locked inside her apartments, it would be impossible for her to use the underground passage without being intercepted by the rebels.

For the first time he considered the possibility that he might die. The massacres of the British at Meerut and Delhi left him with little hope. And yet he rebelled at the prospect. It seemed impossible that he should die. He was neither a soldier nor a hero. He had harmed no one, he knew the Indians liked him, he loved life and he wanted to see Lakshmi again.

At that moment she lay stretched out on her bed, her eyes gazing at the red and gold cloth of the canopy. Kiraun had vanished, Roger was in the British camp; she had to admit, at last, that she was powerless to save him, and she feared the worst for him and for the other Englishmen. Incapable of sleep, her mind restless, she let her thoughts wander in vague daydreams.

Kiraun had still not left Roger's side. She sat close to him, silent in the shadows, trying to make herself invisible.

The young man could not stand another minute on his feet, straining his eyes and ears into the night. He sat down against the parapet next to Kiraun, to take a few moments' rest. The heat, which darkness seemed to enhance, forced his eyes shut, and he fell into a deep sleep.

Kiraun clumsily stroked his cheek, kissed his forehead, and lifted the rifle from his hands. She took his post, holding the heavy weapon with pride.

Everything was still.

3

It was nine o'clock in the morning of 8 June 1857, and the men and women under siege inside the Jhansi fort were on a state of high alert. For the past hour they had been awaiting an attack which, it seemed, would never come.

Kiraun had gone off to sleep not far from Roger's post, on the rampart of the fort that projected closest to the town, only a few dozen yards away. The anxious waiting in the growing heat of the morning had stripped Roger's nerves bare. He wished for only one thing—that the rebels would attack soon and get it over with.

Suddenly, in a chorus of shouts, the insurgents spilled from the alleys of Jhansi and began to climb the hill, shooting at the ramparts. The defenders fired back, beginning a sustained exchange. A group of attackers dragged the enormous mascot-cannon into position with difficulty and pointed it at the spot where Roger stood. He saw the sepoys lighting the fuse. Doubling over instinctively, he had time to tell himself the end had come before a tremendous explosion shook the air. Under the impact, the entire rampart shook. Roger leaned out over the battlement. The cannon-ball had merely chipped the stone wall. He and the other defenders of the fort felt an immense sense of relief. The rebels' artillery could not dislodge them. The old fort built by the Rajas of Jhansi would hold.

Musket-fire intensified on both sides, and the battle grew furious. Despite wave upon wave of attack, the rebels were making no progress. The besieged were hanging on, and Roger began to feel a glimmer of hope.

The battle had been raging for several hours when suddenly, behind him, he heard unexpected musket fire. A group of rebels had invaded the area between the first and second enclosures and were shooting at the defenders from the rear. Caught between two fires, the British experienced a moment of panic. Roger heard a shout: 'Retreat to the third enclosure!'

He ran as fast as he could along the rampart while bullets whistled around him. It was a miracle that none hit him. Propelled only by his instinct for survival, he climbed up and down the narrow stairways carved in the ramparts, crossed the second enclosure, and reached the safety of the third without knowing quite how he had done it.

The rebels had already occupied the areas between the first and the second enclosure. Not far from Roger, Captain Gordon was reassuring his compatriots.

'Don't panic, the fort hasn't been taken. One of our servants betrayed us. He opened a side door allowing the rebels to slip in behind us. But they can't get their cannon in here, and we have the advantage of elevation.'

The forward posts occupied by the rebels were indeed well below the third enclosure, and it was almost impossible for them to fire on the British without coming out into the open.

Roger saw Captain Gordon lean over the parapet to observe the rebel positions. After a few moments, alarmed by Gordon's immobility, a man standing next to him touched his shoulder. Captain Gordon slid slowly to the side and slumped to the ground. He was dead. A bullet had struck him smack in the forehead.

Roger was overcome by discouragement, a feeling that spread to his companions. Gordon had been the soul of the resistance—firm, unshakeable, inspiring in everyone else the hope he seemed to have. His death dealt a terrible blow to morale in the fort. As though they had somehow become aware of the defenders' irresolution, the rebels chose that moment for an unexpected initiative.

They stopped firing all at once; then, an unarmed group emerged from its rocky shelter, surrounding a man who was carrying a white flag. Roger recognized him as Saleh Muhammad, one of Jhansi's Indian doctors. Walking towards the third enclosure, Saleh Muhammad called up to Captain Skene. The patriots, he said, had chosen him to offer the British the promise that their lives would be spared if they surrendered.

Skene answered that he would not lay down his weapons until he had the rebels' word that he and his companions would be allowed to leave Jhansi freely. Saleh Muhammad withdrew, apparently to confer with the rebel leaders. He returned a quarter of an hour later to announce that the patriots swore on what they held most sacred that the British would be allowed to leave unmolested.

For several hours the Rani had been listening to the sounds of the battle. She refused to leave her apartments so as not to come across the rebels. Her attendants came and went, keeping her informed of every development. She could hear the dull roar of the guns mixed with the shouts of an overexcited population and the noisy crackling of fires set off by the insurgents. Confinement, nervousness and anxiety had brought her to the edge of madness. She paced up and down, wringing her hands and pulling at her hair as if to soothe the migraine that oppressed her.

When the shooting stopped, her anxiety knew no limits. Had the fort been taken? Why weren't the British firing? A messenger, gasping for breath, informed her of the rebels' offer. To the Rani it meant that the rebels were not completely sure of victory, and she became somewhat calmer. A few minutes later she learned that the British, accepting the insurgents' promise that they would be allowed to leave Jhansi, had agreed to surrender. Hope awakened in the Rani, and with it initiative. She had her father send servants to the fort to help the refugees and accompany them to the borders of Jhansi's territory. She thought that their presence would dissuade the rebels from mistreating the British.

The surrender of the fort was delayed while the British women packed up. The men waited by the portal of the third enclosure. No sound came from beyond the ramparts. Roger noticed Kiraun among the Indian servants. He had not had time to worry about her since the moment when he had found himself trapped between two fires in the first enclosure. Walking up to her, he said, 'Go find the Rani. Tell her...no, don't tell her anything. She knows how I feel.'

When, at last, the women and children were ready, the heavy portals of the third enclosure swung open. The British stepped back; the esplanade before them was a solid mass of human beings. Hearing of the surrender, rebels had rushed up from everywhere, marching silently. They remained immobile, not speaking, still too astonished to react to the incredible sight of the defeated Englishmen.

Captain Skene began to walk forward, followed by his compatriots. The human wall in front of them did not budge. Then, sepoys emerged from the ranks, walked up to the men in the British group and tied their hands behind their backs, calmly; obviously under orders. The Englishmen, surprised, did not resist. They understood now that the rebels would never allow them to leave Jhansi. Captain Skene protested the breach of promise. The rebels seemed not to hear him. Vainly, he searched the crowd for the face of the Indian doctor who had led the negotiations.

The sepoys tried to separate the men from the women, but the women resisted, clinging to their husbands. The sepoys gave up, and the procession of prisoners moved off. Surrounded by sepoys who were still wearing their British uniforms, they passed through the fort's main portal and headed for the old military cantonment.

Kiraun ran down the slope toward the palace to report what she had just seen to the Rani. Slipping between groups of rebels, she recognized her old customer, Gurlash Singh, in animated conversation with the leaders of the insurgents, Rissaldar Kale Khan and the darogha Bakshish Ali.

Her curiosity was too strong; nonchalantly, she edged closer and listened.

They were too busy to pay any attention to her. A message sent by the rebels in Delhi had just brought bad news; a British army coming from the west was marching on Jhansi to put down the rebellion.

Wherever they had regained the upper hand, the British had exacted a terrible vengeance on the rebels and the people who had supported them. At Benares and Allahabad, they had indulged in terrible slaughter, cold-bloodedly, indiscriminately massacring men, women, old people, even children. In Benares alone, the repression had taken six thousand lives, payment for the few dozen Englishmen who had been murdered at the start of the rebellion.

The columns of the British army that were marching on Delhi to free the capital had left behind them a wake of ruin and death. Entire villages had been annihilated. After hasty trials that defied any notion of justice, the British executed any Indian they considered suspect; and, to British eyes, all Indians had come to be suspect. The victims were either hanged or, in the old Moghul fashion, tied across the mouth of a loaded cannon which, when fired, blew them to a thousand pieces, spattering the onlookers with blood and bits of flesh. Most of the condemned, before their execution, were insulted and tortured under the impassive eyes of British officers.

To keep control of the state of Punjab in western India, the British had resorted to terror. Successive waves of preventive repression had resulted in between forty and fifty thousand deaths; sepoys thought to be disloyal, deserters and villagers accused of sheltering them were hanged and shot, not by the dozen but by hundreds. Entire regiments had been completely exterminated.

Rissaldar Kale Khan and his companions grew more and more excited as they exchanged the tragic news and swore to avenge their brethren. And yet, beneath their fury, there was fear. What would happen to them if the British army marching on Jhansi retook the town?

Kale Khan leaned over and whispered a few words to Bakshish Ali which Kiraun was unable to hear. She saw Bakshish Ali round up a few dozen rebels and leave hurriedly. She followed him on the run.

The procession of prisoners had reached the Jokhan Bagh, the gardens which, despite their name, were merely a vast deserted area of rocky uneven ground stretching between the fort and the British cantonment.

Roger, hands tied behind his back, kept his head down and his eyes fixed on the path, not so much from fear of falling as from shame at the possibility of tripping in front of the rebels.

Since leaving the fort they had been accompanied by a crowd more merry than malevolent that grew by the minute.

Roger noted a number of evil-looking faces. Yet he did not feel threatened. He was surprised by the resignation of his companions when the Indians had gone back on their word and taken them prisoner. And now not one of them complained. The men were impassive and dignified. The women walked briskly in spite of the packages they carried. None of the children cried.

The heat was terrible, but the captives seemed not to notice the sweat that streamed down their faces and soaked their clothes. Roger walked next to Annabelle Phipps. Had it not been for her haughty bearing and her clothes, she could have passed for an Indian, with her dark complexion and straight black hair falling down her back.

She pointed out the Rani's servants, who were following the prisoners. 'Look at them, Roger. She sent them to witness our humiliation. I'm surprised she didn't come herself. She must feel triumphant just now.'

'So you'll be jealous of her until the very end,' Roger answered, raising his head to look at her.

At that moment an arm emerged from the crowd, extended itself between two of the sepoy guards, and grabbed Annabelle. Roger had just time to recognize Annabelle's maid, the servant she had most mistreated. The few people who saw it happen were too stunned to react. Annabelle and her maid had already vanished, swallowed up in the crowd.

Turning his head to search for the two women, Roger saw a group of rebels led by Bakshish Ali moving towards them. He even made out Kiraun's small silhouette behind them.

Bakshish Ali bellowed an order; the procession halted. Another order and the sepoys separated the prisoners into three columns: one of men, one of women, and a third of children.

Roger was wondering what this meant when he heard Captain Skene say to Bakshish Ali, 'You've tied my wrists too tight. Loosen them.'

'What does it matter now?' Bakshish Ali answered, and he plunged his sabre into Skene's stomach.

Skene sank slowly to his knees and then collapsed. He found the strength to whisper, 'Kill me, my country has many more men like me.'

Bakshish Ali stabbed Skene several more times. Skene stopped moving. Roger stared, paralyzed, until something hit him in the back. He did not feel the blade of the sabre run through his body. Blood filled his mouth and he toppled over, face to the ground, his eyes wide open.

Then the slaughter began. Driven wild by the sight of blood, the sepoys and the men in the crowd turned into savages, drunk with killing.

Drawing their weapons, they fell upon the prisoners with shouts of 'Maro! Maro!—Kill! Kill!'

Shoved forward by the crowd, Kiraun did not miss a single detail. She saw Mrs McEgan throw herself in front of her husband to protect him; she saw her dragged back brutally and killed while her husband was hacked to pieces on the spot. She saw Doctor Phipps grab his assassin's blade and try to push it away, cutting his fingers before falling, his chest pierced. She saw Mrs Taylor fall to her knees, begging for mercy before a sepoy, who then cut her throat. She heard little Carshore beg in Hindi for his life, 'Spare me! You've already killed my mother and father.' She heard him scream as a sabre-thrust slashed his forehead. She wanted to escape the terrible scene, but the crowd of spectators would not let her through. She tried to cover her ears against the snarls, the screams and moans. Nauseated by the smell of blood, she felt like vomiting.

It took the rebels a quarter of an hour to finish off the sixty men, women and children, a quarter of an hour of horror and madness.

Only when the last Englishman had stopped groaning did the murderers stop. They stood exhausted among their victims, their faces blank, their weapons and clothing dripping with blood. Kiraun stepped over the corpses, pushing some aside with her foot. She found Roger's body and turned it over. His face had not been touched. His eyes were open, and a trace of a smile remained on his lips. A rip in his bloody shirt exposed a rosary of sandalwood, the one the Rani had given him. Gently, Kiraun took it off his neck and, impelled by an instinctive, powerful force, she picked her way through the human wall surrounding her. She walked away as fast as she could. She had only one thought in her mind—to find the Rani.

It was a little past six in the evening when Moropant entered his daughter's apartments. He found her in the little room near the entrance which she used as an oratory. She was kneeling, sitting back on her heels in front of the statue of her patron saint, the goddess Lakshmi. She did not even turn her head when she heard him come in. After a moment's hesitation, he leaned over her and said, 'They have slaughtered them all.'

The Rani did not react. For a moment Moropant had a feeling that she already knew, perhaps instinctively, everything that had occurred. Then he thought that she had not heard.

'They were *all* killed,' he said. 'None of them survived. Not one.'

The Rani remained immobile as a statue. At that moment Mandar came in with Kiraun. This time, the young prostitute had had no trouble gaining access to the Rani. She came up, knelt beside her, took the Rani's hand, opened it, and placed Roger's rosary in her palm.

'I took it off his body,' she said. 'He was wearing it when he was killed.'

The Rani turned to her abruptly. Eyes staring, her expression was like a madwoman's. Her mouth opened, but no sound emerged. Terrified, Kiraun shrank back. Then Lakshmi regained her regal pose.

Kiraun needed to speak, to tell everything she had seen. She spared Moropant and Mandar no detail, keeping the story of Roger's death for last.

'Once Sahib Roger fell, they continued to stab him. They put their swords through him twenty, thirty times.'

Kiraun fell silent. Then the three of them heard a sound that made them start; the Rani had let Roger's rosary slip from her hands. For a time they anxiously watched this woman, crushed by grief; then furtively, they left the room, leaving her alone.

Taking advantage of the adults' inattention, Damodar had slipped out of his mother's apartments. He ran through the ceremonial rooms, shouting, 'The feringhis have all been killed and I'm king!' The rebels gathered around him, cheered and laughed at his shouts.

Outside, in town, joy reigned. The inhabitants had learned of the massacre of the prisoners and for them, it meant only one, marvellous thing—they were rid of the occupiers. They were going to regain their prosperity and the happy rule of their queen. They embraced in the streets and gathered around posters the rebels had put up at street corners.

'The people belong to God, the land belongs to the Emperor of India, and both religions rule.'

The crowd had invaded the streets around the Rani's palace and were clamouring for her. Later, Mandar returned to the Rani's room and found her in exactly the same position. From outside they could hear the shouts: 'Long live Lakshmi, long live the Rani of Jhansi!'

Without turning her head, the Rani said suddenly: 'Bring me my opium pills.'

Mandar, dumbfounded, hesitated. The Rani's voice rang again, imperiously, 'I know you didn't throw them away. I know you hid them somewhere. Bring them to me immediately.'

Mandar obeyed. When she brought the box, the Rani's hands were shaking so much she could hardly take it.

The next morning the enthusiasm of Jhansi's people began to wane. They had got rid of the British, but now they had the rebels on their hands, and all night there had been violence in the town. Drunk with wine looted from the cellars of the British, the insurgents had run through the streets, shouting, molesting the inhabitants, wrecking everything in their path. They were turning, indiscriminately, on the rich and on anyone else to whom they took a dislike. They invaded people's residences, stole everything they could get their hands on, beat up the owners, and set the places on fire. In short, they were behaving like conquerors, and the inhabitants of Jhansi were not the sort of people to tolerate such behaviour for very long.

They prayed openly that order replace anarchy, that the Rani's authority be re-established, that the rebels leave. Strangely enough, this was a desire the rebels shared. Their leaders understood that there was nothing more to be derived from Jhansi and that their popularity was rapidly decreasing. But they had no money for the journey onward.

At the palace, no one had slept; nor had anyone dared enter the Rani's apartment. Her attendants waited in her antechamber, ready to run in at any summons, but no sound came from the closed door of her oratory. Late in the morning, the situation became so uncertain and so tense that Mandar took it upon herself to go in, followed by Moropant.

They found the Rani in the position they had left her the night before, sitting on her heels before the statue of the goddess Lakshmi. Had she taken any rest? Had she really remained there, immobile, for more than twelve hours? They were never to know. After some hesitation, Moropant broke the silence.

'Listen to me, Lakshmi. Anarchy rules the town. There is no more authority. The rebels make the law. You must assume power. There's no one but you who can do it.'

The Rani neither moved nor answered. Mandar, spurred by the urgency of the situation, exploded.

'How can you let yourself go on like this while your kingdom drifts and your people are in danger!'

Only then did the Rani turn around. Her features were drawn, her eyes set in dark heavy circles, her face a wax mask. They saw that she had been crying. At last, she permitted herself to speak, 'So my people have at last returned to reason.' Her voice was so clear, so firm, that Moropant and Mandar were struck dumb. Then Mandar pressed her advantage.

'Your people are in danger. You must do something.'

Moropant feverishly added, 'The rebels are waiting for you. They're demanding to see you; they want to leave Jhansi.'

There were about a hundred sepoys marching up and down in the throne room, talking in loud, impatient, angry tones.

'Is she never going to come, this Rani? Must we bring her here by force?'

The Rani came in, alone. She was still wearing the soft shirt and trousers, rumpled and drooping, that she had worn the night before. Her face showed clearly her sleepless night, the tension, the ordeal. Her expression was tight, impenetrable. She took her seat on the gaddi and calmly stared at the terrifying-looking men. Their leader, Kale Khan, stepped forward.

'We have freed your kingdom of the accursed foreigners who occupied it. We want to join our brothers in Delhi and fight with them, but we have nothing. Give us some silver, Rani. We deserve it. We...'

The Rani interrupted him with a wave of her hand. 'You are perjurers, thieves and assassins.' She said this in a soft voice, her eyes lowered, as though she were delivering a compliment. The astonished rebels stiffened, falling silent.

'Had you fought the British bravely and openly, I would have been the first to congratulate and reward you. But you stabbed them in the back. You betrayed your word, you assassinated innocent women and children, and now you think only of looting and robbing your brethren. Threaten me all you want, kill me even, you won't get anything from me.'

The Rani then stood up and slowly walked out of the throne room.

The rebels who had remained stiff and silent while she spoke, seemed to recover their wits. They grumbled, became annoyed, then angry. In a corner of the room, indifferent to the tumult, their leaders conferred, receiving messages and sending others out.

The Rani set off in search of Damodar, whom she had once again forbidden to leave her apartments. He was not to speak to the rebels, she explained to him; they didn't love Jhansi, they didn't love his mother and they didn't love him. Then she told him, as gently as she could, that his friend Roger had died. The child's enormous eyes stared at her, filled first with disbelief, and then with tears that silently brimmed over. When he was rejoicing earlier at the death of the feringhis, he hadn't realized that Roger might be among them. Roger was his friend and could not be included among the foreigners that everyone around him despised.

'Even though Roger wasn't a Hindu like us,' he asked, 'do you think he could be reincarnated?' The Rani answered that the gods could do anything.

'In that case,' Damodar concluded, 'in a future life, he will be a powerful Raja.'

In the throne room the rebels' uncertainty and agitation had lasted for two hours when a messenger brought a note to Kale Khan.

'Now we've got her,' he muttered. Then he silenced his troops.

'Brothers, we will not submit to a woman who has made herself the accomplice of the accursed British. We will force her to give us what is ours by right.'

The rebels followed him out of the throne room, crossed the ceremonial chambers, broke down the carved doors of the Rani's private apartments, which until then they had respected. Her courtiers were knocked over and stepped on, her servant-women violently shoved out of the way. They found the Rani in her library. She had changed into a white sari, and as her only jewellery, she had hung around her neck the sandalwood rosary she had given Roger. She was sitting in a corner, reading holy texts to Damodar. She did not even blink when the rebels burst through the door and spilled into the room, furious and menacing. Damodar shuddered, but he did not throw himself into his mother's arms. All he did was move a little closer to her, gently, and she stroked his head.

Kale Khan, towering over her, said, 'Give us some money immediately and we'll leave Jhansi. Otherwise we'll blow up your palace and put Prince Sadasheo on the throne.'

Only then did the Rani raise her eyes from her book. For a few seconds she looked at Damodar. Then she said, 'Before answering, I must consult the goddess Lakshmi.'

Guarded closely by the rebels, she walked to the palace's temple located near the main porchway. She requested that the temple's priests ask the goddess what she must do. They draped a crown of flowers on the idol's head and began to chant the holy texts. Depending on which side of the statue the first flowers fell, they would interpret the goddess's answer.

Minutes passed. The rebels stood motionless, as though fascinated by the glow of the idol's jewels and her silver skin. All awaited the oracle's signal. The Rani was thinking about the rebels' demands; she had only wanted to gain time. The rebels had not frightened her, but Kale Khan's threat to put Sadasheo on the throne seemed serious.

Finally, the goddess made a sign. Not one but two flowers fell, at exactly the same moment, one on each side of the divinity's silver face. The Brahmins were puzzled. They had never seen such a sign before and they had absolutely no idea what to make of it.

Without listening to their pedantic, laborious explanations, the Rani returned to take her seat on the throne, surrounded by the rebels, who seemed both anxious and threatening.

'I have decided to pay you,' she announced.

'We want three hundred thousand rupees,' said Kale Khan immediately.

'Where would I find such a sum? The British seized my fortune and reduced me to misery.'

'Three hundred thousand rupees. Not one less,' Kale Khan repeated.

'Is it worthy of warriors like you to ask so much of a woman alone and in distress?'

Immediately, the Rani sensed that that argument had had some effect and the rebels were softening. Kale Khan tried to change the tide. 'Sadasheo will be more generous than you are, when he's king.'

'Seventy-five thousand rupees,' the Rani hurled back.

Kale Khan burst into laughter.

'You're making fun of us, Rani. Two hundred seventy-five thousand rupees.'

And then began a most shameless bargaining. Where Kale Khan was brutal, the Rani was tough. Finally, they reached the mutually agreeable figure of one hundred thousand rupees. The Rani summoned her chief accountant to bring the balance of her personal exchequer. There were only fifty thousand rupees. Kale Khan grumbled, 'It's not enough.'

The Rani called for her jewel-chest. Opening a drawer, she took out the necklace of pearl twists circled with rubies that she had bought that day long ago from the conspirator-jeweller, and she offered it to Kale Khan.

'Take it. One of your accomplices sold it to me, I shall not need it anymore.'

Before the leader could take it, an arm stretched out from behind him, Bakshish Ali grabbed the jewel. The Rani's eyes flashed. Opening the other drawers of the chest, she began to throw her jewels, one by one, on the carpet before her. Kale Khan, his arms crossed on his chest, remained impassive, but Bakshish Ali, Gurlash Singh and the sepoys in the first row dived to the floor to pick them up. The Rani tossed them necklaces, bracelets, aigrettes, chokers, earrings, the way one tosses pieces of meat to a pack of dogs.

When she had emptied the last drawer, she said, 'That is all I have. Now go.'

Kale Khan suspected the Rani had many more jewel-chests, but he understood also that he had been defeated by this woman, that he had failed to break her. She had turned his men around by gorging them with such riches that he could not expect any more from them. When the rebels retired, some of them wished the Rani a long and happy reign.

When the last rebel had left the room, the Rani turned to Mandar and began to laugh harshly.

'They disgust me, but they're so naive...'

Her advisers and courtiers, who had carefully taken shelter well away from the stormy negotiations, reappeared.

'You will summon immediately,' she ordered, 'the representatives of all castes, all faiths, and all guilds. I want to see them all assembled here before nightfall.'

Then she turned to Moropant, 'My father, there is a sacred task I cannot fulfil myself and which I must ask you to undertake in my place. Take servants and go to the Jokhan Bagh. There you'll find the bodies of the British, where the rebels left them. Have them buried decently in the Christian manner. Pick up all their belongings as well as those they left behind in the fort and bring them to the palace.'

At nightfall the rebels left Jhansi to go fight in Delhi. Their accomplices, led by Bakshish Ali, and some of the Rani's soldiers, followed them.

An hour later Lakshmi convened her improvised parliament. Aristocrats, landowners, bankers, merchants, heads of workers' and artisans' guilds, Hindus and Muslims were all represented, despite the short notice and the disorder reigning in the town. It was the first time that a ruler had addressed herself directly to the representatives of the people to solicit their opinions, and no one wanted to miss this inconceivable innovation.

Perfectly composed, neat and impeccable in her white sari, the Rani, seated on her silver throne, gave a short speech:

'With great difficulty we have managed to save the town from roving bands of sepoys. They are gone from Jhansi for good I hope, but they have left behind them a chaotic situation that we must deal with without delay. We must, at any cost, prevent anarchy from taking over in Jhansi. I have invited you here to give me the benefit of your opinions. Speak frankly.'

A heavy silence followed this exhortation. No one dared speak first. No one was accustomed to speak freely before a ruler. At length, two functionaries, formerly employed by the British, opened the debate. One had been a secretary to Captain Gordon and had known Roger well; the other had been an employee of Captain Skene. They suggested that the Rani write, as soon as possible, to the representative of Britain at

Gwalior to assure him that she was wielding power only in the name of the British.

The head of the carpenters' guild protested. 'British domination of Jhansi is finished. Why ask their representative to put a rope back around our necks?' Murmurs of approbation greeted this sally. The Rani refrained from voicing an opinion.

The head of the oil-sellers' guild spoke up, 'We don't want to be governed by anyone but our Rani.'

The others approved.

'No more foreign domination. We want our own kingdom.'

To everyone's surprise, the bankers and merchants who had most profited by the British occupation shared the popular opinion. One of them went as far as to say, 'This is the day we've been awaiting for so long. It would be suicide to return Jhansi to the British.'

The Rani pointed out that if she accepted the throne offered to her by representatives of the people, she did so only in the name of her son, Damodar, the legitimate Raja.

The people of Jhansi, informed of the historic council, had invaded the small square in front of the palace and the terraces of the neighbouring houses in the nearest streets.

Night had fallen, and the immense crowd, compact in the darkness, stood silent, without moving. The heavy gates of the palace opened at last and Moropant walked out. In a loud voice he declared that the representatives of the people had voted unanimously in favour of the Rani's rule, and that in consequence, the state of Jhansi was once again independent.

He had barely finished when the Rani herself appeared in the porchway. Her small white silhouette was visible from afar, lit by torches around her. She did not speak. She simply greeted the crowd in the Indian manner, joining her hands in an attitude of prayer and bowing her head.

An incredible ovation rose from the shadows.

'Long life to Lakshmi! Victory to Lakshmi! Long live Jhansi!'

All night the town was in delirium. People celebrated their new independence in the brilliantly-lit squares and streets. Every house was the site of an impromptu feast. Temples and churches were jammed with the faithful giving thanks. The orange flag of the Marathas, symbol of liberty, flew from every building. The mascot-gun Kadak Bijli, unearthed by the rebels, was used to crown the celebration; soldiers who had remained faithful to the Rani fired salvos in her honour. When the crowd heard the explosions, their enthusiasm was boundless.

Late that night the Rani assembled in the audience chamber all the aides and advisers she had been able to find and said to them, 'We have neither administration, nor army, nor police, nor treasury, nor communications. It is time to get to work.'

Until dawn, they laboured together to build a state from nothing. The posters the rebels had glued up the day before, she had torn down and replaced by one of her own compositions:

The people belong to God, the land belongs to the Emperor of India, and this kingdom belongs to Rani Lakshmi.

4

By morning the Rani had assembled a subtly-balanced government. Diwan Naransin was returned to the premiership. Old Kashmiri Mull was put in charge of justice. Once again the Rani entrusted the state's finances to her father Moropant. His notorious greed would help perform miracles where they were most needed, the treasury having been emptied by the rebels.

Sanghar Singh, the dacoit who had been the Rani's general, was released from the prison where the rebels had thrown him, and given the task of rebuilding an army with the soldiers who had remained faithful.

Meanwhile, at the Rani's request, volunteers among the inhabitants of Jhansi formed a militia to maintain order and began patrolling the city, day and night. The Rani freed the servants of the British who, after the fort's surrender, had been put in irons by the rebels.

Calm returned to the town, and the state rose from its ashes at the very moment when everywhere else in the region rebellion was in full swing and anarchy spreading. In all the neighbouring towns—Nowgon, Chanderi, Jalaun, Hamirpur and Banda—the British had been expelled and all authority had vanished.

Without consulting anyone, the Rani wrote to the British. Even if the news that an army corps was marching on Jhansi turned out to be false, Lakshmi remained convinced that, sooner or later, the British would try to retake Jhansi and avenge their countrymen through terrible reprisals. It was therefore necessary to explain what had happened. The Rani found it a distasteful task, but now that she had recovered her throne, she had to put political necessity before personal feelings. She dictated to her munshi a letter addressed to Sir Robert Hamilton,

British agent for central India, whom she had met at Gwalior where he lived. Apparently, he was the only British authority remaining in the region.

She did not want to give the impression that she was merely giving excuses. She limited herself to recounting the facts, the sepoys' mutiny, the massacre of the British, her powerlessness to protect them, the threats she had faced from the rebels and the sums she had been forced to pay to make them leave. In order to prevent the anarchy that would spread through a state without a leader, she had been forced to assume power, by doing which she was, besides, only acceding to Captain Gordon's last request. She did not hide the difficulties she was experiencing—Jhansi had been left without funds, without an army and without an administration.

As the Rani placed her seal on the letter, she suddenly felt an immense fatigue. She had been working almost without interruption for thirty-six hours. She retired to her room. Mandar was waiting for her, looking grave, to give her a package. It held Roger's belongings.

The Rani untied the package. She leafed through Roger's sketchbook and found the watercolours of her domestic animals, of her white peacocks, of her owl. She found a portrait of herself that Roger had done, without telling her.

The precious dagger she had once given him had been stolen, but the cloth of his black suit still smelled faintly of him. The emotion strangling Lakshmi became unbearable when she came across a portrait of Roger at fifteen or sixteen, painted by and inscribed to him by his mother.

Unhinged, she burst into sobs. Mandar took her in her arms and stroked her hair. Lakshmi was trembling, half-choking, exhausted by fatigue and grief.

Mandar knew that this was a reaction to the opium Lakshmi had taken the night before. The euphoria and lucidity the drug brought her were invariably followed by depression.

The Rani's attack grew worse. Her entire body was racked with spasms. Mandar panicked. She rushed to fetch the opium box and thrust it before the Rani.

'Never again!' the Rani screamed. 'Do you hear me? Never again!' And she threw the gem-studded pillbox away so hard that it broke a windowpane and fell into the courtyard.

At last the Rani stopped hiccuping and fell silent, white with exhaustion. Her tears continued to flow, abundant, inexhaustible. She muttered incomprehensible words among which Mandar heard only Roger's name. Then, still crying, the Rani began to shout, 'I hate them, I'll always hate them...'

Mandar thought the Rani was speaking of the rebels, of Roger's assassins.

'I hate the British. They're the ones who killed Roger, much more than those brutes, those butchers. If the British hadn't been so ignorant, so blind, so stupid, Roger would still be alive. The British were more the cause of his death than the sepoys. I will hate them until I die.'

From that time on, the Rani was never again to mention Roger's name. Her grief was her's alone.

The court soon returned to the fort, the traditional seat of authority. The living quarters of the palace were located on the upper floors, where they received more light. The first three floors consisted of offices, waiting-rooms and servants' quarters. The ceremonial rooms and the apartments of the Rani and Damodar filled the two top floors, where the view over the ramparts stretched to great distances in all directions.

Lakshmi had found the palace in a distressing state; the rebels, before leaving town, had ransacked this symbol of the British occupation. But in just a few weeks she was able to restore it to its former splendour. First, she discarded the heavy English furniture. She brought out the sumptuous Isfahan and Lahore carpets that the occupiers had kept in storage. On the walls she rehung religious scenes painted on cloth and portraits on glass of Maratha leaders. She kept the large richly-framed mirrors that one of her predecessors had ordered, at great expense, from Europe, the voluminous chandeliers and candelabra of multicoloured Bohemian crystal. It was not only her refined taste which dictated this redecoration but also political considerations. She knew that in India power shows itself also through luxury.

Often she roamed from room to room, wondering which one Roger had used during his stay at the fort. She would stop here and there, silently summoning his spirit. There was never an answer, but Roger's memory floated everywhere in this palace, just as it did in the Rani's heart.

The Rani's days settled into a routine. She rose at five o'clock and took her bath in water scented with the essence of jasmine. Then her servants helped her dress. Invariably, she wore a white sari, her only adornments being a diamond ring on her little finger and, around her neck, the rosary she had once given Roger. Then she went to her private oratory for her puja. After having poured oil and milk on the statue of Lakshmi in order to awaken the goddess, she dressed her, put jewels on her, placed before her offerings chosen by the astrologer according to the position of the sun. In the end she rang the bell marking the fact of the divinity's presence. Before leaving her apartment, she bowed in adoration of the tulsi, which she touched lightly for good luck.

Every morning and afternoon she stepped out onto the gharotra. Far from being a forbidden spot, the fort was a sort of public building now that the sovereign lived there. The populace could enter it freely, and during the Rani's public appearances, they brought petitions that were received by the chamberlains. She always brought Damodar with her, in order that he might learn about the people's needs and the ways of tending to them.

Then she would get down to real work. She went to inspect her army with Sanghar Singh, which was being reassembled. She received her ministers and aides in the audience chamber. It was the hour when she examined fresh news brought from all corners of the empire by couriers and spies.

At Gwalior the large garrison of sepoys had revolted against its British officers, massacring them along with some wives and children, threatening to throw Maharaja Sindhia in prison and blow up his palace if he refused to lead the rebellion.

At Agra, one of the most important British centres in India, the European population had fled the city in panic and taken refuge at the Red Fort, a former residence of the Great Moghuls, now bursting at the seams with six thousand refugees.

South of Jhansi, at Indore, troops of the Maharaja had joined with the sepoys of the garrison to run the British out, smashing one of the most important strongholds of British India.

In the north-east, the cities of Aligarh, Fatehgarh, Shahjahanpur, Bareilly and Moradabad had rid themselves of the British and recognized the authority of the restored Emperor of India, old Bahadur Shah.

At Cawnpore, one of the country's most prosperous commercial centres, Nana Sahib, revealing his true colours, had gathered popular support, and with three thousand natives, he had laid siege to the several hundred Europeans who had retreated into the barracks, submitting them to daily bombardments.

At Lucknow, the former capital of the kingdom of Oudh, both the garrison and the native police had mutinied.

The Rani quivered with joy. She could already imagine the revolution triumphant everywhere and India free of the British, but she was brought back to reality by Sir Robert Hamilton's reply:

> *Until a new superintendent arrives at Jhansi, I beg you to manage the district for the British government, making arrangements such as you know the government will approve. When the new superintendent takes over from you, be assured that he will repay you for all your losses and expenses, and deal liberally with you. We are sending thousands of troops to the areas that have seen unrest and dispositions have been made to restore order to Jhansi in good time. A British army has already retaken the city of Delhi, killing thousands of rebels...*

The Rani had to smile at the magnitude of the lie; but she was also furious. Hamilton had not found a single word to thank her for maintaining order despite the dangers she had faced.

Were the British preparing to bring reinforcements from their homeland to regain control, just as Diwan Dinkar had said they would? It was so difficult to get a clear picture of the situation from Jhansi. In order to find out more, the Rani asked her Prime Minister, Diwan Naransin, to go on a fact-finding mission; not to the British at Bombay or Calcutta—heaven preserve her from sending them an ambassador.

Naransin was to carry his queen's compliments to the Great Moghul in Delhi, to Nana Sahib at Cawnpore, to the other rulers who had gone over to the rebellion. Compliments cost nothing and Naransin could thus evaluate the strength, the capabilities and the future of the revolutionaries.

That meeting in the audience chamber capped the morning. The Rani returned to her apartments, ate a quick meal alone and granted herself an hour's rest. Early in the afternoon, conforming to an old custom of Indian kings, she received gifts her subjects had brought her that morning. They were presented to her on silk-covered silver trays. She kept what she liked and gave the rest to the kotwal, to be distributed among her servants.

At three o'clock she went to the throne room to hold the durbar, seated on the gaddi, often with Damodar at her side, flanked by two immobile pages holding gold maces.

She had changed into a navy-blue shirt, white trousers and turban, and a brocade belt that held the ruby-studded gold scabbard of the sword of the Rajas of Jhansi.

A crowd of almost seven hundred men filled the throne room. Her eye sharp and her memory infallible, the Rani noted who were absent and on the following day, inquired as to their reasons. Facing her were her ministers, arms full of documents, accompanied by the clerks of the durbar who kept minutes of the session. The Rani rapidly examined each matter, made a decision and issued the necessary orders. She concentrated on delivering justice and settled matters of civil or criminal law with remarkable skill. 'She's wise and brave, just and generous,' the people said of her, 'and above all, she is pure in mind and spirit.'

Only at nightfall did Lakshmi retire in order to devote herself entirely to her son.

Before going to bed, she spent an hour or two in the company of Mandar and her other servants. She had installed Kiraun among them, and the promotion of the little prostitute had caused quite a stir at court.

Every Tuesday and Friday the Rani went to perform her devotions at the temple of Lakshmi. As soon as she left her palace the fort's orchestra would strike up; at the other end of town, an orchestra at the temple would take over as the Rani's suite approached. Two hundred soldiers marched with the procession, over which flew orange flags, the symbol of Jhansi's independence.

On these occasions the Rani travelled in a luxurious hand-carried palanquin, followed by her ministers, her courtiers and the heads of the nobility. When she had finished her prayers, she stopped on the threshold of the temple and invariably gazed out over the lake to the pavilion that stood on the other shore. After Roger's death she had had it closed down and had not been there since. It stood in the distance, deserted and melancholy, a stony memory of bygone happiness.

This was the moment awaited by the beggars and the merchants. The Rani liked to walk among them, distributing alms to the former and examining the wares of the latter.

One day an Arab merchant had placed himself in her path in order to show her two horses. She stepped over to take a look, and immediately, a circle formed around her, bystanders mingling with her guards and courtiers.

The merchant knew he was dealing with an expert. The Rani carefully examined the two stallions who were alike as twins, both of them superb, restless, pure-bred animals. Her eyes shone with excitement.

'I'll take them both,' she told the merchant.

'You're making a mistake, Rani. One of them is worth a kingdom and the other isn't worth a handful of sand.'

Astonished, the Rani turned to see who had spoken, a tall young man, gawky but powerfully built. His light skin, his fair hair and blue eyes marked him as a man of the north, probably a member of one of the Pathan tribes, Muslims originally from Afghanistan. The Rani looked at his candid expression and asked, 'And who are you to know more about horses than I?'

'Akbar, at your service, Rani,' he answered, a touch of irony in his voice. 'I've known horses all my life. The one on the right has a weakness in the chest.'

Nettled, the Rani hopped onto that horse and galloped away on the road that led to town. She came back five minutes later, jumped to the ground, and told the merchant, 'This one isn't worth fifty rupees. For the other I'll give you fifteen hundred.'

The horse was bought and named 'Pari'.

Annoyed that the Pathan should have shown himself to be more knowledgeable than she about horses, the Rani looked around for him. He had not moved.

'And now tell me, Akbar, who are you and what are you doing here?' she asked.

'The British took our lands, so I'm travelling; I'm out to see the world...'

'Do you want work?' the Rani asked.

'If the work is interesting and the master good, why not?'

'I'll take you into my cavalry, you'll be in charge of choosing the horses.'

'Rani, I don't want to have anything to do with your officers.'

'You'll answer directly to me. Present yourself at the palace tomorrow.'

The Rani took her seat in the palanquin, and the procession set off.

Traditionalist Hindus frowned on their ruler's decision to take a Muslim into her cavalry, but the majority of the people approved of her tolerance. The Rani herself was certain she had made a good choice. She knew Pathans to be brave, loyal and proud, though extremely touchy and merciless in their vengeance. She liked their lack of servility, their taste for freedom. And perhaps she, too, had been amused by Akbar's impertinence.

When Diwan Naransin returned from his tour early in July, the first thing the Rani asked for was news relating to the massacre of the British at Cawnpore.

Besieged by rebels ten times as numerous as they, bombarded ceaselessly, the British situation had soon grown desperate. Nana Sahib had offered to let them surrender and they had accepted. While the prisoners were being led to the river to be evacuated by barge, the rebels had fired on them at point-blank range. The Rani was appalled that Nana Sahib should have broken his word and have executed men who had surrendered.

Naransin reassured her. He had seen Nana Sahib, his cousin Rao Sahib, and his aide Tatya Tope. All of them deplored the massacre, which had been caused by a terrible accident. Fanatics among the rebel sepoys were responsible, not Nana Sahib's men. Although warned too late, Nana Sahib had still been able to save two or three hundred women and children whom he had locked up in a palace in Cawnpore to protect them from the sepoys' murderous fury. It was still a fact, however, that Cawnpore had been liberated. Tatya Tope, proving himself to be a remarkable general, had run the British out of the whole province and, in particular, out of Bithur. Nana Sahib had returned there and proclaimed himself Peshwa, leader of the Maratha confederation. In the palace that had witnessed the shame and downfall of his father, he had held a solemn durbar during which he re-established the prestigious title which the British had snatched away from him.

Naransin had been present at the historic session which, for all Marathas, marked the resurrection of the former glories of their people.

Nana Sahib hurried to rebuild a court at par with the legendary one of his father's. Despite his triumph, he had not forgotten his old friends and he sent fraternal greetings to the Rani. In order to amuse her Naransin had brought some gossip. At Bithur it was said that Huseinee Hanum still ruled the Peshwa's heart—and, people added, his decisions as well.

Leaving Bithur, Naransin moved on to Lucknow, where the British had just suffered a bloody defeat.

In an attempt to escape the vice that was closing around them, they had counter-attacked, only to be stopped at Chinaat. The ensuing battle had turned against the British, who had been forced to make a hurried retreat towards town. That very evening, the building where the British civilians and military had taken refuge was completely surrounded. The siege had begun.

The man leading the revolutionary army, the man who had defeated the British at Chinaat, was a Muslim holy man, a certain Ahmedullah Shah, known as the Maulvi of Faizabad. The Rani was startled to recognize the name of that powerful fanatic she had once heard preach in Gwalior, whose personal magnetism had made a strong impression on her.

Naransin too had been powerfully impressed by the Maulvi's charisma and his authority over the sepoys, who were quite prepared to lay down their lives for him.

The Maulvi had told Naransin that the besieged building could not hold out for more than a few days. The British there were in deep confusion, especially since the death of the Commissioner, Sir Henry Lawrence, one of the first victims of the siege. The fortifications, hastily raised, were said to be indefensible. What could seventeen hundred Europeans, among them many women and children, do against thousands and thousands of trained, disciplined revolutionaries equipped with powerful artillery that bombarded the besieged day and night?

Apart from that tiny enclave, the immense city of Lucknow belonged once again to the Indians. Then a woman had appeared, Begum Hazrat Mahal, whose story Naransin told the Rani.

Born into a very poor family, she had been trained to become a dancing courtesan, then had slipped into the former king of Oudh's harem as a servant. Very beautiful, she had quickly become one of his concubines, thus taking on the entirely honorary title of Begum. Having given birth to a son, Birgis, she ascended to the enviable rank of Mahal. The ousting of the king of Oudh by the British and his exile to Calcutta had dispersed his court and dashed the hopes of Hazrat Mahal; though not for long, for she was a woman of unquenchable ambition. Deeply involved in the conspiracy against the British, she had taken advantage of the dissolution of their authority to seize the throne and have her son Birgis proclaimed king of Oudh. It did not matter that it was whispered that Birgis was not, in fact, the son of the former ruler, nor that the man Begum Hazrat Mahal had appointed prime minister was rumoured to be her current lover. The kingdom of Oudh had been restored.

The Begum and the Maulvi hated one another. He reproached her for sacrificing everything to her personal ambition, and for neglecting the sacred task of liberating India. She feared the Maulvi's prestige and did everything she could to eliminate him.

Another woman was the absolute ruler of Delhi, the third stop on Naransin's tour where he had been to an audience of the Great Moghul at the Red Fort. The palace had recovered its splendour. Protocol was as refined and as complex as during the reigns of the legendary great Moghuls. Naransin regaled the Rani with his descriptions of the court of Delhi.

But in fact, poor Bahadur Shah was being pressured by everyone. To the sepoys who came every day to demand money, he claimed to be penniless. His sons fought over posts and sinecures. His remarkable general-in-chief, Bakht Khan, was quarreling with his ministers. But everyone—viziers, imperial princes and revolutionaries—trembled before his favourite wife, Zeenat Mahal. A member of the plot against the British, she still secretly harboured hopes of putting her own son on the throne. For the time being, however, she limited herself to dominating Bahadur Shah and terrorizing him with scenes of extraordinary violence. She was present at all his audiences, hiding behind a golden lattice, and she showed no reticence about butting into the conversation and shouting orders.

The Rani interrupted Naransin's account.

'And the British army that was sent to re-take Delhi?'

'A single miserable army corps. It reached the outskirts of the capital about two weeks before I got there, but the great Moghul's troops stopped them and forced them to dig in. Without reinforcements, they can do nothing against Delhi, and they're more besieged than besiegers. Delhi, protected by formidable artillery and forty thousand defenders, has nothing to fear.'

On his way back Naransin had stopped at Gwalior where he had been received by Maharaja Sindhia, who, although officially still in power, was being closely watched by the revolutionaries. As for Diwan Dinkar, he had literally vanished, and some claimed he had taken refuge with the British at Calcutta.

'Did the garrison's sepoys leave to attack the British at Agra as they planned to?' the Rani asked.

'Actually, they remained in their cantonment at Gwalior...the Maharaja gave them three months' advance pay.'

'Then you can be sure Diwan Dinkar is still there, even if he's forced to keep to the shadows. No one else could have inspired Sindhia to do anything as smart as to neutralize the sepoys by showering them with gold.'

At the end of his trip, Naransin had detoured through Mandisore, located southeast of Jhansi. Having remained until then relatively calm, it had recently risen up under the leadership of Prince Firoz Shah, who had expelled the British from the entire province and installed a revolutionary government.

'I don't have to explain to you,' Naransin continued, 'that with this exploit, he cut the British lines of communication between Bombay and Agra, and created a nest of revolutionaries not far from the capital of their ally, the Maharaja of Gwalior.'

'And not far from Jhansi,' added the Rani thoughtfully. 'But Firoz Shah is a nephew of the Great Moghul. Aren't all the imperial princes good-for-nothings?'

'Firoz Shah isn't like the others. One remarkable thing is that he forbids his troops to plunder or massacre. He has even severely punished some soldiers who ignored those orders. He emphasizes that greed and cruelty only tarnish the cause of the revolution. And finally, from what I hear, Firoz Shah is very young, barely twenty-two and very handsome.'

Annoyed by the hidden motive she sensed in Naransin, the Rani asked sharply, 'And what conclusions did you draw from your tour, Diwan?'

'I have seen the Great Moghul put back on the throne, the kingdom of Oudh restored, and the Maratha Empire, under the leadership of the Peshwa, risen from its ashes. Three of the greatest powers of our past have resurfaced in history. Tomorrow, India will be completely free, and the allies of the British will be cursed by the population.'

Sensing by her silence that the Rani was not absolutely convinced, Naransin insisted, 'At Delhi I saw the envoys of the most powerful kings of India pay court to the Great Moghul. There were the representatives of the Maharaja of Patiala, of the Nawab of Rampur and of the Maharaja of Baroda...'

The Rani interrupted this listing.

'And what did they bring the Great Moghul? Troops? Money? No—they brought homage, which is just so much wind. In the meantime, you might not be aware of this, they continue to assure the British of their support. Believe me, Diwan, if we want to safeguard the peace and prosperity of Jhansi, we have to be very careful; let us keep from getting involved and instead watch how the situation develops.'

5

The Rani was finishing dressing when she felt a small hand tug at her sari. That was the method Kiraun used to inform the Rani there was something she wanted to tell her. The Rani looked into the wide eyes of the child-woman, innocent and shy, and, although she was in a hurry, she took her aside and listened to her story.

Kiraun had a friend in the profession she had left, one of whose customers was a sweeper from the street of the grocers. Although he was an untouchable and therefore had no contact with the grocers themselves, the sweeper kept his ears open and was always well-informed about the activities and events in their lives, especially one particularly talkative grocer who had, among his customers, the wife of a tinker who rented two rooms to a poor wretch who had once been a servant to a British family. One thing led to another, and Kiraun had learned that the former servant was hiding in her closets a madwoman, who alternated between hours of immobility and apathy and sudden attacks of indescribable panic during which she sobbed and screamed so loud that she could be heard in the streets.

Could it be there was an Englishwoman hiding in Jhansi, a survivor from the massacre at the Jokhan Bagh?

The Rani waited for evening and the end of the daily durbar to leave the fort. Carefully veiled, she followed Kiraun to the tinkers' street, left her to stand guard outside, and slipped into a dark, squalid stairway. Entering the first room without knocking, she found a servant who immediately fell to the floor and kissed the ground before her.

Without stopping, the Rani walked towards a collection of dangling rags that served as a door, and entered a small windowless room. A woman was sitting on a pallet. She did not even blink when the Rani came in. It was Annabelle Phipps. She had lost a great deal of weight and her skin had turned grey. Her hair fell in a long tangle onto a borrowed sari, filthy and worn. Moved by the sight of this broken woman who had once loved Roger, Lakshmi turned to the servant, who had followed her in, and whispered, 'How did you save her?'

'I was following the sepoys who were taking the British away. This was at the Jokhan Bagh. There were many people around them. At one point I got close to her. I just pulled her roughly by the arm, the others didn't have time to stop me, and I led her away. With the veil I put on her, she could pass for an Indian. For the first few days, I hid her in the empty tombs near the Jokhan Bagh, because I thought no one would dare go into those sacred places. Every day I brought her water, flat cakes and a little flour. But it became too dangerous. A beggar or a fakir could have decided to rest in the tombs, and besides, the police were everywhere. So madam gave me her earrings which I sold. With the money, I rented these two rooms for her and for myself. But now we have almost no money left and I'm afraid.'

The Rani looked at the servant for a long time and then asked, 'Why did you save her?'

'Madam wasn't a bad mistress. She shouted at us, but she wasn't truly nasty. And when I realized they were going to kill them all, I didn't want her to be massacred.'

'I wish that others had done as you did,' said the Rani gravely. And she handed her a heavy purse, adding, 'You'll have even more if you obey me.'

Then she turned to Mrs Phipps, who had still not stirred.

'I've come to save you,' she said in her softest voice.

Annabelle reacted as though she had received an electric shock. She turned away abruptly, her face deformed by hatred and fear.

'You want to kill me the way you had him killed, the way you had my husband and the others killed!'

The Rani's voice shook as she answered, 'I did not have them killed, Mrs Phipps. I was not able to save them.'

'Why then have you been searching for me? There are patrols everywhere, the police checks on anyone entering or leaving the city. Is it me you're after? Or perhaps you're looking for other survivors of the massacre? Well, you needn't worry, because there aren't any but me.'

Annabelle was impervious to reason, but the Rani continued humbly, 'My police has no instructions other than to re-establish the order that was disrupted by the rebels. Come with me, Mrs Phipps. I'll shelter you in the palace.'

'Never! You'll have me killed. Haven't you spilled enough blood already?'

The servant had kneeled next to Annabelle and was stroking her hand.

'Listen to the Rani, Madam, she is good. She'll save you.'

But Annabelle no longer heard. She had resumed her blank, absent expression. 'They're all dead, all of them,' she whispered over and over. The servant took Annabelle in her arms, rearranged her sari, and made her stand up as though she were a very small child. The Rani stepped aside to let them pass.

Annabelle and her servant were settled in two rooms in the outbuildings of the town palace, quieter now that the Rani had moved to the fort. The Rani told Kiraun to go visit Mrs Phipps every other day.

The monsoon, which during the summer drowns northern India under torrential rains, ordinarily has little effect on central India. And yet, late in August 1857, it had been raining in Jhansi uninterruptedly for three days.

That morning at dawn, news had come that Sadasheo, the cousin of the late Raja of Jhansi, had seized the fort and the town of Kurrara, one of the brightest jewels of the Rani's kingdom, located thirty miles east of the capital.

When her advisers gathered around the Rani, there was noisy confusion as each of them tried to relate whatever information he had been able to gather—Sadasheo disposed of considerable manpower; the peasants were prepared to rise up in his favour; the talukdars were behind him, and he had numerous supporters within the town itself; he had already chosen his men for the important posts; he had started minting coins stamped with his name, and issued a proclamation that had been distributed throughout the state:

Maharaja Sadasheo has mounted the throne of Jhansi at Kurrara.

Wanting to prove their importance, the members of the council magnified the situation little by little and analyzed it interminably. Dissecting, conjecturing, splitting hairs, they completely forgot that urgent decisions had to be made. They even forgot the Rani, who had been silent all this time.

Contrary to her usual state, she felt very depressed. Annabelle's reappearance had awakened in Lakshmi tragic memories that, until then, had been kept in abeyance by her feverish activity. The ceaseless rains had also darkened her mood.

She thought of Damodar, in whose name she had to act. He was so young, so vulnerable. How many more years would she have to struggle and fight before he could take over? The fatigue of the past three months, during which she had struggled so hard every day against enormous problems, suddenly overwhelmed her.

Akbar, who, since his recent promotion to equerry, attended the meetings of the council, let the others rattle on while he stared intently at the Rani. Emerging from his silence, he said, 'Let me go to Kurrara, Rani. I'll take three hundred horsemen and make short work of your Sadasheo.'

The advisers protested. A few hundred horsemen would not stand a chance of dislodging the usurper. They needed to wait, to gather more information, raise emergency troops, make sure of the population's feelings. In fact, they didn't trust this new arrival, whose proposal seemed the height of impertinence. Akbar did not bother to answer them, but insisted, 'Let me go there, Rani.'

'Well, go then, if you want to,' murmured the Rani.

Something in Akbar's voice and his attitude had swayed her. The advisers wanted to raise more objections. It was too late. Akbar had already left.

The Rani held no durbar on that day or the next. She refused to see her subjects or hold more councils. She stayed in her apartments, emerging only to walk along the ramparts of the fort. It continued to rain intermittently. Her Kashmiri shawl draped around her head, the Rani ignored the rain. Her steps always led her gradually to the east, towards

Kurrara. Leaning on the parapet, she surveyed the horizon, clouded by rain. Anxiety gnawed at her, for Jhansi, for Damodar, for herself, and especially for Akbar, even though she refused to admit to herself that her preoccupation for one of her servants could outweigh her concern for her entire people. Nevertheless, her anxiety was somewhat attenuated by the trust Akbar had managed to inspire in her. He was neither a dreamer nor a reckless hothead.

He came back the following evening, dripping wet, his clothes caked with mud, grinning madly. With him joy burst into the Rani's apartments. Before she could recover from her surprise, Akbar announced, with ironic solemnity, 'Kurrara lies at Your Majesty's feet.'

'What, already!' cried the Rani.

'It was nothing at all. You see now that you mustn't listen to people who lose their heads so easily.'

'How many were they?'

'A little more than five hundred—amateurs, dacoits, deserters. No artillery, they didn't know how to fight, and we had surprise on our side. We overran the fort in no time at all.'

'And the talukdars who were behind Sadasheo?'

'They had been lured into it with promises, and we had no trouble turning them around.'

'And wasn't the population behind him?'

'Lies, Rani, lies. The peasants want only one thing—peace. They've had enough of trouble and insecurity. They believe in you because you represent stability.'

'And Sadasheo? Was he killed?'

'No. When he saw that things were turning against him, he fled to the north. We weren't able to get our hands on him.'

The Rani felt like keeping Akbar there, listening to him, watching him, drinking in his presence. He looked at her tenderly, and said gently, 'Let me, at least, go change my clothes.'

The next day the rains stopped, and autumn, which in India is a second spring, began. Washed by the rain, the sky had grown deeper and the air was exceptionally transparent. Nature seemed reborn.

That evening was the festival of Janmashtami, which celebrates the birth of the god Krishna. The court observed the feast in the Rani's garden. The fort of Jhansi's three enclosures, running along the uneven flank of the hill, left here and there irregular spaces between them. At the northwest end of the fort was a flat area larger than the others, studded with palm trees, tall flame-trees and a few mango trees; the Rani had added flower beds, two marble fountains and bougainvillea that climbed the length of the rampart, dressing up its austerity. The covered passageway of the second enclosure was level with the garden and thus made a natural pathway. A multicoloured canopy had been raised against a wide portal which once led to a drawbridge, long since disappeared. Brocade pillows had been strewn on Persian carpets that covered the lawns and paths.

When Akbar strolled down the stone ramp leading to the Rani's garden, he was struck by the beauty of the spectacle. The breeze played with the flames of torches set up all along the walls. The murmur of fountains mingled with the melancholy sound of flutes. Courtiers and dignitaries strolling about the paths looked like enormous flowers—pink, red, gold, silver, and most of all, yellow, the colour of the Janmashtami festival. Swings had been suspended from the trees, and in them, as was the custom, sat ladies of the court and wives of dignitaries, their saris floating like banners as they swung back and forth.

The Rani had noticed Akbar's arrival. She had him sit next to her under the canopy. From turban to slippers he was dressed entirely in white, without a single jewel.

'I see,' she told him, 'that you refused to bow to tradition and wear yellow.'

'Just as you did,' answered Akbar.

The Rani was wearing a sari of gold lamé.

She was intrigued by Akbar's personality, by the initiative and authority he had displayed in his venture against Sadasheo. She asked him about his origins.

'Contrary to what you think, Rani, my father was not a peasant. He was a nobleman, though poor.'

Akbar knew his family tree by heart, and Lakshmi and he took pleasure in retracing their genealogies, a favourite pastime of the Indian aristocracy. According to a legend that might have had some basis in truth, Akbar's first ancestor, originally from Afghanistan, had fought Sikander, the fair-haired conqueror who, in Europe, was known as Alexander the Great.

Without preamble, the Rani then said, 'I've decided to entrust you with the command of my cavalry, Akbar Khan.'

Neither the promotion nor the honorary Muslim title seemed to affect Akbar, who merely replied, 'And so, after judging me worthy of commanding horses, you think me worthy of commanding men.'

'I've watched you, you know how to lead men, you're especially good at convincing them. You've certainly convinced me.'

There was a long silence, and then the new sirdar said, 'You didn't ask my opinion, Rani.'

'If you don't want to accept what I'm offering, you're free to leave, Akbar Khan.'

'I'll stay—because you too have convinced me.' His eyes were laughing as he spoke. His attitude, which might have passed for insolence, was just a manifestation of his innate sense of equality. One did not give orders to Akbar Khan; one conquered him only if he allowed himself to be conquered.

Led by Mandar, who was a fabulous dancer in her own right, about forty of the court ladies performed sacred dances while singing the chants of Govinda dedicated to Krishna. They did not display the professional sensuality of the nautch, but reserve, grace and modesty. The Rani leaned towards Akbar, 'Have you noticed they're all wearing the rakhi?'

By displaying this bracelet, a precious jewel or a simple strip of cloth, the dancers showed their fidelity and attachment to the person who had given it, in this instance, the Rani.

'Did you know, Akbar Khan, that when a lady offers the rakhi to a man, it means that he must stand ready to sacrifice everything for her, including his life, and to answer to her every call. It also bestows on him the title of adoptive brother.'

While speaking, the Rani had removed from her wrist a slender bracelet that she now slipped over Akbar's wrist.

'After what you have done for me, I consider you my adoptive brother.'

Akbar gazed at the twelve lucky stones of India set in the thick red ribbon. He stared straight into the Rani's eyes. His blue eyes were both laughing and burning.

'I don't need the rakhi to be faithful to you, Rani. Let us be brother and sister then, since that is all we can be.'

The Rani blushed violently and looked away.

Four days later, Sadasheo himself arrived in Jhansi, in chains, escorted by soldiers of the personal guard of the Maharaja of Gwalior in whose state he had sought refuge. The Maharaja had denied him asylum, arrested him, and sent him back to the Rani. Lakshmi guessed that behind this stood her old friend Diwan Dinkar who, although cooped up in one of his master's palaces, still directed his policy from his hiding place.

Lakshmi had Sadasheo locked up in the fort, in the hanged man's tower, and then went to visit him. Her way lit by a torch that Akbar held, she climbed down the steep spiral stairway and entered a tiny stone-walled cell. Sadasheo was chained to the wall by heavy iron rings. His sorry condition did not affect the Rani. She considered it kindness enough that she had not immediately executed this man who, for the third time, had threatened the throne of her son Damodar. Sadasheo maintained his arrogance, but underneath his haughtiness, there was palpable fear.

'Why did you try to usurp my son's throne?'

'It's mine by right, and you know it.'

'Forget that, Sadasheo, and tell me who put you up to it. I know you didn't act alone.'

'I did act alone but let's say I have a few powerful friends.'

'Who?' shouted the Rani. Sadasheo's only answer was a snigger, and the Rani flushed with anger.

'My late husband, your cousin, developed some very efficient methods to loosen tongues, and if it were necessary, I could find it in me to remember them.'

'You can torture me, I won't tell you anything.'

But Sadasheo was a boastful man, and he was unable to keep entirely silent.

'If I told you who my friends were, you'd be astounded. And when you do find out, it'll be too late, and I'll be on the throne that is mine.'

'In the meantime, your throne is here,' answered the Rani, showing him his cell, 'for life.'

She was furious as she left, furious at having learned nothing, at having seen that schemer stand up to her and mock her. She would wrench the truth from him. She promised herself to remain calm in the future and use guile, but she did not exclude the use, if necessary, of more radical means.

The next day when she returned to the tower with Akbar, she found the guards in a state of terror, begging her to forgive them and spare their lives. Sadasheo was sick—Sadasheo was dying. The Rani rushed to his cell. His body was hanging limply from his chains, his face green and contorted in what was obviously hideous suffering. She ordered him untied and summoned the palace doctors.

They examined Sadasheo and diagnosed a poison for which there was no remedy. The guards admitted that Sadasheo had been sick all night, but terrified of being punished for their negligence, they had alerted no one. Sadasheo died soon afterwards, without having been able to speak.

A five year old memory came back to the Rani as she looked at the corpse lying on the filthy floor of the cell. Like Sadasheo, Mira, the servant who had poisoned the Raja, had died before the Rani could force anything out of her. It had been said that Mira, tortured by remorse, had committed suicide. But in fact, she had been murdered, just like Sadasheo. Sadasheo had been suspected of standing behind Mira's crime. And now it was he who had been eliminated.

'Who has a grudge against me? Who wants to chase me from the throne?'

She had said this aloud, and Akbar answered, 'Our courts have always had their mysteries and intrigues—jealous cousins, or ambitious younger brothers of maharajas. With Sadasheo's death, the plot has failed.'

Gradually, his calm anaesthetized the suspicion with which the Rani now viewed everything and everyone.

6

Although the monsoon season was over, the rains had continued to fall on central India, an extraordinary phenomenon that perplexed the seers immensely. It was raining in Bombay, which forced Roderick Briggs to stay cooped up in his room. His host, Mr Baxter, a merchant friend of his father, had placed at his disposal a huge and comfortable apartment and did everything to make his stay a pleasant one. Despite all this, Roderick fumed at his enforced idleness. The outbreak of the insurrection had kept him from continuing on to Jhansi. In all towns where trouble and violence had struck, it was open season on the British. Upon receiving the news, Bombay had, at first, been astonished. Bombay, the pearl of British colonization, Bombay, the gateway to India, had trembled. Roderick had witnessed the panic of the civilians who, at the news of a revolt of the garrison's sepoys, had taken refuge in the fort and on ships anchored in the harbour.

But the worst had been avoided, thanks mostly to the British chief of police; disguised as a Brahmin, he had been able to arrest the main leaders of the plot during a secret meeting, thus preventing a general uprising. Order had since been maintained.

Nevertheless, the weakness of the British forces stationed in Bombay prevented them from undertaking any campaign against the neighbouring provinces that had gone over to the rebellion. Condemned to idleness, Roderick devoted much of his free time to writing to his fiancée, Sarah Brandon, who had remained in London; distance had only increased his infatuation. The tension of the situation, the depression brought on by his perusal of the *India Gazette* or by the news gleaned from the gossip at the military club led him to pour himself out in interminable letters.

And yet a glimmer of hope has appeared amid the series of reversals and disasters we have suffered. Our troops have retaken Cawnpore. From Calcutta we had sent a small army up the valley of the Ganges to retake from the mutineers the cities of Benares and Allahabad. It was no easy task, and was accomplished thanks only to the heroism of General Neill. From Allahabad, we sent a column to the neighbouring city of Cawnpore. In the course of several violent engagements, our troops broke through the barriers the rebels had placed in their path. A last desperate and furious charge enabled them to seize Cawnpore. The bloody tyrant Nana Sahib fled the city with thousands of his soldiers.

Roderick raised his pen. The downpour outside darkened his room, but instead of freshening the atmosphere only made it more suffocating. Multiplied by the humidity, mosquitoes harassed him. He killed several before resuming his account.

In taking Cawnpore we have furnished proof that a few well-trained, disciplined regiments, inspired by our faith and led by our patriotic ideals, can defeat savages, outnumbering them ten to one, who think only of looting and murder.

Alas! When they entered the city, our troops found horrors such that all of British India is in mourning. After Nana Sahib, going back on his word, had ordered the execution of the heroic defenders of Cawnpore who had surrendered, he had kept two hundred women and children alive, probably to ransom them. He had imprisoned them in appalling conditions in a building known as Bibigarh House. When our troops were about to retake the city, he decided to avenge himself and personally ordered the massacre of every hostage. His henchmen, only too happy to obey, turned the prison into a slaughterhouse. When the last woman, the last child had been killed, their bodies were dragged by the hair and thrown down a well, where our troops found them. We shall make them pay the price for the blood spilled, and not only at Cawnpore but everywhere those barbarians committed atrocities, at Meerut, at Delhi, at Jhansi…

Roderick always returned to dwell on the events at Jhansi. Bombay had learned of the massacre of the British there and, although Roderick had no details about Roger's fate, he had lost any hope that his friend had survived. In an earlier letter, he had mentioned the Rani...

> *It seems she was able to get rid of the assassins and re-establish order while waiting for us to take over. Some say she took advantage of the situation to retake a throne to which she has no right...*

When Roderick finally received precise information on the circumstances of his friend's death, he became haunted by images of that terrible end.

> *The monsters at Jhansi basely subjected the men to torture and raped the women before hacking them to pieces on the spot.*
> *Can anyone imagine such barbarism in our century?*
> *Do they still deserve the label of human beings, those savage beasts who must now be exterminated? I swear to you, Sarah, on what I hold most sacred, that I shall avenge Roger's death. I shall track down his murderers wherever they may hide. And I shall kill them without mercy as they killed Roger. My soul will know no peace until I acquit myself of this sacred task.*

In India the rain is not sad; it is noisy, insistent, violent. It kept the Rani inside, a difficult trial for a woman who so loved the outdoors. She had been brought her lunch, which she took alone in the library, but that day she ate nothing. The fall of Cawnpore had come as a shock. It was a cruel denial of the hope for a free India that had grown in her with the spread of revolutionary successes. Her heart resented the massacre of British women and children at Bibigarh, committed by the orders of her former friends whom she accused of having thus lost their honour. Her whole being resented the atrocious reprisals the British had committed against the vanquished city. India was entering a cycle of blood-soaked horror from which she saw no way out. Diwan Naransin interrupted her gloomy meditations to announce the presence in the city of Tatya Tope.

'He arrived unexpectedly at my house, and I could not refuse to take him in.'

'You have made a mistake, Diwan. He has come here only to force us to give up our neutrality and to compromise us in the eyes of the British. The fact that my Prime Minister shelters him makes my government an accomplice of the murderers of Bibigarh.'

The Rani's vehemence did not stop the Diwan.

'Tatya Tope is the most brilliant general of the revolution. He has just lost Cawnpore, but he'll recapture it. He has already won many battles, and the people regard him as a hero. He is asking to see you.'

'And of course all of Jhansi already knows of his arrival.'

'Refusing to see him would be an insult, contrary to popular feeling,' answered Naransin.

The Rani finally gave in to Diwan Naransin's persistence, but she was determined not to open her doors too wide to Tatya Tope. Instead of treating him as a guest of honour, she would receive him during the daily durbar, shielded by the strict limits of protocol.

She awaited his arrival, surrounded by her dignitaries, her ministers, noblemen and burghers who had come to place before her petitions and arguments needing to be settled. Hearing the cheers of her soldiers and the people massed outside to greet Tatya Tope, she was unable to stifle an expression of impatience. He walked into the throne room, ramrod-stiff, wearing his eternal white turban. The Rani found him even uglier than she had remembered—low forehead, thick nose, eyes sunk deep in their sockets, his mutton-chops, now grey and bristly, lending him a savage look. His teeth were irregular and blackened by tobacco, smallpox had pitted his skin. The Rani did not return his smile. She watched him coldly as he made the customary greetings, and then abruptly asked him, 'Why have you come here, General?'

'To ask you to join us—you and your troops.'

'Jhansi wishes to maintain its neutrality and remain at peace,' the Rani answered curtly.

'Your neutrality in relation to whom, Rani? To the British? Soon, there won't be a single one left in all India. I've just come from Gwalior. There I induced the sepoys to join my troops and...'

The Rani interrupted him, 'But you didn't induce the troops of the Maharaja of Gwalior to join you, from what I've heard, General.'

'The Maharaja is our friend. Breaking protocol, he personally came to visit me in my camp, offering me betel and incense as though to an equal, to a ruler. Diwan Dinkar, who is not reputed to be among our supporters, came with him. The following day the Maharaja sent me carts, horses, elephants, camels and mules for my army.'

'Presents I can give you too, if the circumstances require it. How much meaning do they have?' asked the Rani with irony.

Tatya Tope looked surprised at her hostility. In a low voice he said, 'I would like to speak to you alone, Rani.'

The Rani could feel that the spectators disapproved of her harsh treatment of the hero. She sensed the suppressed fury in Mandar next to her. She looked for Akbar, who sat among the dignitaries on one of the throne room's pillows. He was staring straight ahead, impassive. The Rani rose and motioned to Tatya Tope to follow her, not to her private apartments—that would have been too great an honour—but to the private audience chamber off the throne room.

Tatya Tope went straight to the point, 'You've got something against me, Lakshmi—why?'

The Rani answered with a single name, 'Bibigarh.'

'You lament the fate of two hundred English women and children, and you do not cry for the thousands upon thousands of our brethren dying every day in Cawnpore at the hands of the British? Forget the summary executions, the shootings, the indiscriminate hangings they supervise. But do you know that before killing their victims, the British torture them with refinements of unimaginable perversity? Worse still, they break their castes. They make them lick earth sullied by untouchables, they ram pieces of pork and other impure meats down their throats so as to make them die impure...'

'Enough!' cried the Rani, 'I don't want to hear any more... It is you who gave the British a pretext for their unlimited reprisals. It is Nana Sahib and you who called their vengeance down on the heads of our brethren.'

'Do you really think that I, that Nana Sahib were responsible for the tragedy at Bibigarh? Do you want to know what really happened? While the British troops were approaching Cawnpore, a few voices in the council called for the execution of the female prisoners. Nana Sahib, his cousin Rao Sahib, myself and all the other members of the council rejected the proposal with horror. The women of Nana Sahib's harem heard about it and threatened to throw themselves out the windows if the prisoners were executed. When one of our officers, without consulting us, tried to eliminate embarrassing witnesses as a precautionary measure, all the sepoys of our army refused to obey his orders. Then the battle began and we were all busy defending the city. That was when Huseinee Hanum came onto the scene. You remember her, Nana Sahib's favourite, who in the old days taught you to dance? I've always said she was born with hatred and cruelty in her heart. While no one was paying attention to her, in the midst of the battle, she led her lover to Bibigarh—ah yes, she is unfaithful to Nana Sahib, our friend, with one of his own soldiers. She also brought along two Hindu peasants and two Muslim butchers and she ordered the five men to kill all the women and children. By the time we heard about it, it was too late, we were already evacuating the city. The British immediately put the blame for the massacre on us. For them there was one murderer, Nana Sahib, and his accomplices, Tatya Tope, Rao Sahib and the others.'

Tatya Tope's account sounded legitimate to the Rani. He was a straightforward, honest man, not a liar. The Rani believed him. It was a tremendous relief to her even if she did not show it immediately, for, it was not in her nature to recognize her mistakes easily.

Tatya Tope continued his account, 'After they took the city, some of the British wrote touching inscriptions on the walls of Bibigarh House, passing them off as the last scribbles of the women and children awaiting death, in order to further excite the murderous fury of their compatriots. They've made of the Bibigarh massacre an excuse to allow them to inflict reprisals without restraint.

'And it's the same everywhere. They circulate the most extravagant rumours about our cruelty. Our revolution is responsible for massacres which I am the first to deplore, but we have raped no women, we don't torture our prisoners, we don't roast children, and we're not cannibals. All these accusations would be laughable if they weren't so tragic. The British find in them an excuse to kill with a clear conscience thousands and thousands of innocent people in the name of justice and civilization.'

Tatya Tope felt the Rani coming around. After a moment's silence, he said, 'Come and join us, Lakshmi.'

'Do you believe we can win, Tatya?'

'I don't think about it, Lakshmi. Victory! That's not important. I'm fighting to free our country, to keep it from falling back under the British claws.'

'You have the stuff of a great leader, Tatya—you could win. And you know I don't like the British any more than you do.'

'I know, Lakshmi.'

'Perhaps one day I'll join you. But I can't force my people to run the risk of British reprisals. I don't want Jhansi to meet the fate of Cawnpore, Benares and Allahabad. What's more, the people here don't want to fight. All they want is to work and prosper in peace. I have spared them war—and I must continue to respect their wishes.'

'Do you think your subjects will be able to prosper as long as there is a single Englishman still in India? But perhaps you are right and I am wrong. Stay here, Lakshmi, and rule in peace. Take good care of Jhansi.'

At that moment Damodar ran into the room. He wanted to see the hero whose exploits he had heard about from his attendants. Intimidated by Tatya Tope's fierce appearance, he stopped. The general smiled at him with the same charm that had made him so popular among the rebels.

'O Raja! If you are as brave and as caring for your people as your mother, you shall be a great ruler!'

The child smiled back at him. The Rani was touched.

'I have to go,' Tatya Tope said abruptly.

'Stay, my friend, I'll hold a feast in your honour tonight.'

'We're at war, Lakshmi, I have no time for feasting.' And then, he added, smiling, 'I wouldn't want to compromise you.'

The Rani answered spiritedly, 'A friendship cannot compromise me.'

She insisted on accompanying Tatya Tope to the fort's first enclosure, where he had left his mount, because only the ruler is allowed to enter it on horseback.

Once he was out of sight, Damodar whispered into his mother's ear, 'What an ugly man!'

'Perhaps,' answered the Rani, 'but he's a skilful general, a brave man and a loyal friend.'

Ten days later the Rani learned of the fall of Delhi. Conflicting interests, divisiveness and ineffectiveness among the Indian generals had wiped out the potential of the immense army and powerful artillery they had at Delhi. The British, who for months had held a position above the city, had at last received reinforcements from the region of Punjab, which they had conquered earlier through harsh measures. After intensive shelling and several furious assaults, they had retaken the city on 20 September 1857 and put the octogenarian Great Moghul, Bahadur Shah, inside a cage. Before his trial, the British filed past the sick old man, insulting him grossly and demanding that he be executed immediately. His wife, Zeenat Mahal who, according to Diwan Naransin, had been the real force in Delhi, shared his captivity and cursed him from dawn till dusk.

This particular news affected the Rani less than the fate imposed by the victors on the inhabitants. The British had taken revenge on Delhi with particular ferocity, literally plunging it into a bath of blood and fire so encompassing that the city fell into ruin, from which it seemed unlikely ever to recover. The former capital of the Sultans and Moghuls, which had absorbed so many invasions and occupations, was dead.

And yet the confidence and determination shown by Tatya Tope allowed the Rani to bear the shock. The fall of Delhi was a setback for the revolution, but not a disaster.

7

Making the most of a mild October afternoon, the Rani skipped her usual nap before durbar and instead went to watch the training of new horses for her cavalry. The soldiers had brought the horses to the arid plain that stretched south of the town of Jhansi to the jungle, and galloped them on the Orchha road, not far from the ruins of the former British cantonment.

The Rani was in her element. Her judgement of the virtues and faults of each horse was flawless. She loved them and knew how to earn their love. They stepped up to her and nuzzled her face. She was leaning over to examine the hocks of one animal, whose imperceptible limp she alone had noticed, when a group of peasants appeared in the distance, emerging from the cover of the jungle. Stumbling, staggering, bleeding, they ran straight ahead, dragging the old, carrying the children. The Rani cantered over to them. Prey to some unspeakable terror, they refused to stop at her command. The Rani grabbed one man and held him tightly. He could barely speak. But the Rani was able to glean the appalling news from his stuttering.

That morning at dawn, without warning, a powerful army of the Rani of Orchha had invaded Jhansi. It was commanded by Orchha's Prime Minister, Diwan Nathay Khan. He had already seized all the villages south of the capital as well as the palace at Barwan Sangar, the country seat of the Rajas of Jhansi. Troops were burning villages, slaughtering peasants. Those the Rani had encountered had fled the village of Hazrat Puna.

An hour later the Rani presided over an extraordinary session of her council. The munshis had brought from the archives the treaty of alliance between Orchha and Jhansi, negotiated four years earlier by Diwan Naransin, the letters of friendship from the Rani of Orchha to Lakshmi after she succeeded to the throne, Orchha's century-old claims to Jhansi's territory, the land deeds donated by the early Peshwas. The Rani's advisers argued, shouted, fought, cursed and threw documents at each other's heads. The Rani did not take part in the discussion. Akbar noticed, with surprise, that she seemed to be enjoying herself immensely. A servant entered with a letter that had been brought by an enemy officer. Naransin read it aloud: in exchange for the immediate surrender of the town and fort of Jhansi, General Nathay Khan offered the Rani of Jhansi the same pension she had received from the British.

'Write,' she ordered a secretary, '"Do your worst, Nathay Khan—I'll make a woman of you." Seal it and send it.'

Diwan Naransin stood up.

'My heart bleeds, Rani, but I must speak to you in all honesty. I love Jhansi as you do. But Jhansi, you've said so yourself, wants peace. Do you wish to throw your country into a ruinous, murderous war? Is it not your duty, painful though it may be, to consider Nathay Khan's proposal or at least try to negotiate?'

The Rani smiled ironically, 'You are right and you are wrong, Diwan. My subjects want peace, but they want it under my sceptre, not the Rani of Orchha's.'

Naransin insisted, 'And with what will we oppose Nathay Khan's advance? He has forty thousand men and twenty-eight guns, while we...'

'We have only a few thousand ill-trained men and a few old guns,' the Rani finished. She fell silent while she concentrated. Akbar thought she was going to give in. He rose and was about to speak when the Rani motioned him to be quiet and sit down.

'Jhansi today, all of India tomorrow, is watching us, waiting to see how we handle this test. We shall not give in to the Rani of Orchha or to our other enemies, no matter what. We shall fight.'

With bitter irony, Diwan Naransin asked, 'And which of us will you send to meet the army of Nathay Khan? Who will be your general-in-command?'

'I will, Diwan.'

Her answer echoed in the audience chamber like the crack of a whip. 'After all,' she continued, 'isn't this a war between ladies? Even though the Rani of Orchha, despite her nickname Lackri Bai, the warrior queen, isn't commanding her own army?'

Several of her advisers half-rose in protest. She stopped them.

'There is no time to argue. We must act. You will be informed of my orders.'

The following days were filled with intense activity. Jhansi became a vast military camp as the Rani raised her army. Under Sanghar Singh, the commander of the army, soldiers were being drilled on every square, at every street corner. Sanghar Singh had made this war his own. Had the Rani of Orchha not dared to invade and occupy his territory, the land on which, for years, he had exercised his reprehensible but lucrative activities? Lakshmi had put Akbar in charge of recruiting. He travelled the roads non-stop, riding from village to village; with his gift for persuasion, he signed up all those capable of holding a weapon, asking no questions about their past. So many sinister-looking men appeared in the streets of Jhansi that the inhabitants grew afraid and Kashmiri Mull came to speak to the Rani.

'These soldiers Akbar Khan's been bringing in—no one knows whether they're here to defend or to attack us.'

'War is war,' answered the Rani. 'Sanghar Singh will keep them in line. He knows all about bandits, he was one himself.'

'But that's not the worst of it, Rani. Many of these recruits are deserters who have streamed in from all over the region after hearing that you were hiring. They're people who fought the British. The British might take umbrage—and think you were raising an army against them.'

'If they don't like my army, let them send one of theirs to defend me.'

In the meantime, Nathay Khan and his troops were marching on Jhansi with no great haste. Nathay Khan was taking his time; he obviously considered this war little more than a military excursion.

It was four o'clock in the afternoon. Followed by her staff, the Rani climbed to the top of the tower rising above the first enclosure. Below, she could see her men preparing for battle, milling about the second and third enclosures as well as on the town walls. She wore a turbaned helmet, long metal gloves, and a wide belt of steel. The jewel-studded sabre of the Rajas of Jhansi hung at her side. Masculine but not lacking in feminine grace, warlike without seeming ridiculous—for she was a very small woman—her carefully-chosen uniform filled Akbar with admiration.

Damodar stood close to his mother. Despite Moropant's insistence, she had refused to evacuate him from the town.

'If he's going to be a king worthy of the name, he might as well receive his baptism of fire as early as possible,' she had said.

A dull, growing rumble came from the jungle in the distance. Soon the leading enemy forces emerged from the cover of tall trees. A heavy silence fell over the ramparts of Jhansi, anxious, waiting. Nathay Khan's entire army marched out onto the Jokhan Bagh, the empty area stretching between the town and the old military cantonment, where the British had been massacred. The soldiers seemed beyond number.

Stiff as a statue, the Rani kept her eyes fixed on the human ant colony that was advancing slowly to the sound of drums and trumpets. She was seized by a mixture of fear and feverish intoxication.

Suddenly, Nathay Khan's troops began to run forward, shouting, like a tidal wave ready to sweep away everything in its path. Sanghar Singh grew impatient. 'Give the order to open fire, Rani.'

'Not yet,' the Rani replied.

The human tide rushed inexorably towards the ramparts. The front lines were no more than fifty yards away. Up on the observation tower, the Rani's staff went into a panic. All started shouting at once.

'Let's give the order to shoot immediately, or it will be too late.'

'They're going to rush the walls.'

'If we don't fire the city will be taken.'

Only Akbar remained silent, staring intently at the Rani. He trusted her, but he was not sure what she meant to do.

Sanghar Singh, in a frenzy, blurted out, 'If she doesn't give the order to fire, I'm going to give it myself.'

The Rani wheeled around and barked, 'Be quiet and don't move.'

The enemy's leading ranks were now only twenty yards from the walls and they had already opened fire as they ran. The Rani saw several of her men fall. Then she turned to Ghulam Ghaus Khan, her head-gunner and calmly, said:

'Now—open fire.'

Ghulam Ghaus Khan leaned over the battlement and signalled to his men below, stationed in the second and third enclosures. A tremendous explosion shook the air. The Rani's few cannons had fired, raising a cloud of smoke. When it cleared, the Rani saw that several dozen of the enemy lay stretched out on the ground. But the human tide continued to surge forward, running, roaring and firing. The Rani shouted, 'Fire again! Fire at will!'

The guns began a continuous barrage. The noise was deafening, and smoke hid the battlefield from the Rani and her staff. The attack lasted only fifteen minutes. Nathay Khan's troops, surprised by the vigorous fire of the Rani's gunners, retreated in disorder, leaving behind several hundred dead in the Jokhan Bagh. The assault had been repulsed.

When the last of the enemy soldiers had been driven back, the Rani turned to her staff.

'In the future, generals, you will spare me your impatience. The enemy troops had to be allowed to come close enough to be mowed down by our cannon. We also had to surprise them. Nathay Khan, confident of victory, didn't expect to meet any serious obstacle. It was necessary to let him enjoy that illusion as long as possible so that the surprise would be total and murderous. Perhaps from now on you will have more faith in my judgement.'

The warriors hung their heads, ashamed to have doubted her. Only Akbar stared at her, a happy gleam in his eye.

Night had fallen, and the Rani was comforting defenders of the fort who had been wounded during the attack; she had them brought to the town palace, transformed into a hospital by Mandar and her women. This visit was for her a trial far more difficult to endure than what she had gone through that afternoon. She had an instinctive revulsion for blood, wounds, moans of pain, hospitals and their smells. Tomorrow, flatterers would tell her that her appearance had roused enthusiasm, caused miracles, healed the wounded. For the moment, she saw only men, almost unaware of her presence, agonizing in their own condition, tortured by pain. She envied the composure of little Kiraun, who went from one to another without seeming in the least unnerved by these horrible visions.

Suddenly, the chorus of moans and sighs was interrupted by an explosion outside. The Rani stopped to listen. The thunder of artillery fire rattled the windows; instinctively, she ran to the palace courtyard. Brief, intense flashes of red lit up the sky to the south. The Rani hesitated, unsure of what to do. An officer, gasping for breath, brought her the news.

Nathay Khan had regrouped his army in the shelter of the forest and under cover of darkness, had moved his artillery, which he had kept in reserve during the initial assault, up to Jhansi. His guns had opened fire simultaneously on the fort's third enclosure, where the Rani's own artillery was massed, and on the Orchha Gate, where his troops were massing for an assault. She gave the officer-messenger orders for Sanghar Singh and sent him to the fort.

The Rani paced up and down, nervous, concentrating. Then she summoned one of her aides.

'Go find Akbar Khan. Tell him this is what he must do...'

Three soldiers, their clothes smeared with blood, made a dramatic entrance into the courtyard.

'They're battering down the Orchha Gate!' one of them cried. 'We can't hold out any longer. They're about to invade the city...'

A reflex she would later be at a loss to explain made the Rani leap into the saddle and gallop towards Orchha Gate. She was riding Pari, the horse she had bought on Akbar's advice on the day of their first meeting. The few guards who had time to saddle up had difficulty keeping up with her. Near the Orchha Gate the Rani found herself in the midst of total chaos. Inhabitants of the suburb were fleeing into the town. They neither ran nor shouted, but walked forward in tight ranks, taking steps so small they seemed hardly to move at all; some carrying huge bundles, others pulling rickety overloaded carts, paying no attention to what was coming in the other direction. The guards had to open a path through them for the Rani with blows from the flats of their sabres.

At Orchha Gate the heat and noise suffocated and deafened Lakshmi. Enemy shells were not striking the walls of the town but flying over them to crash into the suburb, setting houses on fire, crushing roofs, causing entire floors to collapse. One shell had ripped a large hole in the town's thick, bronze-braced wooden gate. Wounded and dead littered the ramparts and the ruins of the little square. Flames lit up small pools of black blood, already drying out. The Rani sensed immediately the lassitude and discouragement of the defenders. Several of them, throwing their rifles to the ground, ran down the rampart's stairway to escape. She shouted to stop them, 'Brothers, return to your positions! We shall win!'

She ordered her guards to climb to the ramparts and tell the defenders that she promised them gold, a lot of gold, if they held Orchha Gate against the enemy. Their instinct of obedience to the ruler proved stronger than fear, and they headed back towards the ramparts.

'Hold fast! The Rani promises you gold, much gold!'

The soldiers turned around, recognized the Rani at the foot of the ramparts, and quickly resumed firing with, it seemed to her, renewed vigour. She caught sight of Kiraun who, always hungry for excitement, had followed her from the palace.

'You're mad, get away from here!' shouted the Rani.

'You too, Rani, take cover!' Kiraun answered in her sharpest voice.

The Rani began to laugh. Later on, several witnesses were to express wonder at having seen the Rani of Jhansi, in the midst of the flying cannonballs, break out laughing. She continued to circle in front of Orchha Gate, shouting, 'Hold on, you'll have gold, lots of gold!' even though no one could hear her.

A handful of enemy soldiers had already broken through the Orchha Gate, and one of them charged at the Rani. She had drawn her sabre. One of the soldiers thrust his lance at her. With a flick of her sabre, she deflected the lance and plunged her blade into the enemy's chest. He opened his mouth in astonishment, raised his hands to his wound and fell backwards. His companions were already surrounding the Rani, thrusting at her with their lances. She manoeuvred her horse, twirled her sabre around her head, and suddenly, cleaving the air, swept it down whistling into the wall of flesh around her. The enemy, now pouring through the half-demolished Orchha Gate, threw themselves at her guards and engaged them in hand-to-hand combat, preventing them from coming to her assistance. She was alone in the midst of shrieking devils. Her horse Pari swivelled about, sidestepped a blow, reared to knock down an assailant; it seemed to know how to parry every blow. The Rani was one with the animal, striking out at her attackers as though she were gifted with the eight arms of the god Shiva, as though no weapon could get at her. The blood of Maratha warriors was raging in her. Flames from the burning houses lit up dramatically this dance of death unfolding under the stars of a dark, serene sky. The Rani might have been overcome by sheer numbers if the fort's artillery had not suddenly begun to thunder. The order she had sent to Sanghar Singh had at last been carried out. Immediately, she sensed hesitation in her attackers. Intoxicated by the noise of those cannons promising salvation, she fought even harder, slashing one man's head, lunging through another, cutting in half the arm of a third. The attackers recoiled, then fell back and vanished through the black hole of Orchha Gate. The Rani, her sword still raised, was left alone on her horse, in the middle of a carpet of dead and wounded enemies.

'Good work, Kadak Bijli,' she muttered, exhausted.

The Rani had been back in the fort for several hours. Around her, the officers were describing the battle to one another at the top of their lungs, messengers were entering with news that had become completely irrelevant, and generals were sending away orderlies with orders that were now useless. Damodar, still mad with fear and excitement, refused to go to bed and ran around in and out of the dignitaries' legs, Diwan Naransin stepped over to the Rani and whispered in her ear:

'I didn't see Akbar Khan during the battle. Did he take part?'

'He is where he's supposed to be,' answered the Rani cuttingly. She sensed that Naransin bore Akbar a strong dislike.

At that very moment Akbar strode into the throne room, exhausted, his face blackened by dirt and gunpowder, his clothes torn and streaked with blood. The Rani thought he was wounded, and Akbar read the anguish in her eyes.

'It's just enemy blood,' he reassured her.

And then, in one breath, he said, 'We did it! There's nothing left of Orchha's army. Your strategy was brilliant.'

On the Rani's instructions, Akbar and his horsemen had ridden out of Jhansi from the side of town hidden from the attackers, had rounded the fort through the jungle and taken up positions on the Orchha road without being detected. He had prepared his ambush there following the Rani's instructions; she had not for a moment doubted her victory and Nathay Khan's retreat. Akbar had attacked the enemy in the dark when they least expected it, and despite the small number of his own horsemen, he had turned the Orchhans' retreat into a total rout.

It was late, but fear, in retrospect, and the tension and excitement of the day kept the Rani from sleeping. Tired of tossing and turning on her bed, she got up and slipped out of the palace without being noticed by her many servants slumbering in the rooms and the courtyard. She liked to roam about at night, undetected. She had passed through the gate of the enclosure and was descending the stone ramp that led to her garden when she saw a ghostly silhouette moving soundlessly along an alley. She had heard it said that the garden was haunted. She hesitated slightly; then, steeling herself, she walked resolutely towards the white shadow.

'Did you think I was a ghost, Rani?'

It was Akbar. He did not even apologize for having entered the forbidden garden without permission. All he said was, 'I came here to look for your shadow and I am lucky enough to find you in person.' Without pausing, he continued: 'I'm sorry I wasn't with you at Orchha Gate. People talk about nothing but your heroism. Tell me, didn't you feel any fear?'

'I was too busy hiding it.'

'Commanding an army with that kind of skill and efficiency is not given to everyone. It's as if, all your life, you have been devouring manuals of strategy. Where did you acquire the discipline to evaluate a situation, the self-assurance to make decisions, the imagination to dream up traps for the enemy?'

'If only I knew, Akbar Khan. I don't know what came over me. Perhaps I was inspired...'

Without being aware of it, their stroll had brought them into the dense shadow of a mango tree. Unselfconsciously, the Rani lay down on the grass. Akbar settled next to her. All of a sudden, he laughed.

'You really made me laugh when you scolded your generals after the battle. You didn't frighten me—but why the devil didn't you let them know of your plans beforehand?'

Akbar's habit of not showing any formal respect stung the Rani.

'I did it deliberately. I wanted to keep the same surprise in store for my generals as for Nathay Khan. It was necessary not only that I defeat the enemy but also that I convince my friends. I needed to impress them in such a way that they would immediately come to believe in me. For at first, they had no confidence in me.'

'Why should your friends trust you when you don't trust them?'

'I've never found anyone I could trust.' The Rani's voice trembled.

Akbar sat up and put his hand on her shoulder, a gesture at once tender and protective. She began to cry, quietly. After the tension and the exhaustion of the past few days, everything inside her dissolved into relief that she had withstood the test. Akbar took her in his arms. 'Cry all you want, little girl,' he said. He kissed her hair tenderly. The Rani let her tears flow, then freed herself from Akbar's arms and stretched out on her back.

'I don't ordinarily cry, especially in front of someone.'

Akbar whispered, 'I love you.' He lay down on top of her and sought her mouth with his. They rolled on the grass, kissing and caressing.

That night Akbar Khan, the Pathan, became the Rani of Jhansi's lover.

The following day Nathay Khan, in the name of his mistress the Rani of Orchha, sued for peace on any terms. Lakshmi thought it useless to humiliate a ruler, her equal, and asked only for payment of war-damages. She was re reading the articles of the treaty when, suddenly, she looked up and began to reprimand Diwan Naransin.

'By the way, why did you want me to give in to the Rani of Orchha?'

Her question and her piercing gaze seemed to confuse Naransin for a moment.

'I told you; I love my country above all. I wanted to spare it the horrors of war, and besides, our defences were very weak.'

'One day, several years ago, I accused you of being in love with the Rani of Orchha. Perhaps I was right—perhaps you're still in love with her?'

'You're making fun of me, Rani.'

'You're right, Diwan, I am making fun of you, and that will be the only vengeance I take for your having doubted me.'

8

The Rani was a woman of habit. Every night, after her servants had retired, she rose from her bed, dressed, threw a peasant-shawl over her head, and slipped out of the palace, carefully and quietly. Outside, if by chance she came across a guard or a servant, he would mistake her, as she trotted by, for one of the girls who paid secret calls to soldiers stationed at the fort.

She had allotted Akbar two spacious rooms in one of the buildings erected at various times in front of the palace, against the ramparts of the first enclosure. Traces of stucco decorations showed they had once served some noble function. Akbar was a man of sober tastes. His lodgings were furnished only with a narrow mattress thrown on the bare ground, a few cushions and a desk. The Rani found this unfamiliar austerity highly exotic.

No sooner had the Rani arrived than they settled down to dinner, even though she had already eaten. He made her share his pleasure in eating and she would discover in herself an appetite she would never have suspected. Like a man of the people, he used banana leaves for plates. He stuffed himself with raita. To every dish he added great spoonfuls of ghee, which he doted on. The Rani enjoyed these simple meals, a stark contrast with the refinement of her own table.

Akbar had also introduced her to alcohol. He drank enough to surprise even the most hardened old campaigner. He helped himself to large glasses of rice wine; she settled for a few sips, enough to make her euphoric. As soon as dinner was finished, they made love, there on the mattress, next to the remains of dinner. Then they would spend long hours, lying side by side, chatting tirelessly. She liked to tease him.

'You took me by surprise, Akbar Khan, that first time you threw yourself on me.'

'You're lying, Rani,' he would answer, mocking her. 'You wanted me to make love to you. Your eyes had undressed me more than once.'

Laughing, she would deny it, or sometimes, especially in the early days of their affair, she would begin to cry. Akbar would hold her tighter, asking for no explanation. She offered him one.

'I'm crying, but it's from happiness now. I had to carry so much responsibility these past months, I had to try so hard to be strong... Now I can let myself go because you allow it!'

Akbar did not like to show he was moved. His voice grew hoarse.

'You've been steering a kingdom through danger and uncertainty all on your own, and you'd like never to be tired? A little humility, Rani...'

She stretched voluptuously.

'In all my life I have never felt so happy.'

'And yet,' Akbar replied,' you loved the Englishman. You see, I've made my inquiries, and I know everything.'

'With Roger it was passion, and passion never brings happiness.'

'Perhaps the Englishman was, for you, just the caprice of a queen.'

He refrained from adding that he too might be one. Guessing at his thoughts, she answered them, indirectly.

'My feeling for Roger had neither present nor future. It set me apart. It cut me off from my brethren, who would have considered it shameful and degrading. So I had to hide it, even from Roger, and I couldn't allow it to develop. Through you, Akbar, it is also our country and my work that I love. With you, I am discovering love, a love that is all I need.'

She was not being entirely truthful; she loved Akbar deeply, but much of her love for him was, in fact, friendship. She wanted to say more, but he silenced her with kisses.

Making love with Akbar became the most natural thing in the world. Far from exhausting Lakshmi, the feverish nights revived her, filled her with renewed energy.

As she returned alone to the palace, dawn was spreading a grey light over the countryside and the horizon was turning pink. Lakshmi breathed in the unique freshness of this hour, the odour of trees and grass. She felt rested, 'As though I'd slept twelve hours at a stretch,' she thought, 'instead of spending a sleepless night.'

Blunt as he was, Akbar sometimes offered advice she had not asked for. Like the day he told her, 'You don't take enough care of Damodar.' The Rani denied it. She was supervising her son's training and education and initiating him to his future responsibilities as a ruler. She made it her duty to pay him a visit in his apartments every evening before he went to bed.

'There—you said it. You do it by duty, not by inclination.'

'How can you think that? I love the child—he's so sweet, so affectionate...'

'He's also much more intelligent than you think. He needs to be appreciated.'

Akbar had struck a sensitive nerve, for at times the Rani did indeed worry whether she was a good mother. Secretly she suspected Damodar of being soft; she was unable to detect in him the future hero she wanted for a son.

Perhaps it was because of unconscious feelings of remorse that she decided to invest with exceptional solemnity the ceremony in which Damodar, having reached nine years of age, was to be initiated into the warrior-caste that was his by birth. The government, the court and the nobility gathered in the courtyard of the temple of Lakshmi. The Rani took Damodar by the hand and presented him to the saffron-robed priest, who asked the ritual questions, the last of which is a fitting lesson for all kings:

'Before governing others, will you seek first and foremost to govern yourself?'

And the child had to answer, 'I pledge to make every effort to dominate my passions.'

The priest raised the heavy sabre of the Rajas of Jhansi over the flame and chanted.

'O God, who art within this adolescent, guide him that he may use this instrument for the glory of the truth and the preservation of the good, for the resurrection of thy ancient and infinite compassion in the hearts of all men.'

'Tathasthu, so be it,' shouted the assembled company with a single voice. The priest held out the sword to Damodar, took his hand, and led him seven times around the altar.

That day all the inhabitants of Jhansi, whatever their caste, including the untouchables, ate and drank at the young Raja's expense.

At the entrance to the palace, ladies of the court placed garlands of flowers around Damodar's neck. Then, complying with his mother's wish, he presided over his first durbar. He did not seem intimidated at having to sit alone on the silver gaddi and he received his subjects' homage with the grace of an adult. But it was a child who, afterwards, was reunited with his mother. Perhaps, in the light of Akbar's observations, the Rani noticed that Damodar seemed afraid of her. Would he make a good king, would he be capable of insuring the happiness of Jhansi?

At this time, late in 1857, the revolution was making progress once again. Tatya Tope had seized Kalpi, a town located halfway between Jhansi and Cawnpore. Held by the British for half a century, powerfully defended and dominated by a reputedly impregnable fort, its fall echoed like a clap of thunder. Tatya Tope was already marching on Cawnpore. And Lucknow had been the scene of repeated defeats for the British. They had sent a first and then a second column to retake the city from the rebels, but neither had been able to do more than evacuate their countrymen under siege in the Residence.

Meanwhile, Jhansi remained at peace which, in these troubled times, was a considerable achievement. The Rani was more popular than ever with her subjects. And yet, in the past few weeks, a vague anxiety had been growing inside her. It was almost midnight and she was in Akbar's chambers. He could feel her tension and his love for her enabled him to follow the meandering of her thoughts.

'Why are you uneasy, Lakshmi?' he asked. 'You say you're happy and yet you're always fretting over something for no reason.'

'And what if there were a good reason?' she asked, holding out a printed handbill.

It is forbidden to anyone to shelter rebel sepoys or other declared enemies of the state or those who have opposed British troops with weapons in hand. I warn those who disobey this order that they will be considered enemies of the British government and treated as such.

The proclamation was signed by Sir Robert Hamilton. No longer able to exercise power, he had first taken refuge in Calcutta, and then made it to Bombay by a circuitous route.

When Akbar finished reading, he muttered contemptuously, 'When the British are powerless, they rattle their sabres.'

'If they talk like that it means they must be preparing for something.'

The next morning, 1 January 1858, the Rani sent an official letter to Sir Robert Hamilton, written in gold ink and wrapped inside a small brocade bag.

She quoted the report she had sent him at the time of the mutiny at Jhansi and his response confirming her restoration to her throne. Then she told him of the Rani of Orchha's surprise attack, which had left Jhansi's army and finances depleted. The danger of a similar unexpected attack by any of her neighbours remained a constant possibility, and she feared that next time she would not be able to stop it. Therefore, she asked for British assistance...although she did not point out what kind of assistance she required, which exempted her from placing her troops at their disposal should they demand it. Against the eventual arrival of the British in Jhansi, she was implicitly declaring herself their ally by placing herself under their protection, but she was committing herself to nothing.

As British clouds gathered over central India, she sensed that peace in Jhansi could be maintained only through diplomatic subtlety entirely foreign to Akbar's nature. She did not reveal to him that she had written to Sir Robert Hamilton.

Excerpts from a letter from Roderick Briggs to Sarah Brandon, dated 1 January 1858, Indore.

At last, beloved Sarah, I shall be able to fight, for we are about to embark on the campaign, and I could have wished no better gift from the New Year.

Already the region is being stabilized. Because southern India remains loyal to us, one of our army corps managed to retake from Firoz Shah, a member of the family of the former Great Moghul, the important city of Mandisore, which he had seized a few months earlier. We continue to rely on the unwavering support of the Maharaja of Gwalior, who despite continual pressure, has remained completely loyal and has informed us that he will place his personal army at our disposal as soon as circumstances allow.

And a certain Tatya Tope, the only rebel general of consequence, has just been turned back at Cawnpore, although he came within inches of beating us.

Several times I had asked to be transferred to the army fighting so bravely at Cawnpore and Lucknow. My requests were refused and I have had to wait long months in enforced idleness that has weighed upon me cruelly. Then our compatriots at home, enraged by the newspaper reports of Indian atrocities, enlisted by the thousands, and long-awaited reinforcements have begun to arrive at Bombay. My regiment, the Third Bombay Europeans, has already reached Indore, our army's assembly point, and I have been appointed aide-de-camp to General Rose, who is to command it.

The young man did not mention that he owed the appointment to the influence of his father, an important member of parliament from Devonshire. Nepotism was so entrenched in the mores of the British ruling class that it seemed only natural to those it benefited. Roderick's promotion, besides, was far from honorary, for it brought responsibilities and did not exclude him from actual combat in the field. In his letter Roderick overflowed with admiration for his superior.

...General Rose, a remarkable man, though Scotch and Catholic, is a philosopher and a hero. Tall, lean, and gaunt, he is as resolute as he is compassionate. He fought heroically in Crimea and then served in Egypt and Constantinople, where he acquired a profound knowledge of the Orient. Staggered by the events in India, he did not hesitate, despite his age—fifty-seven—to place his sword, once again, at the service of the nation.

Nor did Roderick have any reservation about Rose's political alter-ego, Sir Robert Hamilton, 'a model administrator whose firmness will prevent any temptation to negotiate with the rebels or pardon the assassins.' Roderick was alluding to the indulgence, much criticized, shown by the Governor General of India, Lord Canning, and some of his associates.

Thanks to his position as aide-de-camp, Roderick shared the secrets of the powers that be. He knew the plan of campaign; his regiment was to head towards the northeast, take Kalpi, and join up with the British army that was fighting in the former kingdom of Oudh at Lucknow and Cawnpore.

He did not hide from his fiancée the difficulties awaiting him and his companions. Their army numbered only four thousand five hundred troops, against thousands upon thousands of rebels spread throughout the region. They would have to cross five hundred miles of difficult country, jungle and ravines, much of it almost impenetrable. How many obstacles await! How many unknown dangers!

> *We have received disturbing information from Orchha, a small state that borders on Jhansi and is our faithful ally. It seems that the Rani of Jhansi might not be the friend of the British she claims to be. An inquiry has been ordered into her actions and additional information requested from Orchha. Jhansi lies on our route, and although the Rani has maintained an apparent neutrality until now, we cannot be certain she will not greet us with cannon fire.*

One morning in late January, as the Rani was returning in state from the temple of Lakshmi, she noticed an unusual gathering around the mosque in Jhansi's principal street. She ordered her palanquin to halt, pushed aside its embroidered muslin curtain, and asked one of her officers what was happening.

'It is Prince Firoz Shah preaching to the Muslims.'

That is how the Rani learned, to her great surprise, of the presence in Jhansi of the Great Moghul's nephew who, after capturing and then losing the city of Mandisore, had led his men into guerrilla warfare against the British, causing them endless trouble in the region. Why had no one told her?

Firoz Shah was staying with a rich Muslim merchant and he had been extremely discreet. On that Friday his troops—a thousand men—

had joined him and were pitching their camp outside the town while he made his first public appearance. Taking advantage of the fact that it was the Muslims' holy day, he had come to the mosque to preach Jihad, Holy War.

A stirring in the crowd alerted the Rani that Firoz Shah was about to leave the mosque. She was able to make out, in the midst of the faithful, a small man wearing the garb of a pious Muslim, a white jellabah without ornament or embroidery. Firoz Shah walked down the steps of the mosque, slowly made his way to the Rani's palanquin, and saluted her by bringing his hand from his heart to his mouth and then to his forehead.

There was a long silence while the Rani examined him. Just as Diwan Naransin had told her, Firoz Shah was handsome. He seemed even younger than his age; one would have put him at around eighteen. His small stature did not detract from the nobility of his bearing nor from his obvious energy. His slightly hooked nose betrayed his breeding; his fleshy lips, sensuality. In his very large dark eyes there was something distant and even haughty.

In a dry voice the Rani asked him the same question she had put to Tatya Tope, 'What have you come here for, Prince?'

'I go where God takes me, Rani.'

'How is it that you've been here a week and did not come to pay your respects, as custom demands?'

'A pious man, a warrior has more important tasks than acts of protocol.'

The Rani lost her temper. 'By what right do you preach in our capital and camp your troops in our territory?'

'The Warriors of Faith, provided they bother no one, pitch their tents where they can. As for myself, Allah has ordered me to spread His word.'

The Rani gestured and her procession set off briskly. She turned, and through the muslin curtain she saw Firoz Shah standing among the faithful watching the palanquin move away, a thin smile on his lips.

Furious on her return to the fort, she sent an order to Firoz Shah to remove himself and his troops from her state without delay. His only answer was a request for an audience. The Rani accepted without asking anyone's advice, on a vague impulse. Firoz Shah's personality intrigued her. Nevertheless, she was careful not to receive him during the daily durbar, which would have been too solemn an occasion. After all, Firoz Shah was a rebel leader. But since he was also an imperial prince, she did not want to receive him in an inappropriate manner. She awaited him late in the morning in her private audience chamber, surrounded by her principal aides.

When he entered, she was once again struck by the nobility of his bearing. Everything about him spoke of his breeding, down to the austerity of his attire. His white jellabah stood in sharp contrast with the complicated uniforms of the Rani's officers and the glittering brocades of her ministers. Only Akbar, as always, was dressed in white, like Firoz Shah.

The Prince's opening statement was almost a challenge.

'This first audience will also be my last, since I am an undesirable.'

The Rani surveyed him carefully before answering, 'Jhansi is at peace and intends to remain so. We do not wish to harbour foreign armies on our soil.'

'And what will you do when the British army arrives from Indore? Will you throw them out too?'

'We shall maintain the neutrality that is our salvation.'

'Neutral! You, Rani? You, the heroine of our revolution?'

The Rani thought he was mocking her. Sensing her surprise, Firoz Shah continued, 'All the revolutionaries admire you for having run the British out of Jhansi and freed your kingdom. Everywhere one hears praise for your courage and skill in war. We all consider you one of us.'

This allegation annoyed the Rani terribly.

'We might be inclined to join the revolution,' she replied, 'if it sometimes won battles instead of losing them.'

Firoz Shah burst into laughter. 'You're alluding to my loss at Mandisore...'

The Rani interrupted.

'To Mandisore and many other defeats.'

The exchange of half-acerbic, half-insolent remarks went on for some time. The Rani's aides were convinced that Firoz Shah was exasperating their mistress. Only Akbar and Mandar, who witnessed the audience, guessed the truth. The Rani's answering the new arrival with such vivacity meant that an instantaneous connection had been established between them.

'I plan to hold a celebration. It's been a long time since we've had one,' the Rani announced a few days later. Akbar, who adored festivities, encouraged her.

It was not late enough in the season, nor warm enough, for the feast to be held in the gardens. The Rani thought the throne room too small, so she had the palace's sunken courtyard transformed into a banquet-hall. A huge, richly-embroidered canopy of red cloth was stretched between the terraces. In each window overlooking the courtyard, a torch lit up the gold of the canopy and the whiteness of the walls. In each arcade on the ground floor stood one of the Rani's guards in a glittering red-and-gold uniform, motionless as a pillar. The whole courtyard was covered by a red carpet on which stood low tables clothed with brocade so sumptuous that its red background was almost buried under the gold. The entire dinner was served on dishes of finely-worked silver. The Rani had invited only men, as much to honour a military leader like Firoz Shah as to allow the ladies of the court to respect the rules of purdah towards a Muslim.

For Firoz Shah had been invited. He had sent away his army, not outside the Rani's territory, but to a more discreet location several miles from the town, not far from the Kalpi road. The Rani had not repeated her request that he leave; nor had he brought it up again. A few advisers, including Kashmiri Mull, had protested the Rani's intention to invite a rebel. The Rani had swept aside their flimsy objections. After all, her neighbour was the Maharaja of Gwalior, the most powerful and prominent of the allies of the British, and had he not personally gone to visit the camp of the rebels' most illustrious chieftain, Tatya Tope? Had he not sent the Nawab of Banda a letter congratulating him on a victory over the British?

Firoz Shah was late and the dinner had already begun. Around the tables dignitaries, covered with jewels and embroidery, looked like circles of gold and gems. To the usual vegetarian fare the Rani had added dishes of lamb in honour of her Muslim guest, and alcohol to satisfy her military officers. She noticed that Akbar, seated at a nearby table, was spurning wines from Afghanistan in favour of enormous glasses of arak. As usual, he was joking with the guests and his laughter was heard often.

Seated next to the empty pillow that had been set out for Firoz Shah, the Rani was wearing her usual white sari, but unusually enhanced by heavy jewellery. That evening her astrologer had allowed her to wear diamonds, ambiguous stones that were not to be worn every day. From her neck hung a breastplate of very large diamonds of different cuts, and from her ears dangled cascades of similar stones. Since Roger's death she no longer wore the ring he had given her but kept it in a chest in her room. On each of her fingers was a diamond ring of a different colour—pink, yellow, blue. Her head tilted at a characteristic angle, she awaited the arrival of Firoz Shah.

At last there he was. He had exchanged the dress of a devout Muslim for that of an imperial prince, and the Rani was struck by his elegance. He wore a long waistcoat and a huge turban of green brocade, the colour of Islam, white baggy breeches and green slippers embroidered with gold. He had casually coiled around his neck several strands of uncut emeralds strung on a thread of gold.

The Rani ate practically nothing, but she noticed that her guest attacked every dish with an apparently insatiable appetite that contrasted with his self-restraint and his frail physique.

Although Indian custom requires that one eat in silence, she wanted to chat with him. A need to vent her feelings made her speak of the difficulties of her task and the burdens of power.

'Come,' interrupted Firoz Shah. 'Don't complain. You love being queen, I know that.'

His insolent frankness did not offend the Rani. She sensed that she intrigued Firoz Shah, that he wanted her to like him.

'Last May,' he said, 'I came back from a long pilgrimage to Mecca and landed in Bombay on the eve of the rebellion. I left for Delhi as soon as I heard that my uncle Bahadur Shah had been returned to his throne. But on the way I learned I wouldn't be well-received there. Competition around the person of the Great Moghul, barely reestablished in power, was very great. And so, wandering here and there, I settled down in a village not far from Mandisore and began to preach holy war against the British. The Maharaja of Gwalior, on whom Mandisore is dependent, sent troops to arrest me. I took refuge in an abandoned temple in the jungle where, soon, I received some pilgrims, dissatisfied believers. One day, these faithful raised the banner of rebellion and I appeared at their head before the walls of Mandisore; the inhabitants were only waiting for a sign... The authority of the Maharaja of Gwalior and the British was overthrown and their representatives taken prisoner. I let myself be proclaimed king...only to have the city retaken from me by those same Englishmen just a few months later.'

He spoke casually, continuing to pick at the various dishes, but then he grew animated as he described the clandestine existence he had led ever since, the jungle camps, the night marches by moonlight, the ambushes laid for the British...

The Rani sighed at the evocation of this adventurous existence. Still, wanting to be sincere, she admitted the truth:

'Yes, I do like to be queen. That's what I was trained for; I wouldn't feel at ease in any other role. Not that this one doesn't have its difficulties, particularly right now—the greatest of them being to maintain the neutrality of my kingdom at any price despite the situation at large and certain untimely visits.'

The allusion did not even draw a smile from Firoz Shah. He answered, 'And you are also neutral in your heart?'

The Rani smiled.

'I cannot pass for a heroine of the revolution, as you so kindly described me, dear Prince, while remaining indifferent to that same revolution. Let me say it again—the interests of my kingdom require that I remain at peace with the British.'

'Then you'll have to hope the British allow you to remain at peace with them.'

'What do you mean, Prince?'

'We will speak about that later.'

They were interrupted by servants bringing the sweetmeats, the high point of the feast. The cooks had wrapped the different pastes in gold leaf.

'If I were the former king of Oudh,' the Rani said, jokingly, 'I would have had them sprinkled with crushed emeralds. But I find those stones hard to digest, even in powdered form.'

During dances by the nautch girls, the Rani resumed their conversation, 'Do you think the British will win?'

'Who knows?'

'What are you fighting for, then?'

'For the faith.'

'Oh no, Prince. You fight not for the faith but for adventure. You were born an adventurer, you've always sought adventure.'

For the first time, Firoz Shah smiled at being unmasked. Lightly, he answered, 'Life itself is an adventure. Why shouldn't the faith be another?'

'Aren't you even afraid of death?'

'I await death, and perhaps, I even seek it. Believe me, death is a more loyal companion than this life you seem to cling to.'

The Rani felt that he had suddenly become distracted. A few moments earlier, he had noticed one of the nautch girls, the most beautiful of them, and now his eyes were following her intently as she danced.

The Rani was more and more intrigued by this young man who concealed the soul of an adventurer, who had seen it all, this pale-faced prince who must have been a great connoisseur of women. The look with which he was undressing the nautch-girl was unmistakable.

The final act of the spectacle awaited the guests on the terraces of the palace. The fireworks display, a vogue imported by the Great Moghuls a few centuries before, was about to begin.

At a signal, thousands of rockets shot up from the fort's three enclosures to mingle above the guests and tumble to earth in multi coloured shooting stars. Then larger-than-life animals, made of a flammable paste, were set afire. Peacocks, elephants, cobras and tigers burst into flames at the top of each tower and, for a few minutes, seemed to be alive. The Rani looked around her. Slightly drunk, Akbar was staggering as he stared up at the fireworks, mouth open, uttering shouts of enthusiasm, like a happy child. Firoz Shah looked on as an expert, immobile, smiling with satisfaction, as though each rocket were a personal homage.

When the celebration came to an end, it was too late for the Rani to join Akbar. It did not upset her. That night she preferred to be alone.

The next morning the Rani moved Firoz Shah into one of the apartments of her palace reserved for the most important guests. To the protests of some of her advisers, she answered that an imperial prince merited such treatment; to others, that honour compelled her to give shelter to a fugitive.

One afternoon, when the women had retired and the palace slumbered through the sacrosanct hours of the siesta, she crept from her room. Like many Indian palaces, this one contained a labyrinth of rooms without end, passages with no apparent purpose, stairways hidden in walls, concealed recesses and entresols. Although the hallways and antechamber were filled with loitering servants, there was always a way, for someone who knew the palace well, to move about without being seen. That is what the Rani did to make her way to Firoz Shah's apartment. Trembling, her heart beating, she hesitated at the door of his room, touching the handle. Then, resolutely, she walked in.

She found him lying on the low wide bed of gilded wood and ornate columns. He was naked save for a small loin-cloth. He looked at her without saying anything as she walked to the bed and lay down at his side.

He did not move. Then he said simply, 'Why do you want to make love to me?'

'Because I desire you.'

'So you wish to add another lover to your collection?'

'I want only you.'

Firoz Shah revealed himself to be a lover of refined and expert sensuality. And yet, immediately after they had made love, he covered himself as though ashamed of his nakedness. This unexpected modesty added spice to Lakshmi's pleasure. She had the delicious impression she had just led the young prince astray.

Convinced that her escapade had gone unnoticed, Lakshmi smiled absently, as though in a dream, while Mandar brushed her hair. That was the last ritual before going to bed and the other servants had already retired. With her usual frankness, Mandar went straight to the point:

'It used to be that you had no lover, and now you have a whole regiment.'

'A regiment! Don't exaggerate! What can I say, Mandar? For the first time in my life I feel desirable.'

'And yet the Englishman desired you. Akbar desires you, and he proves it every night.'

'That's true, but first they fell in love with me. Now I feel capable of having a lover without first feeling affection. During all those years of marriage, I was frustrated; I want to make up for lost time.'

'And so now, it's you who takes the initiative—a queen's privilege, I suppose.'

'In order to cope with my tasks, to withstand the pressures of my position, I need distractions, and I can find them only by going in search of a new adventure.'

'Do you really want to be like those debauched queens who are laughed at by their courts? Is Akbar not enough?'

'I love Akbar as I would a friend. Our affair has become a sort of habit—an exquisite one, of course, but a habit all the same.'

'And how will you avoid making Akbar suffer? I don't want you to hurt him. He's a good man and he loves you.'

'He won't hear anything about it. Trust me.'

9

Three days later the Rani unexpectedly had a decisive conversation with Firoz Shah. It was siesta time, just after they had made love. The Rani was about to leave to preside over the daily durbar when she suddenly asked him, 'Why did you tell me, on the night of the feast, that Jhansi's neutrality was becoming an illusion?'

Firoz propped himself up on his elbows, stared at the Rani pensively, and answered, 'Because the British are going to attack you.'

'Are you mad? Why would they attack me? I'm not their enemy.'

'First, because they're convinced you are responsible for the massacre of their countrymen in Jhansi last June.'

'That's not possible. I told them what happened and they accepted my explanations.'

'Believe me, Lakshmi, I have agents almost everywhere and I'm well-informed on the intrigues at Bombay and Indore. From the very beginning there have been doubts in high places about your innocence. After all, the British had dethroned you, and the revolution put you back in power. But you had restored order to Jhansi and therefore, you were still the most tolerable solution for them. So they pretended to believe you. But recently, they managed to get their hands on some proof, on testimony that incriminates you.'

'And who gave it to them?'

'Who knows? Someone who wants to harm you, out of jealousy, perhaps. Or some ambitious person who wants to rob you of your power. Or else some intriguer paying court to the British. It doesn't really matter. What's important is that the British believed his lies, believed these primitive forgeries because they wanted to believe them.'

'I don't understand.'

Firoz Shah jumped from the bed and stood in front of the Rani, oblivious, for once, to his nakedness.

'Why, you ask? Because the British are masters at twisting the truth. In order to stoke the anger of their countrymen, they have already spread the word that we raped their wives and tortured their children, which is completely untrue. The British speak of nothing else and that, in turn, allows them to massacre and torture us with a clear conscience. Recently, they've invented a redoubtable enemy with whom to galvanize the troops they are massing near Indore. And that enemy is you. They fear you because of your independence. You're not ready to lick their boots like the Maharaja of Indore or of Gwalior.'

The Rani interrupted, 'The Maharaja of Gwalior is on the side of the rebellion. I saw the letter he wrote to the Nawab of Banda congratulating him on having gotten rid of the British.'

'That was just a gesture. Tomorrow he'll be back at the feet of the British as he always has been. Whereas you shall always be incorruptible, proud and independent. And because of that, you are more of a threat to them than the worst of the rebels.'

The Rani stared into Firoz Shah's large black eyes, as though she wanted to pierce the secret of his soul; then she left the room without another word.

That afternoon the durbar was unbearable for the Rani. She had to make a prodigious effort to concentrate on the matters that were put to her. It seemed to her that the stream of petitioners would never end.

Akbar, who had noticed how distracted she was, sought her out after the meeting. The Rani could not be found. At last the guards directed him to the little temple of Ganesh below the second enclosure where, during the siege of the fort by the rebels, she had met Roger for the last time. An old attendant slumbered in a tiny corner of the sanctuary. The Rani knelt before the statue of Ganesh. Was she praying? Her lips were tight, her features tense, her face deathly pale.

'What's wrong, Lakshmi?'

'The British are going to attack us.'

They walked out of the temple and sat down on a bench, roughly hewn out of the rock. The shade of an old tree hid them from the sight of townspeople and peasants who were climbing or descending the paved path linking the town to the fort.

The Rani told Akbar what she had heard from Firoz Shah without, of course relating the circumstances of their conversation. She could not—she would not—completely believe the injustice, the monstrosity the British were preparing. But Akbar, much more wary of them, thought Firoz Shah was quite right.

'It's not possible,' exclaimed the Rani. 'I did not go to fight alongside the revolutionaries even though my heart urged me to do so. I humiliated myself before the British, even going so far as to write them several times. I was even ready to open my doors to them. Against all odds, I have maintained peace in Jhansi. It can't be that all my efforts came to naught.'

'No, not for nothing, Lakshmi. Thanks to you, Jhansi had seven months of peace and prosperity while everywhere else a storm was ravaging India.'

'Perhaps my duty is to surrender to the British in order to spare my people? They'll drag me into a courtroom, but I'll defend myself against their accusations, and defeat their prejudice against me.'

'You, surrender? Never!' cried Akbar. 'I won't let you do it. Besides, it would be useless. We know all about British justice. If they don't want to believe in your innocence, you will never convince them of it. On the contrary, they'll be only too happy to confuse you and prove your guilt. And then, it's just naive to think that giving yourself up would save your people. The British would just enslave them. Is that what you want?'

'All I can do now is what I wanted to avoid at any price—throw my Jhansi into the war. The British are really very skilful,' she added bitterly. 'They make me a murderess at the very moment when they take the offensive.'

'We'll defend ourselves. We defeated the Rani of Orchha. And if necessary, we'll ask for help from Tatya Tope and his army. India is far from beaten and we won't be.'

'And I might actually become the revolutionary heroine I'm supposed to be,' added the Rani with a humourless laugh that was painful to Akbar's ears.

The next morning's session of the council unfolded as usual. Seeing the Rani enthroned among her advisers, seated like bankers on their brocade pillows, it would have been difficult to imagine that the fate of Jhansi was at stake. She had asked Firoz Shah to attend the session to repeat the information he had received. When he had finished, she proposed once again to surrender herself to the British in order to save her people from the disasters of a war. Perhaps she did this more out of clever design than conviction. Just as she expected, her suggestion drew unanimous protests. Diwan Naransin declared that the British must be resisted and Jhansi defended at all costs, without compromise or concessions. Old Kashmiri Mull, who in the name of wisdom habitually opposed the Diwan's proposals, favoured negotiation. He had trouble believing entirely in the heinousness of the British and perhaps he had a more realistic view than his colleagues of their military strength. He suggested that the Rani write them once again to sound out their intentions.

'I've written too often already,' she protested. 'It served no purpose other than to humiliate me. I won't do it again. Besides, the fact that Sir Robert Hamilton didn't answer my last letter is ample proof of the accuracy of Prince Firoz's words.'

Moropant came to his daughter's support.

'The Rani is right. The British are stubborn, and nothing will convince them of our good faith. We will have to defend ourselves,' he added, without conviction.

'With what?' asked Sanghar Singh.

Deep within, the head of Jhansi's army was intimidated by the British, whom he had never seen and who, in his primitive imagination, had grown to assume the size and shape of legendary monsters. One didn't wage war against monsters! And Sanghar Singh began a detailed description of the meagreness of the treasury, of the insufficiency of Jhansi's troops and artillery.

His dispirited remark angered Ghulam Ghaus Khan, the head-gunner.

'With my guns I have enough to stop all the British in the world. Don't worry, Rani. We shall win.'

Unfortunately, his enthusiasm was based more on conviction than reality and fooled no one. The Rani spoke up.

'By assuming power I wanted only to protect the throne of my son, the legitimate ruler, until he comes of age. I could abdicate and the British, who hold me personally responsible for the massacre, would have no further reason to attack Jhansi. Since you don't wish me to give myself up to them, I'll simply disappear.'

Firoz Shah, who until then had not opened his mouth, spoke warmly, 'Come with me, Rani. Let us go with my army, and together we shall fight the British on the battlefields.'

Akbar jumped up from his cushion. Red with anger, his eyes flashing, he answered, 'It's obvious, Prince, that you don't know Jhansi. The people will never allow their queen to go. They are ready to die, all of them, rather than lose her.'

Firoz Shah's large black eyes narrowed as he stared at Akbar Khan with disdain.

'The inhabitants of Jhansi run the risk of losing their queen and their lives.'

The British, he explained, were holding the entire population of Jhansi as well as their queen responsible for her crimes. Jhansi had rebelled, Jhansi would have to pay. Thus, it would be easier for them to crush the kingdom under their boots.

There began between Firoz and Akbar a verbal duel that was the climax of the session. Firoz maintained that neither Jhansi—nor any other city—could be defended against the science and technique of the British armies. He knew this from his own painful experience at Mandisore. It would be necessary to retire with arms and supplies into the jungle, and from there, wage a guerrilla campaign. Akbar insisted that Jhansi could hold off the British with its fortifications, with a newly-assembled army, with weapons that could be bought, and cannon that could be forged.

Firoz Shah did not raise his voice. He spoke deliberately, defending his plan in the name of reason, countering Akbar's objections point by point. The calmer he remained, the more Akbar lost his temper. His eyes flashed lightning, he gesticulated, shouted, trampled logic underfoot.

The Rani put an end to the quarrel, merely raising a hand to silence the two men. Then she called for Damodar. The child came in and stepped forward, intimidated by the grave faces of the advisers. The Rani took his hand.

'Listen carefully, my child. The British want to seize your throne and enslave your people. We shall not accept this. And so, we are going to war. May the gods assist us.'

The week which followed was one of agitation and, to tell the truth, confusion. Morning and evening, the Rani held meetings to prepare for Jhansi's defence. Her afternoons were spent with Firoz Shah and her nights with Akbar. Her advisers, galvanized by her resolution, were now all in favour of resistance. Proposal followed counterproposal during interminable debates. The palace was filled with feverish activity and considerable disorder, but the Rani's confidence was returning.

The war with Orchha had proved to Lakshmi that she could win. Her nature was no longer under the constraints of politics; she burned with the desire to fight. Her imagination fed on epic tradition. She could see herself galloping at the head of her troops like the ancient heroines whose exploits she had admired as a child.

Around Lakshmi everyone was brushed by the same excitement.

Damodar, affected by the general nervousness, no longer feared to barge into his mother's apartment, uninvited, at any hour of the day. He would interrupt her in order to tell her gallantly of the progress he was making in his military training. Lakshmi had entrusted him to one of her officers to initiate him in the art of war. She listened to him with pride, then dismissed him absent-mindedly.

With Akbar, she went from worry that bordered on dejection to optimism that approached outright gaiety. Akbar alternated between jealousy and tenderness. At every opportunity he gave her to believe that he suspected her liaison with Firoz Shah.

'Do what you want, but don't make a fool of me by inventing ridiculous pretexts to be alone with him!'

Akbar's reproaches depressed her and suddenly she would see everything on the dark side. Then he would cheer her up and paint rosy pictures of the future. He made her laugh, he took her in his arms, and together they would fall into his bed.

Akbar affected her; Firoz bewitched her. His seductiveness mixed with cynicism, his lucidness, his mystery were for her a powerful magnet. At siesta time she would rush to him. Sometimes she found his room empty. Perhaps some Koranic lesson had kept him at the mosque long past the noon prayer?

In fact, the Rani suspected him of having gone to call on a nautch-girl. She did not hold it against him; although she desired Firoz Shah and enjoyed his company, she was not in love with him. During one of their conversations, the Rani said, pensively, 'You come from nowhere, on your way to some unknown destination—like a messenger. But a messenger of what? Of destiny?'

'Or of death. I might be the messenger of death.'

'Death! You talk about nothing else. As for me, I am life.'

'And that's why you'll be spared. But death will take me and take me soon, because I am ready for it.'

Troubled, the Rani looked at this very handsome young man who had been born without hope, and whispered, 'You are a prince of darkness.'

One morning at the hour when she went to visit her horses, the Rani was surprised not to find Akbar there. One of the officers explained that he had gone to recruit soldiers in the neighbouring villages. What? Without warning her, without leaving her a note, without having said anything about it last night? The Rani wondered what had bitten him without wanting to admit that it might have been simple jealousy. In the following days she received no news. She remained convinced that he had not gone away for long. But Mandar thought otherwise and did not hesitate to say so.

'You've lost him. And it serves you right. Too bad for you.'

Where were the British? What were they up to? One thing was certain; their army had left Indore. Travellers reported they were force-marching on Jhansi without rest, ten thousand, one hundred thousand strong. Spies claimed they had changed their direction, they were marching east. Indeed, they had already seized Sagar and Garhakota. The Rani pored feverishly over her maps; did they mean to dislodge the rebel Nawab of Banda? Had they decided to leave Jhansi alone?

It was growing increasingly difficult to get reliable news, for between Jhansi and the rebels stretched a vast unsettled region scoured only by uncontrolled bands. Frightened petty kings still faithful to the British, shut up in their palaces, had allowed anarchy to take over.

Akbar had not reappeared. The Rani felt some sadness and remorse, but also a kind of relief at no longer having to bear the brunt of the burdensome rivalry and tension between him and Firoz Shah which had been troubling her peace for some time now. And then Akbar, although a born leader, was not an expert tactician like Firoz Shah, who was giving the Rani precious advice for the organization of Jhansi's defence. Every day she inspected the repairs being made on the walls of the town and the fort. All the trees growing around them were cut down in order to provide their defenders a clear field of fire. She gave orders to stock tonns of rice, grain, flour and sugar against the eventuality of a siege. She ordered the manufacture of gunpowder and munitions, and opened two workshops to make cold steel blades and firearms. Ghulam Ghaus Khan, the head-gunner, worked tirelessly to repair the oldest cannons. Those too rusted to be useful were melted down to make new ones. A special war tax was levied on the population. The Rani set the example by sacrificing her gold and silver dishes in a public ceremony before the temple of Kali. First, she made offerings to the fearsome goddess, whose ornaments include necklaces of human skulls in order to ward off disaster and banish fear. Then, bending under the weight, her servants brought mounds of dishes, cups, and bowls of precious metals which she presented to the priests to be melted down.

Instinctively, she had understood that she was her own best asset in stimulating her subjects to donate money, and she was not above putting herself on view in order to stimulate their imagination.

Following her, the inhabitants of Jhansi came to present their voluntary donations—men, their gold and their dishes; women, their jewels. No one held back. The rich burghers' wives deposited in trays their most opulent necklaces, and the most humble slipped simple gold rings from their fingers.

Finally, the Rani had soldiers recruited from the entire region. Attracted by the reputation she had earned in the war against Orchha, a number of the rebels who had been fighting in the area answered her call. In a few days she had assembled a thousand men, who pitched camp around the town. Every day, accompanied by Damodar, she presided personally at the recruitment. Because Indians are by nature both chivalrous and affectionate towards children, she knew that the image of a woman and her young son, the one symbolizing frailty and determination, the other the future, would make a deep impression on new recruits.

She asked no man about his past or his origins, accepting everyone who came forward. One morning she saw before her Bakshish Ali, Jhansi's former head-jailer, who had presided over the massacre of the British. All his arrogance gone, dressed in rags, he had come humbly to re-enlist. Sanghar Singh, the commander of the army, was about to hire him when the Rani stepped in. She walked up to Bakshish Ali, looked him up and down, and said, 'You have no business being here among us. Go hang yourself elsewhere and never come back.'

Waves of horsemen began arriving in Jhansi, ten, twenty or thirty at a time, to place themselves under the Rani's banner. They were all men of the north, Pathans. Jhansi welcomed them with open arms, for the support of these fierce and loyal warriors was precious. These nomads came either from nearby or from distant provinces, having been notified by messages from their families or their tribes. All had been recruited, directly or not, by Akbar Khan. It was his contribution, his surprise, his gift to the Rani. Where was he? What was he doing? she asked the Pathans. Akbar Khan was travelling tirelessly, and because he was constantly on the move, no one knew where to find him.

At the moment she was thinking of him, Akbar was in a village only a few miles from Jhansi. From the steps of an old temple he was exhorting the peasants to become soldiers of the faith, freedom fighters, defenders of the Rani, whom he compared to Durga, the most seductive incarnation of Kali, the warrior-goddess. As he praised her gallantry, her generosity, her invincibility, the peasants were very surprised to see tears rolling down his face.

One of the scouts sent far to the south by the Rani returned exhausted to Jhansi to announce that, against all expectations, the British had forced through the three passes of Narut, Mandapur and Darooni. And yet, the revolutionaries, outnumbering the British two to one, had been prepared, waiting for them around those famous gorges and their natural defences of jungle more impenetrable than anywhere else, sheer cliffs and unfordable rivers. Still, the British had won through.

So the British had not turned east; they were headed straight for Jhansi. Lakshmi decided to write Tatya Tope, who was waging a guerrilla war in the region, and ask for the support of his army. Then she threw herself headlong into her task, stepping up the preparations for the defence of Jhansi and trying to foresee every eventuality. Learning from the disastrous example of so many leaders of the revolution, she wanted to leave nothing to chance.

In order to deny the British around Jhansi the grain, vegetables and firewood they needed, she decided on a scorched-earth policy.

Both peasants and great landowners were reluctant to allow the destruction of their fields and orchards. The Rani sent deputies to convince them, and where force was necessary, she did not hesitate to use it. Soon the once-green approaches to Jhansi looked like a dreary, uniformly grey desert.

For the first time in Indian history, she conceived the idea of assembling battalions of women—for infantry, cavalry and even artillery.

She rode out from the fort on her royal elephant, that albino envied her by all her neighbours, and went into the town's poorest quarters or into the surrounding villages. She would sit in the lotus position under a canopy of leaves hastily assembled in a square or before a temple. And she would speak without ever raising her voice, which would have been unworthy of a queen. She talked with the hundreds of women seated around her as though they were her equals, and they drank in her words.

The prestige of this queen who had descended from the heights of her palace to converse with her people, added to her natural eloquence, performed miracles. There was not a single woman in Jhansi who did not want to enlist in her army.

One day, she went to her town palace to supervise the stocking of provisions. She walked into the yard containing the outbuildings where, for months, Annabelle Phipps had been living in secret. The Rani had almost forgotten the existence of her former rival. She hesitated at the door, then walked in. Annabelle Phipps had recovered some of her beauty and most of her arrogance.

'I hope,' the Rani said, 'you have everything you need.' The Rani's regal tone of voice, the solicitude that Annabelle took for condescension, irritated her.

'I have everything I could expect to have in a prison,' she answered,

'In prison!' the Rani exclaimed. 'But you're free. Go out, if you want. Leave...'

'It's easy for you to free me now that a British army is nearing Jhansi to chase you out.'

Mrs Phipps's ingratitude stung the Rani.

'Between us, Mrs Phipps—who is it then who saved you?'

'I didn't want to survive Roger. I wanted to die with him. You have forced me to live on in mourning.'

Her bathos goaded the Rani to irony. Forgetting Annabelle's pitiful condition, she skirted the edge of tastelessness, 'Why don't you commit Sati, the ritual suicide of our widows?'

'My religion forbids me to kill myself, and I must live to bear witness to what happened here, to describe the murder of Roger and my countrymen.'

'Mrs Phipps, you're a very presumptuous woman. I could have you killed and thus eliminate the only witness.'

'Principal witness, yes, not the only one. Even in this prison where you keep me, I have contacts with the outside world. I know many Indians who are prepared to testify before my countrymen and expose all your crimes. Be advised, the hour of your punishment is drawing near.'

There was no dealing with this presumptuous, vindictive woman. The Rani shrugged and left her. Could it be true that Annabelle had contacts in town, that there were Indians in Jhansi prepared to crush their own ruler? The Rani preferred to think her former rival had made it all up. Nevertheless, their brief conversation left her shaken.

The Rani had begun receiving Firoz Shah in the sanctuary of her room, where no man other than her father had ever set foot. When the servant-girls had retired, he would arrive wearing the white jellabah of devout muslims or the garb of an imperial prince, dressed in green from head to toe and covered in emeralds. Detesting tobacco, he would inveigh against the smell of her hookah, even though she had taken care to mix rose-water with the bubbling water of the kaliah. Lying on her bed, Lakshmi liked to watch him undress before he came to join her, hugging her with all his strength.

During one of those nights of intense pleasure, as they lay naked among the rumpled silk covers and the gold-embroidered pillows, he said, suddenly, 'I've decided to leave.'

She half-raised herself from her pillows and stared at him, examining his long, pale, well-proportioned body. 'Well, Prince, so you're deserting us!'

Calmly, he explained that he intended to take his troops and head for Lucknow. A third British army had left Cawnpore to march on the former capital of the kingdom of Oudh, which had become the principal hotbed of revolution. The army was commanded by Sir Colin Campbell who, thanks to reinforcements from England, had assembled a considerable force—in fact, the largest British army India had yet seen.

'And you will come with me,' added Firoz Shah. 'I want to see you distinguish yourself on what promises to be the most celebrated battlefield in Indian history and the key to the future of our country.'

'You know well that I will never abandon my people, not even for the best of causes.'

General Rose's victory at the three passes of Narut, Mandapur and Dhamoni had made Firoz Shah doubt that Jhansi could hold out indefinitely against a British army. Instead of hanging on with little hope, it would be better to fall back on more defensible positions and regroup the forces of the revolution. The strategist's cold analysis annoyed the Rani.

'If you want to leave, that's up to you. But I'm convinced that by staying here we'll be able to hold off the British.'

In veiled terms Firoz Shah let her understand that he considered Jhansi strategically unimportant, that the fate of India would be settled at Lucknow.

'What would Jhansi be without you? No one would have heard of it if it weren't for its queen. It is your gallantry, your influence, your prestige that have made Jhansi what it is. Now the revolution needs you where it is going to have to fight for its very life. If Lucknow falls, do you think Tatya Tope will be able to hold Kalpi? Do you think, despite your optimism, that you yourself will be able to hang on here, at Jhansi?'

'There is a difference between us. You have no roots anywhere, and you are free to go where destiny calls you. But I am indissolubly linked—chained, in fact—to Jhansi.'

The Rani knew how much she would miss this lover, this accomplice, this lord who spoke the same language as she, but she did not tell him so. She expressed her regret only at the prospect of losing his advice and his troops. Firoz smiled.

'My troops wouldn't be of much use to you. The Pathan horsemen Akbar is sending you continue to swell the ranks of your army and soon, you won't know where to put them all. Besides, as you know, numbers are unimportant in fighting the British. As for my advice, I'm grateful that you consented to listen to it. But in fact, Lakshmi, you manage admirably well all on your own. You need only people who will follow your orders, and that is something I could never do.'

Now it was the Rani's turn to smile.

'I'll admit it,' she said, 'I'll regret not having gone off to fight with you.'

Firoz thanked her for her hospitality with the graciousness of a grand seigneur and the sincerity of a simple man. He would always think of Lakshmi, whose example would inspire him wherever he went. It was his way of telling her that he loved her, insofar as he could love anyone—a young man already tired of life, a prisoner of his destiny. 'Wherever I might be,' he said, 'call me and I shall come running.'

'Thank you Prince—but it will be up to you to guess when I need you.'

That disguised reproach was the only one she made. They separated without an embrace, without a word. Firoz Shah left Jhansi as dawn was already streaking the sky red.

Strangely enough, it was not Firoz Shah whom the Rani missed when he left, but Akbar. How much longer would he make her pay for her infidelity, when would he return? She felt alone—alone in her fear of the future, alone to face that British army, still only a ghost but whose advance was inexorably towards Jhansi.

10

Excerpts from a letter from Roderick Briggs to Sarah Brandon, dated 18–19 March 1858.

In the last ten days we have marched without encountering a single rebel. But a far more dangerous enemy has sprung up in their place, and that is the Indian summer.

The countryside around us was scorched and desolate. The wells were empty and the leafless trees gave no shade. The thick layer of dust on the roads was a considerable hindrance; the wind swept it up in gusts, blinding us, stinging our eyes, irritating every pore of our skin. At night the temperature in the tents reached a hundred and ten degrees. Like my companions I have had to shave my head entirely so as to avoid unnecessary heat. Sunburn has eaten away at my skin, particularly on my nose; I am not a pretty sight, and for the first time, I am not unhappy that we are apart, for I should be ashamed to let you see me like this. Yesterday we arrived at Chanchanpur, sixteen miles southwest of Jhansi. It has been almost three months since we left Indore. Rose made us lose considerable time on operations that took us far out of our way whenever fancy struck him to dislodge some band of rebels, and then by immobilizing us when he noticed his army was running short of supplies. And if we were able to force our way through the passes at Narut, Mandapur and Dhamoni, it was only at the cost of great, unnecessary losses in human lives. The officers denounce his lack of vigour, his negligence. The men are losing their trust in him. Everyone suspects that age is catching up with him. As for myself, I find it difficult to forgive him for putting off endlessly the moment when we shall give the Rani of Jhansi her just desserts. Not only did she deceitfully launch the rebellion in her kingdom in order to recover her throne, but she personally ordered the massacre of our compatriots. As I have written before, there can no longer be any doubt, for we have received irrefutable proof from Orchha. I have seen orders signed by her own hand, and letters written by her to the rebel leaders, her accomplices. It was she who murdered Roger. It is she whom I will make pay for the innocent victims sacrificed not only at Jhansi but also at Cawnpore, Delhi, everywhere her accomplices unleashed their barbarous cruelty. And it is upon her death that I shall have avenged him. I ask God for only one favour: to let me kill her with my own hands, that Messalina, that Jezebel. She has just furnished us with fresh proof of her duplicity. Sensing that the noose was tightening around her, she sent us an emissary who arrived here at Chanchanpur this morning. He is none other than her minister of justice, a certain Kashmiri Mull. I was with General Rose and Sir Robert Hamilton when they received him. He is a very alert old man, immaculately dressed, with a misleading air of dignity. He spoke decent English and seemed an old hand at legal argumentation, with fearsome powers of persuasion. His mission is surrounded with such secrecy that even the Rani's closest advisers have not been informed of it.

Through her envoy, the Rani offered to put up no resistance in the advance of our army, to pledge obedience to our government, and to return to it all the territories in her possession. She asks that in exchange, we spare her people destruction, looting and reprisals. She promised not to resist us...while at the very same moment she is harbouring one of the most notorious leaders of the rebellion, a man called Firoz Shah, while every day new guns emerge from her arsenals and new regiments of fanatics fill out her army, according to information relayed to us by our spies. I boiled inwardly as I listened to her emissary recite her honeyed promises, and trembled that Sir Robert might fall for it. God heard my prayers—or, rather, Sir Robert showed his customary firmness. It must be said that only a few days ago, he had received instructions from the Governor General of India. He told the emissary there was no need to return the Rani's estates to the British government since, legally, they belonged to us already. He added that the Rani and those suspected of having participated in the massacre would be tried by a commission named specifically for that purpose. If the Rani succeeded in proving her innocence, she would come to no harm. But first, she would have to come here immediately as a gesture of good faith, and remain under guard until her trial. The emissary answered that his mistress would never submit to such injustice and humiliation. She was, he added, innocent. Rather than surrender, she and her people would fight us to the death.

Negotiations then broke off. I hoped that Sir Robert would throw the Rani's emissary in jail, but we let him go. I was assigned to see him off. On our way, he attempted to make a case for her in the hope that I would pass it on to my superiors. I told him he was wasting his time and I didn't hide from him what I thought of his mistress, and I couldn't keep myself from mentioning Roger.

I sometimes wonder whether Rose is the man to fulfil the task that lies before us. At Jhansi, we shall fight not undisciplined gangs commanded by a multitude of inexperienced leaders, but a powerful, organized army directed by the Rani of Jhansi's iron hand. It must be admitted that this unscrupulous woman has proved herself an intelligent and able general. Nevertheless, I have a growing conviction that the hour of her judgement and the hour of my vengeance are approaching.

'19 March: Yesterday, I was filled with hope as I closed my letter. Today it is with rage and disappointment in my heart that I open it once more to tell you of the latest developments.

A week ago, the rebel General Tatya Tope, coming to the rescue of his accomplice the Rani of Jhansi, made a diversion and suddenly headed south east to attack the cities of Panna and Charkhari, whose rulers have always been our loyal allies.

Upon hearing the news, the Governor General in Calcutta became greatly agitated. If we allowed the Rajas of Panna and Charkhain to be beaten, no other rulers in India will rally to our side. So this morning there arrived a formal order from the Governor General Lord Canning instructing General Rose to abandon immediately any plans against Jhansi and rush to the aid of Charkhari.

We are being asked to abandon a target sixteen miles before us in order to attack another one eighty miles off our route. Of course, our

> *general is eager to comply, even if it means ruining our chances of taking Jhansi...*
> *So close to our goal, will it slip through our fingers? Uncertainty and confusion are the rule at the headquarters, and my hand trembles with anxiety as I write to you...*

'There is no room for traitors at the Rani's side,' Diwan Naransin spat out the sentence, staring Kashmiri Mull in the eye.

The Rani answered curtly, 'What my minister of justice did, he did at my express orders, and for the welfare of the state.'

This exchange took place during the council session that was held a few days after Kashmiri Mull's return from Chanchanpur. News of his short trip had quickly spread. Since the old man had always been a partisan of the British alliance, some said that he had tried to surrender to the British, others, that he had wanted to flee Jhansi but had been pursued and caught, and then been forgiven by the Rani. The most zealous of his political adversaries, including Diwan Naransin, went as far as to claim that, for a long time, he had been in the pay of the British.

Several of the talukdars and the noble tribal chiefs who assembled for the daily durbar proved more shrewd than Naransin. They understood that the Rani herself had wanted to negotiate with the British, and without directly challenging her, they demanded that in the future no accommodation with them be sought.

The Rani was forced to submit to the humiliation of agreeing. The failure of Kashmiri Mull's mission affected her in more ways than one. Kashmiri Mull had been less than stoical in his account of his hurried travels over ruined roads, carried out entirely at night so as to avoid attracting attention. He had been offended that the British received him not as the ambassador of a queen but rather as the accomplice of a criminal with whom they refused to negotiate. He had been astonished by the hatred he had felt in one of General Rose's aides. This young man, whose childish features were contradicted by hard eyes, thin lips and bloodthirsty words, had drawn up a bitter indictment of the Rani. He had mentioned having known Roger Giffard. From Kashmiri Mull's description, the Rani knew that he must be that Roderick Briggs of whom Roger had so often spoken. More than once, she had toyed with the idea of inviting him to Jhansi, when circumstances allowed. The absurdity of the war made it possible that now she should find Roger's best friend among the enemies preparing to fight her. She was devastated that, like the rest of his countrymen, Roderick held her responsible for the massacre and, therefore, for Roger's death. The horror of this accusation, which only revived painful memories, overwhelmed her. She sobbed in the arms of old Kashmiri Mull, who was astonished and stupefied to see her in a state so unlike her usual self-control.

Once she recovered, she was thankful for the absence of Firoz Shah. She would have been unable to bear the irony with which he would have greeted her final attempt to negotiate with the British.

Since his departure, the Rani had received news of him only through a proclamation dated from Lucknow itself in which he called on Muslim and Hindu alike to join forces in order to save their religions and exterminate the British.

Firoz Shah asserted that he had enrolled under his banner one hundred and fifty thousand men, sworn to victory or death. This extravagant figure only reminded the Rani of the boastful claims of other revolutionary leaders. Could it be that Firoz Shah was worth no more than the rest of them?

At Lucknow, the decisive battle had begun. Sir Colin Campbell had arrived before the city at the head of his formidable army. He was immediately joined by the Maharaja of Nepal with his Gurkhas, soldiers famous for their fighting spirit and cruelty. They had a tough opponent to contend with, for leading the city's innumerable defenders were the principal chiefs of the rebellion: the redoubtable Begum Hazrat Mahal, who had seized power in the former kingdom of Oudh; the Maulvi of Faizabad, whom the Rani had heard preach in Gwalior; Nana Sahib, whose movements in the last few months had been shrouded in mystery; and Prince Firoz Shah.

Immediately, the fighting reached extraordinary intensity. Each suburb, each enormous temple, each gigantic palace in the opulent city was fought for; the losses on both sides were terrible.

The Rani thought often of Firoz Shah, now in his element, and feared for him. But soon she had other things to worry about. The British army that had arrived at Chanchanpur sixteen miles from Jhansi had not fallen, as she had hoped, into the trap set by Tatya Tope with his diversion on Panna and Charkhari. Her spies, recruited mostly from among the Indian orderlies of the British field officers, had kept her informed of every word that was spoken inside enemy headquarters. From them she learned that, contrary to what Roderick thought, it was on General Rose's personal decision that his army had not gone to rescue Charkhari and instead, had continued its advance on Jhansi. That made the Rani reassess the general's qualities and she knew she would be facing a worthy adversary. The British impatience to attack Jhansi and capture her made her realize how important she was to them. She did not understand why, but she was forced to admit it.

A wave of panic seized Jhansi as the British army drew near. A certain number of its inhabitants fled—not the poor, but the richest who left for Gwalior with their belongings stacked on carts. The Rani did nothing to stop them. 'The beggars and I, we're enough for the job,' she muttered. Nevertheless, she wanted to show she was still as confident as ever.

She decided to give a special lustre to the festival celebrating the goddess Lakshmi, which fell at this time of year. She settled on 20 March, a Friday, considered a very lucky day. She sent Damodar with the men to pray at the temple. Dressed in pink brocade and glittering with diamonds, with the miniature sword Nana Sahib had given him at his side, the child sat proudly on Pari. The Rani never allowed anyone to ride her favourite horse, but she had made an exception for her son on this special occasion. Damodar's appearance on his horse, surrounded by ministers, dignitaries and guards, elicited an impassioned response from the population.

At the palace the Rani received women, without discriminating by caste, for a ceremony barred to men. The gold statue of the goddess had been moved from her private oratory to the throne room, where it was installed on a pedestal covered with lilies, marigolds and roses. On both sides of the idol rose pyramids of fruits and vegetables, and bowls and trays of silver had been placed before her to receive offerings.

The priests had taken from the coffers the goddess's richest ornaments which were used only on feast days, and they had covered her with them so that she seemed entirely encrusted with diamonds, emeralds and pearls. On the walls they had hung large religious paintings, the oldest and the most beautiful in the collections of the Rajas of Jhansi.

The sumptuous display was meant to show that, despite the circumstances, the lavishness of the court and the prosperity of Jhansi remained unchanged. And, as though they had gotten the word, all the guests had brought their best pieces. The wives of the noble tribal chieftains, of the court functionaries and the talukdars wore silk saris embroidered with gold; the women of the people, wives of artisans and shopkeepers, wore carefully-washed cotton saris of lively colours. The ceremony lasted from two o'clock in the afternoon to nine at night, half-social, half-religious. Between the sacred readings, the ladies took time to chat while nibbling sweetmeats, sitting in groups on the ground. The Rani moved from one to the other, wearing her usual close-fitting white sari. Smiling, more gracious and affable than ever, she had a word for everyone. And she achieved her purpose; delighted by her welcome, the women went home in a state of euphoria and confidence, to tell their husbands of their afternoon with the Rani, with an enthusiasm that gave them renewed courage.

No sooner had the ceremony ended than the exhausted Rani was brought a letter that had been thrown over the wall of the first enclosure. It was unsigned and only a few lines long:

> *The queen will go to meet the Captain accompanied by her prime minister and her father. No one else must accompany the queen and she must have no armed escort. She is to meet the Captain within the next two days; and no later.*

The sentinel who had picked up the letter was sent for and questioned. The letter had been thrown by a rider in uniform.

'Whose uniform?'

The sentinel could not say. The bizarre letter, its incorrect style and its anonymity awakened the Rani's suspicions. She sensed a trap and tore it up. Besides, the time for negotiations was long gone.

PART III

THE HEROINE

1

At five in the morning on 21 March, the Rani stood with her staff on top of the highest tower of the fort's ramparts, searching the horizon. The incomparable splendour of the Indian dawn was spreading over the land, bathing the misty countryside in pink and grey light.

Then, suddenly, the sun appeared. It set the tower afire, eased down the ramparts, crept along the ground and lit up the scorched earth and the blackened trunks of burnt trees. Only the screeching monkeys leaping from branch to branch disturbed the silence.

The Rani was the first to see, quite far in the west, a cloud of dust rising slowly between two rocky hills; it was the British army. Her stomach knotted in fear. She would have given anything to have Akbar at her side. Only he knew how to reassure her, only he could communicate his optimism. Where was he? Would he return, or had jealousy and suffering overcome him, driven him away from her forever? With prodigious effort, the Rani managed to remain impassive before her officers, who were watching her from the corner of their eyes. Just as courage is stimulated by the presence of others, so too is courage often no more than its own pretence.

For the next three days the Rani watched from the ramparts as the British army attempted to lay siege to Jhansi. It was clear to her that General Rose would not dare attack the almost impregnable fort. He would be able to take it only by starving it out through a siege that would take too long. As for the town, it was defended by four and a half miles of thick walls, reinforced with towers and bastions, and Rose did not have sufficient troops to encircle it. The modest force sent to him by the Rani of Orchha would not make much difference.

He would have to be content with positioning his batteries here and there and sending out patrols to prevent any attempted breakout. Firoz Shah had been mistaken, the Rani thought. Jhansi could hold out indefinitely—or at least until the summer reached its height to exhaust the besiegers.

The Rani was brought a proclamation that had just been thrown over the ramparts. In it Rose called upon the inhabitants of Jhansi not to resist, reminding them that all the cities taken by force by the British had been subjected to looting and massacre. The same fate awaited them if they defended Jhansi. The Rani saw Rose's use of this psychological weapon as further proof of his impotence, which only reinforced her optimism. Besides, in this field, she was more skilled than he. A queen, shrewd and Indian, she knew the mentality of her compatriots far better than he.

In response to General Rose's threatening proclamation, the Rani once again summoned the spokesmen of the various social classes, knowing that they never tired of meetings and palavers, and that to win them over, one needed only to allow them to express their opinions as long as possible.

She orchestrated this exceptional durbar perfectly. She began by asking the delegates point-blank whether they wanted to defend the city or seek peace. Speaking for her ministers, none of whom disowned him, Kashmiri Mull declared himself for peace but asked the Rani's opinion. She replied that her position did not count; she would place herself in the hands of her people, and accept their decision, whatever it might be.

One after another, the commander of her army, the noble tribal chieftains and the delegates of the town's citizens declared themselves in favour of maintaining Jhansi's independence—in other words, they opted to fight. Then the ministers, through Kashmiri Mull, bowed to the peoples' decision.

'Let us fight then for independence,' concluded the Rani, 'and let us keep in mind the words of our god Krishna, "We shall have freedom if we win; if we die on the battlefield, we shall win eternal glory and salvation."'

She was answered by an ovation. For every man in the room, this frail but indomitable woman seemed to incarnate their threatened city and their determination to defend its freedom.

Where she had been calculating in the staging of the durbar—especially in the intervention of the ministers—the Rani was completely honest with Damodar. She summoned him to the audience-chamber, and through the window, showed him the encampment and guns of the British. Then she sat him on the throne, and standing before him, like one of his subjects, said, 'My son, I govern only in your name. It is you who rules, you then who bears the real responsibility. You must decide whether or not you want Jhansi to be defended at any price.'

'Yes, I want it,' the child said in a low voice.

Damodar had known what his mother wanted to hear. His reply was enough to make her see in him a potential hero. She had not even stopped to wonder what she would have done if he had answered otherwise. Even so, Damodar asked in an almost audible murmur, 'When will Akbar Khan be coming back to defend us?'

'Soon, very soon, my son.' But as she said it she was not sure she believed it herself.

The child was still in the room when Moropant came in, bringing a note that a rider, dodging British patrols, had just brought in. The Rani read.

> *Your friends from Kalpi salute you, Rani. The enemies from outside, the accursed British, are a threat to you; but far more dangerous are the enemies within, who act in the shadows. You are betrayed, Rani, within your own council, there where you least suspect it. Watch everyone; trust no one and listen only to yourself.*

The Rani asked to see the man who had brought the note. But he had left immediately, claiming he had to return to Kalpi without delay.

'You are betrayed within your own council.' But by whom? Kashmiri Mull, the defender of the British alliance, was a natural target for suspicion. But was that not just too obvious? Besides, the Rani had no doubts about his loyalty. Sanghar Singh, the leader of the army? Could one really trust a former dacoit? Instinctively, the Rani rebelled against the thought that he might betray her.

She recalled that someone else had already mentioned the existence of traitors around her. When he had been arrested and imprisoned in the fort, Sadasheo, her late husband's cousin, the unlucky candidate for the throne, had boasted of having powerful friends within Jhansi itself:

'You would never suspect their identity, and when you find out, it will be too late,' he had said.

But today the note had been sent by 'friends from Kalpi'. This could mean only Tatya Tope or members of his inner circle. But nothing confirmed that they had written it. Was it not more likely just a British trick to sow suspicion in her camp and force her into mistakes? Since they had no other means of taking Jhansi, they might try anything. If only Akbar were here! But he had left her on her own, and on her own she would have to keep a cool head, on her own she would have to win.

She looked at her son, who had been watching her anxiously. He had said he wanted to defend Jhansi. And she had given her word—Jhansi would be defended.

On 25 March, the British opened fire on Jhansi. For five days and five nights their guns roared incessantly, echoed by those of the Rani. Sometimes the firing was so intense the ramparts seemed crowned by a wall of flames. At night the red-hot shells flying through the darkness seemed like monstrous fireflies. Together with the torches running along the fort's towers, they made a magnificent spectacle, accompanied by the wild music of drums, which reverberated incessantly.

No sooner would the British carve a hole or open a breach in the wall than the women of the Rani's battalions would rush up under fire to fill the gap, and if by any chance a cannon was put out of commission, they would repair it. Furthermore, they did not hesitate to take the gunners' places and fire cannon at the enemy.

The Rani could not be more proud of her amazons, and she envied them the opportunity to fight alongside the men. She would have liked to have had a specific task of her own.

Everyone, from the tallest to the shortest, had a station to man and a job to do. The Rani no longer had much need even to give orders. This siege was quite unlike battles she had dreamed of, and in sharp contrast to the brief, lively war she had fought against Orchha. As the days went by, the bombardment and even the tension had become routine, and time passed with discouraging slowness. The Rani felt depression begin to gnaw at her optimism. Only Akbar's high spirits could have driven it away. But Akbar had abandoned her. To chase away her dark thoughts, she immersed herself in her duties. She still had to show herself, to praise, to console, to encourage—in short, to set an example.

Every morning she toured the parts of the town most damaged by the shelling, and every evening she inspected her artillery on the ramparts. During the first bombardment the whistling of the shells and the explosions had terrified her; British shells were quite another matter compared to the Rani of Orchha's puny little cannonballs. She concentrated on controlling her nerves and her breathing so as not to jump at each detonation. That enabled her to forget her fear. Then she grew accustomed to the terrible din and even began to find a kind of intoxication in it. And she was fully aware of the bolstering effect her visits had on her troops.

Refusing defiantly to buckle on a battle dress, she wore her richest saris and her best jewels and demanded that Mandar and her other female attendants do the same. These women, dressed as if for a party, strolling graciously among the defenders under a hail of shellfire seemed to make a mockery of the British and of death.

On the evening of 30 March, the Rani had gone to inspect the ramparts that had been hit hardest by the British bombardment. She came to the bastion where Kiraun had been assigned. Kiraun had received permission to enlist in the Rani's batallions and was working furiously to drag sandbags much too heavy for her to fill gaps blasted in the ramparts by British shells. Mostly, however, she kept the entire bastion entertained. She hurled at the defenders her most salacious jokes and at the British the most appalling insults, of which she had accumulated an inexhaustible reserve in her former career.

That evening Kiraun swelled with pride at having been treated by the Rani, in front of her companions, as an old acquaintance. She was putting on airs, gambolling about, provoking the enemy and drawing laughs from the bystanders.

The Rani did not see the shell come in. She ducked instinctively. Next to her she heard a little birdlike cry. Kiraun had taken a direct hit. Her chest crushed, she had died instantly.

A raging desire to kill seized the Rani. She lunged at the nearest gunner, tore a lighted fuse from him and, without even aiming, fired the cannon. The explosion shook the entire bastion, and when the smoke cleared an ovation rose from the ramparts. The Rani had hit the most dangerous of the British batteries, knocking out its cannon and killing its crew. While the defenders of Jhansi cheered her, she knelt beside Kiraun's body and wept bitterly.

She had the corpse carried to the fort for a solemn burial. The Pathans sent by Akbar, whom she had made her crack regiment, served as an honour guard for the young girl who had died for Jhansi. In front of the cavalry in perfectly dressed rows, Kiraun's body was raised to a hastily-built pyre and the priests began to chant. An uninformed spectator might have thought it was a noble woman being buried, and not a miserable untouchable. The guns of both camps had fallen silent, respecting an unspoken truce. During the unexpected silence the Rani watched flames from the pyre rise into the pink and black sky.

With Kiraun gone, the Rani had lost another link to the memory of Roger. It seemed to her that Roger had been killed once again, this time by the British. Her hatred of them, increased tenfold, only strengthened her determination to never give in to them, no matter what happened.

31 March was a terrible day for the besieged. The artillery duel was particularly violent; the din, infernal smoke and dust darkened the air. On the ramparts the defenders were mowed down in entire ranks, to be replaced immediately by fresh troops.

The Rani was about to return to the fort when one of the sentries reported significant movement in the distance to the south. With her officers she rushed to the palace's highest terrace and peered south through her field glass.

About ten miles away an immense army coming from the northeast was advancing along the banks of the Betwa. Behind the russet hills and the dark stretches of jungle, the Rani could make out innumerable ants marching in impeccable formation; Lilliputian cannon and, visible despite the dust, minute orange spots, the flags of the Marathas. Tatya Tope was coming to the rescue. Like General Rose, he had grasped the strategic, and especially the political and symbolic, importance of Jhansi. The British wanted to take Jhansi, whatever the cost; the Indians knew that Jhansi must be held, no matter what the price.

At nightfall, a horseman, taking advantage of darkness and the sudden scurrying about by the British troops, found a way into the city, galloped to the fort, and asked to see the Rani. He was a man named Saltabada, one of Tatya Tope's officers, sent to pay his respects to the Rani and assure her that on the very next day the siege would be lifted. Caught between Tatya Tope's army and the defenders of Jhansi, the British army would be crushed. Captain Saltabada gave the Rani a letter bearing Tatya Tope's personal seal. It contained precise instructions. For tactical reasons stemming from his own plan of attack, the Rani was to limit herself to bombarding the British lines and not to attempt any attack until she had received a precise signal from him. These were orders from the revolution's best general, and the Rani of Jhansi felt both proud and relieved to be serving under him.

The news had spread quickly through the town. The people rushed to the ramparts and an immense shout of joy welcomed the sudden vision on a distant hill of a gigantic bonfire lit by Tatya Tope to announce his presence. The crowd's enthusiasm burst all bounds when on orders from the Rani, the guns of the fort began to fire salutes in return. Unable to bear that kind of provocation, the British replied: despite the darkness; they began to fire blindly into the city.

But the inhabitants of Jhansi could not have cared less. British shells had ceased to be messengers of death, now that deliverance was at hand. From the terrace of the palace where the Rani stood, the scene was magical. The dark sky was streaked with red trajectories of the shells. Intermittent explosions failed to drown out the sounds of drums and trumpets rising from the city, mingling with the joyous murmur of the crowd.

In the distance, in the vast, dark jungle, the campfires of Tatya Tope's army seemed like flickering fireflies, will-o'-the-wisp bearers of hope on their wings.

Excerpt from a letter from Roderick Briggs to Sarah Brandon, dated the evening of April 1.

For nineteen days my regiment has been camping east of Jhansi. My tent is pitched beside Lake Lakshmi. On the other bank is a sort of villa belonging to the Rani where, it is said, she used to stage orgies with her many lovers. Around our camp one sees only burnt fields. The ground is covered with a thin film of ash. There is no firewood, there are no fruits, vegetables or hay. Worst of all, there is no shade; the blackened stumps of trees don't provide any. The sun beats down on us without pity, and the enormous granite boulders reflect its rays and radiate fire. We've been shelling Jhansi since our arrival, wasting our ammunition for nothing. Yesterday, shortly before nightfall, we received messages via the optical telegraph system we had installed in the nearby hills indicating the approach from the north of considerable enemy forces. It was the army of Tatya Tope.

Caught between it and the Rani's forces, our situation seemed hopeless. I had visions of us already beating a retreat but General Rose kept a level head and revealed a firmness and daring I would not have believed him capable of.

He wanted neither to lift the siege of Jhansi nor allow Tatya Tope to march in with impunity. Under the cover of darkness, he sent the first brigade out to the Orchha road to block Tatya Tope's approach. As for the second brigade, which includes my regiment, he had it spread out to contain the besieged. I did not participate in the battle myself, but I was given a detailed account.

At dawn Tatya Tope's army emerged from the cover of the jungle. In apparently inexhaustible waves, cavalry, foot soldiers and artillery men galloped and ran towards our men to the beating of drums.

Rose had positioned our meagre artillery on both flanks so as to enfilade the enemy lines. Then, at the head of his dragoons, he charged the centre of Tatya Tope's army. Stunned by the vigour of this attack, and caught between the joint fire of our flanking artillery, the first enemy lines began to fall back.

Thereupon, Rose sent in our infantry on a bayonet charge. Seeing his front lines smashed, Tatya Tope ordered the rest of his forces to fall back and, to protect them, he set fire to the jungle. On Rose's order our soldiers leapt through the flames in pursuit. They soon trapped the rest of Tatya Tope's troops against the Betwa River and routed them. Tatya Tope was able to take only a few of his regiments with him as he retreated towards Kalpi.

We seized eighteen of his guns, his elephants, his camels, his war treasure and, best of all, an enormous amount of ammunition, which was, by that time, sorely needed. In two hours our fifteen hundred soldiers had put to flight an army of twenty thousand rebels. One can say without exaggeration that Tatya Tope's defeat was nothing short of ignominious. And yet, it was not that his men lacked courage; not one of them asked for mercy, and they left more than a thousand dead on the battlefield. Our side suffered only a score of casualties.

For us, the men of the second brigade maintaining the siege of Jhansi, the day was just as busy. No sooner had gunfire signalled the beginning of the battle than the Rani hurled at our painfully thin lines the most violent fire we had seen since the beginning of the siege, so constant that the towers of the fort were enveloped in fire and flames.

From the top of the ramparts, the rebels, galvanized by the certainty of Tatya Tope's victory, fired their muskets tirelessly in our direction. We expected at any moment that they would try to break out and attack us...

In the opposite camp the Rani's officers had indeed pleaded with her for permission to attack. The Rani continued to refuse, citing Tatya Tope's instructions. Too many battles had been lost by the revolutionaries because of their lack of cohesion. Sanghar Singh grew so angry that he threatened to take the fort's Pathan horsemen and lead them against the besiegers without awaiting orders.

'Who's in command here!' shouted the Rani, her features distorted by rage. 'You or I? I order all of you to remain at your posts until I tell you to move!'

And the Rani's authority was such that they all yielded, hoping for the signal from Tatya Tope which never came.

Suddenly, their attention was drawn to an Indian horseman galloping hell for leather through the British lines, headed for the fort. As soon as the British saw him, they began to concentrate their fire on him. It seemed impossible that he would not be hit. The Rani and her officers were breathless as they watched his mad race, fearing to see him fall at any moment. The horseman seemed to be positively enjoying the hail of bullets whistling around him. He knocked over the red coated soldiers who tried to stop him, reached the ramp that led to the fort and disappeared under the porchway of the first enclosure. A few moments later he made a dramatic entrance on the Rani's observation tower. It was Akbar.

'What are you waiting for!' he yelled. 'Attack immediately!'

Struck dumb by this apparition, the Rani did not know what to answer.

'We're waiting for Tatya Tope's signal.'

'You're mad! For three hours Tatya Tope has been waiting for you to come out.'

He was shouting so loud his voice deafened the Rani even more than the gunfire.

'Tatya Tope sent us an officer with the order to await his signal.'

'That officer is a traitor. Tatya Tope never sent any such order. Hurry up or it will be too late.'

Faced with the urgent necessity to launch an attack, the Rani recovered her composure and gave brief orders. By the time they were transmitted and the Pathans assembled from their posts on the ramparts, thirty minutes had elapsed. When they were ready, the Rani saw through her field glasses several hundred of Tatya Tope's soldiers emerge from the ruins of the old military cantonment and flee, with Rose's men in pursuit. In a flash, the Rani understood that Tatya Tope had lost the battle, that it was too late, that she had made a terrible mistake in believing the officer allegedly sent by Tatya Tope.

Akbar chose this moment to reproach her.

'Who asked you to just sit there doing nothing? If you had attacked, you would have annihilated the British.'

The Rani turned abruptly to face him. There was almost hatred in her eyes. She opened her mouth to answer but then refrained. Turning away, she looked at Sanghar Singh.

'Assemble immediately all the officers of the fort,' she told him.

When they had all gathered around her, she sensed the crushing discouragement the defeat of Tatya Tope had inflicted on them. Her voice firm, she said, 'For the past ten days Jhansi has defended herself heroically without Tatya Tope and we can continue to hold our position without the help of anyone. During all that time you fought with incomparable courage and flawless determination. By that splendid demonstration of your noble qualities you have already attained glory. I count on you to maintain that highest level of discipline and heroism you have already displayed in the defence of our beloved Jhansi. I know you will.'

The meeting took place in the throne room. The Rani had sent for various chests which she now opened, taking out men's bracelets and ceremonial caftans which she distributed to her officers. She also opened bags filled with gold coins which she ordered them to distribute to the defenders of the city. Spontaneously, her officers swore once more to fight to the last man, if necessary. Meanwhile, the gunfire continued on both sides.

The Rani left the fort to tour the defences. Akbar wanted to go with her. A harsh expression on her face, her voice cutting, she stopped him. 'Go rest, Akbar Khan. You really need it.'

Everywhere she went, the Rani distributed praise and encouragement. To everyone she showed her resolve and her optimism. Only after she had revived in her subjects the courage drained by Tatya Tope's defeat did she return to the fort. Akbar was waiting for her at the door to her apartment. She wanted to reply to the anxious, probing question in his eyes.

'We defended ourselves perfectly well on our own and we shall continue to do so. I never asked for assistance from anyone and I was right not to. Tatya Tope's arrival has only made the situation worse.'

In the bitterness of these words Akbar sensed the depth of the Rani's irritation.

'He let himself be defeated ignominiously,' she continued, 'and he didn't even give us time enough to try an attack.'

Akbar understood that in accusing someone else, the Rani was indirectly admitting her own error.

'While you were inspecting the ramparts,' he said, 'I took it upon myself to have a search made for the man who brought you the false order from Tatya Tope. Of course he's disappeared.'

'But who, then, is betraying me!' cried the Rani.

And she told Akbar of the mysterious note she had received before the invasion of Jhansi, warning her of traitors among her own advisers. As far as Akbar was concerned, there were no traitors but the British. He placed his hand on her shoulder.

'Don't worry, Lakshmi, we'll get them another time.'

It was already late and the guns barked only at intervals. The Rani was still awake. On her wide low bed, she watched Akbar seated beside her, resting his back against a gilded column of the canopy. He was drinking glass after glass of arak. His face was crimson, his eyes flashing, and once again she was startled by the quantity of alcohol he could absorb.

'What have you been up to these past weeks, Akbar Khan?'

'I was working for you. I sent you the best Pathans in India.'

'Why didn't you come back when the siege began? As the commander of my cavalry, didn't you belong here?'

'Not really. My cavalry and I are useful only in charges, battles, sorties. During a siege what use would we be to you? And besides, I had more important things to do, such as bringing Tatya Tope's army to your aid. If you think he felt like coming!... He didn't want to hear anything about it. He had other important objectives, and he had no desire to put himself out for Jhansi.'

'So it was you who convinced him.'

'No, it was you, Lakshmi—by holding out so much longer than anyone expected. Everyone at Kalpi was sure the British would take Jhansi in two or three days. Your resistance convinced them.'

The Rani took Akbar's large hand between hers and, in a sudden change of tone, asked, 'Why did you abandon me?'

'I didn't abandon you. It was you who abandoned me.'

She threw herself in his arms, kissed him, and clasped him gently to her. But her caresses could not silence him. Akbar wanted to tell her how he had suffered. He had nothing against Firoz Shah, whom he actually held in high esteem.

'It's you I was angry with, because it's you who had betrayed me. I suffered so, Lakshmi—it was so hard to be apart from you. You're the most precious thing I have.'

But Lakshmi no longer heard him. Soothed, reassured, she had fallen asleep in his arms, a faint smile on her parted lips, her hand in Akbar's. Gently, he lay her down on the sofa and for a long time, he watched her, stroking her long hair spread out on the cushions.

The following morning the British resumed their shelling of Jhansi with an intensity that did not slacken with evening.

From her observation post on one of the towers of the fort the Rani noticed that weak spots were beginning to appear in its defence. She rushed to the sections of the ramparts that had suffered the worst damage.

Her presence and her words had their usual effect. Overturned guns were righted again by female battalions and gunners returned to their posts. Jhansi's morale was holding up better than its walls; the Rani noticed heavy damage in several places.

The British bombardment, more visible in the darkness, seemed to double in intensity. In her refuge in the town palace, Mrs Phipps was on the brink of hysteria. Her guards kept her informed of the situation, although with some distortions. Divided between the hope of soon being freed by her compatriots and the fear of being murdered by the Rani before that could happen, the past few days had put a great strain on her nerves.

And now, she was in danger of being killed by British artillery, whose main target was the town palace.

Every explosion shook the walls of her tiny room, filling it with an infernal roar. She crouched in a corner as though the ceiling were about to fall on her, her hands over her ears. Suddenly, a shell landed very close by. The windowpanes shattered, the lamp hanging from the ceiling crashed to the floor, and Annabelle was knocked to the ground.

When she stood up, shaking, her ears ringing, she saw that she was bleeding heavily. A shard of glass had cut her ear and cheek. Thinking she was mortally wounded, she ran screaming into the courtyard; her guards were too panicked to stop her.

Everywhere, people were carrying away the bleeding, wounded and the horribly mutilated bodies of the dead. The lawns were strewn with fragments of furniture, pieces of mirrors and chandeliers, shreds of tapestries. One shell had crashed through two stories and burst in the palace's temple, killing or wounding the faithful who had gathered there to pray, knocking over the statue of the goddess Lakshmi, shattering precious liturgical objects.

The panic in the courtyard was so great—everyone running in all directions—that no one paid any attention to Mrs Phipps. Haggard, she staggered about aimlessly, muttering, 'Here they come, here they come.'

Suddenly, she thought she saw the Rani. She shrieked and ran away as fast as she could. It was indeed the Rani, with Akbar, who would not leave her side. British shells kept coming in without interruption. Here, a section of the wall collapsed; there, a group of wounded people screamed in pain. The Rani was not afraid. But she was discouraged.

'It's all over, it's just a question of time now,' she said.

Akbar protested hotly:

'Our numerical superiority over the British is almost crushing. We still have three times as many men and our artillery is just as powerful as theirs.'

'You want it spelled out, Akbar Khan? Our numerical superiority means very little. We had to enlist all those who volunteered—in other words, we accepted anyone. Our soldiers have neither the discipline nor the fighting skills of the British. As for our guns, they have none of their power and accuracy.'

An officer came up with two dangerous-looking men, two of the spies that were sent out each night to the British lines.

The information these two spies brought the Rani, that night of 2 April, was so astonishing that, at first, she could not believe her ears. The British had exhausted their ammunition. Forced to break off the siege of Jhansi, they were to strike camp tomorrow morning. The Rani had so much trouble believing what the two spies had just told her that she questioned them at length, right there in the midst of the bombardment.

They repeated their information several times, insisting that they could not be mistaken. They had been able to crawl close enough to a group of British officers to overhear their conversation, and they understood enough English to be certain of what they had heard. The officer who had brought them to the Rani confirmed that other spies had observed unusual movement all along the British lines that might well mean the beginning of a withdrawal.

The Rani's mistrust gave way before so much matching testimony. She had always known that the British force had only limited reserves of ammunition, and they might well have exhausted them in the battle the day before. Tatya Tope's intervention might, therefore, not have been entirely useless, she thought. The marvellous news might be true. She ordered the two spies not to spread it, to avoid causing a relaxation of vigilance or a premature celebration among the defenders.

The tension of the past ten days relaxed all at once. Akbar walked with Lakshmi to the door of her apartments and was about to take his leave, when she murmured, 'Stay.'

She dismissed Mandar and her other servants and drew Akbar into her room. Later, half-asleep, she said, 'It was hard, but we held. Jhansi held.'

'It's you who held, Lakshmi. You alone. Jhansi only followed. I admire you as much as I love you. Now, rest. From now on, I will always stay by your side.'

2

Mandar had to shake the Rani several times to arouse her from her slumber.

'Rani, wake up, the British have taken the southern ramparts. They're beginning to spill into the town.'

Without fully understanding what she had heard, the Rani leapt from her bed, threw on her mannish clothes, sprinted up the steep, narrow staircase and burst onto the terrace of the palace. She needed no spyglass to see. At the southern edge of the town, near Orchha Gate, hundreds of red coated ants were rushing towards the walls, raising ladders, clambering up, joining other ants running along the ramparts, invading towers and bastions, knocking down defenders... Other clusters of red ants were already making their way into the neighbouring streets, shooting at anything that moved. The Rani understood the situation immediately; her spies had been tricked by a skilful performance by British officers who, rather than lifting the siege, had launched a general assault. How had they silenced the batteries on the south ramparts? How had they gained entrance to the walls? How had they smashed the defences? The contrast between the certainty of deliverance she had taken to bed a few hours earlier and the terrible reality that greeted her upon awakening was too violent—her nerves gave out.

For a moment she stood transfixed, her mouth open in a scream that would not come, her eyes bulging. Her whole body began to tremble convulsively. Her mind seemed to have deserted her. Her staff did not dare say anything. Even Akbar did not know what to do. Never before had he seen her lose her composure like this. British shells were crashing all about them and the Rani might be hit at any moment.

Akbar pulled her backwards, violently. She turned to him, and little by little, she stopped shaking. She took his spyglass, leaned out over a battlement and stared at the southern ramparts. Straightening up, she turned to Akbar, 'Let's set your Pathans on them.'

It did not take her long to get her weapons. She appeared before the hastily-assembled horsemen wearing her light helmet, her steel gloves and wide steel belt. She mounted Pari and raced down the fort's ramp in a furious stampede. Galloping at the head of her horsemen, the Rani saw, at the end of a wide street, hundreds of redcoats on the smashed rampart.

It seemed to her she was reliving the battle against the Rani of Orchha. But this time she was utterly unafraid. She was already upon the British soldiers, her sabre drawn, when they turned and ran off without a fight. Were they really such cowards? The Rani thought she had won. Crazed by the action, she raced after them, but a volley of bullets made her horse rear and pull up short. The British had not fled; they had merely taken shelter in neighbouring houses. The Rani dropped her sabre, took the reins between her teeth, drew her horse-pistols and fired them both, at random, at the now invisible enemy. This was not how the Maratha were trained to fight. This was not how the Rani had fought the soldiers of Orchha. Her horse Pari spun about, jumping, sidestepping among red coated corpses. Around her the Pathans, trapped, were being shot down one by one.

Akbar, using his body to shield the Rani, saw her suddenly knocked back on her horse. He thought she had been hit—but no, she sat up again on her mount, shaking her head violently. A British bullet had hit her helmet just above her forehead and torn it off. The shock left her shaking and dizzy. Akbar grabbed Pari's reins, dragging the horse to lead Lakshmi to safety behind the corner of a house.

'It's absurd to stay here!' he shouted at her. 'There's no point in your waiting here to be killed by one of their bullets. Go back to the fort!'

Though she could see the Pathans falling in increasing numbers not far from her, she could not resign herself to giving up the fight. But Akbar dragged her, by force, away from the area. Only then did she give in.

'Order your horsemen to fall back.'

Soon afterwards, General Rose appeared on the ramparts, surrounded by his staff, which included Roderick Briggs, and ordered that priority be given to the capture of the Rani's town palace.

That was easier said than done. Every house had become a fort. The rebels were firing with such intensity that their bullets raised showers of dust in the streets.

They hurled slabs of stone, tree-trunks, and even pots and pans at the British. They, in turn, tossed grenades through open doors and windows, and then set fire to the houses in order to flush out the rebels. The British advanced between two walls of flame whose heat, added to the sun's, was pitiless. As soon as they came within the line of fire of the fort, cannon and muskets opened up on them but were unable to stop their advance. Arriving at the palace, they blew up the gates. In the first court—the stables—they were met by the elite troops of the rebels who, having nowhere to escape to, were ready to fight to the last man.

Hand-to-hand fighting began immediately. Soldiers of the 35th Regiment rushed into a building, only to be blown up by rebel grenades. Other men of the same regiment were hacked to pieces on the spot. Then the British went berserk. They charged, ignoring the muskets pointed at them.

Rattled, the rebels fell back and ran to barricade themselves in the stables. General Rose, upon his arrival, ordered the stables to be set on fire. Rather than be burned alive, the rebels rushed out, their weapons raised. Shot by the British at virtually point-blank range, not one escaped. There were still a handful of them inside the rooms of the palace, on the terraces, in the outbuildings, but the back of the resistance had been broken. The Rani's palace was almost entirely occupied by the British. It was noon. Without a thought for the corpses littering the yard or for the wounded groaning in pain, the victors stretched out on the ground, overcome by exhaustion and heat. Many had piled on their heads a few turbans torn from rebel corpses, in order to protect themselves from the sun. Others made weak efforts to put out the fire raging in the stables. General Rose sent several small groups to mop up resistance inside the palace, a scene of utter devastation. All the windows were shattered; the doors had been knocked down or smashed by grenades. The ground was strewn with broken boxes, crushed furniture, shards of crystal and glass. In a corner one officer found a coffer filled with jewels and had it brought to General Rose.

Roderick Briggs continued to explore the site with a few men, knocking down, one by one, all the doors on the ground floor. Reaching the last one, he kicked it open and stepped into a dark room, his pistol in one hand, his sabre in the other. Facing him was a woman in a sari, whom he took for an Indian.

'Don't kill me, I'm an Englishwoman!' she screamed.

Her accent convinced Roderick immediately. Briefly, she explained that she was Mrs Phipps, the widow of the Jhansi doctor and the sole survivor of last June's massacre. The poor woman seemed half-dead from the hardships and the confinement the Rani had imposed. She broke down, crying incomprehensible words. Roderick ordered two of his soldiers to lead her to General Rose.

Suddenly, he heard hurrahs and shouts of joy. In the building where the Rani's Pathans had hidden, soldiers had found a Union Jack sent fifty years earlier by the Governor General to the Raja of Jhansi, with permission to have it carried before him, an honour never before granted to any Indian prince.

Captain Darby of the 86th Regiment brought the flag to General Rose and asked permission to raise it. Rose consented, entrusting him with the honour. It was well-deserved; Darby's regiment had suffered heavy losses and he himself had been hit several times. Despite his wounds, he climbed to the terrace and hoisted the British colours over the palace, drawing a volley of cannonballs from the fort.

The Rani wanted no witness to her despair. The Union Jack now floated above her former residence, and she locked herself in her room and fell on her bed, sobbing. So many of her soldiers had already died. More were dying every minute. Gulam Ghaus Khan, the head-gunner, hit by shrapnel, had fallen beside his beloved cannon, Kadak Bijli.

Sanghar Singh had tried to save the remnants of his army. With a few hundred infantry and two dozen horsemen, he had left the town by the western wall, overcome the British patrols, and taken refuge on a rocky height. The British cavalry had pursued him and surrounded the hill. His foot soldiers fought heroically, with cold steel when their ammunition ran out. None asked for mercy; none survived. Sanghar Singh then led his cavalry to the top of the hill. There, they too put up a spirited resistance. When they were overwhelmed by sheer numbers, they blew themselves up with their own powder horns.

The battle continued to rage throughout the city. Civilians had joined the remaining soldiers of the Rani's army to fight on from house to house. The British had to storm them, one after the other. The inhabitants invariably refused to surrender, forcing the British to kill them all with bayonets. Rather than let themselves be captured, the men threw their wives and children down wells and jumped in after them. The British hauled up a few of the survivors in order to massacre them on the spot. Halwaipura, the richest quarter of the city, was in flames. Hundreds of cows, buffalo, horses, camels, donkeys and dogs tore through the streets, crazed with terror. Men, women and children were burned alive in blazing houses they dared not leave. Their screams covered the noise of the fire and rose all the way to the fort where, in her bedroom, the Rani covered her ears to try to shut them out.

But she had no right to give in to despair while so many were suffering and dying. She rose from her bed and, without a thought for her appearance, made her way to the throne room. There, she found Diwan Naransin, Moropant, Akbar and old Kashmiri Mull, the last loyal circle; they explained the situation to her. The British had established a line of patrols from the south rampart, where they had attacked that morning, to the north rampart. In addition to the town palace, they had seized two-thirds of the city and were methodically setting about taking the last third below the port. By nightfall they would be masters of all Jhansi.

The Rani seemed not to be listening. Her eyes rested on the large mirrors and crystal chandeliers she had once ordered from Lucknow, on the precious religious miniatures on the walls, on the gaddi where she had so often sat enthroned.

Her advisers stared at her anxiously. Akbar was the first to break the silence, 'The town has been taken, but not the fort. We can withstand a siege here. We still have a few hundred of my Pathans, several cannon, more than enough food, and our ramparts are stronger than those of the town. We could hold out for a very long time.'

The Rani murmured an answer, 'What's the use? The city has been taken, and with it all reasons for resistance. Listen to the screams of the men, the women, the children being killed. You want us to lock ourselves in here while all around us my people are dying? Why defend the fort if Jhansi is dying?' She let a few moments pass before continuing calmly, in a soft voice, her head tilted in her characteristic manner, 'I've thought about it and I've made my decision. I will not surrender, and I have no wish to outlive my people. Tonight I shall blow myself up with the fort. That is what our ancestors did rather than submit to defeat, and that is how they earned eternal glory. May those who wish to follow me into death stay here; let the others leave the fort at nightfall and escape as best they can.'

There followed a silence so heavy it seemed to blot out the noise and the shouts from outside.

Moropant walked over to his daughter and took her hand.

'Have you forgotten Damodar? You have no right to abandon him to his death. It's for him that you fought. It's to preserve his future that you must go on living.'

'Take him away,' she cried, 'save him, watch over him. But I will never be able to live with the fact that I was unable to defend Jhansi.'

Akbar returned to the attack with vigour, heightened by anxiety.

'Jhansi is dying, but the revolution still lives, and so does India. Our brothers who are carrying on the fight elsewhere need you, your prestige, your gallantry. And instead of helping them, you want to discourage them by your death?'

Naransin backed him.

'Akbar Khan is right. Join Tatya Tope's army at Kalpi and continue the fight at his side. As long as there is any hope, that is where your duty lies.'

Suddenly Kashmiri Mull felt very old and very tired.

'How will you escape?' he asked. 'The British are in control of the town and have patrols around the fort. You'll never get through.'

Akbar answered dryly, 'There's only one way—boldness. There's no doubt the British think we're digging in for a siege. They don't expect us to try to break out. We'll take them by surprise and rip our way through their net.'

One by one these arguments wore down the Rani's resolve, but still she did not consent. Then Akbar shook her up. Defying protocol which, despite the circumstances, shocked all the others, he gave her orders.

'Enough arguing,' he said. 'Go, get ready. We have two hours.'

What surprised the others most was the docility with which the Rani complied.

At midnight British fire and British steel continued to deal out death in the town of Jhansi. At the fort everything was ready. The Rani was to take with her only Damodar, Moropant and Mandar, under the protection of Akbar and fifty Pathans. The five of them loaded their horses with heavy sacks containing the gold and jewels that had remained in the coffers of the fort.

It was not a clandestine departure. All the occupants of the fort came to bid the Rani goodbye. Her ladies-in-waiting, the dignitaries who had remained at her side, all begged her to take them along. She refused; it was too dangerous. She advised them instead to take refuge in the town, where they would have more room to hide and a better chance to survive.

'Don't worry about us, we'll be all right,' said Kashmiri Mull. 'Take good care of yourself.'

There were tears in her eyes as she embraced him. She distributed jewels and silver, some going to the few hundred Pathans who had sworn to defend the fort to the last man. Diwan Naransin had asked to stay behind with them and had requested the honour of leading them.

'No! I want the British to find the gates wide open and the fort empty. Desperate resistance would only encourage their murderous rage. An easy victory will appease them. Disperse and disappear,' she ordered the Pathans. 'Save yourself, Diwan, and may God be with you!'

'May God keep you, Rani.' And Naransin bowed, more solemnly than usual.

She had exchanged her battledress for a man's attire—white shirt and breeches; around her head, a turban wound to conceal her long hair and in her belt, two pistols and her sword. She mounted Pari.

Her son Damodar was lifted up behind her and tied to her back with a silk shawl. She crossed the first, then the second enclosure.

Near the temple of Ganesh was a little door cut into the third enclosure, through which she left the fort. With her escort she scrambled down the slope, crossed the outlying areas of the town and took the long street of the cotton-merchants that led to the northeastern part of the town. This route had been chosen as the safest, since the British soldiers were busy looting the town palace and mopping up in other parts of town.

When they reached Pandery Gate, the Rani and her escort pushed their horses into a wild gallop. From the ramparts the British fired at random into the darkness, but the riders had already disappeared.

To slip through the net of British patrols around the city, they split up, as agreed beforehand, into several small groups. The Rani kept with her Mandar, Moropant, Akbar and about ten Pathans, including the five in charge of carrying all that remained of Jhansi's treasury. They had almost reached the cover of the jungle when, coming around a rocky hillock, they bumped into a patrol which was moving along silently, guided only by the luminosity of the night.

'Halt! Who goes there!'

There were about thirty of the enemy and the Rani heard the bolt action as they cocked their rifles. She kept her composure and, assuming a masculine voice, answered, 'We're on our way to rescue the village of Tehri which is threatened by the rebels.'

'All right, pass on.'

They were off at a gallop without a second bidding and soon reached the jungle. At least, thought the Rani, one could always rely on the naiveté of the British. With all her heart she hoped the other group of Pathans would be as lucky as she.

When they arrived at the village of Aari, ten miles northeast of Jhansi, the Rani and her companions rested their horses. The five Pathans carrying the treasure were having trouble keeping up with the rest, so an elephant was brought from the villagers and the precious cargo shifted to its back. Moropant offered to lead them to safety. He would head north, where the British would not be looking for him. In the city of Datya he had a friend, a rich merchant, who would give him shelter. There, Moropant could hide the treasure and await further developments.

The Rani was unable to repress a bitter smile. Between protecting his daughter or the treasure, Moropant, faithful to his principles, had not hesitated.

There was no time to lose. The British could, at any moment, become aware of the Rani's flight and send patrols to find her. She gave half her escort, five Pathans, to her father, and set off again, covering another ten miles at top speed.

Upon reaching the village of Pandery, she decided to give the men and animals a little more rest. The British would certainly not dare venture this far in pursuit. The men threw themselves on the curdled milk and chapattis the peasants brought. Akbar congratulated himself on the success of his plan.

'You see, Lakshmi, we were right to take our chances.'

She sat silently on a low wooden chair the village elder had brought her, not eating, not moving, lost in thought. She had saved her son, Akbar and her own life. But Jhansi had been taken from her and her people were dying...

Excerpts from a letter from Roderick Briggs to Sarah Brandon, dated 4 April 1858.

> *Late in the afternoon of 3 April 1858, we could say, at last, that we had conquered the city of Jhansi. Some areas of town, especially in the north, were not yet under our control, but resistance was dying down. It was about six o'clock. General Rose, with another aide, Lieutenant Lyster, and myself, was touring the town palace, contemplating the bedlam inside with an air of detachment. I thought it wise to seize the moment to congratulate him on the capture of Jhansi which, despite the errors and the cost in lives, constituted a remarkable exploit. The General stopped, and said to me pensively, 'The city has been taken, that's true, but the fort is still holding out.' 'We shall take it, General, as easily as we took the city,' I answered. 'You are very innocent, Briggs. With those Pathans determined to fight to the last man, with the Rani to command them, and the guns they*

still have, the fort is almost impregnable except through hunger and thirst. And we have neither the time nor the supplies to undertake a long siege. Any suggestions, gentlemen?'

'Try corruption, General. It was more than a help in our taking of the city,' Lyster suggested.

'You don't know the Rani, that's plain. She keeps a firm hand on her elite guard. None of them could be bought. I fear your solution might bring only complications.'

'Do you have another, General?' asked Lyster, not without impertinence.

'Perhaps. What we need is for the Rani to escape from the fort. Don't look so startled, Briggs, and listen to me instead. We won't control the north of the town until tomorrow morning. If we widen the mesh of our net of patrols around the city, the Rani will soon hear about it from her informants. She'll jump at the opportunity and decide to flee. We will make sure she is successful. Once she thinks herself safe, the cavalry we will have posted along the roads will go into action and take her, alive. We cannot fail, because no woman can gallop as fast as our cavalry.'

Lyster, through either conviction or flattery, approved the General's plan. I ventured to raise an objection. Was it not dangerous to try to outwit a woman as diabolical as the Rani? She just might slip through our fingers.

'In any case,' answered the General, 'there is no other solution except a long siege, and that is something I cannot contemplate. We shall do what I have decided, and you, Briggs, will personally carry the necessary orders to the patrols north of town.'

I had to comply. We settled down for the night in the only part of the town palace that was more or less intact. The General had his camp-bed set up in a room which I was told had been the Rani's private audience chamber. Since he wanted me to remain nearby, I threw my bedroll in a corner of the throne room next door. I needn't tell you I did not get much sleep.

At two o'clock in the morning, two scouts I had sent out came to wake me. The Rani had escaped, just as General Rose had predicted. Our soldiers had seen her pass through Pandery Gate; they had fired on her escort, but in the air carefully, to avoid hitting her. Later, she and her companions must have split up, for our soldiers stopped a group of her Pathans and, seeing the Rani was not with them, killed them all. One of our patrols ran into the Rani herself. Despite the fact that she had disguised herself as a man, the officer leading the patrol immediately recognized her from descriptions he had been given. Following instructions, he let her pass, pretending to believe the extravagant explanation she gave him. He sent the stipulated signal immediately to the men of the 14th Dragoons posted behind our lines in order that they might stop the Rani and bring her back alive.

I immediately roused the General and brought him up to speed. There was no more to be done except wait for our cavalry to return with their catch. They were slow in coming. I envied the General his coolness as he went back to sleep. I couldn't do it and so paced up and down the vast deserted throne room.

Day was breaking when a runner from the 14th Dragoons arrived. Our cavalry had combed the entire twenty miles north of the town without finding anything. The only thing they had to report was that at the village of Aari, having interrogated the peasants in a somewhat brutal fashion, they learned that the Rani had stopped there. It was too late, and our men had to give up the chase. Just as I had predicted, Rose's plan had failed and the Rani had slipped through our fingers.

I then asked him for permission to go after her myself. I was so furious that I imagine I might have done so, even if Rose had refused. But by this time, there was nothing left to lose and he told me to do as I saw fit. I quickly glanced at a map. The Rani had stopped at Aari. From there she could have gone northwest to Datya, but she would not have dared—the ruler of that small state is one of our loyal allies. She must then have taken the northeast route towards Kalpi to rejoin the army of her accomplice, Tatya Tope.

With twenty horsemen I rode out of the city in the direction of Kalpi. I had only one hope—that the Rani, reassured by the distance she had covered, would stop to rest. Despite the early hour, the heat was intense, but I hardly noticed it. It was eight o'clock in the morning when we reached the village of Pandery, thirty miles from Jhansi.

We spilled out into the square like a tidal wave. The Rani had been there all right. Unfortunately, the villagers, alerted by the noise we made, had warned her of our arrival. She and her companions were already in the saddle and off before we could reach them.

Then began the wildest of chases, worthy of the novels of Sir Walter Scott that you love so well. The fugitives were riding flat out, but almost imperceptibly, we were gaining on them. I rode at the head of my men and saw the Rani lose ground little by little. I could have fired at her, but Rose had insisted he wanted her alive. I spurred my horse again and again and managed to draw almost parallel with her; I was about to jump on her when she suddenly turned and struck me on the arm with the flat of her sabre, so hard that, surprised and unbalanced, I was thrown out of the saddle and my horse fell on me. The Rani stopped, raised her sabre to finish me off; but then she saw one of my men coming straight for her. She turned about and, in a flash, caught up with her companions. Instead of going after them, my men stopped to help me to my feet. I shouted at them to leave me alone and get on with it—but it was too late. The Rani's group was too far ahead. My arm was badly hurt in the fall and I cannot hold a pen. You mustn't be surprised by the handwriting. I am dictating it to one of my colleagues and I couldn't wait to tell you everything that happened.

Although the General's reasons not to lay siege to the fort were valid, his plan to capture the Rani was no less than absurd. We took the city of Jhansi but, thanks to General Rose, the Rani has escaped us.'

3

Chirgaon, Amara, Moht, Orai, the villages streamed by, crowned with ancient forts. The Rani of Jhansi, followed by her escort, had been galloping for several hours when the thick jungles gave way to a succession of narrow, deep ravines. They were not far from their goal.

In the darkness the Rani could make out the domes of the eighty-four temples, which were actually old tombs of forgotten dynasties, that marked the approach to Kalpi. In front of her she saw the glow of innumerable campfires of Tatya Tope's army. Just another hundred yards and she would reach the protective embankment. Suddenly, her horse staggered and fell forward. A consummate horsewoman, the Rani rolled herself into a ball, and stood up immediately, only slightly shaken. Damodar had slipped out of the silk shawl that held him to his mother, but he was also unhurt. The Rani leaned over Pari who had so valiantly carried a double load. His nostrils were steaming; a whitish foam emerged from his mouth. His flanks were a mass of wounds from the Rani's spurs. He was panting and making pathetic attempts to move his legs, as though he wanted to run on. The Rani stroked him.

'Thank you, Pari. Without you, we would never have made it.'

She rose, gathered in her arms Damodar, who was almost unconscious with fatigue, and went to meet the sentinel who was approaching cautiously.

'I am the Rani of Jhansi.'

The sentinel rushed off to alert his officer. Mysteriously notified, soldiers came out of nearby tents. The report flew from mouth to mouth, 'The Rani of Jhansi, Lakshmi.'

All seemed carried away with admiration before this legendary woman in whom they saw almost a divinity. They held out their hands timidly, wanting to touch her. An officer rushed over. Again, Lakshmi said, 'I am the Rani of Jhansi.'

The officer grew frantic. He had to warn his superiors, assemble an honour guard... The Rani stopped him.

'Later. For the moment we need only one thing—sleep. Give us some beds, any beds, and mind you take good care of my horse.'

The officer led the Rani and Damodar to his own tent after chasing out his orderlies. She felt hands relieve her of her son, whom she was still holding, other hands helping her stretch out on a narrow bunk. Then she sank into a deep sleep. Having left Jhansi at midnight, she had arrived at Kalpi twenty-four hours later, after riding one hundred and fifty kilometres on horseback with her son behind her, a feat everyone claimed was impossible, even for a man.

She emerged briefly from her sleep at nightfall the next day, saw, through a haze, the faces of Akbar and Mandar, and heard Damodar speaking volubly. Reassured, she turned over and fell asleep again immediately.

When she woke up the next day, the sun was already high in the hazy summer sky. Akbar and Mandar had been watching over her. Damodar was playing outside, perfectly rested; he had recuperated much more quickly than his mother. For the child their odyssey had been no more than a thrilling adventure. Tears streamed down Lakshmi's cheeks as she dressed; they had not been able to save her horse Pari, dead from exhaustion.

'He held out until he had carried us to safety... never will I find another Pari,' she kept saying.

But already Tatya Tope, informed that she was awake, was striding into the tent. They threw themselves into each other's arms, like long-lost siblings.

'Come, I'll take you to the Peshwa. He's waiting for you,' he said.

'The Peshwa! Nana Sahib is here!' the Rani exclaimed.

'No. It's his cousin Rao Sahib who carries the title and has assumed the powers of the head of the Maratha confederation.'

'So Nana Sahib has died.'

'To tell you the truth, we don't know.'

The Rani was considerably surprised. Tatya Tope gave her an explanation which, nevertheless, left her feeling confused. Ever since last July, when the British had retaken Cawnpore and his capital of Bithur, putting an end to his brief reign, Nana Sahib had virtually disappeared. His presence had been reported here and there, even in Lucknow, and proclamations signed by him had been issued; but in fact, he had not been seen by anyone close to him. From Tatya Tope's uneasiness, the Rani suspected there was underneath it all a considerable mystery to which, perhaps, not even he had the key.

'We shall speak about that and many other things,' said Tatya Tope evasively.

But in fact the Rani was never to know the final word on the fate of Nana Sahib.

For her audience with the Peshwa she spurned the saris and the armour that had been brought her. She donned instead the modest clothes in which she had left Jhansi—a white shirt, white breeches, white turban. Emerging from the tent with Tatya Tope, she found an impressive spectacle. The tents of his camp stretched out of sight; around the camp were several trenches and a solid embankment bristling with guns. His army seemed numberless and powerfully armed. In the background rose the walls of the city of Kalpi, dominated by the fort which served the rebels as an arsenal and treasury. Soldiers and officers ran up to catch a glimpse of the Rani. All of them stared at her with veneration, almost adoration, which surprised her.

'What are they gaping at?' she muttered. 'I'm only a defeated queen who has lost everything.'

Tatya Tope answered, 'For the British, perhaps. But for us, you're a heroine, Lakshmi.'

The Peshwa's tent was enormous, sober on the outside, sumptuous inside. Velvet tapestries richly embroidered with gold, brocade pillows and Persian carpets made it fitting surroundings for a powerful monarch.

Glittering with jewels, the Peshwa sat on a gaddi, surrounded by numerous officers and dignitaries in ceremonial dress. While they exchanged the customary compliments, the Rani noted that he had not changed much in the many years since she had last seen him. Rather short, he had the same large round eyes as his cousin Nana Sahib, and the same tendency to portliness. Very black whiskers joined to his sideburns tried, without success, to lend him an air of fierceness. The Rani remembered him as a deeply kind and rather retiring young man.

Seeing him on a throne in the midst of his army, that same army which had been beaten on the Betwa River and whose ineffectiveness had caused the loss of her Jhansi, the Rani felt a deep bitterness. She drew her sword, the weapon with the gem-encrusted hilt and gold scabbard of the Rajas of Jhansi which never left her. Placing it at the Peshwa's feet, she said, 'The illustrious ancestors of Your Highness gave us this weapon. With their powerful aid we always did what was just and right. Now that we can no longer have your help, I ask your permission to return it to you.'

No one dared look the Rani in the face. Tatya Tope stared at a spot in front of him, high above the Rani. The Peshwa, his eyes lowered and fixed on his gold-embroidered slippers, answered, 'For days and days, you gallantly and successfully defended Jhansi against the powerful British, and when it became necessary you managed to escape, despite enemy traps. That shows your skill and your courage. We can realize our ideal of independence only with leaders like you. I beg you to take back this sword and lend me your assistance in our struggle.'

The Rani was moved, less by the Peshwa's compliments than by his humility.

He leaned towards her, 'Tell me what you want and you shall have it.'

'Give me men for the deliverance of Jhansi.'

The Peshwa seemed taken aback. He thought a moment before answering, 'Alas! The situation does not allow us to spare any part of our army.'

That is how the Rani learned of the fall of Lucknow, which had taken place while she was besieged and cut off from all news. The Peshwa spoke at length of the heroism of the defenders, perhaps in order to take the Rani's mind off his refusal to grant her request.

Lucknow had fallen on 21 March. The British had not found its capture easy. Day after day the leaders of the revolution had hurled violent, attacks against them, retaking their positions and inflicting heavy losses.

Nevertheless, the British had moved forward step by step, quarter by quarter, palace by palace. When they were masters of practically the whole city, the Maulvi of Faizabad and Prince Firoz Shah had returned to the attack, launching the most furious assault of the campaign. The British had contained it only at the price of a bloodbath; bombarding the attackers without mercy, they had finally broken the city's resistance.

The Rani had remembered only one name, that of Firoz Shah, but she refrained from asking about him for fear of attracting the attention of Akbar, who was seated nearby. The Peshwa told her that Begum Hazrat Mahal had fled north with her young son whom she had placed for a few months on the throne of Oudh. The Maulvi of Faizabad was still fighting a guerrilla war against the British in the region. At last, after having kept the Rani hanging, perhaps deliberately, the Peshwa told her that Prince Firoz Shah had travelled northwest with his army, beating back forces sent against him by the Nawab of Rampur, a British ally, and had taken refuge in the city of Bareilly, a revolutionary stronghold.

The Rani hoped that no one heard her sigh of relief at the news that Firoz Shah was still alive. 'So the kingdom of Oudh is lost,' she said, making a face.

'Far from it,' retorted Tatya Tope.

Indeed, in the entire region, the talukdars, the great landowners, had, at last, joined the battle. Until then, the majority had maintained a cautious reserve. But British repression had forced them into open opposition. They had begun violent guerrilla war in all of northwest India. Although the British trumpeted their victories as loud as they could, they were far from having reconquered the whole country. And then, there was still the Peshwa's army at Kalpi.

The Rani caught the ball in mid-air, 'Since Lucknow, alas, has no more need of our help, and since the talukdars are taking care of the kingdom of Oudh, let us take this beautiful army and march on Jhansi.'

The Peshwa's only answer was an invitation to a formal review of the troops.

'Our men are eager to pay you homage,' he added.

The courtiers and dignitaries were surprised; granting such an honour to a woman, even a queen, was unheard of. The Rani saw it as no more than a means of side-stepping her demands.

In her simple volunteer's outfit, she stood out sharply among the Peshwa's officers, glittering with brocade and jewels. In front of her paraded the contingents sent by rulers who had sided with the rebellion, the personal army of Rao Sahib, and sepoys who had kept their British weapons, red tunics, and even the brass plates on which were engraved the numbers of their old British regiments.

Instead of taking their salutes, the Rani would have given anything to lead these fresh troops in the recapture of Jhansi. Her ignorance of what was happening at home ate at her. Everyone she questioned told her there was no news; no messenger had come. An impenetrable wall of silence seemed to surround the vanquished city that wept deep in the Rani's heart.

Once the review was over, the Peshwa brought her to a tent almost as large and sumptuous as his, which he had had arranged for her and her son. Toilet necessities, various perfumes and an entire wardrobe of women's clothes and battle dress had been set out for her, including all the objects necessary to a woman's beauty and the comfort of a queen. The Rani glanced at it all with disdain and dismissed the numerous servants who had prostrated themselves before her when she entered.

She accepted only the honour guard around her tent, for she wanted to maintain her rank out of regard for her son, the legitimate Raja of Jhansi.

Once she was alone with Akbar, she spoke bitterly, 'They want to smother me with honours and put me to sleep with comfort. They're trying to make me understand that above all, they don't want me to meddle.'

Refugees from Jhansi began to arrive the next day, singly at first and then, in small groups. It was extremely painful for the Rani to receive them, but she knew that listening to the accounts of atrocities they had witnessed was the only way to give them some relief. Wanting only to stop up her ears, to run outside, she had to remain seated on the pillows in her tent, asking questions, listening, trying to show sympathy and project an image of hope while inside, she was a wasteland of despair. Little by little, she was able to reconstruct a picture of what had taken place in Jhansi after her departure.

The British had avenged themselves simultaneously for the town's resistance, for the Rani's flight, and for the massacre of their compatriots the year before.

The killing had lasted three full days. According to the more credible estimates, there were five thousand victims: men, women, and children.

The looting that followed was as methodical as the killing had been random. The British soldiers had been given precise orders to ignore ordinary goods and concentrate only on objects of value—precious gems, gold, silver, jewels and coins. They combed the city and seized booty amounting to several million pounds sterling. Naturally, the sacred jewels of the temples, the most precious of all, received special attention. The goddess Lakshmi was stripped to the last of her ornaments and her gold statue taken away to be melted.

What distressed the Rani most was to hear that her library had been completely destroyed. Assembled by generations of Rajas of Jhansi, enlarged by her husband and considerably enriched by her own efforts, the library had been one of the richest in India, open to all learned men in the country who wished to consult it.

To protect the precious manuscripts, the Rani had had them wrapped in richly-embroidered silk cases. It was their gold ornamentation that attracted the British soldiers. They pulled out the manuscripts, threw the pages to the wind, and carried off the cases. Not a single volume had survived.

Once the masters had had their fill, their servants—the sepoys, all from south India who had remained loyal to the British and served in General Rose's army—were given permission to help themselves to what remained. On the first day, the Madras contingent was allowed to pay itself in pots and pans and plates of copper and bronze. They even took door handles and window-latches.

On the second day, the sepoys of the Hyderabad regiment looted everything that was made of cloth—beds, mattresses, sheets, covers, clothing, carpets. On the third day, another sepoy regiment was allowed to haul away grain—rice, wheat, maize and beans—which they poured into sacks and jars they had brought for that purpose.

On the fourth day, the inhabitants of Jhansi had almost nothing left, but there were still some sepoys who had not had a chance to reward themselves. They were given permission to carry off anything they wanted. They needed no further encouragement; they seized chairs, tables, rope-beds, millstones, and even ropes from wells.

Not a single possession, not a single useful object, not a scrap of food was left to the inhabitants of Jhansi who had survived the massacre. Once everything was gone, General Rose ordered the posting of a proclamation that parodied the famous one the Rani had put up upon assuming power after the departure of the rebels:

'In the name of God, the country belongs to Queen Victoria and the government belongs to the British.'

It finally occurred to the new authorities to get rid of the corpses that were rotting in the streets and threatening the town with epidemic. Teams of firemen doused the smouldering ruins. British soldiers and sepoys assembled hundreds of bodies in the town's square in large piles which they covered with wood, planks and all kinds of debris before setting them on fire. The whole town seemed a single vast crematory field. The stench of burnt flesh, mingling with that of rotting animals, soon became unbearable.

Thousands of carcasses of camels, elephants, dogs, horses, cats, buffalo, donkeys and cattle were picked up and thrown into an immense ditch dug for that purpose and then covered with earth.

Her voice shaking, the Rani asked the refugees for news of her friends, 'Kashmiri Mull?'

'He was stabbed to death with bayonets in the temple where he had gone to pray.'

Thus the faithful supporter of cooperation with the British had died at their hands.

'And Diwan Naransin?'

The man she was questioning hung his head.

He was a former functionary in her husband's court, a cunning little man she had always been wary of. He had already managed to annoy her with flattery and thinly-veiled requests for money.

'And Naransin?' she asked again.

The man's voice became almost inaudible.

'He is collaborating with the British. He betrayed you.'

'Naransin, betray me! Impossible!'

Suddenly Lakshmi shouted, 'Why do you come here to tell me such lies! Have the British paid you for this? It's you who are the traitor! Get out!'

The man fled. Aghast, the Rani repeated his monstrous allegations to Tatya Tope. He suddenly seemed embarrassed, looking at Akbar as though asking for his help. Then, after taking a deep breath, he said, 'I would have liked to spare you the truth, Lakshmi. Your informer wasn't lying. Naransin did betray you.'

The Rani flushed with anger.

'You jest, General!'

'Alas no! There is not a shadow of a doubt...'

'Do you have any proof for this fantastic allegation?' The Rani was calm, but Tatya Tope could feel the rage building inside her. Akbar, impassive, was of no help. There was nothing to do but plunge in.

'Strangely enough, the first inkling we got came from Diwan Dinkar, Gwalior's Prime Minister. We are not good friends, but he seems to have some affection for you and, as you know, he's the best informed man in India. He sent us a message, in his usual rather mysterious style, "Watch over the Rani of Jhansi. Tell her to beware. There might be traitors very close to her." Of course, I ordered an immediate inquiry, but you know how those things go. One spy contradicted another. I could gather only hints and suspicions. Nevertheless, all those suspicions pointed to Naransin. That is why I sent you a message of warning, just before Jhansi was invaded.'

The Rani interrupted. 'Your message was so unclear that we mistook it for a trick of the enemy.'

There followed a long silence in which the Rani lost herself in her own reflections. Then she began to think aloud, finding in her own memory long-buried suspicions. 'Naransin must have betrayed me from the very beginning. He must be the one who had my husband murdered. He must be the one who stood behind Sadasheo's attempt to steal the throne, and then had the witnesses dealt with. I have to admit it—no one was in a better position to commit those crimes... But, no, it's impossible! Naransin always supported me. From the very first time I was deposed by the British, he encouraged me to resist. He always did everything he could to prevent my being dispossessed. He always encouraged me to fight back.'

'So that you would be more deeply compromised,' interjected Tatya Tope. 'In fact, he might well have been the source of the lies told about you to the British in order to draw them to Jhansi.'

'I know Naransin,' she said, 'and I know how he loves Jhansi.'

'Perhaps—but he hates you,' answered Tatya Tope. 'At any rate, I've learned in the past few days that he was one of the people most responsible for the fall of Jhansi. He was the one who forged that order instructing you not to launch an attack while I was battling the British. He's the one who allowed the British to gain a foothold on the ramparts.'

'I refuse, do you hear me, General, I refuse to believe that Naransin betrayed me!'

The Rani continued to deny evidence which, deep inside her, she had already accepted.

'Why? Why?' she cried, when the others had left and she was alone with Akbar. 'Because one day, years ago, I refused to yield to him? Could he have kept and hidden such hatred for so long? Why did he betray me? I want to know. Tell me.'

But Akbar, tight-lipped, had no answers.

Naransin's treachery struck the Rani deeply. After so many years of close collaboration, the betrayal of this man who had desired her, who had probably loved her, affected her like a moral rape. The humiliation of defeat was even more painful for having been inflicted by a friend, rather than by a thousand enemies.

Lakshmi refused to see anyone, even Tatya Tope who came every day, even newly-arrived refugees. She had Damodar kept away from her because she could not bear his childish exuberance and she no longer left her tent, which the sun had turned into an oven. All day long, she sat on her pillows, dripping with sweat, doing nothing, saying nothing. She paid no attention to her appearance; she hardly ate at all.

Not even the tragic news about her father roused her from her apathy.

Moropant had managed to reach Datya with his precious cargo and take refuge with his friend Modi, but the latter's friendship had not withstood his greed. Guessing at what Moropant had brought in those heavy sacks, Modi denounced his guest's presence to the Maharaja of Datya, a faithful ally of the British. The Maharaja had arrested Moropant, kept the sacks, and hurried to send Moropant, in irons, to General Rose at Jhansi. Moropant was brought to trial before Sir Robert Hamilton. After summary judgement, he had been hanged from a tree in the Jokhan Bagh, the site of the massacre of the British.

Moropant had refused to defend himself before the judges and had died courageously, without a prayer or a complaint. A few faithful retainers of the Rani had ventured to request Moropant's corpse in order to burn it according to the requirements of their religion. The British had refused and left the body to rot on its rope. They were aware that for Hindus this kind of foulness would prevent reincarnation.

The outrage perpetrated on Moropant's remains required reparation. The Rani went to perform a puja at the temple of Shiva. The crowd that had massed in the streets of Kalpi for her passage saw a robot with waxen features and a spastic walk, who seemed to see nothing, hear nothing. She performed the ritual gestures and presented her offerings like a sleepwalker. When she left the temple, she was greeted by an enormous ovation. She did not even notice that it came from her former soldiers. It was Akbar who explained it to her once they had returned to her tent. A number of chieftains of local tribes had been able to flee Jhansi. Leaving their women and children in villages sheltered by the jungle, they had hastened to Kalpi with their men for the purpose of resuming the fight led by the Rani.

As for Akbar's Pathans, about two hundred who had escaped the British cavalry had also arrived in Kalpi to continue the struggle.

'They're all burning to fight for you,' Akbar added. For the first time in days the Rani seemed to react.

'The British forced me to become a fighter. I'm not cut out for it. I was beaten, and I caused my people infinite misfortune.'

'Don't you understand, Lakshmi, that despite defeat, you won a resounding moral victory? Remember that the greatest heroes in our history are often the vanquished. It isn't victory that counts, but bravery. And perhaps our country loves unlucky heroes. From now on you are an incarnation of the spirit of resistance. You must continue the struggle for the sake of those who expect it of you.'

'And how am I to do that? I have been given neither command nor responsibility. No one trusts me.'

'The leaders, perhaps. Because they're jealous of your prestige. But their men, officers and soldiers alike, all have faith in you. It is your duty to act. Your duty to them and to yourself.'

The Rani's voice, until then only a murmur, recovered its natural quality.

'Why do you give me so much support, Akbar Khan? I'm not worthy of it.'

'Because I love you and because I believe in you.'

4

Excerpts from a letter from Roderick Briggs to Sarah Brandon, dated 20 April 1858, Jhansi.

...Certain inhabitants of Jhansi willingly showed us the place where the victims of the massacre had been buried.

I decided to go with sappers to that site, which is called Jokhan Bagh. After a little digging, we quickly found a mass grave and brought up sixty-two bodies. I shall spare you a description of the sight that presented itself to us.

I had come to look for Roger's remains. It was not an easy task, since the bodies were blackened and almost unrecognizable. And yet, I did recognize him, by his hair and his size. Upon returning to the camp I had to swallow several glasses of whiskey—I admit it to you—to compose myself. On the fourteenth of this month a service was held for the souls of our dead, and it has been decided to erect a memorial. In the Rani's town palace we found crates filled with their clothes, their books and other personal things, including children's toys. In a corner of the room she occupied until her flight, I discovered, thrown in a corner, Roger's sketchbooks, and a little box containing a sapphire ring that had belonged to him and must have been pulled off his body. So much kindling to inflame our vengeance. Yet, punishment was dictated only by justice.

We executed only the Rani's proven accomplices, her father Moropant, her dignitaries, her ministers, her courtiers and officers. We spared all those, even the guilty, who had shown us the slightest spirit of cooperation.

Her former Prime Minister Naransin surrendered after offering us his collaboration. He did not hide his hatred of the Rani and his revulsion at her crimes. He explained the claims that the state of Orchha would make on the territory of Jhansi. I have to admit that these quarrels between native princelings are too complicated for me. General Rose also wanted to reward a certain Du'lajita Kur, who provided the information that enabled us to take the town ramparts. He was awarded two villages taken from one of the Rani's partners-in-crime.

If it is true we wanted to make an example, to ensure that one of the rebellion's worst massacres not be forgotten, at least we did so with restraint worthy of a civilized people.

Once the city was taken, our soldiers showed the unfortunate native women and children, as well as the aged, a degree of Christian charity that is even more to their credit than their feats of arms, and which no other European nation would have shown in the circumstances that had brought us before the walls of Jhansi. I do not exaggerate when I say that I saw some of our men sharing their meals with natives who had lost everything.

We organized an auction of certain objects seized in the Rani's palace. There were small jewels, turbans, tunics and other baubles, some of them rather pretty. I bought for you a cashmere shawl which I hope you will like and which I am sending you by mail.

I confess to you, my dear Sarah, that I am bored.

Our General, resuming those habits he had stifled during the siege, wastes precious time. He waits patiently for the necessary food and munitions. Having got wind of rebel movements quite far northeast of Jhansi, he is toying with the idea of leading us there. Are we going to sweep out every rebel nest in India, no matter how small, before we can attack Kalpi and flush out the Rani of Jhansi?

Though she continues to scheme against us, and we have already accumulated so much damning proof against her, we do not wish to condemn her without giving her a fair trial. Sir Robert Hamilton is heading a commission of officers appointed by him. General Rose has delegated me to represent him and attend the hearings. For several days we met in a room in the fort to question witnesses. We had been able to find several of the Indian servants of our slaughtered countrymen, including the orderlies of Captain Skene and Gordon. Arrested by order of the Rani and condemned to death, it was a miracle that they survived.

We were also able to get our hands on a number of former sepoys who had gone over to the rebellion, all of whom insisted they had acted on express orders from the Rani. From all this testimony it became evident that, long before the rebellion, the Rani had contacted conspirators in the hope of recovering her throne. During the events of last June she incited the rebels to attack the fort where our compatriots had sought safety, providing for this purpose an enormous cannon she had kept hidden in one of the courtyards of her town palace. On several occasions she refused to intervene to guarantee the safety of our compatriots. She was heard to say, 'I won't have anything to do with those English pigs.' Only one witness told a different version of the events—a certain Bakshish Ali, once the town's jailer who, with a few of his companions, actually perpetrated the massacre.

Denounced by a native, he was found by our men hiding in a nearby village. We condemned him to be hanged, not without hearing him out beforehand. His fanaticism was such that, even facing death, he did not hesitate to defend the unworthy queen he had served so well. According to him, the Rani, far from acting in concert with the rebels, was, in fact, their prisoner. Far from having ordered the massacre of our compatriots, she had violently reproached them for it and did everything she could to make them leave Jhansi, going as far as to pay them off with her own jewels. Could one believe a man who has on his conscience the murder of sixty-two men, women and children—especially when we had the deposition of the widow of Doctor Phipps? You will remember that I myself had freed her from prison, the sole survivor of the massacre. General Rose took her under his personal protection. We were all deeply affected by her appearance before the commission. She was dressed in black, as though in mourning for all our compatriots. She knew the Rani well, having once given her English lessons. Early on she had detected in her pupil a mad ambition and an inveterate hatred of all Englishmen.

With her own eyes Mrs Phipps saw a guarantee for safe conduct in the Rani's handwriting on the strength of which Skene and his besieged companions consented to surrender. We know the fate they met for having trusted the Rani's word. We asked Mrs Phipps why she had been spared. She told us that the Rani had preferred to submit her to psychological torture, threatening almost daily to have her executed, which she would certainly have done had we not arrived in time.

On the strength of her testimony the commission concluded that the Rani was guilty on all counts. I paid a call on Mrs Phipps, knowing that she had lodged Roger. She knew exactly who I was, for Roger had often spoken about me.

You will recall that, in his letters, Roger had told me that he had fallen in love with an Indian woman. I wanted to find this person, but Mrs Phipps, whom I asked about it, was completely unaware of the affair and seemed very surprised to hear about it.

'Your friend was very secretive,' she added.

I smiled, for that was typical of Roger. Mrs Phipps is about to leave for Bombay, from where she will embark for England. I have given her your address, as I would like you to meet such an interesting woman...

'How can Memsahib Phipps be so fiercely implacable towards you when you saved her life?' asked Akbar. The Rani answered in a tired voice, 'It's an old story!'

Then she added gloomily, 'A woman's jealousy doesn't fade with time and it stops at nothing.'

Spies and refugees who continued to arrive at Kalpi had eagerly brought to the Rani every detail of her trial 'in absentia'. Although the sufferings of her people burned her like a red-hot iron, she greeted the outrageousness of that parody of justice with icy disdain, explaining to an indignant Akbar, 'Trying to escape punishment, rebel sepoys took shelter behind my name. As for the former servants of the British, they were not harmed during my rule, and some of them even did very well. So they wanted to portray themselves as victims in order not to suffer the fate of other civilians. That, alas, is human nature.

'The British believed their testimony because they needed to justify their own actions. They made me their principal enemy before even knowing if I was guilty. Once they'd done that it became necessary to find proof, even at the cost of the most shameless lies.'

The Rani returned to Mrs Phipps and her accusations.

'To dare to claim she saw that notorious safe-conduct letter in my handwriting! Everyone in India knows that a queen never writes any official document in her own hand but only puts her seal on it. I should have had her executed.'

And in the same tone of voice, she reeled off a chain of insults against her accuser that were so coarse they left Akbar flabbergasted. Nevertheless, her violence seemed to him a sign that she might be emerging from her apathy.

The following morning, from inside her dark and stifling tent, the Rani heard the clattering hoofs of horses, the rattle of weapons, and orders barked in a voice she recognized as Akbar's. Intrigued, she stepped out of her tent and found him putting former soldiers of the army of Jhansi through their drill. There were a good thousand Pathans as well as men from local tribes and refugees who had arrived at Kalpi in successive waves and been rounded up by Akbar. They were a smart-looking lot, those turbaned horsemen, armed to the teeth and manoeuvring in flawless order. Still, the Rani made a face and, after observing them for a few minutes, she ran into the centre of the square they had formed and shouted, 'Is that how I trained you to fight? Where is your vigour? Where is your spirit? You can do better, I know it. Show me!'

She did not see the triumphant smile that lit up Akbar's face. She stayed to the end of the drill, chiding, making comments, and finally, she took command of the now galvanized cavalry. When they were dismissed, Akbar walked back to her tent with her. The Rani was smiling.

'Don't think I didn't see through your crude tricks, Akbar Khan.'

He began to laugh.

'What tricks? We weren't about to let your men rot among the slugs of Tatya Tope's army.'

The Rani grew solemn.

'It's your love that will bring me back to life.'

'Because you are my life.'

And they slid down together onto the pillows, their bodies bathed in sweat, and abandoned themselves to a sensuality that had been stifled far too long.

Having decided to turn her horsemen into a crack regiment, the Rani watched them drill every day. Their discipline and combat technique made them stand out sharply from the rest of the Peshwa's army. Little by little, soldiers from other regiments would come over to watch them train. Having nothing else to do, wearing motley uniforms, they would approach timidly and look on with a curiosity tinged with envy.

Then their officers came to stare with surprise and interest at this strange spectacle—an Indian regiment trained in the European manner. It did not take long for the Rani to notice that some of those officers had begun to imitate her methods, spontaneously but discreetly adapting their own regiments, training to approximate hers.

One day Tatya Tope came to ask her on behalf of the Peshwa to train his entire army. The Rani thanked him for the honour but declined; she did not want to put herself in a position where she would have to criticize indirectly other generals' methods, drawing their resentment and creating disunity and intrigue. Nevertheless, she did not spare Tatya Tope her advice on how to transform his army into a weapon capable of squaring off against the British.

Tatya Tope agreed enthusiastically, promised to follow her instructions...and as Lakshmi noticed in the days following, did nothing. The Rani returned to the attack, this time when the Peshwa invited her to dinner with his staff in his vast ceremonial tent. Once again, she listed the urgent reforms necessary to lift their troops—certainly brave and ardent men, but undisciplined—to the level of the British army. Once again, Tatya Tope backed her.

'The Rani is right,' he said. 'She has learned the art of warfare from the best master there is—experience. It was a hard lesson, as we all know, to see the British take Jhansi despite the numerical imbalance.'

The barb in that allusion might not have been deliberate, but the Rani chose to think so. Impulsively, she replied, 'We held out for fourteen days with inferior armament and ill-trained soldiers, recruited anywhere we could. That's certainly better than letting an army of twenty thousand be routed in two hours by fifteen hundred Englishmen.'

The Rani immediately regretted what she had said. She knew that Tatya Tope would never forgive her this reminder of his ignominious defeat. The Peshwa, however, seemed delighted by the shocking remark she had uttered. He was, that night, in an expansive mood that contrasted with his usual shyness. Sitting next to him, the Rani wondered if he had perhaps increased his usual dose of opium. Rao Sahib leaned towards her and said, loud enough to be heard by their closest neighbours, 'I've made my decision. Tomorrow, I shall give you the command of our army. Never mind those who will criticize my choice of a woman for the post. You are the most qualified—and besides, your exploits have earned you a prestige among our men that no one else enjoys.'

The Rani kept her reserve, but she was vibrating with hope. She yearned for action. She wanted to take in hand that enormous army, mould it, perfect it, to whip the British and liberate Jhansi.

When she awoke the following morning, she learned that Rao Sahib had appointed Tatya Tope commanding general. News had also come that night that two days before, on 25 April, General Rose had left Jhansi at the head of his army and was marching on Kalpi.

'I can't help noticing,' the Rani said, 'that the Peshwa thinks me good enough to train troops but not to lead a campaign.'

Akbar did not hide his thoughts. 'Instead of preparing themselves to win, those incompetents can think of nothing but petty jealousies. Tatya Tope must have forced Rao Sahib's hand. He fears your power.'

'You're mistaken. The Peshwa is just a weakling, and he fears for his own power.'

The council of war to which the Rani was summoned was held at Fort Kalpi in a massive isolated building which the natives believed was haunted. Several centuries earlier it had served as a tomb for a Sultan Lodi of a quite forgotten dynasty. Built at the edge of the cliff that rose sharply from the river Jumna, it consisted of a single vast square room capped by a large cupola. Its inordinately thick walls, with no openings except for a narrow door, sheltered it from prying ears.

Forgetting her bitterness and her disappointment, the Rani, urged to speak first, tried to be as persuasive as possible. Until now, the revolutionary armies' greatest error had been to remain always on the defensive. It was essential that the British not be allowed to lay siege on Kalpi. One could beat them only by taking the offensive and coming out to confront them. To her great surprise, both the Peshwa and Tatya Tope gave in to her arguments without any discussion. They even asked her to choose the best spot at which to stop the enemy advance. Leaning over maps—British, of course, for Indian maps, although beautifully painted, were not very precise—she suggested the small city of Kunch; the unusually dense forests there would provide strong natural defences and be a considerable obstacle to the enemy.

Again, Tatya Tope and the Peshwa immediately agreed. The army would leave for Kunch without delay.

'We take your advice as orders,' added Rao Sahib, 'and it is to you we shall owe our victory.'

Akbar noticed that the Rani seemed transformed, almost joyful, when she returned to her tent and said to him, 'I don't know whether they meant it, but if we do take the offensive as they agreed, if they really do change their tactics as I've urged them to do, then yes, I believe we will win, and everything becomes possible once again.'

Excerpts from a letter from Roderick Briggs to Sarah Brandon, dated 8 May 1859.

At last, we have set off for Kalpi.

Although I had cursed our delays, our advance has been so painful that I have almost come to wish we had stayed at Jhansi. The nights are short and stifling, and by day, the sun is so fierce we can scarcely bear our uniforms. Even under the double cloth layer of our tents, metal objects become so hot you can't touch them with bare hands.

We are crossing flat and arid country. Apart from a thin row of small mango trees along the road, there is not a single trace of greenery. Only thorny, dry bushes break the monotony of the plain.

Early in the afternoon we had stopped and pitched camp when, suddenly, the horizon was darkened by prodigious masses of clouds, composed of the yellowish dust that covers the plain. It was a sandstorm, heading for us faster and faster, higher and higher, like an immense curtain dividing the universe. Sudden, swirling gusts of wind knocked over bushes and trees. The storm was advancing with a terrifying rumble, like an avalanche.

And then it fell on us. The animals had lain down, terror-stricken, trembling spasmodically. All our tents collapsed. The reflected heat and glare of the sun, so unbearable, brusquely gave way to darkness, and every human being, every object seemed hidden in a yellowish fog. You couldn't see a yard away. The wind was so strong that none of us could stand up. We threw ourselves to the ground like the animals. I took refuge under a cart loaded with munitions. Dust seeped in everywhere, under my clothes, into my nostrils, my ears, my eyes. For almost half an hour it was hell. Then it began to rain, in large drops so refreshing they seemed like pearls from heaven. The temperature plummeted.

The rain stopped almost as suddenly as it had begun. There followed a deafening concert of cicadas and toads. Large insects whirred about us; we were attacked by white ants, crickets, fireflies, cockroaches, mosquitoes, and especially by beer bahuti, gliding like a multitude of red velvet swatches. The rain had so increased the weight of our tents that we were unable to push on the next morning.

When we did leave, two days later, the heat had returned with a vengeance, even more intense than before as though to avenge itself for the brief respite the rain had provided. Animals are dying in the dozens from hunger and the heat. The men aren't faring much better. Many have been struck down with fever.

We march now only by night. We lie down at six in the morning and rise again three hours later. Water can be found only at narrow, deep wells, almost exhausted, at interveals of ten miles. Around each one there is the heartbreaking spectacle of thousands of men with dried, shrivelled skin waiting anxiously for their turn to fill their leather flasks. The warm, muddy water does little to quench their thirst.

Yesterday, after marching all night, we reached the village of Pucha to learn that the enemy was waiting for us at Kunch. We had to set off again, cover the sixteen miles in daylight, under a merciless sun, and after a sleepless night. The savannah had given way to jungle. But what a jungle! Thorny, grey, devoid of lushness or greenery. The branches snagged our uniforms, scratched us, pulled us up short. Here and there a tall leafless tree dominated the undergrowth, half-scorched by the heat.

The men were so exhausted we had to order a halt. Since there was no source of water around, they were given brandy to quench their thirst. Can anyone imagine anything more stupid! Alcohol, after quenching thirst for a few moments, only makes it worse. A single glass was enough to have a disastrous effect on exhausted men, making their bodies feel even heavier and multiplying their fatigue.

Still, there was no choice but to move on. This morning we halted one mile from Kunch. The little village stands alone in the embrace of the jungle. On the left we could see, in the distance, a lovely lake whose glittering waters tugged at us like a huge magnet. It was, of course, only a mirage, an illusion that added to our torment. Through my field glasses I could clearly see turbans and rifle-barrels moving about behind the low brick wall that protects Kunch. The rebels were there. Our scouts returned to tell us that Tatya Tope and the Rani of Jhansi herself awaited us with their army. General Rose sent the greater part of our forces around their lines, leaving only a screen of troops, my regiment among them, facing the centre.

The hours crawled by interminably while our two flanks marched through the jungle to take up their positions. We wait under a terrible sun, in waves of dust that seem to escape from hell itself.

The condition of our men grows worse by the minute. I saw some collapse and fall to the ground with heatstroke. Others stand up, throw down their weapons, stagger a few steps, and faint; seven have already died like that. Panic is beginning to infect even the healthy men, and I have just given them permission to seek shade and water in a nearby village where there are two wells that are not yet completely dry.

To escape the inevitable tension that precedes combat, I think of you as I write…

5

'Why did you concentrate your forces in the centre, Tatya Tope? Why did you make the same mistake as you did at the battle of the Betwa? Why didn't you follow the tactics we had all agreed upon?'

It had taken only one hour for the British army to maul the rebels, throw them out of Kunch, and force them to retreat. As soon as they returned to Kalpi, their leaders met in the Sultan's tomb.

Behind the Peshwa on his silver throne and behind Tatya Tope were their respective retinues, groups of officers magnificent in their brocade, with their jewels and gem-studded weapons. Only Akbar, dressed in simple white, without a single ornament, stood like a statue behind the Rani's pillow. The light of blazing torches flickered in the elegant dome that dominated the room and made shadows dance in the corners, enhancing the natural mystery of the place. But the Rani had no thoughts for the ghosts that allegedly haunt it. She had risen to her feet, gesticulating, and her voice became so unusually piercing that it grated on the ear.

'Not only did our strategy—or rather our absence of strategy—turn out to be disastrous, but our army, even though I had brought your attention to this matter time after time, showed a wretched lack of discipline. The men of the Gwalior contingent, of whom you are so proud, Tatya Tope, opened fire without orders, and then they allowed themselves to be run through and abandoned their positions in a hurry.'

No general likes to be criticized, especially by a woman. And Tatya Tope too could be impulsive. He replied sharply, 'And what about your horsemen, Lakshmi, where were they during the retreat? Instead of staying behind to protect our rear from British attacks, they were well in front, hurrying off to shelter before anyone else!'

The Rani's rage built up again before she answered, 'How do you know where my cavalry was? You weren't even there! Without striking a blow, you abandoned us in full retreat.'

'You know very well, Rani,' interrupted Rao Sahib, 'that Tatya Tope went to see his father, who is very ill, in the village of Charkhi. Moreover, the retreat of our army was carried out in perfect order, undoubtedly attributable to the advice you wasted on us.'

'Retreat! That's all you ever talk about! Retreats are all you can lead. Yes! It was a beautiful retreat, and it cost us six hundred lives that would have been spared had Tatya Tope been there to order a counter-attack.

Once again, the Peshwa came to Tatya Tope's rescue and answered the Rani in a cloyingly sweet tone, 'Why didn't you order that counter-attack yourself if you thought it necessary?'

The veiled accusation incensed the Rani, who now turned on Rao Sahib.

'And you, Peshwa, what were you doing at the time? I understand why you didn't come to Kunch, since you stayed here with part of our troops. But what did you do to stop them from deserting at the first news of our defeat? Why didn't you hold them back instead of letting them scatter all over the countryside?

'We returned here to find a desert. I've been told that, apart from your servants and your aides, there were exactly seven sepoys left in the camp.'

Tatya Tope looked weary all of a sudden and spoke sadly, 'If you don't wish to fight with us anymore, Lakshmi, you're free to leave with your troops.'

The Rani's rage had still not subsided when she returned to her tent with Akbar.

'And on top of it all, he takes me for a coward. Does he really think I'm going to abandon him? Though perhaps, I should—I was burning to fight at his side, with his army, but it has caused me only heartache and bitterness.'

'These disputes, these reproaches between you are useless. We'll never win if we remain at odds.'

'Nothing will stop me from speaking my mind, especially when I'm in the right.'

'You're not always in the right. Why, as the Peshwa asked you, didn't you yourself order a counter-attack during our retreat?'

'I wasn't about to risk my horsemen for no reason when the battle had already been lost through Tatya Tope's fault and he had already abandoned us.'

'And you let those poor foot soldiers be mowed down by artillery without going to their aid as I begged you to. I could have cried, watching whole groups of them topple over.'

'Those foot soldiers were Tatya Tope's men.'

It was a reaction typical of a chieftain, and it angered Akbar, 'It's not a question of your men and Tatya Tope's men or those of the Peshwa. There is only one army, our army, which is fighting to liberate our country. What the leaders don't see, the men do. All those you call "Tatya Tope's men" ask me: "Why did the Rani forsake us at Kunch?"'

'All right, Akbar Khan, I promise! You'll never again see me and my cavalry stand aside!'

But since she never found it easy to surrender, she added, 'Judging by your advice, it seems that in the future I will have to charge even when the battle is lost—even when things are hopeless—just for honour.' And she gave an ironic laugh.

'No! To set an example, Lakshmi.'

They challenged one another with their eyes. They were alone in the Rani's tent; it was siesta time and everyone was trying to rest wherever he could. Damodar, fearing his mother's mood, had gone to sleep in Mandar's tent. The silence outside was broken only by the neighing of a horse tormented by flies. Inside the tent, the heat was slightly mitigated by the swaying back and forth of a punkah. Akbar stroked the Rani's arm with a tender, sly gesture that signalled his desire. The Rani snatched her arm away.

'No, not now, I'm too upset.'

He caught her, threw himself with her onto the pillows and began to tear off her clothes. She struggled, she scratched him, she tried to squirm away—then, giving in, she let him undress her and caress her, and then, she gently took him in her arms and drew him close.

Later, he turned to her, his blue eyes laughing. 'I love you, I admire you, that's why I always want you to be the best.'

The Rani looked at Akbar's muscular body and ran her hand through his fair hair. 'If I am, it will be thanks to you... And now that you have raped your queen, you may leave.'

When he had gone, she remained stretched out on her pillows, languid, glowing. She discovered suddenly that she loved Akbar, and was astonished by the revelation, astonished too that it had taken her so long to realize it. Their sensual friendship, their work-related complicity and their shared trials had prepared, without her being aware of it, fertile ground for love to burgeon and bloom. It was not the same passion that Roger had inspired in her, nor the spiritual hold Firoz Shah had exercised over her. What she felt for Akbar was love. Understanding it made her value more clearly, more deeply the love that Akbar bore her, and she was immensely relieved. It seemed to her that once again energy and optimism were surging in her veins.

When Damodar returned to the tent, he was astonished to find his mother in a joyous mood. She welcomed him gaily, played with him as she had not done for a very long time. Happy, the child relaxed; for once, in front of his mother, he gave full play to his natural tenderness and exuberance.

That night, at a dinner given by the Peshwa for his high command, the atmosphere remained tense. The harsh reality of their situation weighed on the guests; within a few days General Rose's army would be at Kalpi, the rebels' last stronghold. They were now driven into a corner at a time when desertions following the defeat at Kunch had reduced their strength by a third.

A clamour from outside broke the silence. There was the noise of a procession, shouts, acclamations. The flaps of the tent were unceremoniously thrown open and a tall, fat man with a long greying moustache entered, wearing as many jewels as the Great Moghul and carrying as many weapons as a dacoit. Barely pausing to greet the Peshwa and Tatya Tope, he made straight for the Rani, lifted her off her cushion and pressed her to his ample breast.

'At last I see her,' he shouted, 'the heroine all India talks about! The flame of our revolution...'

Then, releasing Lakshmi, he seemed to remember the Peshwa's presence, bowed before him and announced in a piercing voice, 'I bring Your Highness two thousand soldiers and powerful artillery. With that we shall surely defeat the British.'

He was the Nawab of Banda, the Muslim ruler of a small state southeast of Kalpi. Recently, he had been the object of much talk. Dethroned by the British, he had, nevertheless, in the early stages of the revolution, protected British lives and interests.

Then, faced with the uselessness of his efforts and the unanimity of his former subjects, he had gone over to the rebels and retaken his throne. Since then he had been one of the more tireless and active adversaries of the British. A formidable man in size as well as temperament, he created a stir wherever he went. His arrival had an immediate and radical effect on the Peshwa's army; the very next morning, deserters began to come back, en masse, from the villages where they had been hiding.

On 20 May, the high command assembled for the last time before the battle. In contrast with the meeting held after the defeat at Kunch, this one was dominated by optimism. The Peshwa began by painting a confident picture of the situation.

'General Rose's army has arrived before Kalpi. Another British army corps from the south is now camping on the far bank of the Jumna, separated from us by a valley too deep for them to cross. Rose will probably attack us tomorrow; his guns are already in place around the city. But what matter! We couldn't care less about the British and their guns. Behind us, we have a cliff that plunges straight into the river. All around us for protection are miles of deep, narrow ravines the enemy cannot possibly cross. I've had trenches dug and embankments built on the Kunch road, which is their only access. And finally, we have our staunchest and most effective ally—our summer, which drives the British mad and makes them fall like flies. Let us wait behind our ramparts while their army crumbles and disintegrates of its own weight.'

He paused to judge the effect of his words and was annoyed when the Rani spoke up.

'Wide is the experience and deep the wisdom of the Peshwa. Therefore, we shall do exactly as he says. Tomorrow Rose will begin to pelt us with shells, and then he will throw his cavalry at us. We will not fire; we will let them come as close as possible. At the very moment when they are sure of their victory, our guns will open up and mow them down. Then, we shall attack. Our cavalry will finish the job our guns began. We will run the British cavalry back, we will break their lines, and thus, if God wills it, we shall gain the victory.'

The Rani had just proposed a strategy entirely opposite to that of the Peshwa, an offensive rather than defensive strategy. Tatya Tope nodded several times to show his approval. The Nawab of Banda loudly agreed—the idea of a furious charge delighted him; he was bored by sieges and dreamed only of blows and blood. Faced with such unanimity, Rao Sahib, already appeased by the politeness with which the Rani had contradicted him, gave in, 'So it will be,' he said and adjourned the meeting.

It was with a lighter heart that the Rani with the other leaders stepped out onto the terrace that ran in front of the 'Little Fort,' the old tomb of a Lodi Sultan, standing three hundred feet over the Jumna River as it ran between sheer cliffs.

They could see, downstream on the other bank, at the spot where the river began to curve, the distant fires of the British army that had come from the south. They leaned over the parapet to watch the lazy waters of the Jumna flow by, reddened by the setting sun and slowed by summer. The sandbanks were swarming with their soldiers who had come in pilgrimage to the river—the holiest of India after the Ganges. The Rani was even able to make out among them Damodar, whom Mandar had brought to perform his devotions. The child imitated the men around him. He plunged his miniature sword into the Jumna and three times called upon Kali, the goddess of war, repeating the pledge he heard his neighbors speak, 'We shall win or we shall die; but we shall not step back.'

Excerpts from a letter from Roderick Briggs to Sarah Brandon, dated 24 May 1858.

Forgive me, dear Sarah, for not having written for so long. More than lack of time, exhaustion is the true reason for my silence. After the engagement at Kunch—one can't decently call that skirmish a battle—we had only one day of rest, during which we were too exhausted to sleep and spent the time in a sort of torpor.

The next morning, when we set off again, our native soldiers—even they were suffering terribly from the heat—began to collapse in droves. In one regiment, half the men were struck down by sunstroke in a single day. Out of a detachment of thirty-six men sent to forage, seventeen fainted and remained in a coma for about two hours. Our General himself was not spared; at Kunch he fell off his horse three times and suffered a mild attack. About half our army was completely incapacitated, and the other half were not in much better shape.

And yet, we did advance. We looked more like a horde of gypsies than a British army, with our extraordinary assembly of vehicles of all sorts, all of them more or less broken, pulled by sick and exhausted buffalo, led by terrorized natives or by peasants impressed into service. We could not stop. General Rose was in a hurry to reach Kalpi. He feared the arrival of the rains, which would have turned the ground into impassable swamps. The chief medical officer was adamant; even the healthy men would not hold out much longer. We had to win immediately or watch our army disintegrate.

So our Via Dolorosato the Jumna was also a race against the clock. We realized we were approaching the river when the plains were replaced by ravines. Intersecting one another without interruption, they were impassable to everything but mountain goats and light infantry.

The rebels awaited us on the road linking Kunch to Kalpi, which they had fortified by digging trenches and raising embankments behind which they had placed part of their artillery. The obstacle seemed insurmountable. The General decided to simply go around it. He had the entire army turn right, in order to attack the town from the south. The rebels were not expecting this tactic, which had the added advantage of allowing us to link up with the southern army camped on the other bank of the Jumna.

During the night before the battle, General Maxwell, the commander of that army, managed, through some miracle, to create a bridge of boats across the river just south of the town. He immediately sent us some of his men, and we were able to send him our sick and wounded to be evacuated to Cawnpore and Calcutta. The arrival of fresh and rested comrades did wonders for our morale.

On the following morning, 22 May, we were quite ready when, at ten o'clock in the morning exactly, the rebel forces appeared outside the walls of the city. They were the combined armies of the man they call the Peshwa, of Tatya Tope and of the Rani of Jhansi who were lined up before us. Suddenly they charged, yelling. We let them come. When they were far enough out to be no longer protected by their artillery, Rose gave the order to fire. A barrage of shells and grenades struck them, sowing confusion among their cavalry and breaking up their infantry lines. The General ordered a counter-attack. We galloped our horses at the enemy at full tilt. No sooner had we reached them and begun to fight than they turned tail and ran.

Already I could see in the distance the cluster of orange flags marking the presence of their Peshwa as they retreated towards the city. An easy victory was most welcome, for even this brief engagement had drained us all. The thermometer read 119 degrees in the shade and there was a scorching wind that literally suffocated us. Officers and soldiers fainted or fell as though struck by lightning. Summer's furnace was doing more damage than the rebels. Later, I learned that our General had had a heart-attack, and that his chief of staff had been transported unconscious to the rear; as for the senior chaplain, he had gone mad. We could already taste success when swarms of rebel cavalry came thundering down on us, weapons in hand, at breathtaking speed. From afar, I recognized Pathans and the cavalry of the Gwalior contingent. One of my companions pointed out the Rani of Jhansi, who was leading the charge in person. Their soldiers must have been drugged on opium or drunk with brandy stolen from our garrisons, for they seemed to pay no attention to the bullets and grenades that fell on them like hail.

They had begun to overwhelm our front lines when Rose called in our reserves to break their momentum. The rebels continued, nevertheless, to fight furiously and they might have gained the upper hand had other rebel units followed their example. But in the distance, hundreds of their foot soldiers were fleeing towards the nearby villages, even jumping into the ravines.

Soon the Rani's cavalry began to pull back. She herself had disappeared. I tried to ride off in pursuit, but my horse refused to move—and I too was completely exhausted. The rebel army was in full flight, and in a daze, I managed to understand that we had won.

All evening and part of the night, Rose pounded the city in preparation for the next day's battle.

At three in the morning we set off to wheel around the town of Kalpi in order to prevent the enemy from escaping along the road to Kunch. We were approaching the village of Rehree when sustained fire broke out from the mud houses. It was only an isolated cluster of rebels. We flushed them without much difficulty and, at the same time, killed a panther and two hares who had the misfortune of crossing our path. At dawn, very far in the distance, we could see columns of rebels hastily retreating towards the jungle.

We took Fort Kalpi and the rebel camp without firing a single shot. Both were completely abandoned, the rebel army having evacuated during the night. Tatya Tope had advised the inhabitants of the town to flee if they wanted to save their lives.

Here and there, in the silent empty streets, pigs and mangy dogs were fighting over rotting corpses. In houses still standing after the bombardment, we found absolutely nothing. On the other hand, the fort yielded a great deal of varied loot: tents, ceremonial umbrellas, rifles, mortars, cannonballs, repair-workshops filled with tools made in England, uniforms of all types and sizes, most of them stolen from British soldiers and still bearing the numbers of their regiments. We even found two ladies' bonnets among trombones, horns, trumpets, drums, flags, hats, bags, belts, flasks, powder-horns. But best of all, in an underground vault, we found sixty thousand pounds of gunpowder. The rebel army had evacuated Kalpi in such a hurry that they left us their arsenal. In a curious building which in past centuries, we are told, was a tomb, and more recently, served as the council room for the rebel chiefs, we found that they had even abandoned their files. The General handed them over to the experts to be examined for any useful information.

Today is the birthday of our Queen. In her honour, we raised our colours over Kalpi. Governor General Lord Canning sent General Rose a cable that was read before the entire army:

'Your capture of Kalpi crowns an uninterrupted series of brilliant achievements. I thank you and your brave soldiers with all my heart.'

We have fulfilled our task. We have taken Kalpi. We have annihilated the rebel army and linked up with the army of the south. Our army corps is soon to be disbanded, and General Rose is not unhappy at the decision. He plans to return to Bombay and take a bit of rest.

Around me, I see nothing but joyous relief, although exhaustion and the heat keep the men from any expansive demonstration. As for myself, I am torn between the relief of being able finally to rest and the frustration of not having avenged Roger's death by killing his murderess, the Rani of Jhansi, as I had sworn to do. We are told that she fled in a palanquin, surrounded by a handful of her Pathans, along the Jumna, heading north. What remains of the army with which she hoped to defy us? Just a few hundred men, dispersed in an impenetrable jungle, sentenced never to come out because all the surrounding areas are held by the armies of our allies.

Rather than surrender, the Rani will, no doubt, choose to remain among the wild animals. How long will she live, in solitude, want and fear? If she does indeed finally elude the British noose, she may, one day, be devoured by a tiger.

From what I hear we shall soon return to our base in Bombay. I will then ask for leave to return to England to marry you if you will still have me.

In truth, I am rather like our General in that I have no desire to remain in India or even come back again to serve. For me, the Indian chapter is closed. I am so happy to be able, at last, to end my letter by telling you, dear Sarah, that I look forward to seeing you soon.

6

Between Kalpi and Gwalior stretches a vast barren region called the Chambal Valley. It is a flat reddish savannah cut by gullies, ditches and uneven dunes of windswept sand, sparsely dotted with thorny bushes. One afternoon in late May 1858, two riders were galloping along a sandy road, apparently indifferent to the suffocating heat that cast a pale grey veil on the sky at the horizon. They descended the cliff, low but steep, that bordered one of those wide streams, irregular and capricious, that cut beds far too wide for their meagre flow. They jumped from their horses and threw themselves, fully clothed, into the water, which was shallow and exceptionally clear, and lay there stretched out for a time, their bodies submerged, their heads resting on the wet sand of the bank, happy to cool themselves and wash away the dust. One was dark and tall, the other rather frail. Both had their hair cut short in the back and wore the white turban typical of Pathans. They seemed oblivious to the danger of the place; the Chambal Valley was dacoit territory, where no one dared venture.

But no dacoit would have raised his hand against a ruler; and one of the young Pathans was none other than the Rani of Jhansi, accompanied by Akbar. It had been four days since they had left Kalpi. Contrary to the vague rumours reported by Roderick Briggs, the Rani had not fled in a palanquin. She had begun by cropping her hair so that she would not be taken for a woman. Then, with Damodar tied to her saddle with a silk scarf, she had left on horseback, accompanied by Akbar, a handful of Pathan horsemen and faithful Mandar. They had worked their way down the cliff to the Jumna over a steep goat path and then ridden off northwards along sandbars that streaked the river.

Later, they turned right and pushed into the jungle to head for

Gopalpur, forty-six miles from Kalpi in the middle of the Chambal Valley desert. The rebel leaders and the remains of their forces had linked up in that small town, where particularly hostile natural surroundings protected them from their British pursuers. The local Raja—there was a Raja at Gopalpur, a protector and accomplice of the dacoits—had had no choice but to welcome them.

The Rani emerged from her daydream and inched deeper into the water, so that only her face remained above the surface.

'At last, here I can breathe,' she said. 'I couldn't have stood another minute of those arguments between our generals blaming each other for the defeat at Kalpi.'

Akbar sat up.

'Why didn't they listen to you as they'd promised to?' he asked heatedly. 'Why didn't they follow your instructions when, the day before they all agreed to? Why...'

'Stop that, Akbar. I know all that, and you're boring me. Don't be like them, don't rehash the past. There's no point to it. It certainly won't do anything for us now.'

The silence returned. For a long time the Rani was lost in meditation. Then she began to think aloud, 'The great revolt of India is about to fail—it's already failed. I didn't want to have anything to do with it, the British forced me. It became my cause and now it is a lost cause. Whoever would have thought—a hundred and fifty million Indians against forty-five thousand Englishmen!'

'Not all of India revolted, Lakshmi. The south didn't stir, the west didn't stir.'

'In the east, Bengal didn't stir because the British crushed it by preventive repression.'

'But the rulers, Lakshmi, the kings of Rajasthan, those in the south, and even your friend the Maharaja of Gwalior? They were afraid to get involved and cautiously remained in the British camp. They are the guilty ones. When our people have leaders worthy of them, who can plan and organize, who will stop being jealous of each other, then we shall find the energy to win our freedom!'

'Let's stop arguing, Akbar! We're behaving exactly like those generals we've been criticizing.'

She spoke with such lassitude that Akbar immediately softened.

'At Kalpi, during the battle, you were magnificent. You've never looked more beautiful. Several times I was almost killed because I couldn't take my eyes off you. I was afraid for you, but at the same time, I felt that you were invincible. I saw you as someone new, someone I didn't know, a legendary figure beyond the reach of enemy blows. Never, Lakshmi, never have I seen you fight as you did that day at Kalpi.'

Akbar's admiration did not raise the Rani's spirits. In a melancholic voice, she said, 'I was right when I refused to join the revolution. I lost Jhansi. I brought misfortune to Jhansi. There's nothing more I can do. There's nothing more to be done.'

'Is it worthy of you to moan like that—you, the fighter, the unconquerable? Do you want me to think the British have finally won, that they've robbed you of your courage? Instead of going around in circles wasting our time analyzing our defeats with the generals, instead of rotting here—let's go.'

'And where will we go, Akbar Khan?'

'To my country, to the north, in the mountains—there where the British will never come looking for us, where men live hard but free lives by the eternal snows.'

The Rani smiled. She stretched almost voluptuously and in a light voice, said, 'But I don't like to travel, Akbar.'

He noticed the quick transformation in the Rani's mood and continued with enthusiasm, 'I'll teach you to travel. I've been doing it since I was a child. We'll go here one day and there tomorrow. We'll be as free as the wind. Adventure will be our daily bread. And perhaps one day, we'll be able to resume the struggle.'

The day was waning; the shadows of the thorny branches were lengthening. The slanting light turned orange in the languor of late afternoon. The Rani shook herself and stood up, her wet clothes sticking to her body.

'Let's go, Akbar, soon it'll be the hour when the tigers come to drink, and I don't wish to meet one. We don't want to give the British the satisfaction of letting ourselves be devoured.'

The long peasant houses, with mud walls and thatched roofs laid out like ramparts, defended the entrance to Gopalpur. In the neighbouring fields stood the tents of the improvised camp of those soldiers who had been able to reach the town. The Rani and Akbar rode along the main street, shaded here and there by tall trees. Only the children came out onto the doorsteps to watch them go by. The adults continued to go about their business, sometimes turning their heads to look at them.

The Rani, again sunk in thought, let her reins dangle on her horse's neck. Then, turning to Akbar, her voice firm and almost joyful, she said, 'You're right, Akbar Khan. There is still time for adventure.'

The building where the Rani had settled was far from being a palace. It was more a villa, recently built in the bastardized style introduced in India by European architects. In deference to the Rani's sex, the Raja had allotted her the apartments of his women, whom he had dispatched to another residence. The purdah consisted of a series of narrow, low-ceiling rooms located in the highest and most remote area of the palace. On the windows and balconies, latticework protected women from inquisitive gazes. Through it the Rani stared out on the limitless flat and bush-studded desert of Chambal Valley.

'Find me a white sari, one whose silk isn't too transparent, so that my shorn hair won't be seen through the veil,' she told Mandar.

This sudden attention to appearance surprised Mandar; she was even more astonished when her mistress added, 'And call the servants to get me dressed.'

It was the first time since her flight from Jhansi that the Rani had demanded the care owed to her beauty and her rank. The servants of the Rani of Gopalpur were very young peasant women, paralyzed by shyness. They gawked devotedly at the famous Rani of Jhansi who was the talk of the whole country and did their best to execute the complicated rites of her dressing.

Relaxed, dreamy, the Rani let them tend to her, like a queen in full glory surrendering to the thousand delights of affectation. Observing her mistress's amused smile, Mandar, though accustomed to her unpredictable moods, thought her mind must be wandering. When the servants had finished their task as well as they could, she heard the Rani order, 'And now, Mandar, give me a massage, only you can do it well.'

While massaging the scented flesh of her mistress, Mandar told her, as she always did, the rumours she had culled from as high up as the command staff.

'I hear that "they" have decided to go to Nepal. Nana Sahib, the Begum of Oudh and so many of the other leaders of the revolution have taken refuge there. They say the Maharaja of Nepal protects them, even though he did send troops to help the British. It's a beautiful country and perhaps we can be happy there while we wait for better days.'

'I will certainly not go to Nepal. The Maharaja has been blackmailing our friends who have sought asylum there. He never stops threatening them and fleecing them shamelessly. I don't want to have to submit to his whims. In fact, I don't want to be a refugee at all.'

Surprised, Mandar stopped the massage, straightened up and mopped her brow.

'Don't stop, it does me good.'

Mandar resumed her work, an expression of consternation on her face.

'So you're going to stay here, alone? Is that really what you want?'

'I wouldn't stay in this horrible hole for anything in the world.'

'So then what, since everything is lost and there's nothing left to do?'

The Rani smiled disarmingly, like a child.

'That is why we'll have to think of something.'

That very evening, Tatya Tope, having fled Kalpi by a road different from the Rani's, arrived in Gopalpur. The Raja wanted to give a banquet in his honour, despite his modest means.

It was held in the 'Raja's Garden', a small walled orchard at the entrance to the town, where a cluster of mangoes faced lemon and orange trees lined up neatly between irrigation canals. In the middle, on a platform, a tiny pavilion sheltered the musicians. Below them stretched a lawn on which carpets and pillows had been thrown about for the honoured guests. Behind the enclosure's low wall were massed the soldiers of the rebellion, their fierce appearance enhanced by their torn and ragged clothes.

The Rani's arrival caused a sensation. Immaculate in her white sari, her face carefully painted, her bearing graceful, she was, though she wore no jewels, the image of refinement and luxury. Where were the officers' and generals' glittering brocade uniforms and jewels? Today, they were fortunate to have a change of clothes. And here came the Rani looking as though she were going to some celebration at court, leaving behind her a scented trail.

The Raja of Gopalpur gave them a simple country meal of rice, potatoes, lentils and vegetables swimming in ghee or seasoned with the hottest of peppers, with half-curdled yoghurt to drink and water that seemed slightly brackish. Neither of those liquids were enough for these rough warriors, who passed flasks of guj from hand to hand and did credit to every flask. And yet, that comforting drink failed to lift the spirits of the military leaders of the rebellion. With a sort of morose glee, princes and generals enumerated the facts of their disaster.

'We've lost all our strongholds... We've lost our artillery, our weapons, our munitions. British armies await us in the south, the east and the west, surrounding the Chambal Valley. In the north, their ally the Maharaja of Gwalior stands with his personal army, blocking that way out. We are in a trap. Either the British will send their columns to dislodge us, or we will have to capitulate.'

'Capitulate? Never!' shouted the huge Nawab of Banda. 'We shall continue to fight! We still have troops.'

The Peshwa Rao Sahib guffawed.

'You call that an army—those few hundred men, disarmed, defeated, demoralized? Come, king—we had better think of fleeing to Nepal like the wiser of our peers.'

The Rani did not even pretend to listen to them. She still wore that light ironic smile that had so intrigued Akbar and Mandar. Suddenly, without turning, she spoke to Mandar, who stood behind her, 'Dance, Mandar, dance to cheer up our friends.'

Astonished, almost shocked, Mandar remained rooted to the spot. The Rani turned around and stared at her. 'Dance!' she repeated.

Mandar rushed off to change her clothes. Where did she find baggy breeches, a tight bolero and anklets hung with bells? When she returned, the guests stopped talking—and Mandar started to dance.

She moved her neck, her arms, her hands, her waist, her legs according to the strict rules of India's great sacred art. Her movements were now slow, now fast, now linked, now separate. Each of her gestures gained significance from her grace and precision. Watching her, one forgot how thin she was and how angular her features were. The insistent sound of the bells on her anklets mingled with the notes of the stringed instruments and the bracing rhythms of the tambourines. Her dance exuded a concentrated and subtle sensuality, and the warriors watched in fascination, as though she were the most beautiful nautch girl they had ever laid eyes upon.

When the Rani felt that the spectators were completely carried away, she raised her hand suddenly and stopped Mandar. There was surprise and almost anger among the spectators. Without looking at anyone, Lakshmi spoke in a clear, strong voice, 'Let us remember the history of the Maratha, our history. We have been victorious because we had impregnable fortresses. What was true yesterday remains true today. Wasn't it fortresses such as Jhansi and Kalpi that enabled us to hold out against the British for so long? Now we have lost them. There is no sense in attempting to flee; the enemy will follow and destroy us. As for surrender—that is a word never used in our tradition. What we must do, therefore, is capture a fortress in order to continue the fight until victory. But it must be a fortress important enough that our exploit will resound all over India, terrify the enemy, and reawaken the enthusiasm of our friends. Which fortress? That is for you to decide. Give me some suggestions.'

The guj and Mandar's dance had done their work. The rebel chiefs were in no state to think, but they were ready to listen to such a proposal. The Rani waited a long time, prolonging the silence almost gratuitously. Then, in the same even voice, she said, 'We shall take Gwalior.'

Gwalior, the pearl of central India, one of the country's most formidable fortresses, in everyone's opinion, impregnable! Maharaja Sindhia and especially his Prime Minister Diwan Dinkar were more vassals than allies of the British, and they still had an army of eight thousand men.

A stunned silence followed the Rani's proposal. It was broken, at last, by the Nawab of Banda.

'Bravo! Let us march on Gwalior immediately!'

Tatya Tope burst out laughing, 'You always have extravagant ideas, Lakshmi. We couldn't possibly take Gwalior—but we shall do it.'

The Rani sensed that Rao Sahib was reluctant and turned her attention to him:

'Gwalior has always belonged to the Peshwa; your ancestor gave it to Sindhia's ancestor, his vassal, and Sindhia is there only through your good graces.'

That appeal to Rao Sahib's vanity worked immediately. In a solemn voice he said, 'We shall take Gwalior.'

The Raja of Gopalpur, only too delighted at the prospect of being relieved of his not altogether welcome guests, noisily approved the proposal.

'I've always said so, Rani! The only man among us is you!'

Everyone had immediately accepted the plan to take Gwalior, but no one had thought about the means to carry it out. Only Akbar seemed worried.

He had accompanied the Rani into her apartments, to the great scandal of the servants in the purdah. Lakshmi noticed how shocked they were and was amused by it; Akbar seemed oblivious. His brow furrowed, his lips pursed, he wore the expression of concentration he always assumed when puzzled.

'And how are we going to take Gwalior?' he asked the Rani.

'We'll think about that tomorrow. First, I had to find a striking idea that would whip up those men—they'd gone soft and timid as women.'

'Do you think we can do it?'

'We must take one last chance. What do we have to lose? Anything is better than staying in this dreadful Gopalpur!'

Then Akbar smiled, and the Rani asked him his own question, 'And you, do you think we'll make it?'

'No, according to all logic. Yes, since you say so!'

'So you don't think I'm mad?' He shrugged, and, suddenly serious once again, said, 'You must be careful, Lakshmi, not to become a prisoner of your image!'

'Am I not already a prisoner of my destiny?'

Never before had the Rani loved Akbar as she did then. He had given her back her fighting spirit, her thirst for action. Once again she dominated the situation, alone with her image, alone with her destiny. When he took her in his arms, she protested, 'Let's not shock the servants—and they have orders from their master to stay with me all night.'

And she struggled out of his embrace with a laugh tinged with despair.

For that moment she felt a need to be in his arms. 'No, stay,' she whispered. And with a quiet gesture, she motioned the horrified servants to leave.

When she rose the following morning, she learned that Tatya Tope had left Gopalpur during the night. He had returned to Charkhi to see his father, a reason that was certainly honourable, but to abandon his army under the circumstances, seemed somewhat bizarre—filial devotion, after all, should have its limits. On that same day, like a good omen, a few hundred sepoys arrived at Gopalpur to enlist in the Peshwa's small army. With them came one of Nana Sahib's former aides, bringing a hundred and fifty horsemen and three guns. The rebels, whom the British thought isolated in the hostile jungle, were in fact regrouping.

The Peshwa's army had begun its march on Gwalior. It had filled out rapidly and now comprised three thousand five hundred men; that was still far short of the number needed for such a foolhardy enterprise. In place of armed force, however, the troops had high morals. The Rani, the symbol if not the inspirer of their enthusiasm, rode at their head, the sun glinting off her helmet and armour among the orange Maratha banners.

On 24 May 1858, the Peshwa's army had already entered the Maharaja of Gwalior's territory and pitched camp in the village of Amin Mahal.

Tatya Tope had returned that morning and had immediately closeted himself with Rao Sahib in the latter's tent. The Rani had not been invited to the meeting, which angered her. But that evening she sat at Rao Sahib's side when he received Lala Bahari, the Maharaja of Gwalior's Grand Chamberlain. Surrounded by their staff, the leaders of the rebellion sat on pillows in front of the Peshwa's tent.

The Grand Chamberlain approached, bowed deeply before Rao Sahib and said, 'His Majesty my master requests that you leave his territory immediately.'

Rao Sahib answered with amused condescension, 'We wrote to your master that we were coming in a friendly spirit. Let him remember our age-old ties. We expect from him support that will allow us to continue south towards our objective. Besides, we have received at least two hundred letters from inhabitants of Gwalior warmly inviting us here.'

So, Rao Sahib had written to Sindhia. The Rani was surprised to hear this. Does one warn people before coming to overthrow them? The Grand Chamberlain, embarrassed, spoke with difficulty, 'I can only repeat what my master the maharaja ordered me to tell you—leave his land.'

Rao Sahib seemed surprised. 'Surely you are aware,' he answered, 'that we had been given to understand that your master's attitude towards us was quite different.'

The Grand Chamberlain bowed his head, and speaking so low he could barely be heard, said, 'If you continue to advance, we shall attack.'

'Attack us—I have twenty thousand men with me,' replied Rao Sahib.

This time the Grand Chamberlain became arrogant and, in a sharp voice, spat out, 'For the last time, my master the Maharaja orders you to withdraw.'

The dignitary's tone enraged Rao Sahib.

'Order? Who are you to give orders! A two-bit servant of some two-bit merchant drunk with opium! And who are your Maharaja and his Diwan Dinkar? Christians!'

'Christians!'—the worst insult Rao Sahib could have come up with.

'We are the Peshwa,' he continued. 'Maharaja Sindhia is no more than the bearer of our slippers. It is we who gave him his kingdom. Instead of fighting us, join our cause—there is a place among us for him as well as for you.'

Before retiring in haste, the Grand Chamberlain forgot to bow to Rao Sahib. Rao Sahib's anger gave way to anxiety. Turning to Tatya Tope, he asked, 'What is the meaning of this?'

Before Tatya Tope could answer, the Rani jumped in. 'I don't see why you are so surprised. We come here to take Gwalior, and you want Maharaja Sindhia to open his gates to us?'

Rao Sahib was about to answer the Rani, but a peremptory look from Tatya Tope restrained him. 'You're right,' he said simply. 'There's nothing very surprising there.'

7

Excerpts from a letter from Roderick Briggs to Sarah Brandon, dated 1 June 1858.

We shall not be married as soon as I had hoped. What can I say, Sarah my love, we can only be patient, stand fast and continue to think of each other.

Yesterday evening, Sir Robert Hamilton took a stroll with General Rose and his aides. It had rained earlier. The ground was muddy, slick, but the light had grown extraordinarily limpid. A large red sun sank behind the tomb. From the terrace we could see the cliffs of the Jumna bathed in the powdery shadows of evening. Below, between the banks of sand, the steel-grey river seemed immobile. Around us, in the trees, was a great clatter of birds, those birds Roger so loved to paint.

I had already packed and made ready to leave in the morning for Bombay and then for England, when a runner brought the General a cable from the Nawab of Rampur, one of the region's important rulers who has always been our faithful ally; a rebel army was on the march to take Gwalior.

How could a few hundred soldiers isolated in the jungle even think of attacking India's most formidable fortress? Sir Robert was convinced the Nawab of Rampur had let himself be taken in by one of those insane rumours that ever haunt this land, but then another runner brought a cable from the Maharaja of Gwalior himself. It was an urgent plea for help; an immense rebel army was approaching Gwalior and the Maharaja begged us to send troops immediately to save him. With that, Sir Robert was convinced. General Rose had no doubts that the Rani of Jhansi was behind this suicidal initiative.

'It's she!' he cried. 'She's their best general. I underestimated her when I imagined her in the jungle, a desperate fugitive.'

We had to act as soon as possible, before she could reach Gwalior. I admired Rose, who did not hesitate for a moment to cable Lord Canning, offering to lead our army to the rescue of Gwalior. The Governor General accepted with alacrity.

'Defeat them, General, and do it soon,' he added. 'If Gwalior falls, then I might as well pack my bags.'

That shows you the spirit that rules in Calcutta.

'You're coming with me, aren't you, Briggs?' the General asked.

How could I refuse? I returned to my tent. The rain had seeped in, turning the floor into a quagmire. My Irish orderly was asleep, dead drunk. Insects of every variety were so thick inside that they swirled about in a dense cloud. As I write, there is an annoying buzzing around me, and I must interrupt this letter every few seconds to kill a few bugs. I am weary, Sarah. I thought it was over. I feel no enthusiasm for taking up the fight once again. I had almost forgotten my oath to avenge Roger's death. I felt at peace with myself, happy to return soon to England and see you again. If only General Rose had been firmer, if only he hadn't let the Rani escape several times, we would not have reached this pass. So I won't be leaving this accursed country so soon. Duty must be done, but I must admit it has become singularly irksome.

The morning of 1 June the rebel army reached the river Morar, hardly more than a stream. Gwalior was only a few miles away. Here, nature was kinder. The easier terrain and welcome shade of tall trees made the march of the Peshwa's troops less painful, and the proximity of their goal contributed to their state of excitement.

Riding at their head, the Rani suddenly saw between the tree trunks, half a mile away, a considerable number of regiments lined up in battle formation on the plain.

Maharaja Sindhia himself had taken personal command of his eight thousand troops. It was not their crushing superiority, both in numbers and equipment, that weighed on the Rani's heart. Never before had she seen one Indian army preparing to fight another, and the monstrosity of this fratricidal conflict overwhelmed her.

The rebel leaders, who had joined her, watched the deployment in front of them. Tatya Tope, perplexed, muttered, 'I don't understand, this wasn't what...'

He never finished the sentence; a huge explosion shook the air. The Maharaja's artillery had opened fire.

'It's a salute in our honour,' exclaimed Rao Sahib.

The Rani began to laugh.

'You're mistaken, Peshwa. They're firing at us.'

One needed only to see the panic spreading through the first ranks of foot soldiers to realize that. Even though no shells had yet reached them, they were visibly reluctant to engage, and several were already turning back. The crucial moment of this mad undertaking willed by the Rani was at hand, and she had to act. She galloped up to the men in retreat and blocked their paths with her horse.

'Don't run away like cowards! Those who want to fight—follow me!' she yelled. Then, without delay, she led her two hundred Pathan horsemen in a charge on the Maharaja of Gwalior's gunners. She bore straight down on the enemy, fearing at any moment the cannonball that would carry her off, the bullet that would wound her. For the first time, she was afraid, so afraid that she shut her eyes, letting her horse gallop on its own. Akbar and the cavalry around her were shouting the war-cry of the revolution. 'Deen! Deen!' she heard them shout. And suddenly, she heard the same cry coming from in front of her. Astonished, she opened her eyes. The Gwalior troops were no longer firing. They were shouting, 'Deen! Deen!' They were laughing, waving their rifles happily above their heads, fraternizing with the rebels. The Rani had reached their front line and was immediately surrounded by ten, twenty, fifty of the Maharaja of Gwalior's soldiers. For a moment she feared they wanted to drag her from her horse and kill her. Instinctively on the defensive, she began to fight them off. But in fact, her assailants wanted only to be near her, to touch her.

'Long live Lakshmi, long live the Rani of Jhansi!' they shouted.

Around her, her horsemen became part of the same enthusiastic wave. The soldiers of both armies threw themselves into one another's arms, clutching, embracing, all the while shouting, 'Deen! Deen!' The Rani burst out laughing and, joining in the general merrymaking began to shout 'Deen! Deen!' with the others.

The news of the flight of the Maharaja of Gwalior and Diwan Dinkar, who had gone to seek safety at Agra, left the Peshwa Rao Sahib and Tatya Tope highly puzzled. Lakshmi could not understand their surprise.

'You seemed to find it strange that Sindhia should try to stop us with his army, and now you seem astonished that he's fled. What did you expect him to do? Open the gates of Gwalior? Wait for us there and greet us with open arms?'

'In any case, that would have been highly convenient,' said Rao Sahib.

'You're losing your mind, Peshwa,' snapped the Rani.

The entire rebel army, loitering on the lawns of the Phoolbagh, the flower garden southeast of the city, awaited orders that did not come. The Rani watched as Rao Sahib and Tatya Tope hesitated.

'What are you waiting for!' she said. 'Let's march into town!'

Rao Sahib took his time before answering, 'We don't know what kind of welcome to expect.'

'But we'll get the warmest of welcomes! Sindhia's troops fraternized with ours, and we know the population of Gwalior is with us—didn't we get hundreds of letters asking us here? Let's go,' she said, spurring her horse.

Tatya Tope stopped her, 'The city might be hiding enemies who could put up fierce resistance.'

'Then let me go in as a scout.'

'Take a regiment with you in case of attack,' advised Rao Sahib.

'Don't fear for me, Peshwa, my horsemen are enough,' she answered ironically.

Escorted by her two hundred Pathans, the Rani entered the city of Gwalior. The doors and shutters of the houses were closed, the streets deserted. The Rani's cavalry fired salutes in the air in her honour, the shots echoing strangely in the ghost town.

The Rani was pensive, thinking about the curious and almost inexplicable events of this day. First, the too-easy victory over the

Maharaja's troops. Then, Tatya Tope and Rao Sahib's hesitation. And finally, these shuttered houses, these empty streets. What was the meaning of this reserve—hostility or fear?

The Rani rode along the street of the jewels' bazaar, which led to the Gurki Palace, the Maharaja of Gwalior's residence. All the shops, like those in the neighbouring bazaar, were shut. Lakshmi could feel eyes watching her from behind blinds and lattices. In the silence a sort of humming began to rise: 'Rani...Jhansi...Rani...Jhansi...' A few men emerged from a dark side street. They walked parallel to the Rani, looking at her with shyness and curiosity. Others joined them, first by the dozens, then by the hundreds. They slipped between the Pathan horsemen who were advancing at a walking pace, drew close to the Rani and surrounded her. And the humming became stronger, 'Rani... Jhansi...Rani...Jhansi...' words of recognition that finally culminated in a shout from thousands of throats, 'Long live the Rani of Jhansi!'

The shutters opened, women's heads appeared in the windows, on the balconies, joining their acclamations to those of the men. By the time the Rani had reached the palace, she was surrounded by an enthusiastic crowd.

The gate was wide open. She entered the immense forecourt, bordered by whitewashed buildings where servants and courtiers of the Maharaja Sindhia seemed to be waiting for something to happen, standing quietly in the sand of the courtyard. In their attitude there was not only definite anxiety but also a kind of haughty indifference that the Rani found disconcerting. One chamberlain stepped up and asked that she not disturb the wing of the palace that housed the purdah, for it was still occupied by Maharani Bazee Bai, the widow of the Maharaja's grandfather. The Rani gave orders that her soldiers stay away from it. Then she dismounted.

Not one of the courtiers made a move to help her. She looked around, taken aback by their attitude, so in contrast to the popular enthusiasm shown her in the town, impressed by the enormous size of the palace, a formidable symbol of the prestigious monarchy of Gwalior.

Her eyes sought Akbar's, seeming to ask him what to do.

'Give them a little jolt,' he whispered, 'that's what they're waiting for.'

She noticed that some of the Maharaja's dignitaries were still staring at her with a gaze both curious and impenetrable. With an abrupt gesture, she motioned them forward.

'Send public criers immediately to every crossroads to order shops and bazaars to open their doors. I want this town to have recovered its normal appearance within one hour.'

An hour later the bazaars had resumed their normal activity and the city its usual animation. The Rani sent a messenger to the Phoolbagh to notify Rao Sahib and Tatya Tope that they could come. Night had fallen, and the streets were lit with torches as the entire population of Gwalior pressed forward to cheer them.

The garrison left by Maharaja Sindhia in the formidable fortress that dominated the city opened its gates to the detachments sent by Tatya Tope. The revolutionaries found sixty cannon and an important stockpile of munitions, loot that seemed all the more extraordinary because it had been won without a fight. While the Peshwa made his triumphal entrance, his men took possession of Gurki Palace. Dignitaries and servants of the Maharaja of Gwalior bustled about, apparently overburdened with work. In the midst of all this agitation, only the Rani remained idle, a faraway expression on her face.

The day had been filled with emotion, surprise, bizarre impressions. It left the Rani puzzled, her mind filled with complex, contradictory thoughts.

Surrounded by his staff, the Peshwa made his entrance into the forecourt where the Rani was standing. Tatya Tope noticed her.

'Come, Lakshmi,' he said, 'we're going to open Maharaja Sindhia's treasury.'

They walked towards the Sindhia dynasty's temple, located within the palace walls, not far from the main portal. The Rani had already visited it when, before the rebellion began, she had come to hold discussions with Diwan Dinkar.

Inside, they were met by an austere, dry-looking old man, Amar Chand, the Maharaja of Gwalior's minister of finance. They stepped around the large black marble statue of the god Shiva at the rear of the temple, and entered a little chapel, completely bare. A narrow stairway had been sunk into the ground. Climbing down, they followed the minister of finance through a labyrinth of crypts and cellars with sweating walls until they came to an iron door studded with nails. This was the entrance to the treasury, guarded far better by the sanctity of the temple than by hidden entrances of complicated secrets. The minister of finance produced several enormous keys which he turned in the door's various locks. They entered a large, low-ceilinged square room containing neat rows of chests of different sizes, all of them carefully numbered. The minister opened them, one after the other. The large ones contained gold and silver coins, the smaller ones were brimming with jewels. The Rani was unable to repress a feeling of covetousness. Never had she beheld such a collection of precious stones. By the light of the torches held by some of the Peshwa's officers, they seemed to come to life, throwing off rays of red, blue and green, while the diamonds glowed with multicoloured fire. The minister, who had taken out his inventory lists, awaited Rao Sahib's instructions. The Peshwa wanted enough to give his army, as well as Sindhia's troops and functionaries, three months' advance pay. He named the sum. The minister, Amar Chand, examined his lists and pointed to two wooden chests bound with iron hoops. The Peshwa's officers dragged them with some difficulty to the centre of the room, and the minister began to count out the amount. This operation seemed interminable to the Rani. The heavy silence was broken only by the clinking of the coins, which echoed dully in the stuffy atmosphere of the cellar.

The Rani watched Sindhia's minister counting them methodically as they slid through his hands. Pointing him out to Tatya Tope, the Rani whispered, 'Why didn't he follow the Maharaja to Agra? Why did he show us where the treasury is hidden? I can't believe he betrayed his master.'

'He didn't betray anyone. He's obeying Maharaja Sindhia's express orders.'

The Rani's stupefaction made Tatya Tope smile. Dropping his usually severe expression, he looked at her with an ironic air.

'Naive Lakshmi,' he said, 'you've been asking yourself too many questions. It's time for me to answer them.'

'For a long time I've been thinking of taking Gwalior. As soon as we lost Kunch, I came here in utmost secrecy. I invented the pretext of a visit to my sick father at Charkhi—which, as you know, drew some criticism and accusations. Of course, Maharaja Sindhia and his Diwan Dinkar were to know nothing of my presence at Gwalior. But I've had contacts here since last September, when I came to enlist the sepoys of the British contingent. I called again on my friends, officers, and especially, the chief of police. They gave me fascinating information. The army was faithful to Sindhia, but secretly, it sympathized with our cause, along with a good portion of the population. Then, after the feast at Gopalpur, when you suggested that we take Gwalior, I came back here that very night, and I learned some very surprising things about Sindhia's state of mind. For a long time the Maharaja had been eager to join our side and thus shake off the burdensome influence of his Prime Minister Dinkar. It was Sindhia alone who sent, without consulting with Dinkar, that letter of congratulations to the Nawab of Banda after his victory over the British. Through third parties, in order not to awaken Dinkar's suspicions, I negotiated with Sindhia until we reached an agreement. Sindhia wouldn't put up any resistance to our troops and he would remain at Gwalior once we occupied it.

'Nevertheless, in order that the British not think he had gone over to our side, he would send them messages begging for help.

'You see, Lakshmi, you wanted to take Gwalior. I wanted its Maharaja. If he walked into our camp, all the Maratha kingdoms—Indore, Baroda—would follow his example. Soon, they would have been followed by the large states in the south, and the revolution would have spread to all India...'

The Rani interrupted him, 'Why did you exclude me from those dealings? I imagine you informed Rao Sahib. Why not me? Why didn't you trust me?'

Tatya Tope smiled again—this time a patronizing smile that disgusted the Rani.

'Your very character forbade it. You are too direct, too straightforward to approve of our intrigues. I was afraid that you might betray the secret by your attitude. Had you known the truth, perhaps you wouldn't have accepted to lead our troops as though it were really a matter of conquering Gwalior; and our deal with Sindhia required, above all, that we give the impression of truly forcing his hand.'

'In other words you manipulated me like a puppet.'

She had raised her voice, and Tatya Tope gestured to her to speak more softly. They continued their conversation in such a low whisper that Rao Sahib could hear nothing. Pretending to be absorbed in the minister of finance's counting of gold coins, he watched them out of the corner of his eye, and on the Rani's face he could read disappointment and rage. Once the sum demanded by the Peshwa had been assembled, he inspected the chests of precious wood encircled with worked bronze which contained the gems. These included the purdah jewels, which were reserved exclusively for the use of mothers and wives of Maharajas—the collection of historic precious stones, famous throughout India; the jewels of the Maharajas of Gwalior; jewels that belonged to the temple and were used to decorate the gods during festivals. Rao Sahib dipped only into the chest that held Sindhia's personal jewels. A glittering cascade of diamonds, rubies, pearls and emeralds poured out onto the velvet cloth that had been placed over one of the nearby chests. According to the minister's inventory, there were 365 articles, some of European manufacture. Rao Sahib hesitated among the necklaces, the belt buckles, the men's bracelets, the pendants, the jewel-studded weapons, and then ordered most of them set aside to be distributed as rewards to his officers and his aides. For himself he kept little—several rows of enormous uncut emeralds and a necklace of diamonds of extraordinary size and brilliance. He invited Tatya Tope to help himself. Not being fond of jewels, the latter picked out a dagger with an emerald-encrusted handle and a sword whose hilt and scabbard were made of carved gold studded with cabochons. Rao Sahib asked the Rani to take whatever she liked. She refused. During the whole scene she had stood silently, arms crossed, back straight, stiff, haughty, the image of contempt. Rao Sahib was anxious that she take at least one or two pieces, as he had done. He was acting not out of greed, he explained, but for revenge—the only revenge he would allow himself on Sindhia for his opposition and flight.

It was an act he wanted the Rani to participate in. She would hear nothing of it. Rao Sahib, more embarrassed than surprised, insisted. The Rani understood that her refusal would create the impression that she was disassociating herself from him; so, leaning over the glittering array, she picked out a single piece, a necklace of three rows of perfectly matched pearls of extraordinary lustre, each one the size of a hazelnut.

'That is a very ancient piece,' the minister of finance commented. 'It is said to come from the Crown Jewels of Portugal, and was bought in London by an agent of the ruling Maharaja one hundred and fifty years ago.'

Akbar had been waiting for Lakshmi in the temple of the dynasty. Seeing her tight lips and her eyes blazing with anger, he questioned her anxiously. Lakshmi sat down cross-legged on the bare stone of the floor and silently began to finger the pearls of the necklace she had taken from the treasury.

Inside the building it was dark. Only a few oil-lamps set out here and there in front of the statue of Shiva provided the illumination. On that evening, the evening of the rebels' arrival at Gwalior, the temple was almost deserted. From time to time, an old man or a group of women would enter; walking silently on bare feet, they would place their modest offerings before Shiva.

At last, the Rani seemed to make up her mind, and spoke in a clear voice, 'Akbar, I'm going to tell you a tale, a story. The story of an oriental intrigue—the sort of thing you Pathans, warriors from the north, are unfamiliar with.'

And she related everything Tatya Tope had told her.

'But,' she concluded, 'things didn't turn out quite the way he expected. He thinks I'm naive, but he's, in fact, much more so; he doesn't realize he was tricked by Diwan Dinkar. Had he trusted me, I could have shown him that Dinkar is stronger than all of us put together. In spite of Tatya Tope's secrecy, Dinkar must have learned of his negotiations with his master. He pretended to know nothing and let matters run their course. What else could he do? Resist us? Either Sindhia's army would have been defeated or, worse still, Gwalior would have become revolutionary and mutinied against Sindhia. But as soon as Tatya Tope left Gwalior, Diwan Dinkar regained control of both Sindhia and the situation. He convinced Sindhia to wage the mock battle on the Morar, in order to convince the British he was still on their side. Then he encouraged his master to flee to Agra and place himself under British protection.

'On top of Tatya Tope's intrigue, Dinkar has built another, far more subtle, which has allowed him, as always, to keep a foot in each camp without committing himself to either.'

She was amused, despite herself, by the old fox's cunning, but it was with deep bitterness that she added, 'Why did Tatya Tope not trust me? Why?'

'He's jealous of you,' answered Akbar. 'Who gave courage to our demoralized troops? Who led them into that impossible venture, the attack on Gwalior? Who disarmed the people of Gwalior of their fear and suspicion and aroused their enthusiasm? Who is the soul of this venture?'

The Rani was stubborn, 'The taking of Gwalior was a fraud.'

'How many people know that? You, me, and a few others. All of India sees it as a startling exploit. With Gwalior as our base, we can march victoriously across the country and liberate all India.'

'Let's begin with Jhansi,' the Rani said in a voice suddenly clear and joyful.

8

The day after his entrance into Gwalior, Rao Sahib became an immensely popular man. He had begun by forbidding his troops to indulge in any violence or looting, which immediately reassured the population. He took for himself only Diwan Dinkar's palace, which he handed over to the Nawab of Banda. The Nawab set to work conscientiously with his troops, smashing the furniture, ripping up chests, tearing down the tapestries, stealing everything of value; then he moved in.

Rao Sahib also freed the prisoners of state, who had been thrown in jail arbitrarily by Diwan Dinkar and left to vegetate, forgotten for years. This liberalism made an excellent impression. The three months' advance pay that Rao Sahib had distributed to the Maharaja of Gwalior's troops as well as to his functionaries and dignitaries also earned him a good number of supporters. Furthermore, he had reappointed the employees of Sindhia's administration to their old posts, thus ensuring the friendship of that influential class. He had promised the Brahmins as well as the mullahs free meals in perpetuity and had given them handouts of laddoos and more concrete gifts in the form of rupees—Rao Sahib obviously knew how to deal with the clergy. Finally, the Peshwa wanted to lure back to Gwalior its fleeing Maharaja, whose incomparable prestige would greatly increase the Peshwa's own power. He wrote Sindhia a letter which he hoped would get to him by way of the Maharani Bazee Bai. She had refused with disdain to follow her grandson in his flight, but surely she would find a way to get Rao Sahib's letter to him. Asked to undertake the mission to Bazee Bai, the Rani, devoured by curiosity to meet her, accepted.

In her husband's day, twenty years earlier, Bazee Bai had been a most influential person not only at Gwalior but also well beyond its borders. It was said that ten years before the great revolt, she had fomented one against the British, conspiring like mad with the Maratha princes. The affair had been hushed up and Bazee Bai had gone away on a long pilgrimage to Benares, the elegant way of sending princes into exile. She had lost even more power when the grandson of her husband, the present Sindhia, had come to the throne and Diwan Dinkar, the avowed friend of the British, became the real power.

But since the beginning of the rebellion, she had recovered some of her influence. People came from everywhere to solicit her support and advice. Bazee Bai was an old woman who was said to be shrewd, wise, fierce and utterly independent.

One of the Maharaja's officers led the Rani from courtyard to courtyard until they came to a doorway cut in a high wall. Respecting the rules of purdah, he did not follow her in.

She entered a small courtyard shaded by a single large tree and overflowing with hibiscus and bougainvillea, then walked towards a narrow facade terribly finicky in decor and painted raw yellow, its windows covered with marble lattices. One of Bazee Bai's ladies-in-waiting, almost as ancient as the palace, was waiting for her at the threshold of the purdah. She led the Rani through a series of very large rooms, empty except for a few pillows and some vast carpets of great value. The whole impression was of extreme austerity. The lady stopped, motioned to the Rani to wait, and disappeared.

Unwritten protocol required that an old queen keep a younger one waiting. A few moments went by, then suddenly, Bazee Bai was in the room, having appeared silently from behind a screen of carved wood. Bazee Bai was a stout woman of medium height. She had the pale skin of people who never breathe fresh air, a wide nose and piercing eyes. Her grey hair was pulled back, she wore neither paint nor jewels, and her sari was of white cotton embroidered in a matching tone. She exuded authority. She greeted the Rani with distant courtesy, sat down on a pillow and, with a wave of the hand, invited her to do the same. The Rani explained her request; would Bazee Bai be prepared to lend her support to the cause of the liberators of India, to use her influence to persuade Sindhia to return to Gwalior, and send him this letter from

Rao Sahib which she was free to read? Without a word, Bazee Bai took the document from the Rani and began to read it in a semi-whisper:

> *Everything is well here, Maharaja Sindhia; in my opinion, your departure was a mistake. I have already written you, but I received no answer. That should not be. This letter I send through Rani Bazee Bai. Come back and take your place on the throne. I took Gwalior with no purpose other than to meet you, then I shall move on. That is my goal. And thus, it is necessary that you come back.*

When she had finished, Bazee Bai dropped the letter on a nearby pillow without comment, and said abruptly, 'So you are this famous Rani of Jhansi. Without knowing you, I sympathize with you, but I don't like your friends.'

'Why not, Maharani? They fight the British oppressor, just as you once wanted to.'

That reminder of her subversive activities did not seem to please Bazee Bai.

'Your friends have taken what doesn't belong to them. They've stolen Gwalior from my grandson.'

'Would you rather have the British at Gwalior? The British...and Diwan Dinkar?'

The allusion to Bazee Bai's legendary hatred for Diwan Dinkar seemed to perk her up. The Rani noticed that Bazee Bai never raised her voice and clearly enunciated each word. In a nervous gesture she constantly pulled the veil of her sari over the lower half of her face. For a long time she said nothing, apparently lost in meditation, and the Rani was wary of breaking the silence. Then Bazee Bai spoke, 'Your friends are conceited fools. They're all puffed up about having taken Gwalior, and are ready to sleep on their meagre laurels. Gwalior is not an end but a beginning. If they want to succeed, your friends must hurry to rouse the southern princes. Otherwise, they'll have taken Gwalior for nothing.'

'I beg you to tell that to my friends, Maharani, they'll listen to you.'

'I don't want to see them and I won't receive them. It's you who must convince them. And I'm told you're good at that sort of thing.'

Once more, Bazee Bai smiled, but her eyes were cruel:

'My little one, you had better think of pulling out of the whole affair.'

The Rani bowed her head, then asked, 'Will you transmit our message and Rao Sahib's letter to Maharaja Sindhia?'

Bazee Bai's only answer was to rise from her pillow, indicating the audience had come to an end.

3 June was declared by the astrologers to be a day that augured well for the enthroning of Peshwa Rao Sahib. The ceremony was meant to show India that the revolution, once beaten, was now more triumphant than ever, and it brought to the Peshwa's throne his former vassals, the kings. Still exasperated with him and with Tatya Tope, the Rani had decided on impulse to stay away. Akbar did not insist. Pomp and protocol were so alien to him that he was delighted to be spared the ceremony. A man who never bowed even to the Rani and served her only out of love, was not about to go down on his knees to pay homage to the Peshwa. The Rani suspected he would much prefer going off to some tavern to get drunk with his cronies.

She was feeling somewhat sorry not to be among her companions on this glorious day when she received an unexpected invitation from Bazee Bai to watch the ceremony with her from the windows of the purdah. She joined the old Maharani at her observation post, a balcony overhanging the main courtyard of Gurki Palace. Pink granite lattices protected the women from being seen. A few grey-haired ladies-in-waiting, ageless, who seemed in constant terror of their mistress, stood around her as she sat on her pillows. She barely greeted the Rani and seemed not to notice Mandar at all.

Stands had been raised for a thousand spectators in the courtyard. Mango branches and garlands of flowers hid their wooden pillars, and above them flew large orange Maratha banners.

The guests arrived at the palace through a tunnel of greenery made from branches of banana trees. Army officers, noblemen, officials, merchants, bankers and representatives of guilds climbed into the stands and took the seats assigned to them by protocol. There were no women. The sun glittered on the men's jewels and played over vast beds of turbans, of waistcoats and caftans of red or pink brocade embroidered with gold and silver. On a raised dais was a gaddi of solid gold taken from Maharaja Sindhia's storerooms.

Tatya Tope swaggered in the place of honour, surrounded by a large staff. The jewels they wore, the gems embedded in their weapons, and the precious materials of their garments transformed them into a kind of glowing cloud. A fanfare sounded the Peshwa's arrival as he emerged from the palace. Everyone rose and bowed very low. Rao Sahib came forward, preceded by courtiers in red-and-gold robes. He himself wore a caftan in white and gold brocade; a breastplate of diamonds and emeralds covered his wide chest and hid the trace of a round belly. From his ears dangled two gold hoops, each supporting an enormous pearl, like those of his cousin Nana Sahib. On his turban he had stuck the Sheerpesh and the Kalagitura, a brooch of very large diamonds and a pearl pompom, symbols of sovereignty. Although his stride was too short, there was a certain majesty in his appearance. He climbed the steps to the dais while a chorus of Brahmins chanted Vedic prayers and the cannons of the fort fired a 101-gun salute. After taking his seat on the gold throne, Rao Sahib made a short speech thanking all those present for their help and support. The spirit of freedom was reborn in India, the detested foreigners were about to be expelled, the country was free. The ancient glory of the Maratha had revived and the Indian empire was reestablished. Although the audience had some trouble hearing him, the end of his speech was greeted with thunderous acclamation.

Then, in homage to the Peshwa, Tatya Tope and the officers of the revolutionary army placed their swords on a gold platter before him. Rao Sahib merely touched the weapons before returning them to their owners. Finally, the representatives of the different castes stepped forward, by order of protocol, to pay their respects to the Peshwa and bow before him. The ceremony, which until then had moved at a good pace, began to drag. Bazee Bai shifted nervously on her pillows, growing bored. She seemed suddenly to notice the Rani's presence. She examined the white sari that clung tightly to the Rani's body, the necklace of jasmine flowers she had placed around her neck, the subtle make-up that enhanced and enlarged her eyes.

'You are very pretty, my child.'

But Bazee Bai's compliments never came without thorns, for she added, 'It's a good thing you're taking no part in this masquerade.'

'Masquerade, Maharani! An entire people applauds the rebirth of freedom in our country and you call it a masquerade!'

'The people!' Bazee Bai shrugged. 'They would applaud if Sindhia came back tomorrow with the British.'

She stared at the Rani, made a wry face.

'So, little queen—you were betrayed at Jhansi.'

This sudden attack stunned the Rani.

'Diwan Naransin didn't betray me. He betrayed Jhansi.'

Bazee Bai smiled.

'I wasn't thinking of that little man. I was thinking of the Rani of Orchha, whom he was working for.'

'How do you know that?'

The informality of the Rani's aggressiveness seemed to delight Bazee Bai.

'That vile Dinkar is not the only one to be well-informed. If you had asked me for an audience when you came to see him, I could have enlightened you.'

She pursued her advantage. 'Who ordered the murder of your deplorable husband and the attempts on the throne by his stupid cousin Prince Sadasheo, if it wasn't the Rani of Orchha? When she failed, she launched a war against you, which she lost. Would she then renounce her designs on Jhansi? That wouldn't be like her. She decided to seize Jhansi through the British. She fabricated the evidence that misled them. On her orders Naransin encouraged you to resist in order to draw them to Jhansi and then made certain its gates would be opened to them.'

'Why did Naransin serve her?' It was a question Lakshmi was addressing to herself as much as to Bazee Bai, who took pleasure in her distress before answering.

'Because, needless to say, they are lovers. Orchha is not far from Jhansi, and Naransin could go there often, in secret. Having been denied the charms of a young queen, he had to make do with those of an old, withered one, because she flattered his ambition and fed his hatred for you. You were defeated not by the British but, without realizing it, by my friend the Rani of Orchha, Lakri Bai.'

Thereupon, Bazee Bai stood up, bid her goodbye with unexpected grace, and retired with her ladies. Lakshmi had not even noticed the ceremony of enthronement was over. The dignitaries had left, and only a few idle servants wandered in the vast courtyard. A sudden gust of wind swayed the garlands of flowers and leaves that hung from the deserted stands, raising whirlwinds of red dust around the new Peshwa's empty throne, whose gold, under the rays of the sun, seemed to be melting. The Rani felt incapable of moving. Faced with the hatred of women—first Annabelle Phipps, and now the Rani of Orchha, or Bazee Bai, Lakshmi felt disoriented and depressed.

Mandar, who until then had remained silent, spoke with a disdain she had never before shown a ruler, 'The old queen is too ancient to act and too deeply compromised to regain power. Beware of her, she's quite capable of betraying us, not out of friendship for the British nor self-interest, but out of pure spite.'

Excerpts from a letter from Roderick Briggs to Sarah Brandon, dated 4 June 1855, Kalpi.

> *The news is bad, Gwalior has fallen into rebel hands. Maharaja Sindhia tried to stop them, but a great part of his army deserted. He himself made a desperate stand with his cavalry, which left sixty dead and many more wounded on the field. No sooner had the rebels entered Gwalior than the Maharaja's minister of finance opened the gates of the treasury to them. They stripped everything, down to the last rupee. They even carried off the jewels of the Maharaja's women and the sacred jewels of the temple. The fall of Gwalior took us by surprise. The letters we received from the Prime Minister Diwan Dinkar in Agra, who was to keep us informed of developments, were far from alarmist. Perhaps he believed our troops would have the time to stop the rebels before they took the town. Luckily, we can count on his unconditional loyalty as well as that of his master Maharaja Sindhia. From Agra, both of them have been bombarding us with protestations of friendship. Sindhia has even sent us several unopened letters written to him by the rebel leader Rao Sahib, who calls himself 'Peshwa of the Marathas'.*
>
> *To our great surprise, we have also received unexpected support from the Maharaja's grandmother, the old Maharani Bazee Bai, who remains very influential in the region and whom we had always considered*

an adversary. She sent us an unopened letter which Rao Sahib had asked her to transmit to Sindhia. She also informed us of the offers the rebels made to try to get her to join them. Nevertheless, the situation remains extremely dangerous. Communications between Agra, Bombay and the northwest provinces have been cut. The rebels have seized a formidable amount of loot at Gwalior, as well as an immense arsenal—enough to forge a new army incomparably more powerful than the one we defeated.

Every hour counts as we hurry to rebuild our army. However, it will be several days, at best, before we can set out. Our men, who were looking forward to a well-earned rest and thought their hardships over, obey without sulking. I draw strength from their example to fight my own lassitude. It is not without sadness that I recall the impatience with which I awaited this campaign a few months ago. Today, I am just as impatient, but only to lay down my arms and leave India.

In celebrating the accession of the new Peshwa, Gwalior gave free rein to its enthusiasm, while the soldiers indulged in a universal and monumental orgy. The three months' pay they had been given was squandered in alcohol, drugs and women. Everyone was having an excellent time—except the Rani of Jhansi.

She was living in the house of Kashgi Ali, one of the Maharaja's ministers, who had been only too pleased to turn over his residence, a string of houses linked by a tangle of stairways and crooked corridors. The Rani placed Damodar under Mandar's supervision in the best apartment while she, curiously, chose to live at the very top of a remote wing. A series of tiny whitewashed rooms opened onto a small terrace hidden by a high wall.

The Rani had to stand on her toes to see the domes and turrets of a nearby temple and the cramped terraces of the old quarter. Letting her hosts take care of Damodar—in other words, spoil him outrageously—she remained locked up in her apartment, and her thoughts invariably drifted back to Jhansi which, in pain, was still awaiting liberation.

Action was becoming an increasingly urgent necessity for the revolutionary army in order not to lose the advantage it had gained in taking Gwalior. But Lakshmi was the only person who thought so. Even Akbar was no help. He disappeared all day to get drunk in the taverns, and when he returned in the evening, in a more or less advanced state of inebriation, his high spirits and laughter no longer amused her.

Several times she had asked for an audience with the Peshwa, only to be told that he was very busy but would see her at any moment.

He spent his days presiding at durbar and receiving delegations, or else, he would make solemn visits to some temple or other, surrounded by an ostentatious procession. Rao Sahib was playing at being Peshwa. Although no one told the Rani, she knew that he also spent long hours every day with the Nawab of Banda at the old palace of Diwan Dinkar in interminable orgies with the most beautiful of the Maharaja of Gwalior's nautch girls. Exasperated by his evasions, she finally forced her way in to see him.

She found him in one of the rooms of Gurki Palace, examining the gifts he had received upon his accession to the throne, surrounded by his usual retainers. Wanting to do justice to Gwalior's reputation for fabulous wealth, the guilds and noble families had contributed mounds of brocade, embroidered caftans, an array of gem-studded weapons, and entire trays of jewels.

The appearance of the Rani in her war clothes—white breeches and white shirt—without a single ornament, without a single jewel, caused some surprise among the attendants. Their presence induced her to moderate her language.

'O Peshwa, the priests say prayers for you, the population blesses you, your army cheers you—but it yearns to fight.'

Rao Sahib answered in honeyed tones, 'O Rani, give our valiant warriors time to rest after their victory; have they not just taken Gwalior?'

He uttered that last sentence, savouring each word, as though he did not quite believe it himself. The Rani, despite the audience, lost her self-restraint, 'We must act, Peshwa, instead of giving ourselves up to the delights—and the illusions—of Gwalior. Let us march south immediately, there where the British are weakest. Let us liberate Jhansi.'

'Your plan, as always, is excellent, O Rani. We shall discuss it.'

Rao Sahib's noncommittal answer made the Rani impertinent.

'Do you think that you are master of the country because you conquered Sindhia? You aren't yet, but you could be if you take immediate advantage of your success to extend it before the British have time to recover. When are we going to war, Peshwa?'

'When we decide in council to do so.'

This haughty answer made the Rani understand how offended he had been that she had stayed away from his enthronement. She ignored it.

'You mustn't underestimate the enemy's strength and resources. The British are crafty and skilful, and it would be a mistake to think we are completely safe here.'

'You're wrong, Rani, the British are much too busy trying to put down our brothers who are harassing them in the neighbouring provinces. You ought to know, for Prince Firoz Shah is their leader. Isn't he a close friend of yours?'

Seeing the courtiers smile obligingly at the allusion, the Rani lost her temper.

'Instead of taking yourself for the Peshwa, you'd do better to imitate your ancestors by earning the right to the title on the battlefield.'

And on that parting shot she walked away without bothering to bow to him.

She walked home with Akbar. His colour was high, his eyes red, he was talking much too loud, and the Rani could see that, once again, he had had too much to drink. Night had fallen and no one paid them any attention. Taverns, brothels and a few brilliantly-lit houses rang with laughter and shouting and drinking-songs. The sidewalks and gutters were strewn with men drunk on alcohol or drugs. Others staggered by in groups, trying to hold each other upright. Courtesans with bare midriffs and vast multicoloured skirts hailed the soldiers in hoarse voices and clung to them as they passed. Two of them grabbed at Akbar and the Rani, mistaking her for a boy. Akbar found it amusing, but the Rani pushed the girl away roughly. Akbar lost patience with her disgusted attitude.

'Come, Lakshmi, smile, be happy. We've taken Gwalior.'

The Rani answered in a muffled voice, 'The Peshwa's puffed up like a peacock. Tatya Tope chews his cud over his success. The army's dead drunk and you sleep yourself drunk.'

'For you there's never a day of rest!'

'Everything is lost, Akbar.'

He did not answer, for liquor had clouded his mind. She felt more alone than ever, alone with her dark thoughts, with her responsibilities.

The Rani was suffocating in the house placed at her disposal by Kashgi Ali, Sindhia's minister, in the old quarter of dark streets and narrow compact houses. She could no longer stand the disorder and debauchery in town. The atmosphere of luxury her hosts had blanketed her in seemed unreal.

Kashgi Ali treated the Rani and Damodar like powerful ruling sovereigns. They applied all their resources of flattery, which the Rani loathed by nature—but behind their bowing and scraping, she imagined a sort of haughty irony.

Feeling the need for fresh air, and the presence of her men, she had had her tent pitched at the Phoolbagh, where the rebel army had set up camp. She could not have foreseen what she found there. Nothing remained of the splendour of the park. Men, camels and elephants had ripped up the lawns, trampled the flower beds, pulled out scented bushes, stripped the trees bare. The graceful pavilions set in groves had been laid waste by the soldiers. In the pools garbage floated in the midst of decapitated lotus flowers. The men seldom emerged from a stupor, induced by drugs, opium among the better-off and, for the poor, paan. Swarms of prostitutes, who had installed themselves in the camp, buzzed about them.

The Rani could hear, coming from inside the tents, the wail of sitars and the laughter of women.

'So this is the army burning for action!' she said to Akbar. 'How can one blame them, the example comes from higher up.'

She resumed the training of her own troops with a harsh strictness she had never shown before. She had the men repeat an exercise twenty times and rained punishments on them for the smallest offenses. She ignored Akbar when he begged her to go easier on his men.

One day when Damodar—who had remained in town—came out to watch the drill, he whispered in Akbar's ear, 'My mother frightens me.'

Akbar made up his mind and approached Lakshmi.

'Go, see Tatya Tope, talk to him again.'

'Why would he listen to me this time any more than all the other times?'

There was also a certain embarrassment behind her reticence. Tatya Tope, once so close, had become almost a stranger to her. Akbar insisted. The urgency of the situation demanded that the Rani put aside her personal feelings. She gave in to this argument and, in deep grief, walked to the pavilion in the park where Tatya Tope had taken up residence.

She found him puffing at his hookah, wrapped in a haze of blue tobacco smoke, lost in reverie, in one of those faraway states which she noticed more and more often in him. He seemed not even to see her come in.

'For once, listen to me, Tatya Tope. Instead of rushing south, we've wasted ten days. We've lost the advantage of surprise and initiative. Now we are reduced simply to waiting here for the British whenever they decide to come.'

'That's exactly what I was thinking,' said Tatya Tope, casually.

Like the Rani, he was in despair because they had not capitalized on their success. He was just as disturbed, even terrified, as she was by Rao Sahib's inertia and the dangers to which it exposed them all.

As he talked, he got up and began pacing up and down, talking of past engagements, of possibilities for the future, of his dreams for India, of the misunderstandings that had come between him and the Rani. Finally, he stopped in front of her and, humbly, beseechingly, said, 'Help me, Lakshmi, there's no one else I can count on.'

His plea immediately swept away any resentment she had against him. Warmly, they discussed the measures to be taken. They would not allow themselves to come under siege in Gwalior fort—sieges did not seem to profit the revolutionaries—but they would march out, instead, to meet the British as soon as they showed up. Large detachments of cavalry would be sent to the north, the south, the east, on all the roads that might serve as approaches for the enemy. The talukdars, the great landowners, would be entrusted with recruiting in each village a certain number of able-bodied men. Not only was Tatya Tope open to the Rani's suggestions, but she could feel their former ties renewing themselves through their collaboration. In the midst of their discussion, he even found the opportunity to joke with her as he had in the old days. Akbar, who had been waiting anxiously, noticed that she was radiant when she emerged from the pavilion. She had recovered an old friend as well as the potential for action. All at once, she was considerably more optimistic.

That afternoon she and Akbar went up to Gwalior fort to examine its defences. They visited the barracks of Maharaja Sindhia, now inhabited by revolutionary soldiers, and surveyed the ramparts and towers bristling with guns. Then they entered the Man Mandir, the most ancient and most beautiful of the fort's abandoned palaces, which rose straight from the cliff facing southeast. It was famous for the varnished yellow and blue friezes that ran along its ochre stone walls. The Rani and Akbar walked through the courtyards, sculpted with graceful bas-reliefs, and the adjacent apartments. The woodwork and tapestries had disappeared a long time ago. Occasionally, the Rani, brushed by the wings of a bat, would scream and duck away. Half-hidden in a wall, they found a steep little stairway which they followed up to a terrace on the palace's highest tower. The view from the parapet took their breath away. Below them lay an infinite expanse of peaceful fields and quiet jungle, lit by the low slanting rays of a late-afternoon sun.

At the foot of the cliff, a road from the old city snaked south between low hills. It was the road to Jhansi. The Rani stared at it for a long time, in silence. Then she studied the horizon in all directions, as though she were searching for the cloud of dust rising above the trees that would signal the arrival of the British army. Without turning around, she grumbled, 'Wait, always wait! When we ought to be running out to meet the enemy! Our only hope lies in attacking, and still we remain on the defensive, waiting for the British as we chew on our paan...'

'We're ready to receive them,' replied Akbar. 'Our army, Sindhia's, his artillery and this fort. All the troops of the British Empire couldn't take Gwalior.'

At that moment a Pathan horseman joined them on the terrace. He had been searching for them all over the palace and he was carrying two letters for the Rani. She took the first one, a simple crumpled piece of paper, and read.

Does the Rani of Jhansi still remember the man she called the Prince of Darkness? Have the palaces of Gwalior softened her too much, or does she still like the outdoor life? If so, let her abandon the imbeciles around her and come join the Prince in his lair.

The letter was unsigned, but the Rani recognized the name she had given Firoz Shah. For a moment she dreamed that she had escaped from Gwalior, that she had joined Firoz Shah, and with him was leading a life of danger and adventure in the jungle. At least, Firoz Shah knew how to fight.

'It's from "the other one", isn't it?' asked Akbar, having guessed from her melancholy smile. She handed him the letter. He read it carefully; then, without raising his eyes, he said, 'You would like to join him.'

She shrugged, touched, tender.

'How could I abandon our men? How could I abandon you?'

She grabbed the paper from him, crumpled it up, and threw it on the ground. Then she took the red brocade bag containing the second letter and examined the seal attached to the gold ribbon that tied up the bag. It was Bazee Bai's. What could the old Maharani be writing her? Inside was nothing but a handbill printed in English and in Hindi.

Lord Canning, Governor General of India, offers ten thousand rupees for the capture of the Nawab of Banda and twenty thousand rupees for the capture of the Rani of Jhansi.

'I'm flattered to be worth more than good old Banda, but it's not very nice for him,' said the Rani. 'Isn't that too much of an honour, having my head worth that much?'

Despite her jest, the Rani's voice was shaky.

'What do you expect, Lakshmi,' answered Akbar. 'You've become a legend. Do you know what the people have been saying about you? They claim that during the siege of Jhansi, when you ran out of ammunition, you used your jewels for grapeshot.'

The Rani burst into laughter.

'If diamonds and emeralds could kill Englishmen, I would certainly have done it.' Then, serious once again, she said, 'I don't want to be a legend, I never wanted to be one. It is destiny, the British, who created this image that is beyond me. I don't like legends...they end badly.'

And then she threw herself into Akbar's arms, suddenly desperate for protection.

'Don't worry, Lakshmi. Whatever happens, we, you and I, will come out of it together.'

9

The following morning, 16 June 1858, the Rani gave her officers their orders for the day. As always, she was an object of curiosity, and soldiers from other regiments—at least those who were awake at this early hour—gathered around to look at her. Untidy, dirty, haggard, their eyes stared vacantly. Some were laughing derisively, their teeth red from chewing betel leaves. Suddenly, the echo of gunfire rolled in from a great distance away.

'The British,' the Rani shouted.

'It's from the east, they're attacking Morar,' said Akbar. Morar, seven miles east of Gwalior on the river of the same name, was a former British cantonment.

'They've reached the gates of Gwalior without our having been warned,' muttered the Rani, overwhelmed.

She was summoned to a council of war. In the streets the crowds were so thick she had to fight her way through. Groups of cavalry, artillery-trains, infantry regiments hurried in all directions. At Gurki Palace, Sindhia's courtiers and dignitaries were still as numerous, but the Rani immediately sensed in their attitude a new and almost imperceptible distance. The officers of the revolutionary army were rushing about, carrying orders. The council room gave onto the courtyard that, just thirteen days earlier, had seen the enthronement and triumph of Rao Sahib. When the Rani entered, he was arguing with Tatya Tope.

In spite of his splendid clothes and sparkling jewels that marked his rank, he had lost all his arrogance, and it was a frantic man who turned to the Rani.

'Come, Lakshmi, I beg you—tell me what you think, what should we do?'

'Peshwa, several times I told you what I thought, and you didn't listen. You've destroyed all our chances for victory by deliberately ignoring my warnings, by neglecting to prepare for war, and by devoting all your attention to trivialities. The enemy is upon us and our army is not ready. Everywhere I turn I see disorder and chaos. How do you expect to win this battle now?'

After the whiplash, the caress, meant for Tatya Tope to whom she now turned:

'Nevertheless, there is still hope. The only thing to do now is attack—all our troops together in a single glorious charge. An attack sudden, unhesitating, overwhelming. The enemy must be repulsed, and he will be. I am ready to do my duty; do yours,' she concluded, turning back to Rao Sahib. 'Let's go, and may God be with us.'

'We'll all go with you!' cried Tatya Tope.

She put her hand on his shoulder, looked him in the eye, and said in a solemn voice, loud enough to be heard by all the officers around them, 'I beseech you and your troops, do not leave the battlefield no matter what happens. I will not retreat, I would rather die than save my life by running away.'

She accepted the responsibility of personally organizing the defence of the eastern part of the city, and returned to the camp through the still-crowded streets.

Akbar was enraged.

'Tatya Tope assigned you the most dangerous position. You should have refused. It's suicide.'

'On the contrary, it's an honour. He knows me. He anticipated my request and gave me the position I wanted. There is a part of the Bhagavad Gita that says, 'If we die in battle, we enter paradise; if we win, we dominate the world.'

At that moment she met Ganghadar on the road. Everyone in Gwalior knew this wise man who had built himself a small monastery outside the city, on the road to Morar, at a spot near a river called Kotaki Saray. The Rani had been there, several times, to avail herself of the holy man's wisdom and also to meditate alone in the bucolic surroundings. Baba Ganghadar seized the reins of her horse to stop her, looked at her with his piercing eyes, and said, 'Now you grow weaker with every minute. Now pray for your life, O Rani, for the sword of India is broken for all time.'

'As long as there remains a glimmer of love and faith in the hearts of our heroes,' she replied, 'the sword of India will remain sharp, and one day it will strike as far away as the gates of London.'

The Rani immediately had her camp transported to the eastern part of town, and with her personal troops she took over the position assigned her by Tatya Tope. All afternoon was spent digging trenches, raising embankments, positioning troops and guns. In the evening she sent for Damodar, whom she had left until then under Mandar's care. She explained why she had summoned him.

'If you wish to be king one day, you had better learn now to show your courage on the battlefield. You've already seen and endured a great deal, enough to harden your heart. But I want you to be present at the decisive battle that will be waged here so that you may learn to master the fear natural to your young age.'

It was long past midnight. In their tents the soldiers slept or tried to sleep. Night had restored its magic to nature that had been laid waste by the soldiers. In the milky darkness the bushes recovered their shape and the trees their mystery.

Strolling with Akbar, the Rani broke the silence around them.

'You see those hills over there—you can just make them out... they're out of the reach of our guns. The British can climb those hills from the rear, put their artillery there, and shell us without our being able to do anything about it. Those hills worry me...something's going to have to be done,' she added with a heavy sigh.

The Rani was deeply weary. Weary of having to be the spearhead of the revolutionary army. Weary of having to fight not only the enemy but also her friends. Weary of acting alone. She ached for her Jhansi, the peaceful, happy Jhansi she had known before the revolution. She would have given anything to return there and live quietly—even dethroned, even dispossessed—as long as she could be among her own people. But Jhansi would never be the same, and perhaps she would never see it again. She stopped walking. Akbar, not wanting to interrupt her thoughts, began to sing.

'You fought well, brave Rani of Jhansi.

The guns were placed on the towers, the magic cannonballs were fired.

O Rani of Jhansi, you fought well, brave one.

All the soldiers were fed on sweets, she herself had nothing but rice.

O Rani of Jhansi, brave one, you fought well.

She ran to the army where she sought water and found none.

O Rani of Jhansi, brave one, you fought well.'

Akbar sang off-key, but there was such intensity in his voice that it took on a singular poetry in the silence of the night. The Rani listened to his song with emotion, and when he was through she asked, ironically, 'And where did those words come from?'

'Some soldiers made them up. The whole army's been humming it.'

'Come, I want to make love to you.' They walked hand-in-hand into the Rani's tent, past the Pathan sentries, rigid as stones.

Excerpts from a letter from Roderick Briggs to Sarah Brandon, dated 16 June 1858.

After leaving Kalpi on 6 June we travelled as swiftly as possible, marching by night to avoid the heat of the day. Early yesterday, we came to Morar. In the distance I could see, rising from the plain, the formidable rock of Gwalior fort. Close by I could make out, between the trees, the houses and the steeple in what had once been our countrymen's cantonment. There, the rebels had posted a thousand men, all of them deserters from the army of the Maharaja of Gwalior. They did not see us until the very last minute. Their guns opened fire immediately, but our artillery, more powerful by far, quickly silenced them. There was a brief but furious hand-to-hand fight from which we emerged on top. It must be admitted we were far superior in number. It took us a little more than two hours to earn this victory. When we entered the former cantonment, we found it empty. The rebels had fled, leaving behind them two hundred dead. I was astonished by the ghost town. An alley planted with trees at regular intervals led to the church. On both sides were rows of houses, or rather bungalows, all identical, each surrounded by its little garden. Grass had taken over the paths and the flower beds were overgrown with brambles. There was no glass in the windows; the church had been sacked.

But at first glance, it seemed as though nothing had changed, as though our compatriots had left only the day before. The sensation was at once strange and reassuring, this discovery of a familiar setting lost in a foreign and hostile land. Grateful for the shade, our men pitched their tents beneath the tall trees. The officers moved into the houses. I myself have a little dollhouse that my orderlies quickly tidied up and made liveable.

Very nearby there is a well which, by some miracle, is not dry. I strolled in the garden, enjoying the contrast with the desert we had just crossed. The tiny lawn is covered with flowers; bushes of jasmine perfume the air. As though in paradise, I stare tirelessly at the pomegranate trees, the fig trees, the lemon and guava trees that surround the house. It is hard to imagine we are still at war.

This morning General Rose decided to press the advantage we had acquired last night. He was convinced that the rebels would try to escape Gwalior from the southeast and he wanted to prevent that. A vanguard led by Major Smith marched to within three miles of Gwalior, which lay beyond a row of low hills, rocky but not steep, behind which the Major planned to put his troops. They were beginning to pitch camp when, suddenly, they came under sustained fire from the nearby hills.

The rebels in ambush were firing at them at almost point-blank range. At the same moment a host of cavalry swarmed from the hills and launched a furious charge. They were upon our men before they could react. Although they fought valiantly, our men were beginning to be in a tight spot when the bugler sounded retreat. They were able to fall back in good order, even though that brutal engagement had cost them a good number of casualties...which they owe to the Rani of Jhansi. Who else but she could have conceived such a sudden and murderous attack? Who else could have led, just as at Kalpi, such an insanely daring charge? Who else could have forced our troops back? I can't say it often enough—that woman is a scourge, and as long as we haven't destroyed her, there will be no rest...and rest is what all of us here long for...

I must interrupt this letter, for I have just been summoned to a council of war. It appears that tomorrow we shall have a tough battle, for our spies have informed us that the rebels are concentrating their entire army. I pray this will be the last battle—but I doubt it. When will this campaign end? To my surprise, I find myself hating this career of soldiering I chose. Still, I was happy to participate in the Crimean War; there, at least, one fought by the rules. Whereas here, the land, the climate, and especially our adversary—everything conspires to surprise us and keep us off balance.

That evening the Rani had returned to her camp satisfied and even optimistic. By taking the British by surprise before they could occupy the hills that had worried her the night before, she had scored a success which, though limited in scope, was unequivocal and promising. It was almost enough to make her forget her impatience, her disappointment at having watched Tatya Tope who, in completing his preparations with exasperating tardiness, let another day go by without giving the signal for the general attack on the British.

She praised Mandar warmly for her behaviour in the fighting. Though she too had been trained to warfare from childhood, her mistress, to protect her, had never before allowed her to fight.

'You see!' said Akbar, 'Once again you were wrong to worry. We won, and without any trouble!'

'Just as we shall win tomorrow,' she replied, suddenly carried away by a strange feeling of exaltation. 'Now I'm sure that tomorrow will see our triumph.'

Then they retired to her tent. The trials of the day had frayed their nerves and tension only increased their desire. Without a word Lakshmi threw herself into Akbar's arms, and he held her to him with almost uncontrolled violence.

'Lakshmi, no night is long enough to prove how much I love you. Let's forget everything for a few hours.'

She quivered under his caresses, their senses inflamed by shared desire. Never before had they known such fever. They could not tear their bodies from one another, and this madness seemed to last a lifetime. Then, exhausted, Lakshmi suddenly fell into a deep slumber. For a long time Akbar watched her, distressed to see her so alone and trusting in the midst of such danger. He himself could not sleep. To quiet his anxiety, he put the Rani down gently on her pillows, pulled a silk cover over her, and stepped outside for a walk.

Mandar too was suffering from insomnia, and they met in one of the camp's alleys.

Perhaps because of fatigue, Akbar had tears in his eyes and felt the need to confide in someone.

'Lakshmi's slipping away from me. She already belongs to history, whether she is victorious or not. Tomorrow, in a few hours, she will no longer be mine. Now, she's strong, she's invincible, out of reach, and I've lost her.'

Mandar answered him gently, 'She loves you, Akbar.'

'Perhaps. But her love for me, no matter what I do, what I say, won't turn her one inch away from what she calls her destiny. And I am no more than a grain of sand.'

'Without you, without your love, could she ever have borne her burden?'

And as though speaking to herself, Mandar added, 'Our destiny, yours and mine, isn't it linked permanently to hers? I know that I myself am destined to follow her everywhere, forever.'

'Not I! One day, when this war is over, I shall leave. No matter how humble and obscure my path may be, I will follow it because it will be mine.'

In the east the sky was turning that matchless sweet pink of an Indian dawn. Around them, darkness was slowly giving way to a grey impalpable mist that clung to the bushes and drifted between the trees. It was that brief sweet hour between the mugginess of the night just ended and the heaviness of the coming day, and the air was made fresh by a light, gentle breeze.

It was still early in the morning of 18 June 1858, but the Rani was ready. She savoured a lemon sherbet in her tent, chatting with Mandar and Akbar while awaiting Tatya Tope's order to march on Morar. Damodar was rushing in and out, toying with his mother's weapons, and showing unusual excitement. The Rani was wearing the same clothes as the day before: a jacket of red velvet embroidered with gold, white breeches and a white turban. On her neck she had once again hung the pearl necklace that was now her only wealth.

After her victory of the day before she had improved the positions she was responsible for. On the low hills, from which she had swooped down on the British, she had placed six batteries of artillery and a large part of her infantry.

'Besides,' she commented, 'after the damage we did yesterday, the British aren't ready. As usual, they're going to take their time, and it's we who will surprise them.' At that very moment her guns opened fire. The British had not taken their time, they were right there. Major Smith had returned, this time with General Rose and twice as many men and guns. While their artillery shelled the Rani's batteries in the hills, half their troops launched a frontal attack and the other half raced off to take the rebels from behind. The Rani leaped into the saddle. Immediately she sensed that her horse was afraid. If she only had Pari; he, at least, had known how to behave in battle.

Before leaving, she leaned towards Damodar:

'Watch closely, my son, it will be quite a sight. I will see you soon.'

After rallying the four hundred men of her cavalry, she galloped straight for the British. On her right, off in the distance, she could see the major force of the rebel infantry, led by Tatya Tope, marching slowly in the same direction.

'Are you afraid?' Akbar shouted to her.

'I'm terrified,' she answered, with a hysterical laugh.

Major Smith's troops had taken the hills. From the crest of one of them Roderick Briggs saw the tents of the Rani's camp,

'Perfect terrain for a charge,' he said to himself just as the bugles sounded the charge. The rebel cavalry had already covered half the empty field. Roderick Briggs hurtled down the slope in the middle of the British cavalry and infantry. The collision with the rebel troops took place at the foot of the hill. It was appallingly violent. The fighting immediately became confused, fierce, indescribably chaotic. It broke up, then closed up again; the rebels were pushed back several times and several times returned to the attack. Later, Roderick Briggs was to wonder how he had survived; the fighting had been so furious, it seemed impossible that he had warded off all the blows. He was forced to conclude that only providence had saved him. He struck out almost blindly, without a thought for defending himself against his attackers.

Despite the fierceness of the rebels' attacks, their ranks were beginning to thin. Roderick felt that they were beginning to weaken. Soon, they did fall back, but only in order to regroup and then, once again, charge with redoubled fury. It was then that Roderick saw the Rani. He was the only one to recognize her, for the others, in the heat of battle, saw only her masculine attire. Roderick was unable to suppress a feeling, brief as lightning, of admiration for her. Holding the reins of her horse in her teeth and a sword in each hand, she struck out to the left and right at the same time. Next to her, another woman was fighting with consummate skill. A sort of giant with pale skin and blond hair protected the Rani, lunging at attackers she had not had time to notice. Roderick wanted to fight his way to the Rani and tackle her himself. But each time, rebel horsemen surrounded him, attacked him, diverted his attention. He wounded some, killed some; others he pushed aside and then he spurred his horse on, again in her direction, but invariably, other rebels would stop him. In his disappointment he believed they had all got together to prevent him from getting near the Rani. He became weary, discouraged. His sword arm hurt, he had a headache, he was afraid, he was furious. His vengeance was there within reach, and now, it seemed she would escape him yet again. He felt that his men, too, were weakening.

At that moment General Rose's camel-corps appeared behind Roderick. This was the crack regiment, the one held in reserve for the ultimate counter-attack. All of a sudden, the advantage swung to the British camp. The Rani understood this immediately. More and more of her Pathan horsemen were falling. They did not retreat, preferring to be killed on the spot, but their numbers were rapidly decreasing. Yet, the Rani did not lose all hope. Her instinct for survival spurred her on more than her hatred of the enemy. If Tatya Tope and the bulk of the army stood as firmly as she and her cavalry, victory was still possible.

But out of the corner of her eye, she saw in the distance that the British had pushed back Tatya Tope's infantry and were now stretched along the empty field where she was fighting, gradually overtaking her right flank. It was clear that she ran the risk of being surprised from behind, surrounded...and taken alive, along with the survivors of her regiment.

'Follow me!' she yelled and, with Akbar, Mandar and fifteen riders, she galloped off to the left, to ride around the British infantry and join the main force of the rebel army. She had broken away from the battle so suddenly that it took the British several seconds to react. They fired at the group galloping off and a volley of bullets whistled by Lakshmi's ears. Roderick, whose eyes had been on her all the time, was the first to notice her flight.

'That's the Rani of Jhansi, catch her!' Roderick shouted to the horsemen around him.

Followed by about thirty of them, he rushed off in pursuit. Rage had swept away his weariness and restored his energy. He spurred his horse who was literally flying. The Rani and her group had covered the better part of a mile before Roderick and his men caught up. At the site known as Kotaki Saray, not far from the small convent built by Baba Ganghadar, the holy man, the Rani and her horsemen wheeled about to face them. The battle began anew, one rebel against two British. Suddenly, the Rani felt a slight pain, like the bite of a snake, in her left breast. A British soldier she had not seen approach had pricked her with his bayonet. She turned towards her attacker, ran him through with her sword and killed him. Her wound, although shallow, was bleeding profusely. The fight was too unequal; the rebels would all be killed or captured.

'Get away, on the gallop, quick!' she yelled.

Once again, she dashed off—so rapidly that the British were unable to hold her. Behind her she heard a scream, a woman's scream. She turned around. Mandar, struck by a bullet at point-blank range, had fallen from her horse. The Rani turned back, raced towards the man who had killed Mandar, and struck him so violently with her sword that she cleaved his head in two. Already, she was off again.

She found her path barred by a wide and deep ditch at the bottom of which ran a stream—an obstacle only a rider as good as she could clear. A single leap and she would be safe, for she knew that most of the British would be unable to follow her. She spurred her horse. Instead of jumping, it stopped so short that she almost flew over its neck. She dug her spurs in again, but the horse refused to move. It pawed the ground and turned about in circles. The British were upon her. Once again, the Rani had to face them.

It was then she saw him—a particularly tall Englishman, pink, blond. Despite the distance, she saw the hatred and determination in his eyes. He was coming straight at her, his sword raised. Three Pathans rode up to protect her. At that moment she felt a violent blow in her left hip as though someone had struck her with his fist. She had been hit by a rifle bullet.

She dropped the sword she was holding in her left hand to squeeze the wound, while continuing to fight with her right hand.

The tall pink and blond Englishman had managed to fight off the Pathans who were trying to stop him. He had reached the Rani. He raised his sword. She raised hers to deflect the blow.

'Here, this one's for Roger!' he yelled.

Astonished, she wavered for a split second. The Englishman's sword came down on her head so forcefully that it opened her forehead and eyebrow. The pain was immediate and terrible. The Rani was blinded by blood.

By an instinct stronger than will, she fought back but, weakened by her wounds, she was able only to strike his shoulder before slipping sideways and falling to the ground.

Akbar had seen her. 'Cover me!' he shouted to the four horsemen still there. Together, they rushed the British. Akbar jumped from his horse, gently picked up the Rani, and carried her in his arms as he ran to the little monastery nearby. The door opened before him; he ran inside with his precious burden, just as the last of his men fell. Baba Ganghadar, the holy man, had recognized the Rani. It was he who had opened the door to Akbar. Carefully, they placed the wounded woman on a pallet in a prayer-hall, whose low ceiling was supported by columns of pink plaster. The monastery included a very old temple, so small it seemed a miniature, one or two rows of cells, and some outbuildings. Everything was covered in flowers and shone with order and cleanliness. The crooked courtyard was jammed with the monks, who were Baba Ganghadar's followers, and with their cattle, which they had brought in from the fields to shelter them from the fighting.

'Hold the British back!' Baba Ganghadar ordered his disciples with unexpected vigour.

From some secret corner they produced a number of old rifles. They ran to take up positions behind the monastery wall; it was evident these monks knew what they were doing, and the wall was solid. Perhaps they might just hold out long enough? Baba Ganghadar had opened a flask of Ganges water and with it he moistened the Rani's shrivelled lips, to freshen and purify her. Blood continued to flow from her forehead, but more slowly, covering the entire right side of her face; it also seeped from wounds in her left breast and hip, darkening the red velvet jacket and spotting the white breeches.

'What a pity...what a pity...' she whispered; then she lost consciousness.

Akbar thought she was dead, but Baba Ganghadar reassured him, 'She's only fainted.'

Behind the monastery wall the firing continued, sustained, intense. Akbar's retreat had been so swift that most of the British had not even seen it. Having killed the last Pathan, they thought the job done, but Roderick shouted at them, 'They've taken refuge inside, we must attack! The Rani of Jhansi is still alive!'

And so, they attacked the monastery, but the monks were putting up a stiff fight.

The Rani's breathing grew slightly stronger. She was regaining consciousness. Her eyes closed, she whispered a prayer, 'In the name of the goddess Lakshmi...' She opened one eye; the other, hit by Roderick's sabre, remained closed. Her gaze was glassy, then it lit up when she saw Akbar standing at the foot of her pallet. With a weak gesture of her hand, she signalled him to come closer. He knelt and leaned over her. She could hardly speak. Between hiccups, she managed to mouth words, jerkily, 'Damodar...I leave him to you...under your protection... go to the camp...run...take him...carry him away...'

Clumsily, slowly, she tried to take from her neck the pearl necklace from Sindhia's treasury. She was unable to manage and fell back, moaning. Baba Ganghadar gently lifted the necklace from her. She put it in Akbar's hand. 'Keep it...for Damodar...'

The effort of speaking had exhausted her. She was gasping; her breathing grew more and more uneven. A thin trail of blood began to run from her mouth. She saw two large tears roll down Akbar's cheeks. With effort she managed to whisper, 'It couldn't have ended any other way.'

She seemed to be choking. The blood from her wounds was seeping into her lungs and slowly drowning her. Baba Ganghadar gently wiped away the sweat that beaded on her face. Suddenly, she seemed to return to life. She straightened up, leaning on an elbow and, without looking at anyone, said in a halting but quite strong voice, 'The British, I don't want them to find my body...'

Her head slid back and a spasm shook her entire body. She slumped backwards. There was one more contraction, and then her body stiffened. The Rani of Jhansi was dead.

Akbar stood up, his arms hanging at his side, staring like a madman at the Rani's face. Baba Ganghadar was muttering prayers. Without moving, he said to Akbar, 'Go, fetch some wood to build a pyre.'

Akbar, as though lashed by a whip, leapt outside, shoved the cattle aside, plunged into the woodshed, and came out again, looking lost. 'There's no wood, we won't be able to burn her.'

'Yes we will, get the cattle's hay.'

Between the two of them they soon built a pyre out of bales of dried grass. Delicately, they placed the Rani on top and set it on fire. Around them, the rifle fire was growing more and more intense. On the other side of the wall there were now hundreds of British cavalry firing at will. The monks were still holding on, but they were falling, one by one. There were only ten able-bodied men left. Akbar stared into the flames that were already enveloping the Rani and dancing upon her corpse. Baba Ganghadar placed his hand on Akbar's shoulder.

'Obey the Rani, go save Damodar.'

In a hoarse voice, Akbar answered, 'The body won't have time to burn, the British will find it.'

'Don't worry, I'll find a way. Now go.'

Baba Ganghadar resumed his prayers and did not even look up as Akbar walked away.

Roderick Briggs was almost insane with impatience. For two hours he had lain siege to the monastery without being able to seize it. At last, the gunfire from the invisible defenders seemed to be weakening. The British renewed the intensity and precision of their own fire. Soon, there were only three rifles firing from behind the wall, then two, and then only one. A few more spasmodic shots rang out; then, from the monastery, only silence. The British rose, left their shelter, and walked towards the monastery in close ranks, cautiously.

The doors opened slowly and oxen, cows, zebus, and buffalo, by the dozen, emerged. Pushed by an invisible hand, excited, panicky, they stampeded, lowing and roaring, into the British ranks. The startled soldiers opened fire to try to stop them, but the animals, wild with terror, knocked them over, trampled on them, creating indescribable disorder. Roderick Briggs was thrown to the ground and, while trying to protect his face, was kicked in the elbow. It took the British half-an-hour to extricate themselves from the animals who ran in circles, kicking and butting. 'Another half-hour lost,' Briggs mourned.

Once order had returned, the British resumed their march towards the monastery. It seemed abandoned; there was no sound, no movement. Roderick was the first to go in. Against the wall he saw several dozen bloodied corpses of monks. It seemed there was no one alive within the enclosure.

And yet, searching frantically, he found, behind a woodshed, a sight that made him stop short. A large fire was slowly dying, and next to it sat an old man, cross-legged on the ground, the palms of his hands turned to the sky, staring straight in front of him and muttering. He did not move as Roderick approached.

With the tip of his boot Roderick Briggs scattered the embers, uncovering a few fragments of human bones, almost completely reduced to ashes.

Postscript

With the Rani, the very soul of the rebel army had been killed. The following day General Rose took the city of Gwalior after a five-hour battle. The rebel leaders were able to escape, and the allegedly impregnable fort surrendered almost without a fight. On the next day, 20 June, Maharaja Sindhia re-entered his capital to the triumphal cheers of the same crowd which, twenty days earlier, had applauded the arrival of the Peshwa Rao Sahib.

One of the first measures taken by the British was the arrest of Amar Chand, Sindhia's minister of finance who, on his master's secret orders, had opened the treasury to the rebels. Tried and condemned for having betrayed his master, he spoke not a word in his own defence and was hanged.

That evening Maharaja Sindhia gave a dinner—an English dinner—at Gurki Palace in honour of General Rose, Sir Robert Hamilton and their staff. His guests stinted neither on praise nor thanks. Rose called the Maharaja 'the best friend the British had in India'.

'If you hadn't been so faithful to us,' Hamilton said, 'this would have been the end of the British presence in India.'

Many compliments were addressed to Diwan Dinkar, who sat next to his ruler. In order to protect his modesty, he suddenly interrupted, without losing his customary impenetrable and cynical expression, 'The end of the Rani of Jhansi didn't surprise me. She herself told me one day that her horoscope predicted an early death. She believed it... Certainly, General, you had to destroy her, and we shall allow historians, present and future, to claim that she was your most implacable and treacherous foe. But I myself am not convinced she would have fought you if circumstances hadn't forced her to...I was told that before the mutiny, she had even fallen in love with a countryman of yours, a young lawyer, who was killed with the others during last year's massacre...'

In the silence that followed, the guests heard the sound of shattered crystal. Roderick Briggs had crushed the glass he was holding in his hand. He rose from his chair, pale as death, in the grip of some terrible vision. He opened his mouth as if to speak, then sat down again, heavily, in silence.

Later, he was to be awarded the Victoria Cross, England's highest military decoration, for his heroic deeds. He did not marry Sarah Brandon. Their engagement was broken as soon as he returned to England. He asked her to return to him the letters he had sent her from India. He published them, and his book on the Great Mutiny enjoyed considerable success.

General Rose received the congratulations of the House of Lords and the House of Commons on his victorious campaign, but legal complications created by enemies he had made in the army prevented him and his men from receiving the material rewards they had a right to expect.

With the fall of Gwalior the rebellion's back had been broken. Yet, it continued to struggle for another year. The fire would flare up here and there, but each time it became more and more feeble.

Tatya Tope was the only one to refuse to accept defeat. For many months he harassed the British and their princely allies throughout central India, always on the move, surfacing where he was least expected and still scoring an occasional small victory. The British covered more than eight hundred miles in his pursuit.

In April 1859, he was betrayed by his best friend the Raja of Nawar and arrested. Brought to the small city of Shivpuri, not far from Gwalior, he was tried, sentenced, and hanged from a tree. But was this the real Tatya Tope? Indians claimed that the Raja of Nawar would never have betrayed his friend. It was said that it was Tatya Tope's double who had been handed over to the British in order to protect the real one, and that the victim had allowed himself to be killed out of loyalty to his leader.

Rao Sahib, the Peshwa, became a hermit and wandered from one hiding place to another. In 1862, he was discovered in the hills of Punjab by British spies disguised as pilgrims. He was brought back to Bithur and hanged in front of his own palace.

The fate of Nana Sahib was to remain an impenetrable mystery. Had he committed suicide by throwing himself into the Ganges, or had he been able to flee to Nepal? Long after the rebellion numerous successive Nana Sahibs were to be recognized in India, and some were even arrested. None convinced the authorities he was really the man who had led the rebellion. The British authorities grew so tired of these false sightings that, in 1895, when a young officer in a remote station wired excitedly to Calcutta to say, 'Have arrested Nana Sahib. Wire instructions.' The cabled response, which left him flabbergasted, was, 'Release him at once.'

Prince Firoz Shah did not die young, despite his own predictions. For a long time he wandered the jungle at the head of a steadily dwindling band of rebels. When he saw that all was lost, he went into exile, wandered from Muslim land to Muslim land and finally settled in Mecca. When he died in 1877, at the age of forty-five, he was a broken man, abandoned by all, destitute and blind.

On 1 November 1858, a proclamation signed by Queen Victoria was posted throughout India. A general amnesty was granted to all those who had fought the British. The Most Honourable East India Company was abolished and henceforth, England would rule India directly. A few years later Queen Victoria became Empress of India, thus succeeding the last Great Moghul, Bahadur Shah, who was rotting in exile in Rangoon, in Burma.

Akbar managed to get Damodar out of Gwalior to prevent his falling into British hands. He brought him to Indore, sold the Rani's pearl necklace to raise money for the child's keep, and entrusted him to the Brahmins of a temple. Then he disappeared and all subsequent efforts to trace him were fruitless.

At Indore Damodar was to lead a long and obscure life. The British refused to return the six hundred thousand rupees they had held in trust for him since the annexation of Jhansi and the deposition of his mother in 1853. All the petitions he sent the government in an effort to get the money were returned to him with brief negative replies—the last one in 1936. Eleven years later, the British Empire vanished and India became independent.

Bibliography

Most British historians have portrayed Rani Lakshmi of Jhansi as an ambitious, unscrupulous woman, vindictive and power-hungry and responsible for the massacre of the British at Jhansi. As this book attests, the truth is quite otherwise. And yet, the truth is hard to pin down. Almost all the documents relating to the Revolt of 1857 that were favourable to the Indians have completely disappeared; only the accusatory and incriminating ones remain. A few of the former have survived, however, and the unexpected light they throw on the revolt reveals something quite different from the standard image painted by British historians.

My main sources have been:

On the Rani herself, *The Revolt of 1857 in Bundelkhand* by Shyam Narain Sinha. Lucknow, 1982.

On the British military campaign against the Rani, 'The Last of the Paladins, Sir Hugh Rose and the Indian Mutiny' by F.E. Whitton. Blackwood's Magazine, June 1934.

Cavalry Surgeon—The Recollections of Deputy Surgeon-General John Henry Sylvester, F.G.S. London, 1971.

On the Sepoy Rebellion in general, *Freedom Struggle in Uttar Pradesh; 6 Vols.* by S.A.A. Rizvi and M.L. Bhargava. Lucknow, 1957, 1961.

These six large volumes of period documents are the richest source of information. Then comes the classic *History of the Indian Mutiny of 1857-8* by Kaye and Mallesson. London, 1889.

The works on the Sepoy Rebellion that are the most pleasant and easiest to read (although they put forth only the British point of view) are:

Red Year: The Indian Rebellion of 1857 by Michael Edwardes. London, 1873.

The Great Mutiny: India, 1857 by Christopher Hibbert. London, 1980.

The most classic work on the Sepoy rebellion, seen from the Indian point of view is, *The Indian War of Independence—1857* by V.D. Savakar. Bombay, 1957.

Finally, the richest source of information on the Sepoy Rebellion remains oral tradition. As far as the Rani of Jhansi is concerned, I am chiefly indebted to the following people who have kindly shared their knowledge with me: Professor Bhagwan Das Gupta of Jhansi; the Sirdar Angry and Mr Diwedi of Gwalior. I am, moreover, grateful to Miss Maruk Tarapur for her brilliant portrait of daily life in princely India of the nineteenth century, and for her patience in reading this manuscript.

Glossary

Attar	natural perfume
Ayah	nurse
Bhagavad Gita	A religious book of the Hindus, part of the Mahabharata
Bhajan	daily session of musical prayers
Blis	sandalwood
Bania	rich merchant
Chapatti	flour-cake that is the staple of Indian food
Chillum	long clay pipe
Chota lathi	a sort of team-fencing using long poles instead of foils
Chowkidar	village watchman
Dacoit	highwayman
Darogha	head-jailer
Dal	Indian lentils
Dhoti	a kind of large loincloth worn by Indian peasants
Deepavali	festival of lights, an important festival on the Hindu calendar
Durbar	session during which the ruler exerts his power in the presence of his people
Feringhi	foreigner
Gaddi	low, wide throne
Gharotra	balcony located above the main entrance to the palace, on which, following a very ancient custom, the ruler showed himself to the people twice a day
Ghee	strong-smelling clarified butter, India's favourite condiment
Gita	see Bhagavad Gita
Gilli-danda	a game played with a stick
Guj	Indian arrack

Howdah	box in which riders sit on an elephant
Hookah	Indian water-pipe
Jihad	Muslim holy war
Kalian	lower half of the hookah, containing scented liquids
Kshatriya	Indian belonging to the warrior caste
Khotwalla	minister of presents
Kitkit	an Indian game
Laddoo	an Indian sweet
Mehandi	Indian henna
Mullahs	Muslims holding religious or judicial duties
Munshi	secretary, scribe
Nautch girl	female dancer
Paan	digestive masticatory of betel and areca nuts
Peshwa	leader of the confederation of Maratha kings
Puja	daily prayer-session
Punkha	large cloth fan swayed by a rope
Purdah	women's apartment
Raita	mixture of yoghurt, cucumber and spicy herbs
Rakhi	bracelet symbolizing loyalty and attachment
Ramayana	sacred Hindu epic on the life of Prince Rama, an incarnation of Vishnu
Rissaldar	Indian cavalry officer
Sati	ritual suicide of widows
Sepoy	Indian soldier serving under the British flag
Sherat	Afghan wine
Sindar	Indian high-ranking officer
Talukdar	great landowner
Tamashagar	puppeteer
Thali	a metal plate
Thug	member of ancient secret societies based on mysticism and ritual murder by strangulation
Tika	dot between the eyebrows (red for married women, black for widows)
Tulsi	basil
Vedas	holy books
Zamindar	landowner

www.ingramcontent.com/pod-product-compliance
Lightning Source LLC
LaVergne TN
LVHW041101080826
845145LV00007B/1649

* 9 7 8 8 1 2 9 1 2 9 6 2 8 *